STUCK
IN THE
MIDDLE

STUCK in the
MIDDLE

Seventeen Comics from an UNPLEASANT Age

edited by
ARIEL SCHRAG

VIKING

VIKING

Published by Penguin Group

Penguin Group (USA) Inc., 345 Hudson Street, New York, New York 10014, U.S.A.

Penguin Group (Canada), 90 Eglinton Avenue East, Suite 700, Toronto, Ontario, Canada M4P 2Y3

(a division of Pearson Penguin Canada Inc.)

Penguin Books Ltd, 80 Strand, London WC2R 0RL, England

Penguin Ireland, 25 St Stephen's Green, Dublin 2, Ireland (a division of Penguin Books Ltd)

Penguin Group (Australia), 250 Camberwell Road, Camberwell, Victoria 3124, Australia

(a division of Pearson Australia Group Pty Ltd)

Penguin Books India Pvt Ltd, 11 Community Centre, Panchsheel Park, New Delhi – 110 017, India

Penguin Group (NZ), 67 Apollo Drive, Mairangi Bay, Auckland 1311, New Zealand

(a division of Pearson New Zealand Ltd)

Penguin Books (South Africa) (Pty) Ltd, 24 Sturdee Avenue, Rosebank, Johannesburg 2196, South Africa

Penguin Books Ltd, Registered Offices: 80 Strand, London WC2R 0RL, England

First published in 2007 by Viking, a member of Penguin Group (USA) Inc.

10   9   8   7   6   5   4   3   2   1

LIBRARY OF CONGRESS CATALOGING-IN-PUBLICATION DATA IS AVAILABLE
ISBN: 978-0-670-06221-8

Manufactured in China
Set in Neutra Display Drafting Alt and Neutra Light
Book design by Jim Hoover

GREAT THANKS TO JOY PESKIN
FOR ALL HER WORK AND FOR MAKING
THIS BOOK POSSIBLE.

• FOREWORD •

IN THIS COLLECTION, sixteen talented cartoonists have come together to share some of their deepest, darkest stories about some of the deepest, darkest years of their lives: the middle school years. The years when you're too old to play with toy cars but you're too young to drive a real one; the years when your best friend suddenly decides you're not cool enough for her, or vice versa; the years when you think no one—*no one*—has ever felt this way before. Well, *Stuck in the Middle* is here to tell you that someone has. The real and fictional characters in this book survived their middle school years, and so will you.

Let's face it: thirteen is an unpleasant age. But that doesn't mean you can't laugh about it, whether you're still dealing with the issues in this book or are far beyond them. Misery loves company, so start reading.

CONTENTS

VANESSA DAVIS

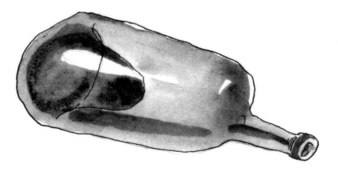

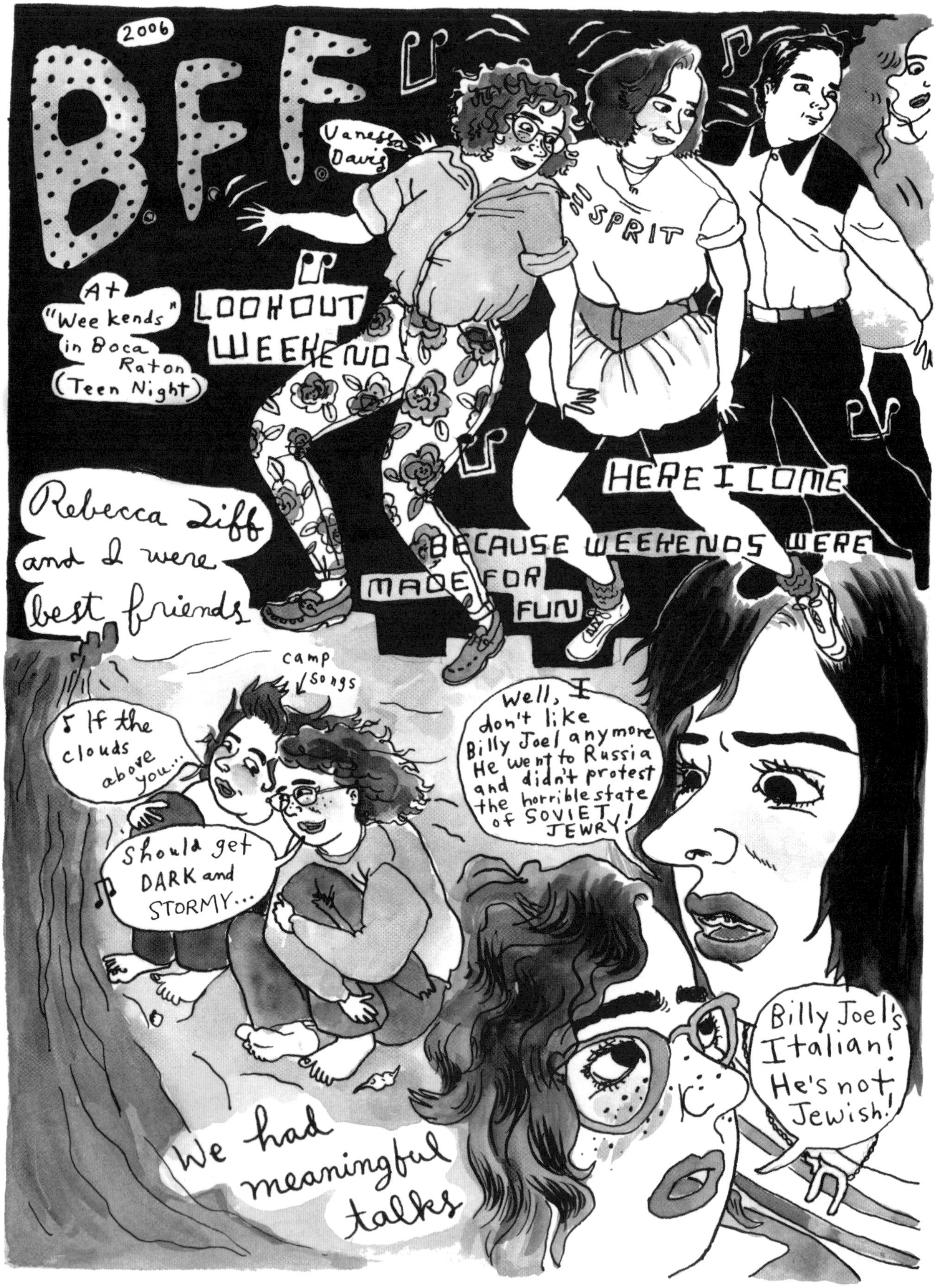
2006
B.F.F.
Vanessa Davis
At "Weekends" in Boca Raton (Teen Night)
LOOKOUT WEEKEND
ESPRIT
HERE I COME
BECAUSE WEEKENDS WERE MADE FOR FUN
Rebecca Ziff and I were best friends
camp songs
If the clouds above you...
Should get DARK and STORMY...
Well, I don't like Billy Joel anymore He went to Russia and didn't protest the horrible state of SOVIET JEWRY!
Billy Joel's Italian! He's not Jewish!
We had meaningful talks

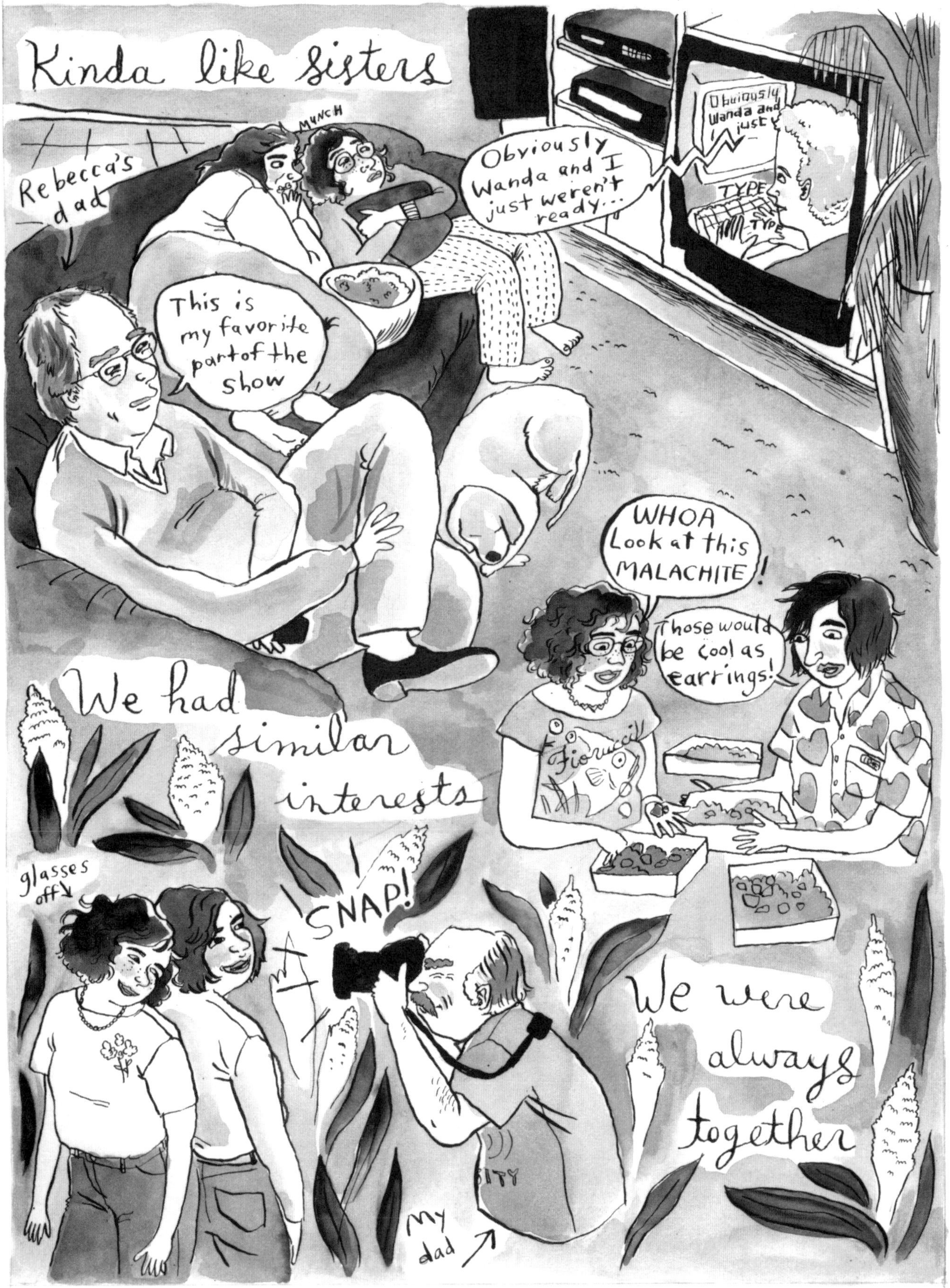
Kinda like sisters
Rebecca's dad
MUNCH
Obviously Wanda and I just weren't ready...
Obviously Wanda and just
TYPE
TYPE
This is my favorite part of the show
WHOA Look at this MALACHITE!
Those would be cool as earrings!
Fiorucci
We had similar interests
glasses off
SNAP!
We were always together
My dad

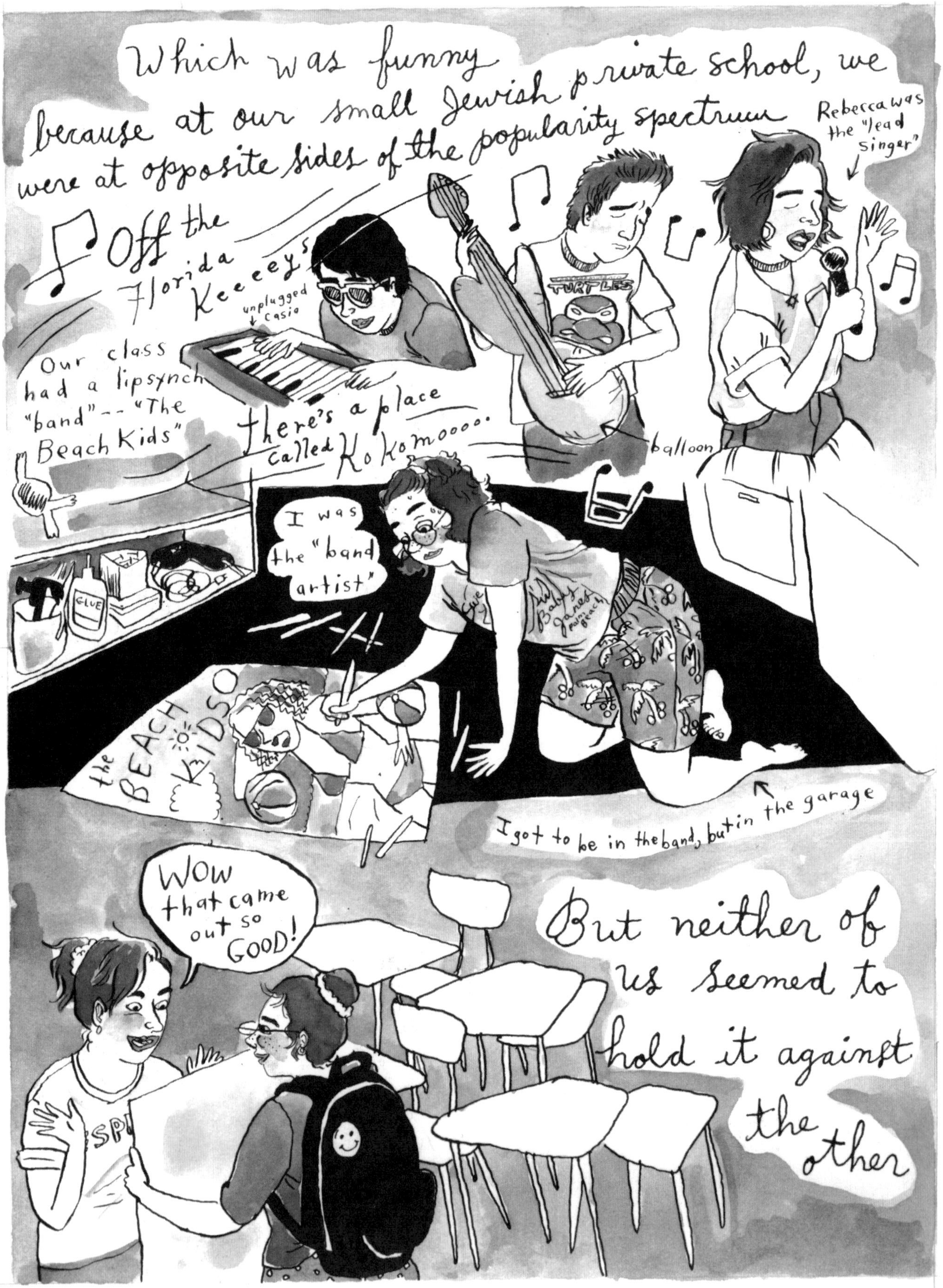
Which was funny because at our small Jewish private school, we were at opposite sides of the popularity spectrum
Rebecca was the "lead singer"
Off the Florida Keeeey's
unplugged casio
TURTLES
Our class had a lipsynch "band"-- "The Beach Kids"
There's a place called Kokomoooo..
balloon
GLUE
I was the "band artist"
the BEACH KIDS
I got to be in the band, but in the garage
WOW that came out so GOOD!
But neither of us seemed to hold it against the other

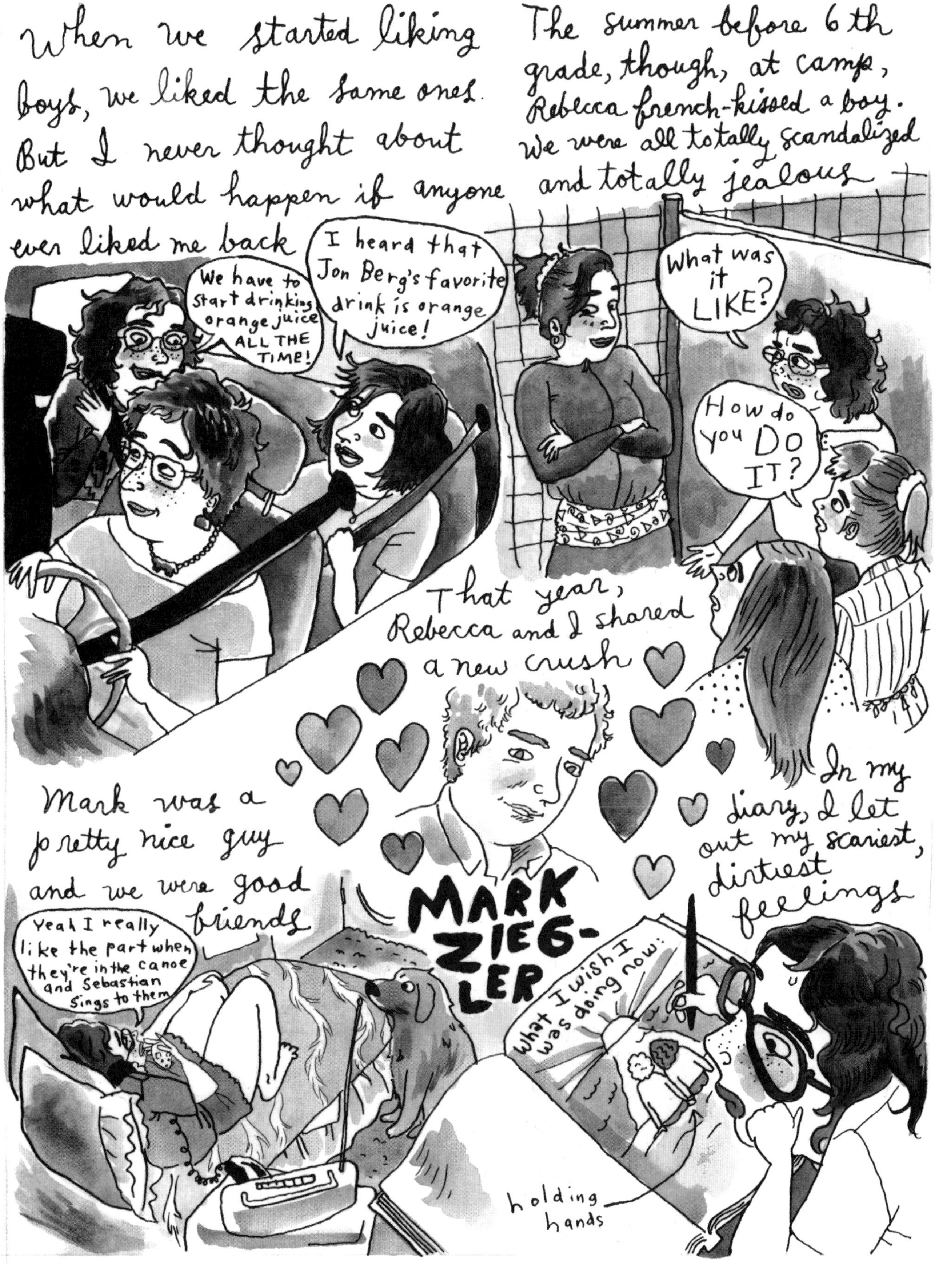

When we started liking boys, we liked the same ones. But I never thought about what would happen if anyone ever liked me back
We have to start drinking orange juice ALL THE TIME!
I heard that Jon Berg's favorite drink is orange juice!
The summer before 6th grade, though, at camp, Rebecca french-kissed a boy. We were all totally scandalized and totally jealous
What was it LIKE?
How do you DO IT?
That year, Rebecca and I shared a new crush
Mark was a pretty nice guy and we were good friends
MARK ZIEG-LER
In my diary, I let out my scariest, dirtiest feelings
Yeah I really like the part when they're in the canoe and Sebastian sings to them
What I wish I was doing now:
holding hands

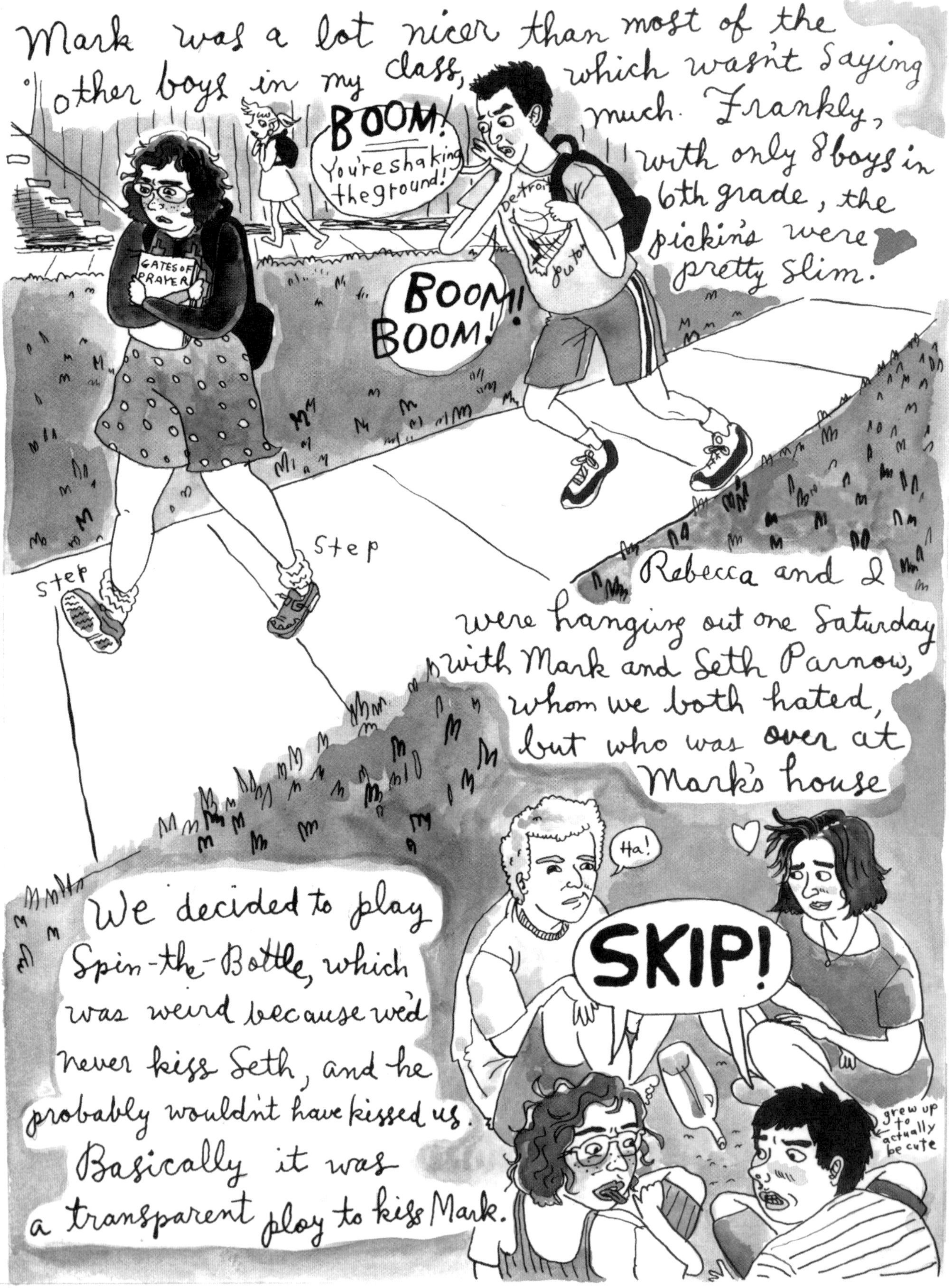
Mark was a lot nicer than most of the other boys in my class, which wasn't saying much. Frankly, with only 8 boys in 6th grade, the pickins were pretty slim.
BOOM! You're shaking the ground!
BOOM! BOOM!
GATES OF PRAYER
Detroit Pistons
step
step
Rebecca and I were hanging out one Saturday with Mark and Seth Parnow, whom we both hated, but who was over at Mark's house
Ha!
We decided to play Spin-the-Bottle, which was weird because we'd never kiss Seth, and he probably wouldn't have kissed us. Basically it was a transparent play to kiss Mark.
SKIP!
grew up to actually be cute

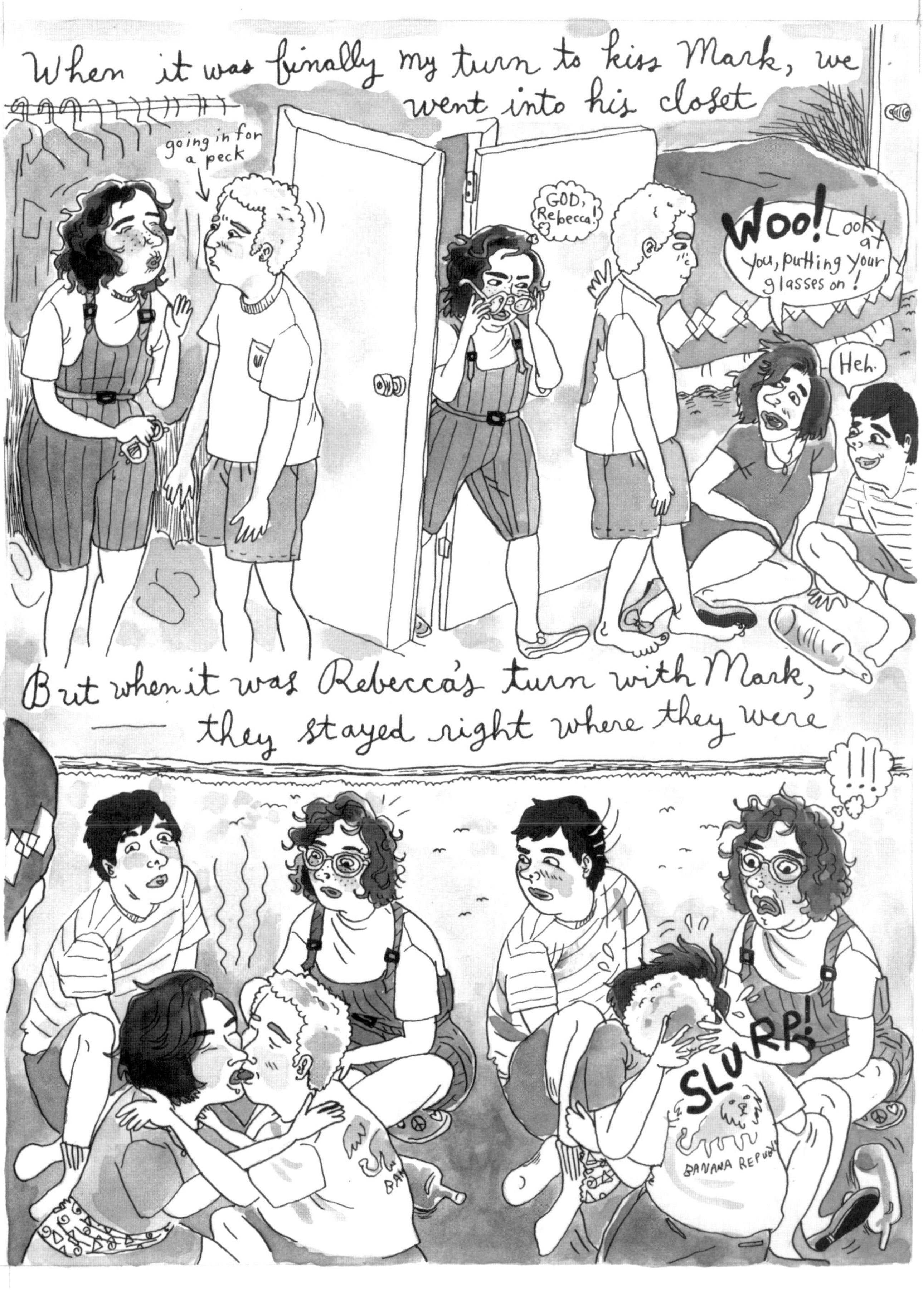
When it was finally my turn to kiss Mark, we went into his closet
going in for a peck
GOD, Rebecca!
WOO! Look at you, putting your glasses on!
Heh.
But when it was Rebecca's turn with Mark, they stayed right where they were
!!!
SLURP!
BANANA REPUBLIC

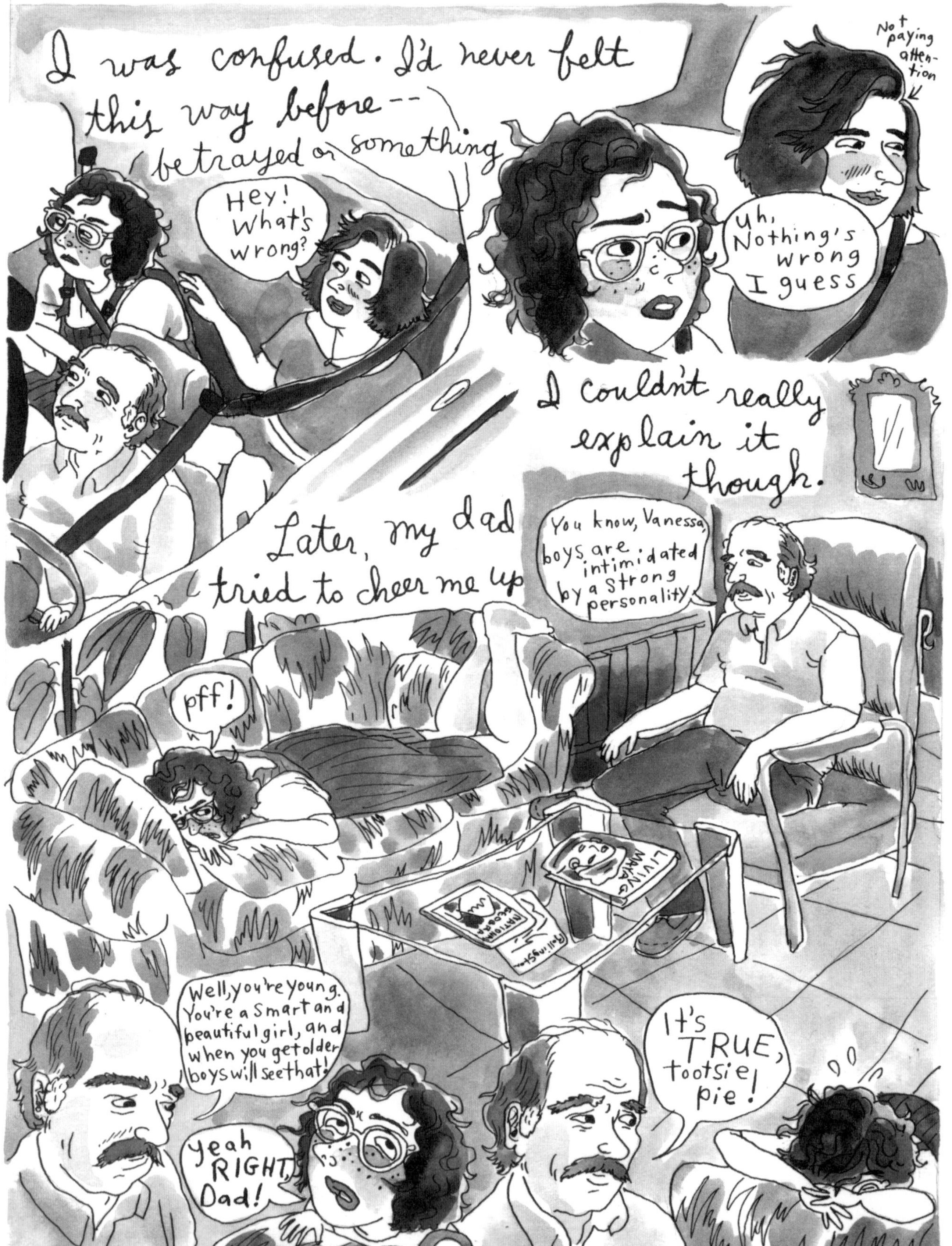
I was confused. I'd never felt this way before-- betrayed or something
Hey! What's wrong?
Not paying attention
Uh, Nothing's wrong I guess
I couldn't really explain it though.
Later, my dad tried to cheer me up
You know, Vanessa, boys are intimidated by a strong personality.
pff!
Well, you're young. You're a smart and beautiful girl, and when you get older boys will see that!
Yeah RIGHT, Dad!
It's TRUE, tootsie pie!

JOE MATT

FROM *Fair Weather* **JOE MATT**

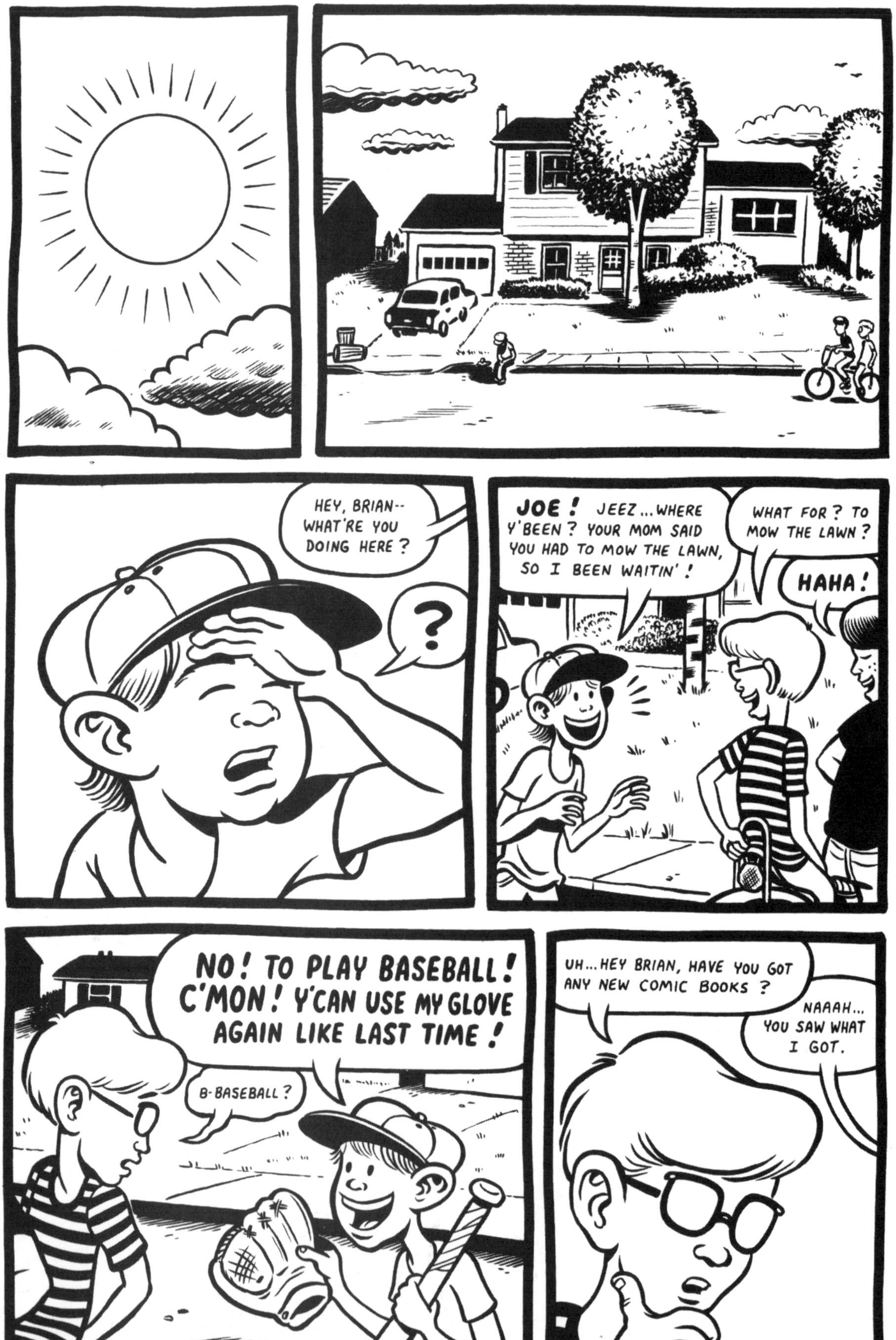
HEY, BRIAN-- WHAT'RE YOU DOING HERE ?
?
JOE ! JEEZ... WHERE Y'BEEN ? YOUR MOM SAID YOU HAD TO MOW THE LAWN, SO I BEEN WAITIN' !
WHAT FOR ? TO MOW THE LAWN ?
HAHA !
NO ! TO PLAY BASEBALL ! C'MON ! Y'CAN USE MY GLOVE AGAIN LIKE LAST TIME !
B-BASEBALL ?
UH... HEY BRIAN, HAVE YOU GOT ANY NEW COMIC BOOKS ?
NAAAH... YOU SAW WHAT I GOT.

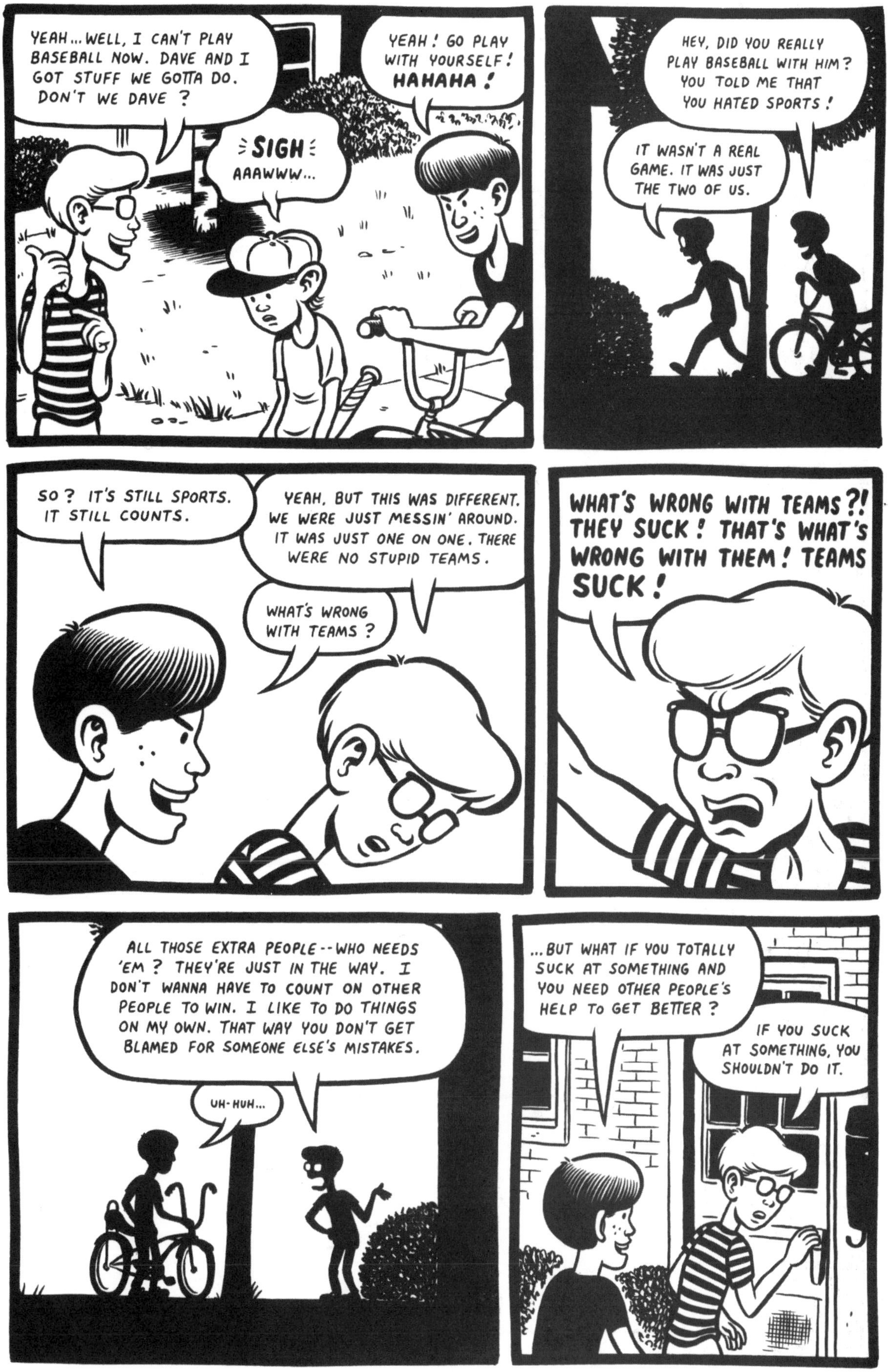
YEAH... WELL, I CAN'T PLAY BASEBALL NOW. DAVE AND I GOT STUFF WE GOTTA DO. DON'T WE DAVE ?
SIGH
AAAWWW...
YEAH! GO PLAY WITH YOURSELF! HAHAHA!
HEY, DID YOU REALLY PLAY BASEBALL WITH HIM? YOU TOLD ME THAT YOU HATED SPORTS!
IT WASN'T A REAL GAME. IT WAS JUST THE TWO OF US.
SO? IT'S STILL SPORTS. IT STILL COUNTS.
YEAH, BUT THIS WAS DIFFERENT. WE WERE JUST MESSIN' AROUND. IT WAS JUST ONE ON ONE. THERE WERE NO STUPID TEAMS.
WHAT'S WRONG WITH TEAMS ?
WHAT'S WRONG WITH TEAMS?! THEY SUCK! THAT'S WHAT'S WRONG WITH THEM! TEAMS SUCK!
ALL THOSE EXTRA PEOPLE -- WHO NEEDS 'EM? THEY'RE JUST IN THE WAY. I DON'T WANNA HAVE TO COUNT ON OTHER PEOPLE TO WIN. I LIKE TO DO THINGS ON MY OWN. THAT WAY YOU DON'T GET BLAMED FOR SOMEONE ELSE'S MISTAKES.
UH-HUH...
...BUT WHAT IF YOU TOTALLY SUCK AT SOMETHING AND YOU NEED OTHER PEOPLE'S HELP TO GET BETTER ?
IF YOU SUCK AT SOMETHING, YOU SHOULDN'T DO IT.

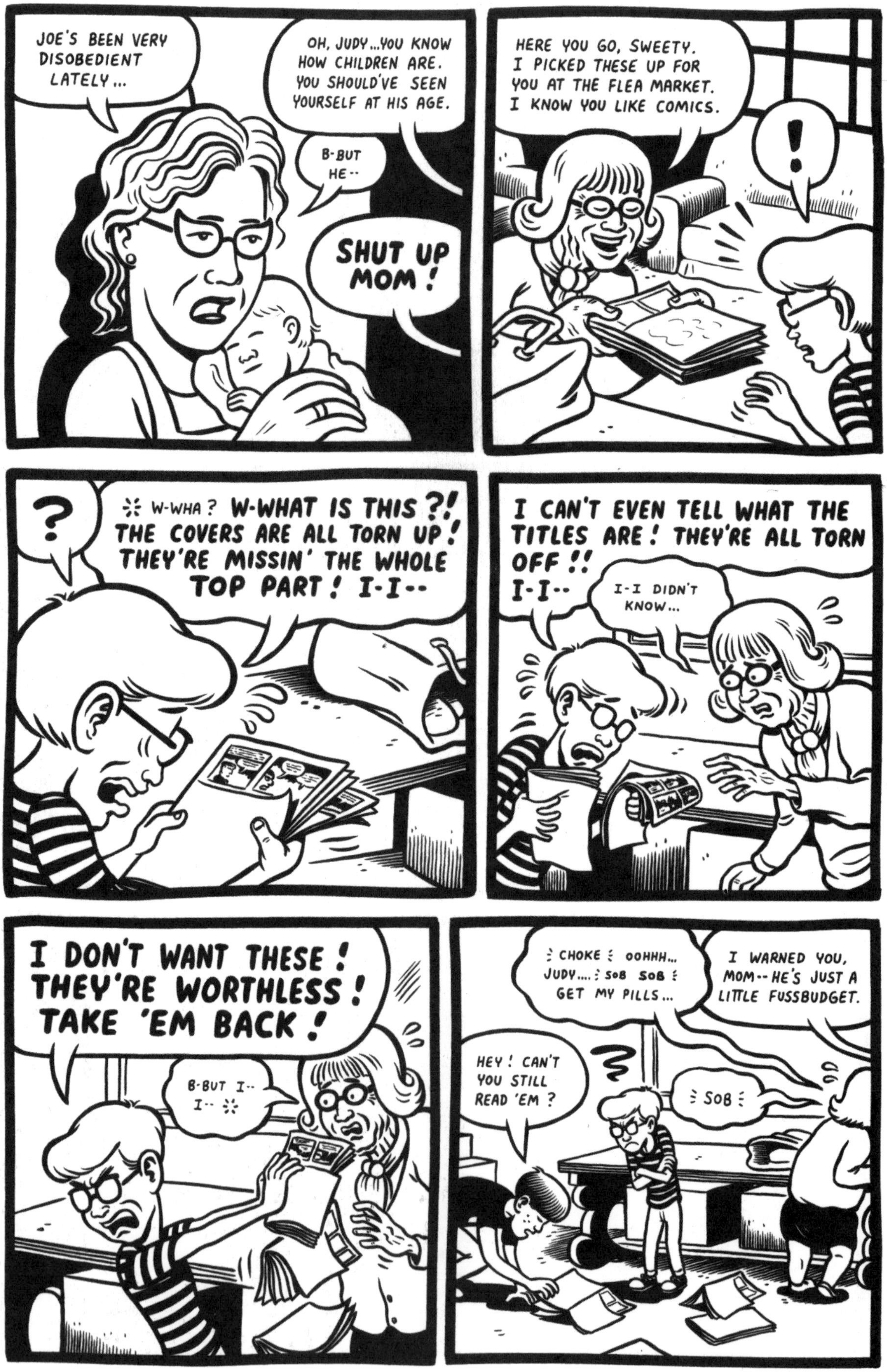
JOE'S BEEN VERY DISOBEDIENT LATELY...
OH, JUDY...YOU KNOW HOW CHILDREN ARE. YOU SHOULD'VE SEEN YOURSELF AT HIS AGE.
B-BUT HE--
SHUT UP MOM!
HERE YOU GO, SWEETY. I PICKED THESE UP FOR YOU AT THE FLEA MARKET. I KNOW YOU LIKE COMICS.
!
?
W-WHA? W-WHAT IS THIS?! THE COVERS ARE ALL TORN UP! THEY'RE MISSIN' THE WHOLE TOP PART! I-I--
I CAN'T EVEN TELL WHAT THE TITLES ARE! THEY'RE ALL TORN OFF!! I-I--
I-I DIDN'T KNOW...
I DON'T WANT THESE! THEY'RE WORTHLESS! TAKE 'EM BACK!
B-BUT I-- I--
CHOKE OOHHH... JUDY.... SOB SOB GET MY PILLS...
I WARNED YOU, MOM--HE'S JUST A LITTLE FUSSBUDGET.
HEY! CAN'T YOU STILL READ 'EM?
SOB

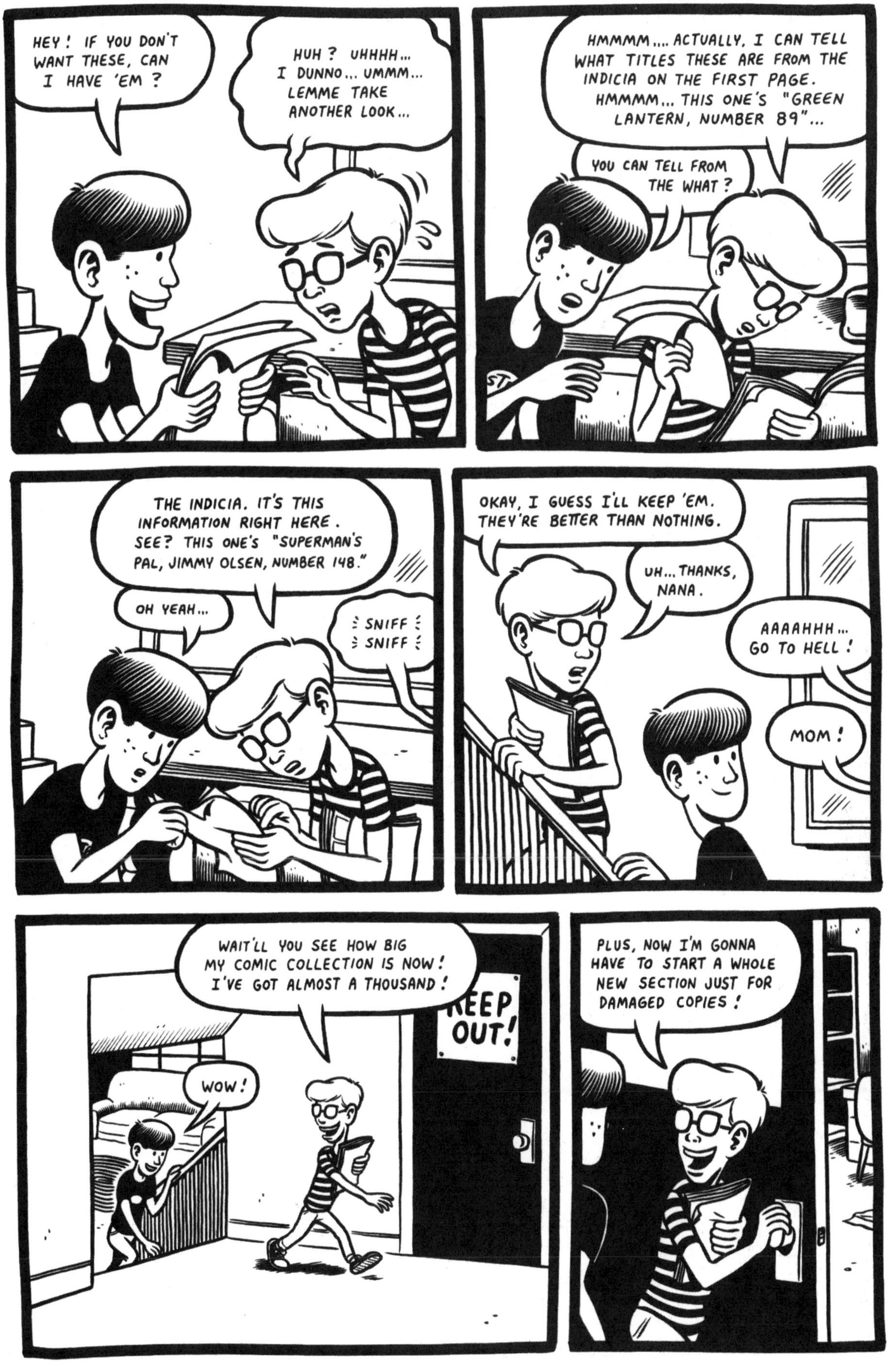
HEY! IF YOU DON'T WANT THESE, CAN I HAVE 'EM?
HUH? UHHHH... I DUNNO... UMMM... LEMME TAKE ANOTHER LOOK...
HMMMM.... ACTUALLY, I CAN TELL WHAT TITLES THESE ARE FROM THE INDICIA ON THE FIRST PAGE. HMMMM... THIS ONE'S "GREEN LANTERN, NUMBER 89"...
YOU CAN TELL FROM THE WHAT?
THE INDICIA. IT'S THIS INFORMATION RIGHT HERE. SEE? THIS ONE'S "SUPERMAN'S PAL, JIMMY OLSEN, NUMBER 148."
OH YEAH...
SNIFF SNIFF
OKAY, I GUESS I'LL KEEP 'EM. THEY'RE BETTER THAN NOTHING.
UH... THANKS, NANA.
AAAAHHH... GO TO HELL!
MOM!
WAIT'LL YOU SEE HOW BIG MY COMIC COLLECTION IS NOW! I'VE GOT ALMOST A THOUSAND!
KEEP OUT!
WOW!
PLUS, NOW I'M GONNA HAVE TO START A WHOLE NEW SECTION JUST FOR DAMAGED COPIES!

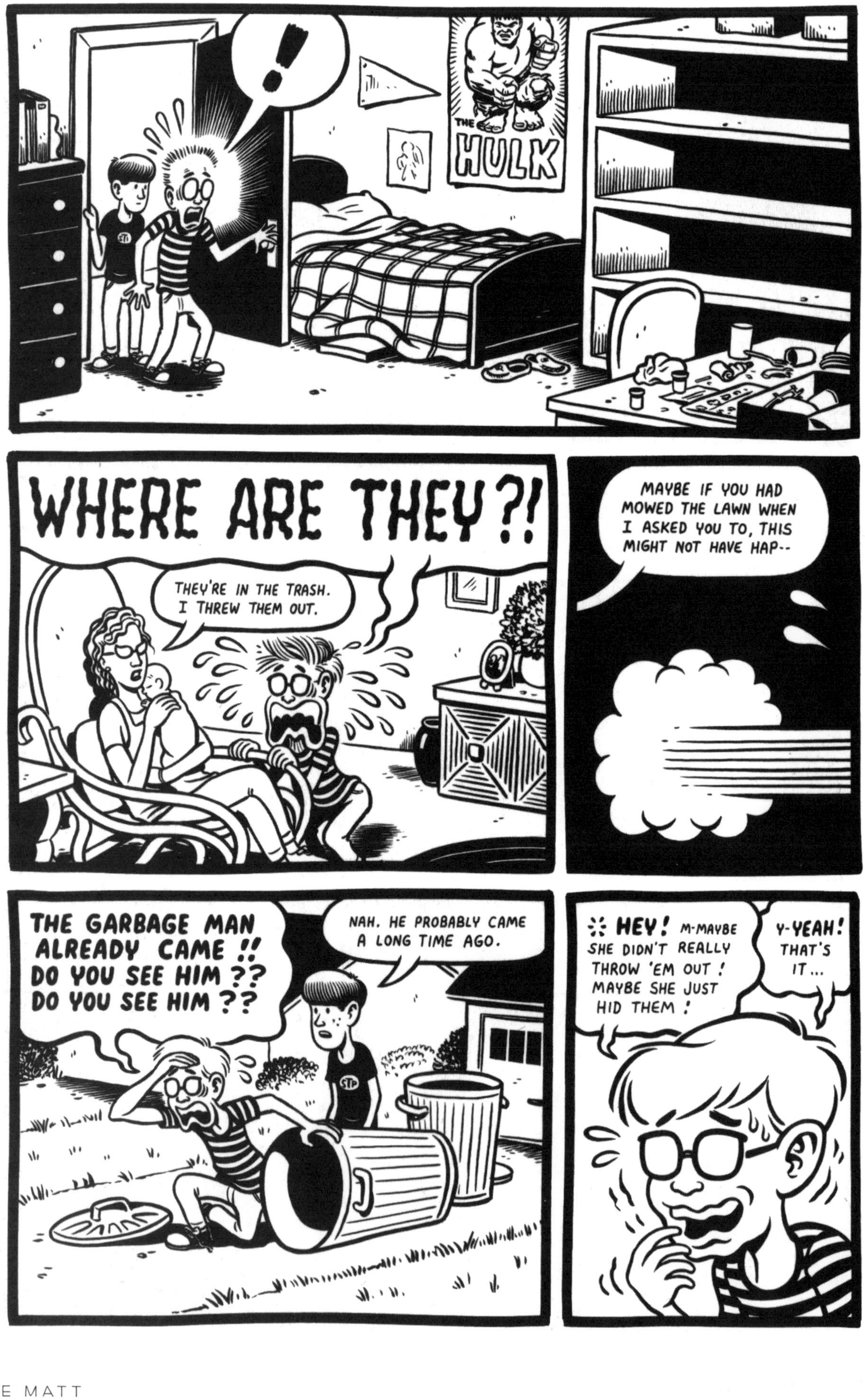

THE HULK
!
WHERE ARE THEY?!
THEY'RE IN THE TRASH. I THREW THEM OUT.
MAYBE IF YOU HAD MOWED THE LAWN WHEN I ASKED YOU TO, THIS MIGHT NOT HAVE HAP--
THE GARBAGE MAN ALREADY CAME !! DO YOU SEE HIM ?? DO YOU SEE HIM ??
NAH. HE PROBABLY CAME A LONG TIME AGO.
HEY! M-MAYBE SHE DIDN'T REALLY THROW 'EM OUT! MAYBE SHE JUST HID THEM!
Y-YEAH! THAT'S IT...

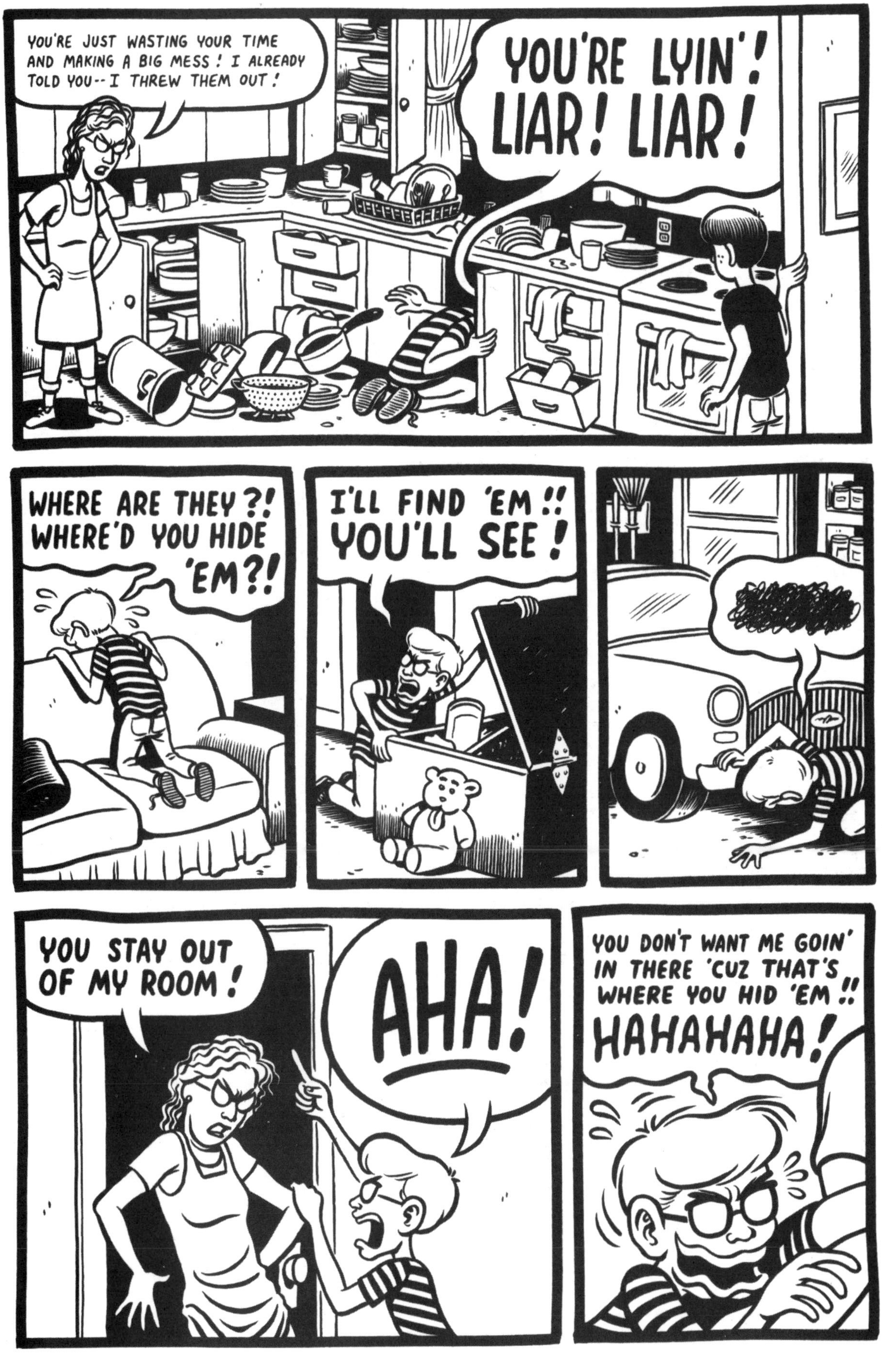
YOU'RE JUST WASTING YOUR TIME AND MAKING A BIG MESS! I ALREADY TOLD YOU-- I THREW THEM OUT!
YOU'RE LYIN'! LIAR! LIAR!
WHERE ARE THEY?! WHERE'D YOU HIDE 'EM?!
I'LL FIND 'EM!! YOU'LL SEE!
YOU STAY OUT OF MY ROOM!
AHA!
YOU DON'T WANT ME GOIN' IN THERE 'CUZ THAT'S WHERE YOU HID 'EM!! HAHAHAHA!

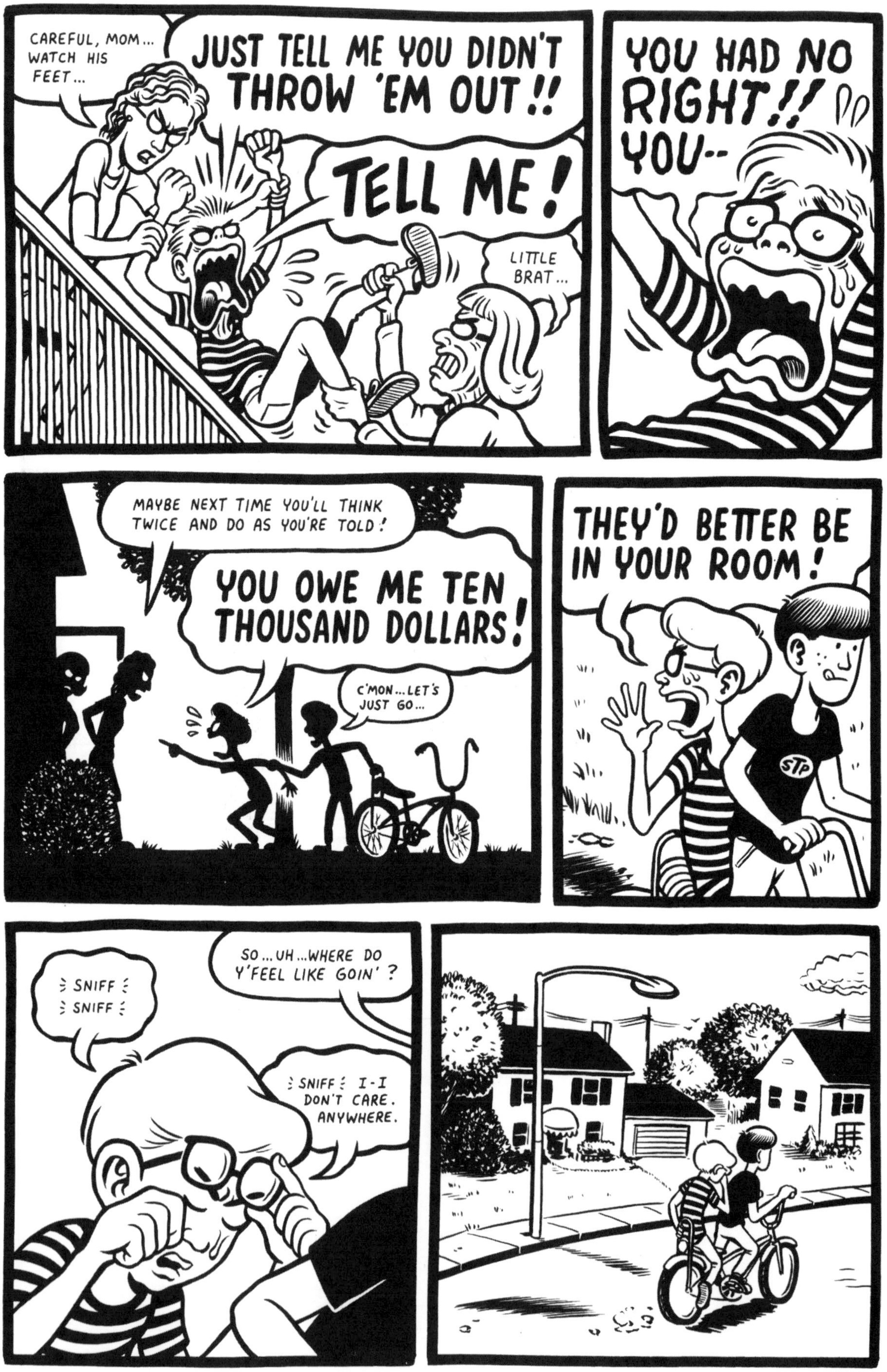
CAREFUL, MOM... WATCH HIS FEET...
JUST TELL ME YOU DIDN'T THROW 'EM OUT!!
TELL ME!
LITTLE BRAT...
YOU HAD NO RIGHT!! YOU--
MAYBE NEXT TIME YOU'LL THINK TWICE AND DO AS YOU'RE TOLD!
YOU OWE ME TEN THOUSAND DOLLARS!
C'MON... LET'S JUST GO...
THEY'D BETTER BE IN YOUR ROOM!
STP
SNIFF SNIFF
SO... UH... WHERE DO Y'FEEL LIKE GOIN'?
SNIFF I-I DON'T CARE. ANYWHERE.

TANIA SCHRAG

SNITCH

TANIA SCHRAG

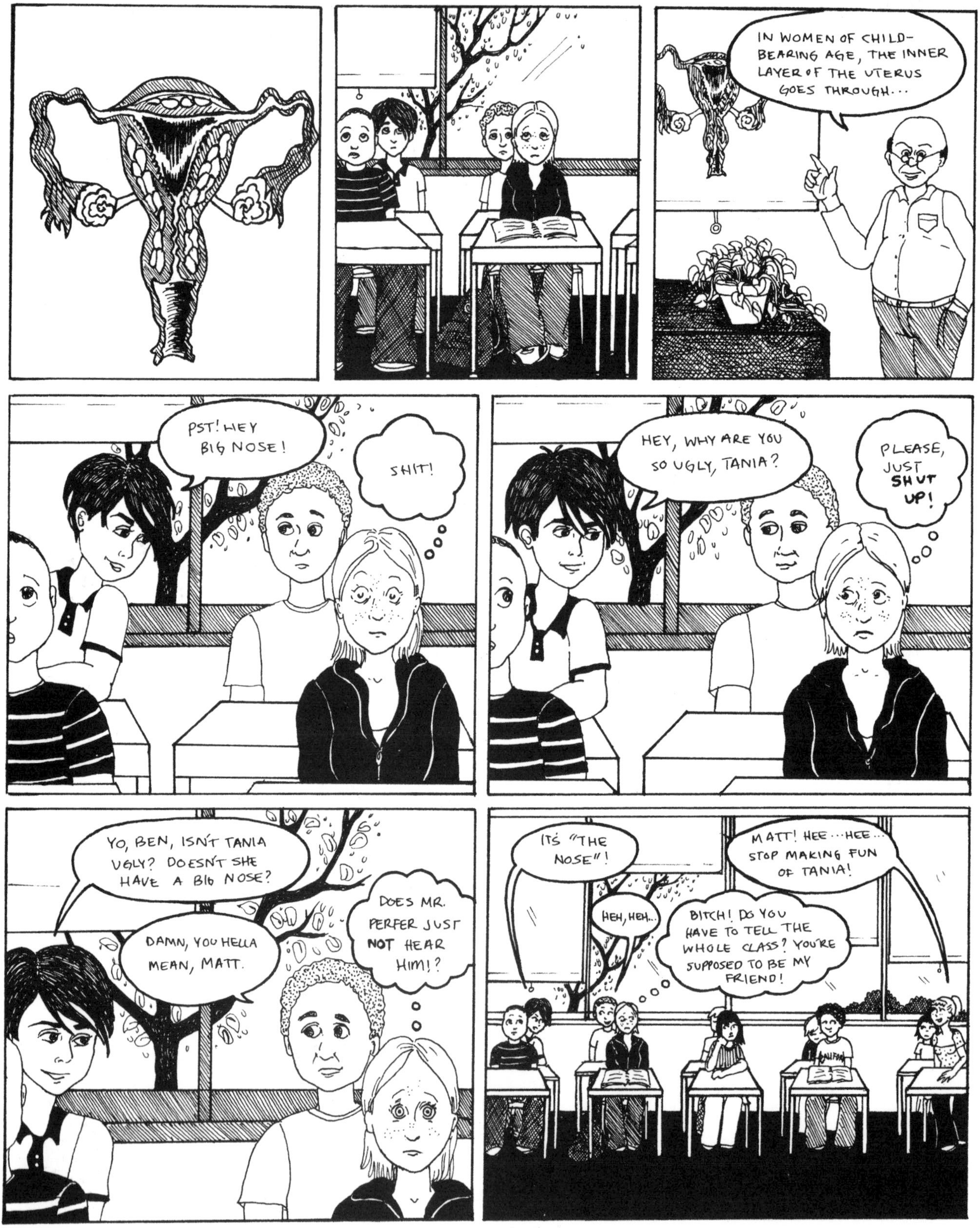
IN WOMEN OF CHILD-BEARING AGE, THE INNER LAYER OF THE UTERUS GOES THROUGH...
PST! HEY BIG NOSE!
SHIT!
HEY, WHY ARE YOU SO UGLY, TANIA?
PLEASE, JUST SHUT UP!
YO, BEN, ISN'T TANIA UGLY? DOESN'T SHE HAVE A BIG NOSE?
DAMN, YOU HELLA MEAN, MATT.
DOES MR. PERFER JUST NOT HEAR HIM!?
IT'S "THE NOSE"!
HEH, HEH...
MATT! HEE...HEE... STOP MAKING FUN OF TANIA!
BITCH! DO YOU HAVE TO TELL THE WHOLE CLASS? YOU'RE SUPPOSED TO BE MY FRIEND!

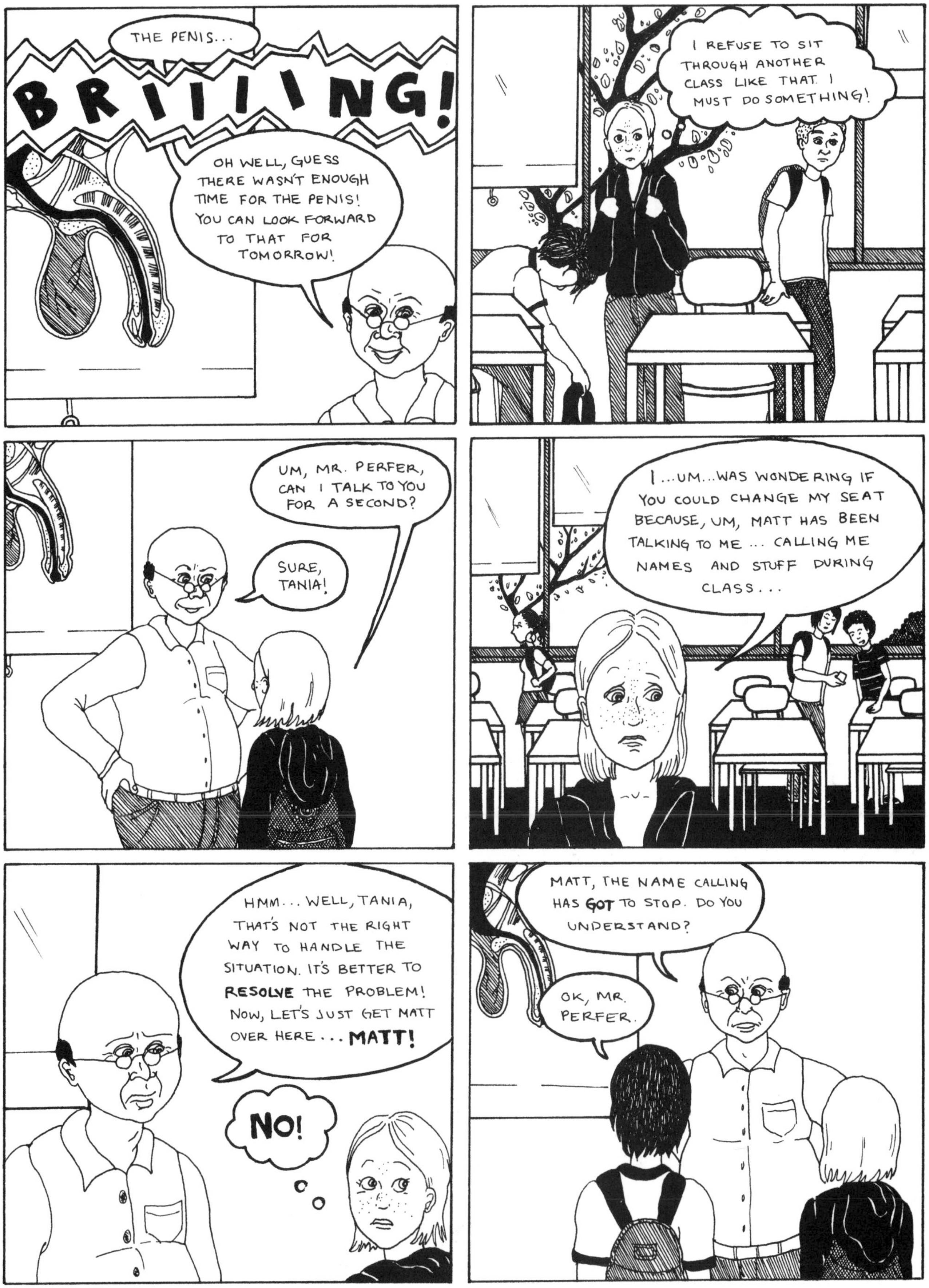
THE PENIS...
BRIIIING!
OH WELL, GUESS THERE WASN'T ENOUGH TIME FOR THE PENIS! YOU CAN LOOK FORWARD TO THAT FOR TOMORROW!
I REFUSE TO SIT THROUGH ANOTHER CLASS LIKE THAT. I MUST DO SOMETHING!
UM, MR. PERFER, CAN I TALK TO YOU FOR A SECOND?
SURE, TANIA!
I...UM...WAS WONDERING IF YOU COULD CHANGE MY SEAT BECAUSE, UM, MATT HAS BEEN TALKING TO ME ... CALLING ME NAMES AND STUFF DURING CLASS...
HMM... WELL, TANIA, THAT'S NOT THE RIGHT WAY TO HANDLE THE SITUATION. IT'S BETTER TO RESOLVE THE PROBLEM! NOW, LET'S JUST GET MATT OVER HERE... MATT!
NO!
MATT, THE NAME CALLING HAS GOT TO STOP. DO YOU UNDERSTAND?
OK, MR. PERFER.

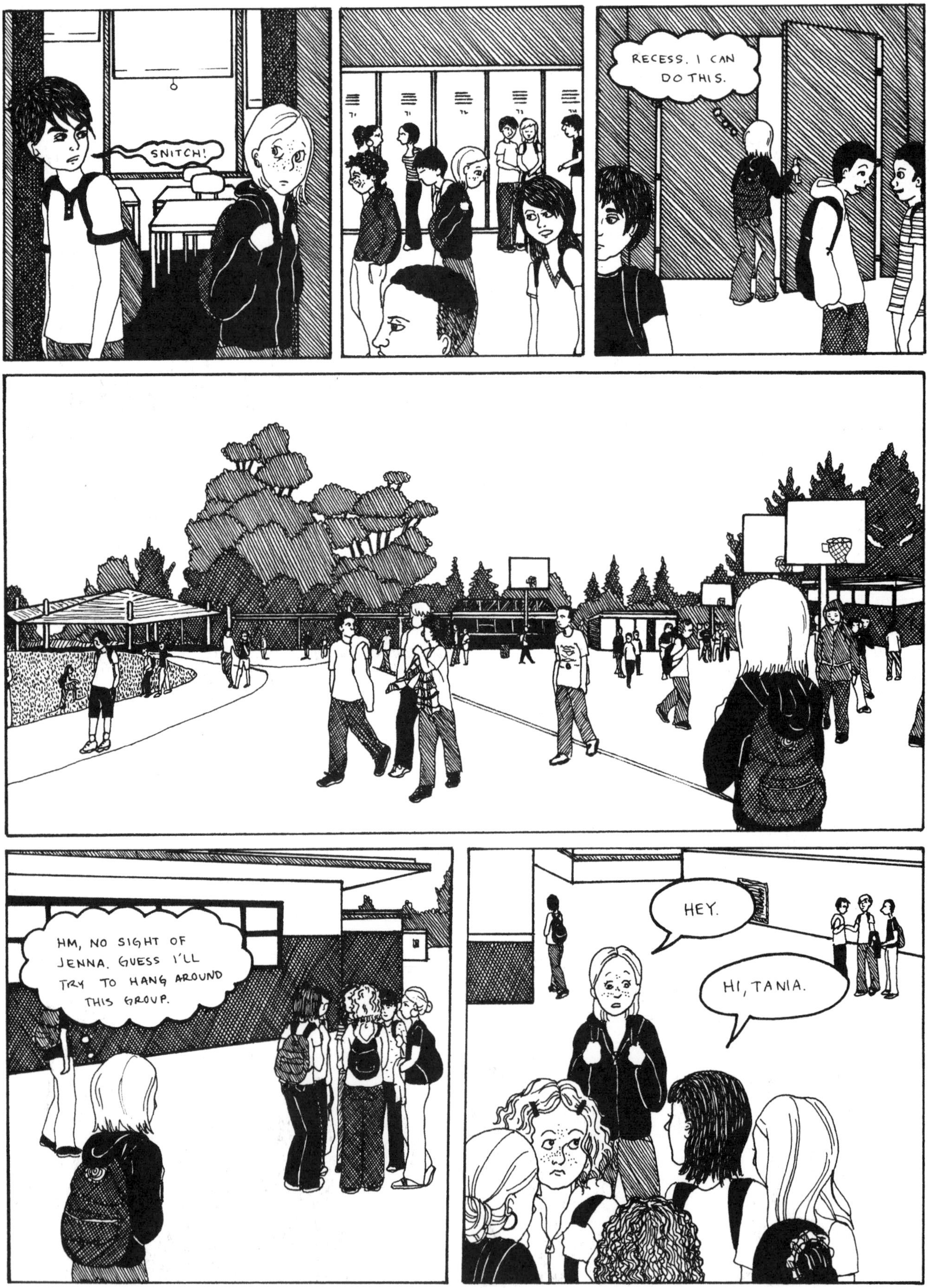
SNITCH!
RECESS. I CAN DO THIS.
HM, NO SIGHT OF JENNA. GUESS I'LL TRY TO HANG AROUND THIS GROUP.
HEY.
HI, TANIA.

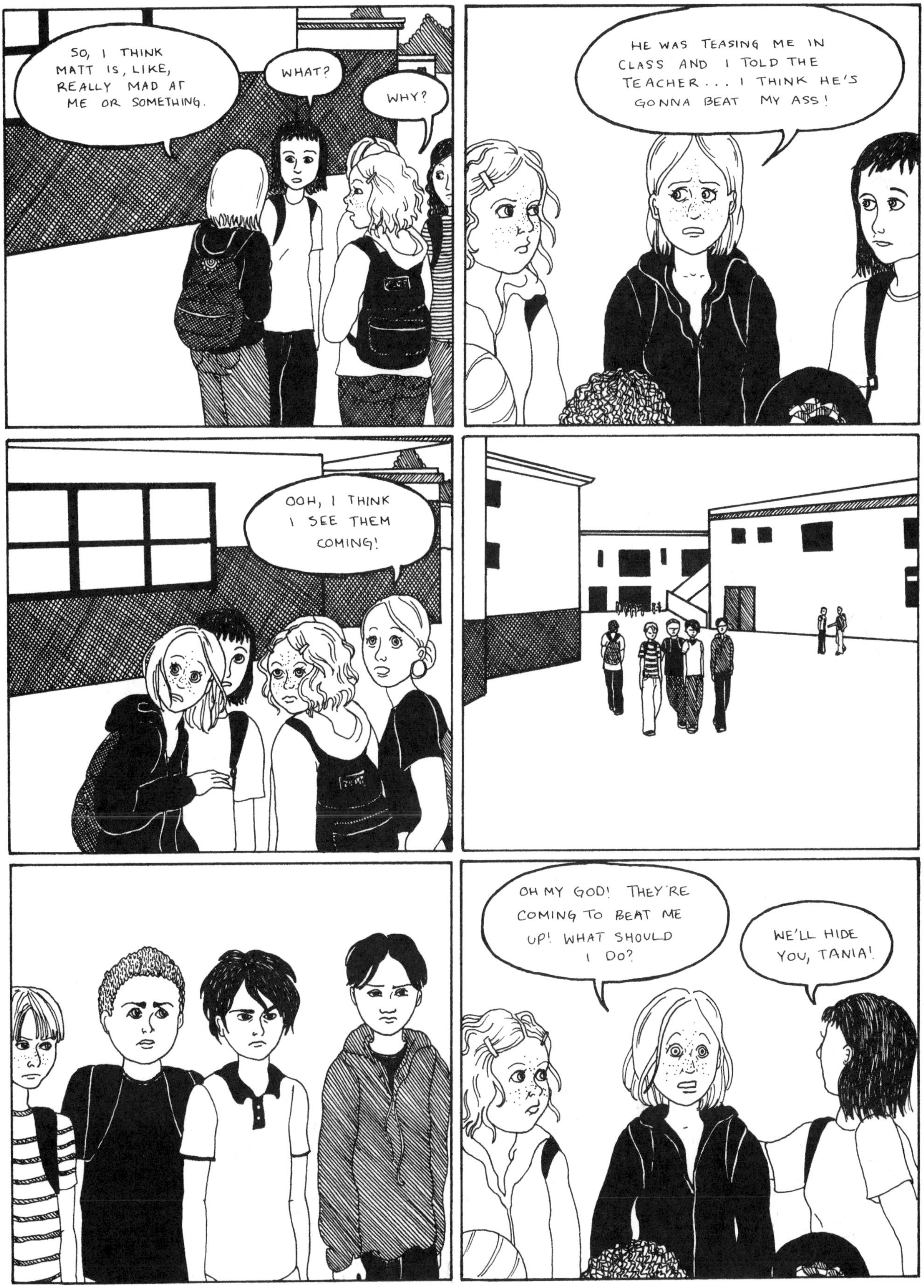
SO, I THINK MATT IS, LIKE, REALLY MAD AT ME OR SOMETHING.
WHAT?
WHY?
HE WAS TEASING ME IN CLASS AND I TOLD THE TEACHER . . . I THINK HE'S GONNA BEAT MY ASS!
OOH, I THINK I SEE THEM COMING!
OH MY GOD! THEY'RE COMING TO BEAT ME UP! WHAT SHOULD I DO?
WE'LL HIDE YOU, TANIA!

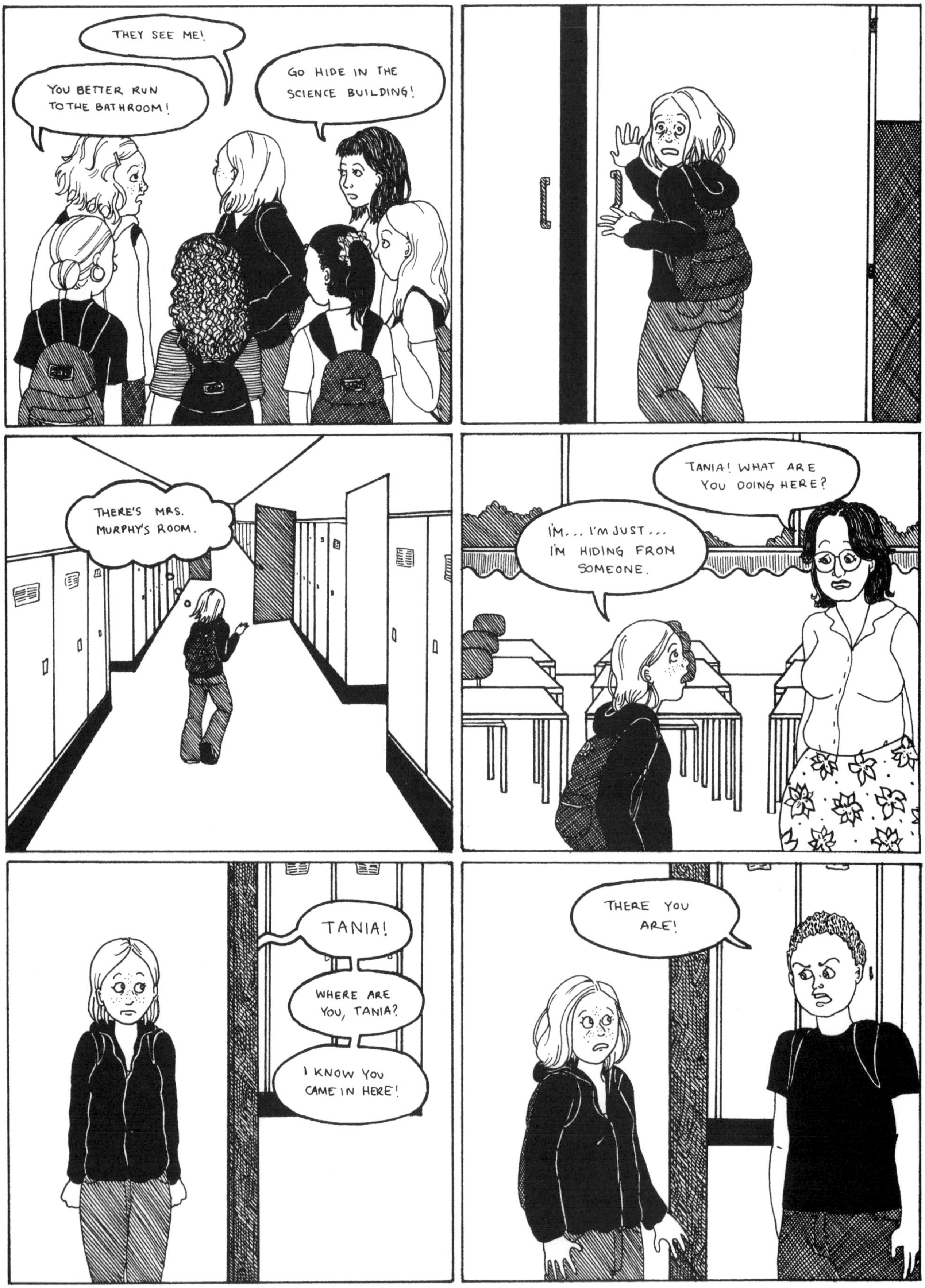
THEY SEE ME!
YOU BETTER RUN TO THE BATHROOM!
GO HIDE IN THE SCIENCE BUILDING!
THERE'S MRS. MURPHY'S ROOM.
TANIA! WHAT ARE YOU DOING HERE?
I'M... I'M JUST... I'M HIDING FROM SOMEONE.
TANIA!
WHERE ARE YOU, TANIA?
I KNOW YOU CAME IN HERE!
THERE YOU ARE!

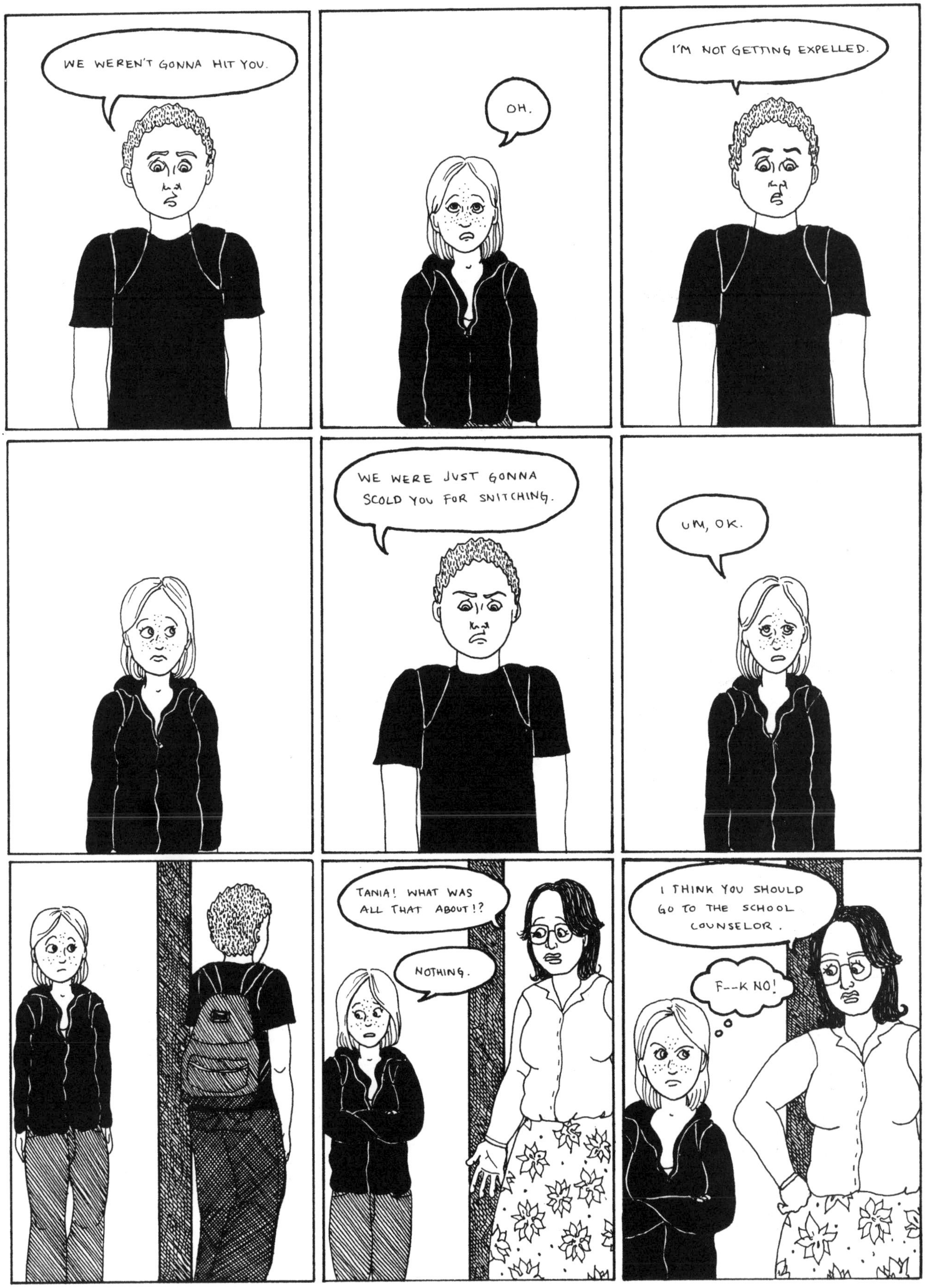

WE WEREN'T GONNA HIT YOU.
OH.
I'M NOT GETTING EXPELLED.
WE WERE JUST GONNA SCOLD YOU FOR SNITCHING.
UM, OK.
TANIA! WHAT WAS ALL THAT ABOUT!?
NOTHING.
I THINK YOU SHOULD GO TO THE SCHOOL COUNSELOR.
F--K NO!

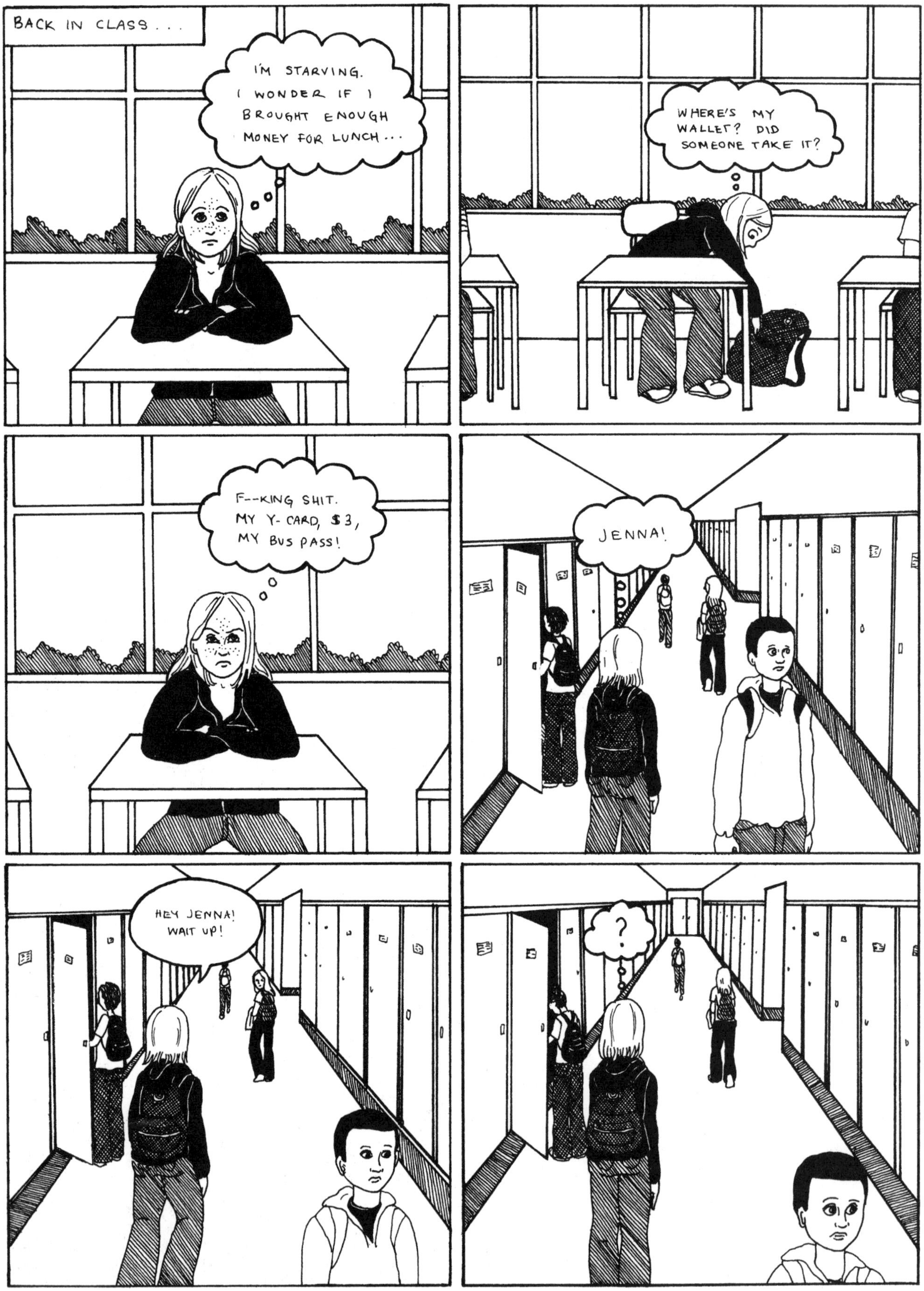
BACK IN CLASS . . .
I'M STARVING. I WONDER IF I BROUGHT ENOUGH MONEY FOR LUNCH . . .
WHERE'S MY WALLET? DID SOMEONE TAKE IT?
F--KING SHIT. MY Y-CARD, $3, MY BUS PASS!
JENNA!
HEY JENNA! WAIT UP!
?

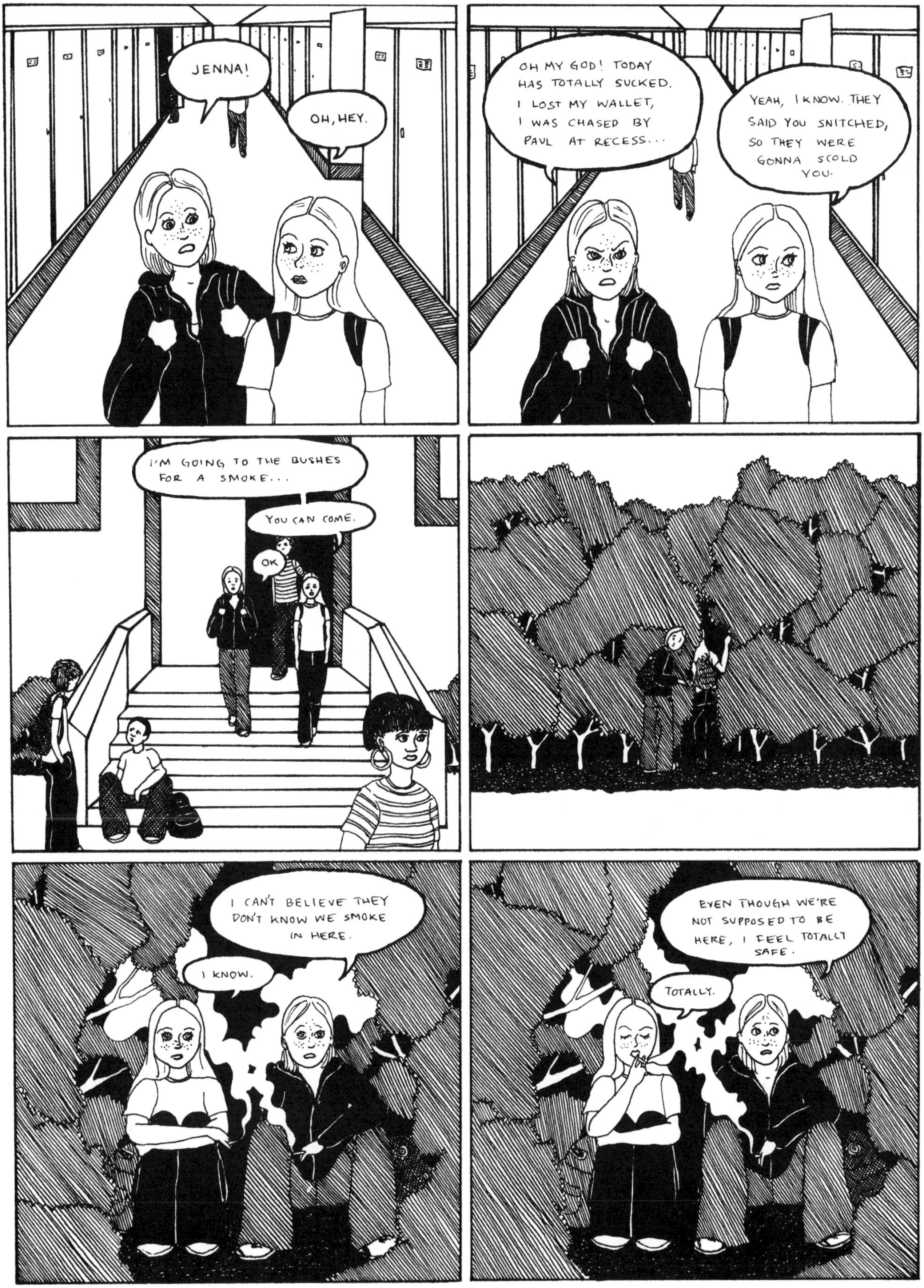
JENNA!
OH, HEY.
OH MY GOD! TODAY HAS TOTALLY SUCKED. I LOST MY WALLET, I WAS CHASED BY PAUL AT RECESS...
YEAH, I KNOW. THEY SAID YOU SNITCHED, SO THEY WERE GONNA SCOLD YOU.
I'M GOING TO THE BUSHES FOR A SMOKE...
YOU CAN COME.
OK
I CAN'T BELIEVE THEY DON'T KNOW WE SMOKE IN HERE.
I KNOW.
EVEN THOUGH WE'RE NOT SUPPOSED TO BE HERE, I FEEL TOTALLY SAFE.
TOTALLY.

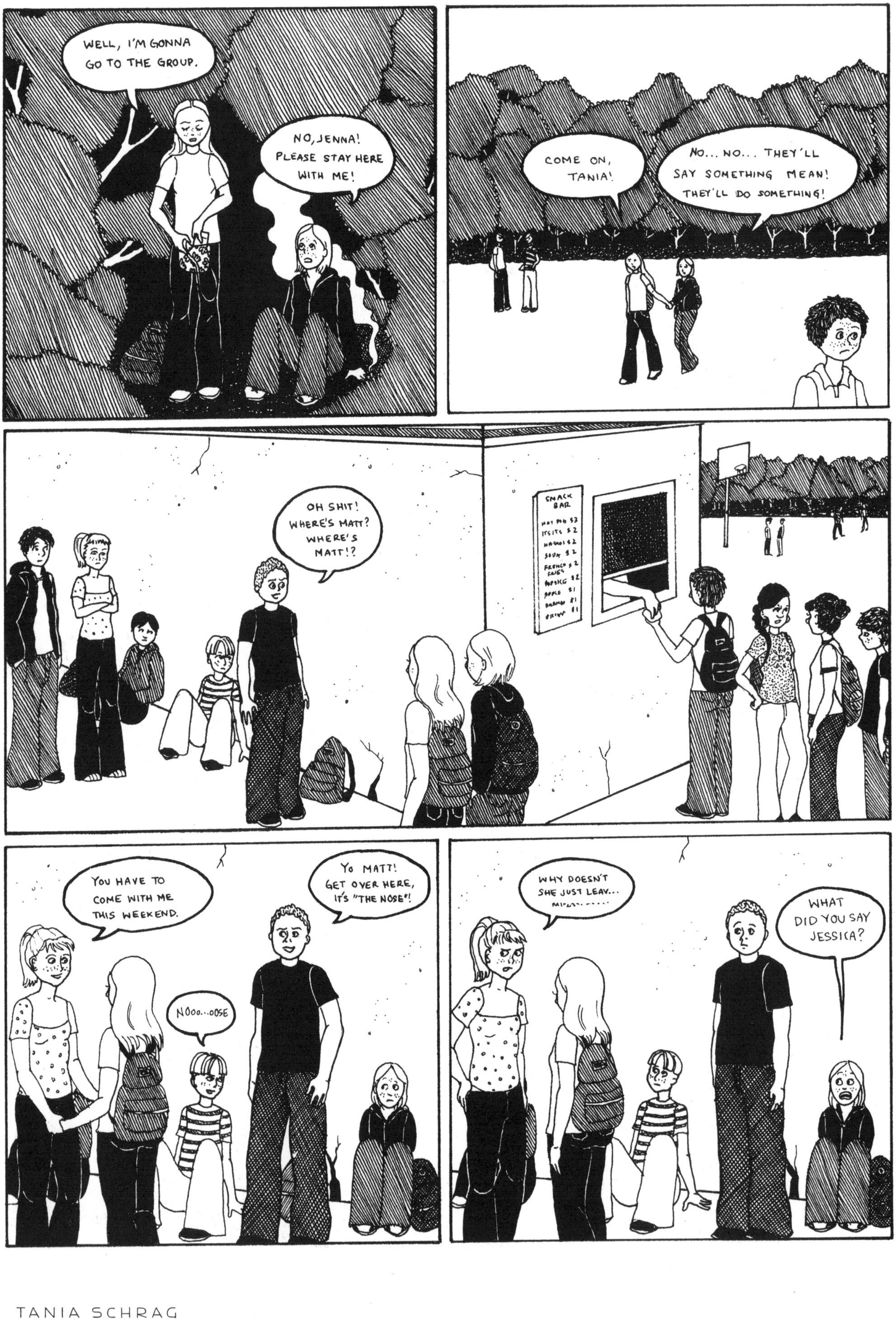
WELL, I'M GONNA GO TO THE GROUP.
NO, JENNA! PLEASE STAY HERE WITH ME!
COME ON, TANIA!
NO... NO... THEY'LL SAY SOMETHING MEAN! THEY'LL DO SOMETHING!
OH SHIT! WHERE'S MATT? WHERE'S MATT!?
SNACK BAR
YOU HAVE TO COME WITH ME THIS WEEKEND.
YO MATT! GET OVER HERE, IT'S "THE NOSE"!
NOoo...OOSE
WHY DOESN'T SHE JUST LEAV...
WHAT DID YOU SAY JESSICA?

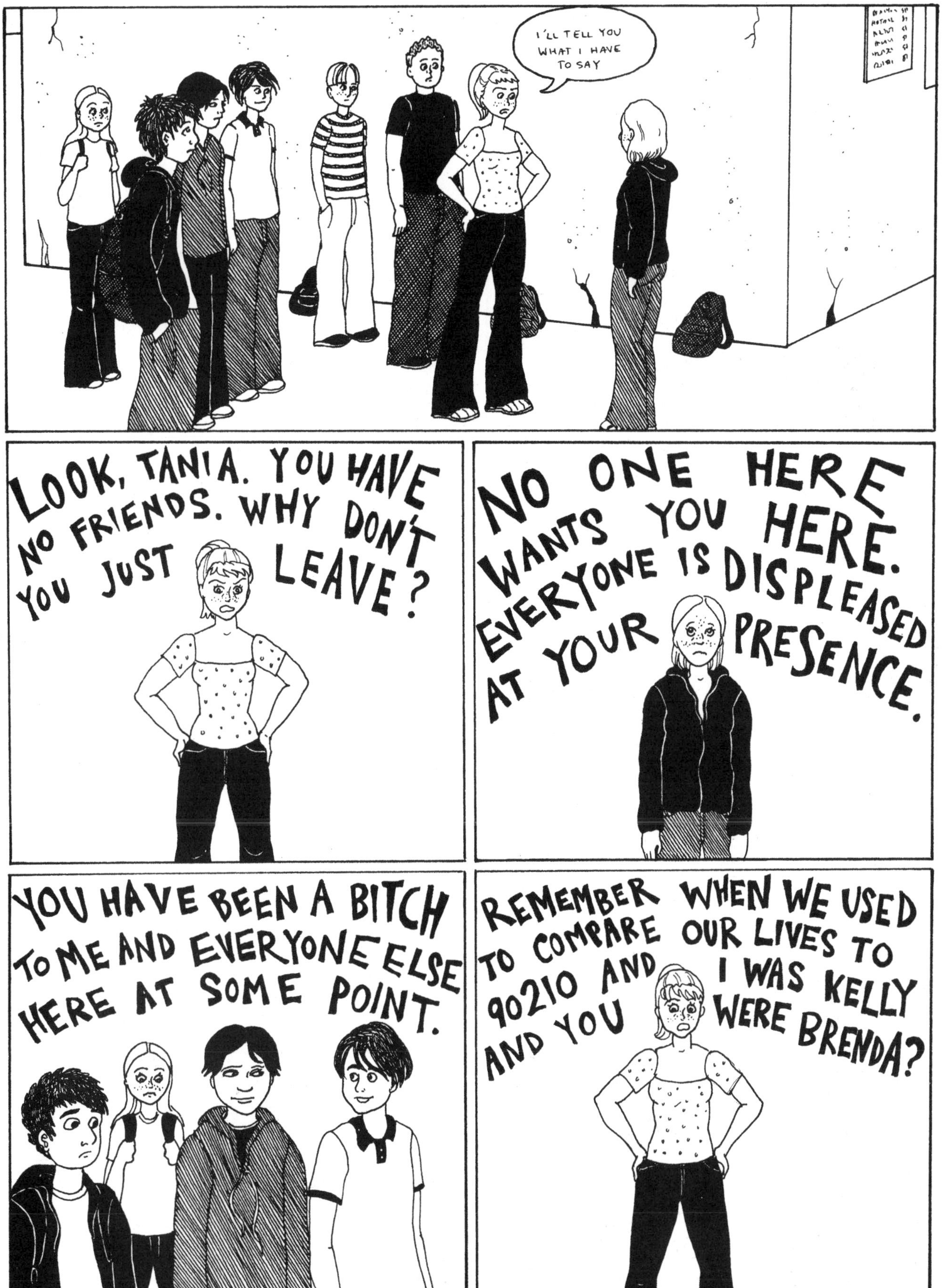
I'LL TELL YOU WHAT I HAVE TO SAY
LOOK, TANIA. YOU HAVE NO FRIENDS. WHY DON'T YOU JUST LEAVE?
NO ONE HERE WANTS YOU HERE. EVERYONE IS DISPLEASED AT YOUR PRESENCE.
YOU HAVE BEEN A BITCH TO ME AND EVERYONE ELSE HERE AT SOME POINT.
REMEMBER WHEN WE USED TO COMPARE OUR LIVES TO 90210 AND I WAS KELLY AND YOU WERE BRENDA?

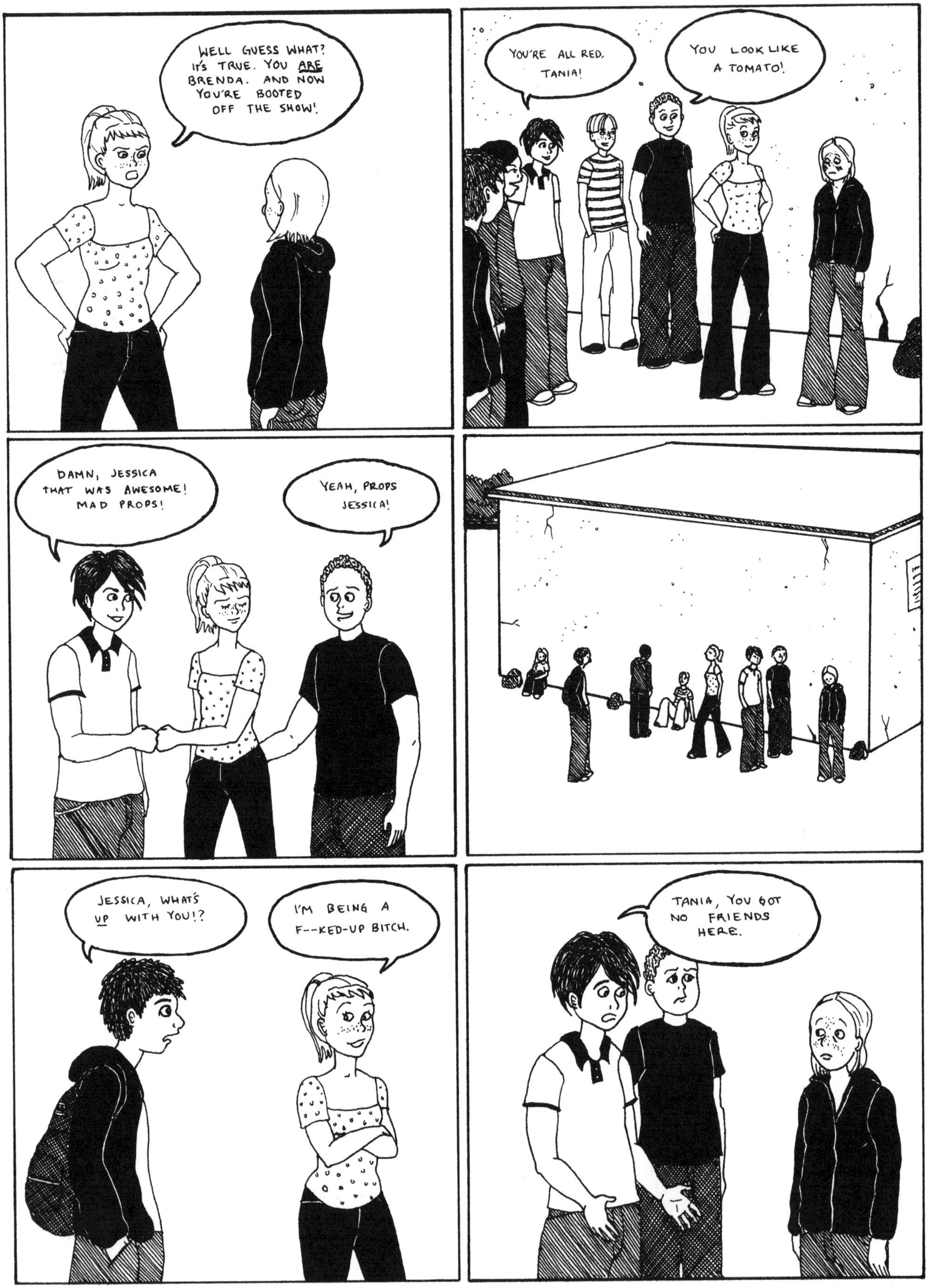
WELL GUESS WHAT? IT'S TRUE. YOU ARE BRENDA. AND NOW YOU'RE BOOTED OFF THE SHOW!
YOU'RE ALL RED, TANIA!
YOU LOOK LIKE A TOMATO!
DAMN, JESSICA THAT WAS AWESOME! MAD PROPS!
YEAH, PROPS JESSICA!
JESSICA, WHAT'S UP WITH YOU!?
I'M BEING A F--KED-UP BITCH.
TANIA, YOU GOT NO FRIENDS HERE.

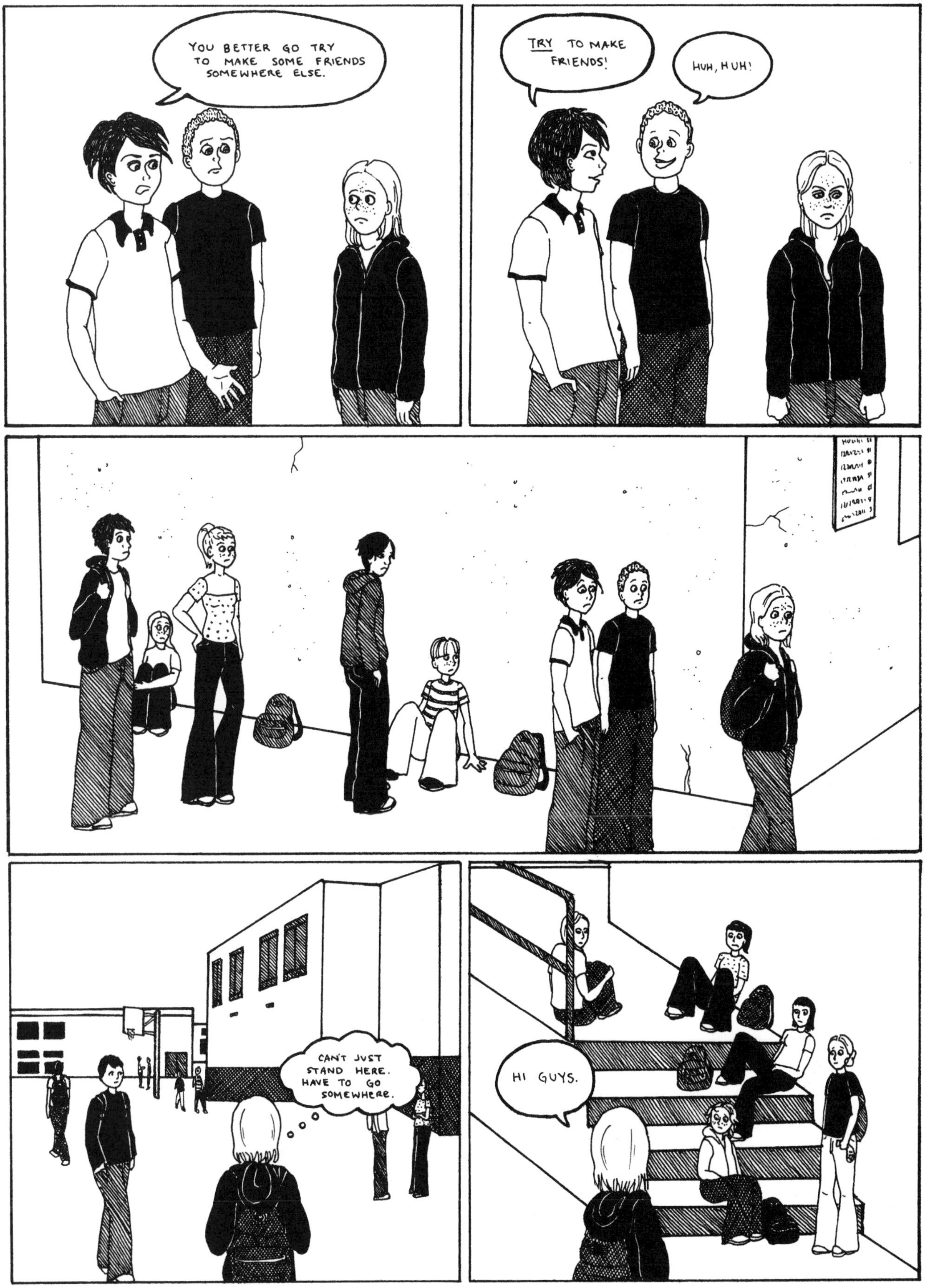
YOU BETTER GO TRY TO MAKE SOME FRIENDS SOMEWHERE ELSE.
TRY TO MAKE FRIENDS!
HUH, HUH!
CAN'T JUST STAND HERE. HAVE TO GO SOMEWHERE.
HI GUYS.

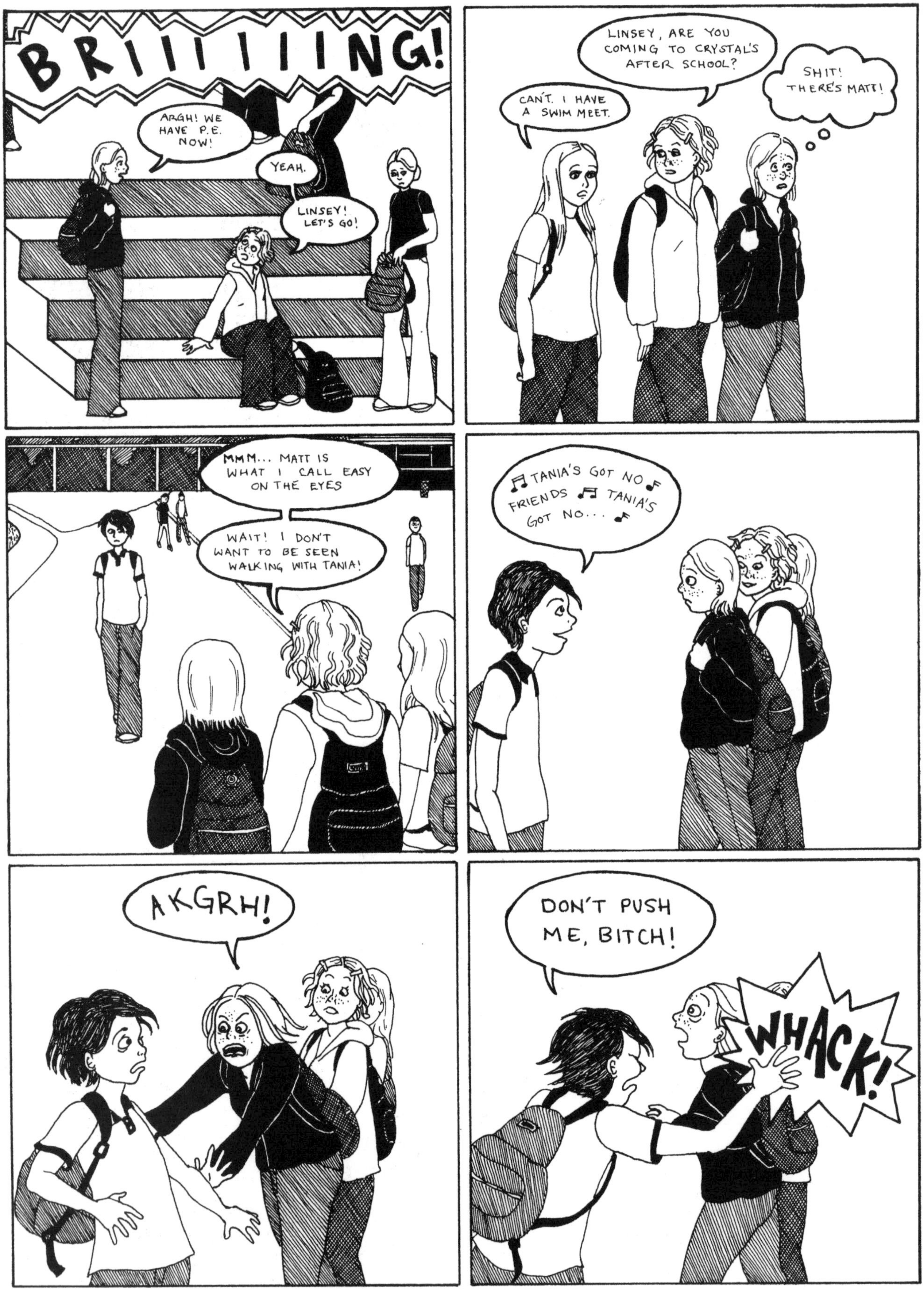
BRIIIIING!
ARGH! WE HAVE P.E. NOW!
YEAH.
LINSEY! LET'S GO!
LINSEY, ARE YOU COMING TO CRYSTAL'S AFTER SCHOOL?
CAN'T. I HAVE A SWIM MEET.
SHIT! THERE'S MATT!
MMM... MATT IS WHAT I CALL EASY ON THE EYES
WAIT! I DON'T WANT TO BE SEEN WALKING WITH TANIA!
TANIA'S GOT NO FRIENDS TANIA'S GOT NO...
AKGRH!
DON'T PUSH ME, BITCH!
WHACK!

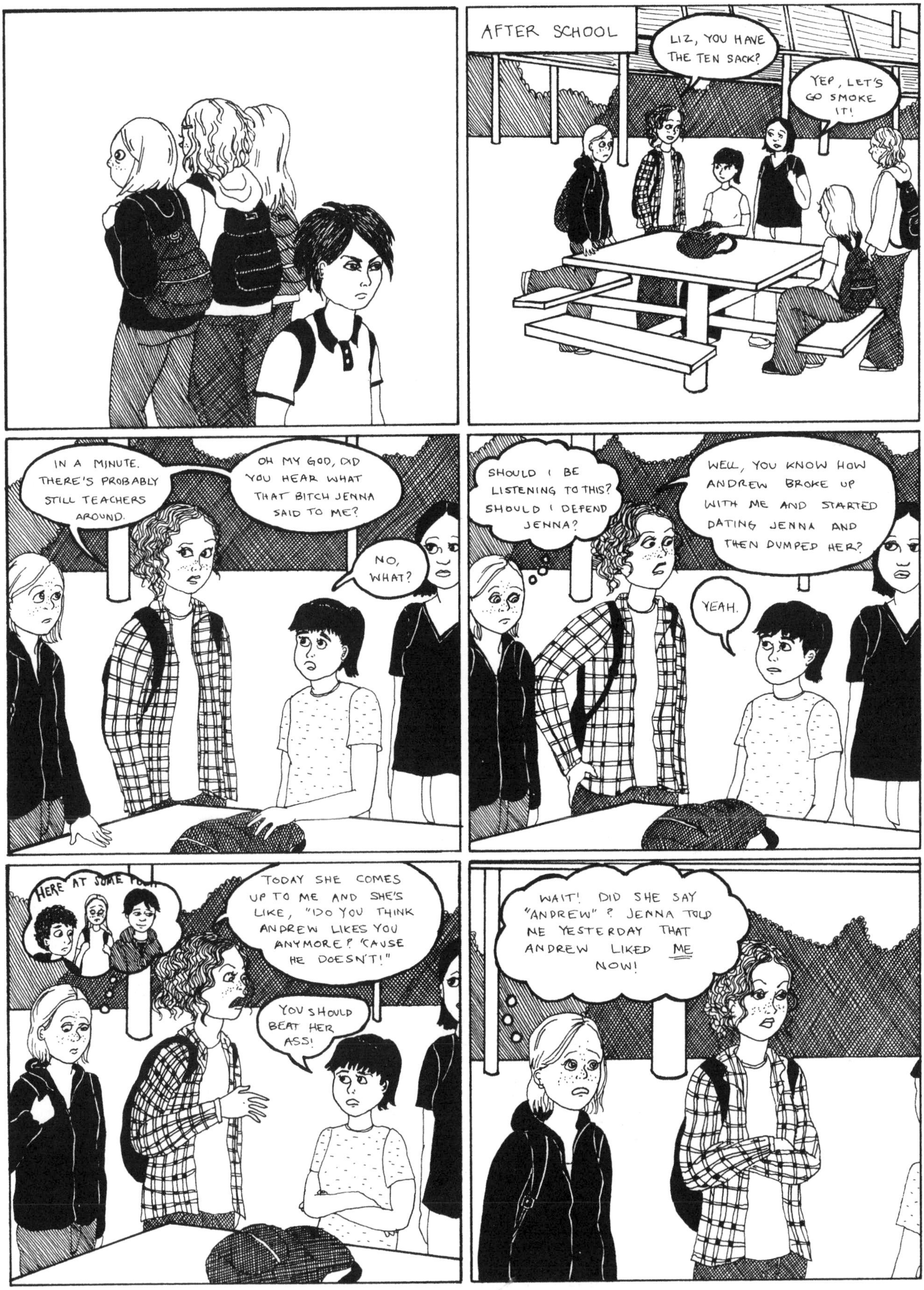
AFTER SCHOOL
LIZ, YOU HAVE THE TEN SACK?
YEP, LET'S GO SMOKE IT!
IN A MINUTE. THERE'S PROBABLY STILL TEACHERS AROUND.
OH MY GOD, DID YOU HEAR WHAT THAT BITCH JENNA SAID TO ME?
NO, WHAT?
SHOULD I BE LISTENING TO THIS? SHOULD I DEFEND JENNA?
WELL, YOU KNOW HOW ANDREW BROKE UP WITH ME AND STARTED DATING JENNA AND THEN DUMPED HER?
YEAH.
HERE AT SOME
TODAY SHE COMES UP TO ME AND SHE'S LIKE, "DO YOU THINK ANDREW LIKES YOU ANYMORE? 'CAUSE HE DOESN'T!"
YOU SHOULD BEAT HER ASS!
WAIT! DID SHE SAY "ANDREW"? JENNA TOLD ME YESTERDAY THAT ANDREW LIKED ME NOW!

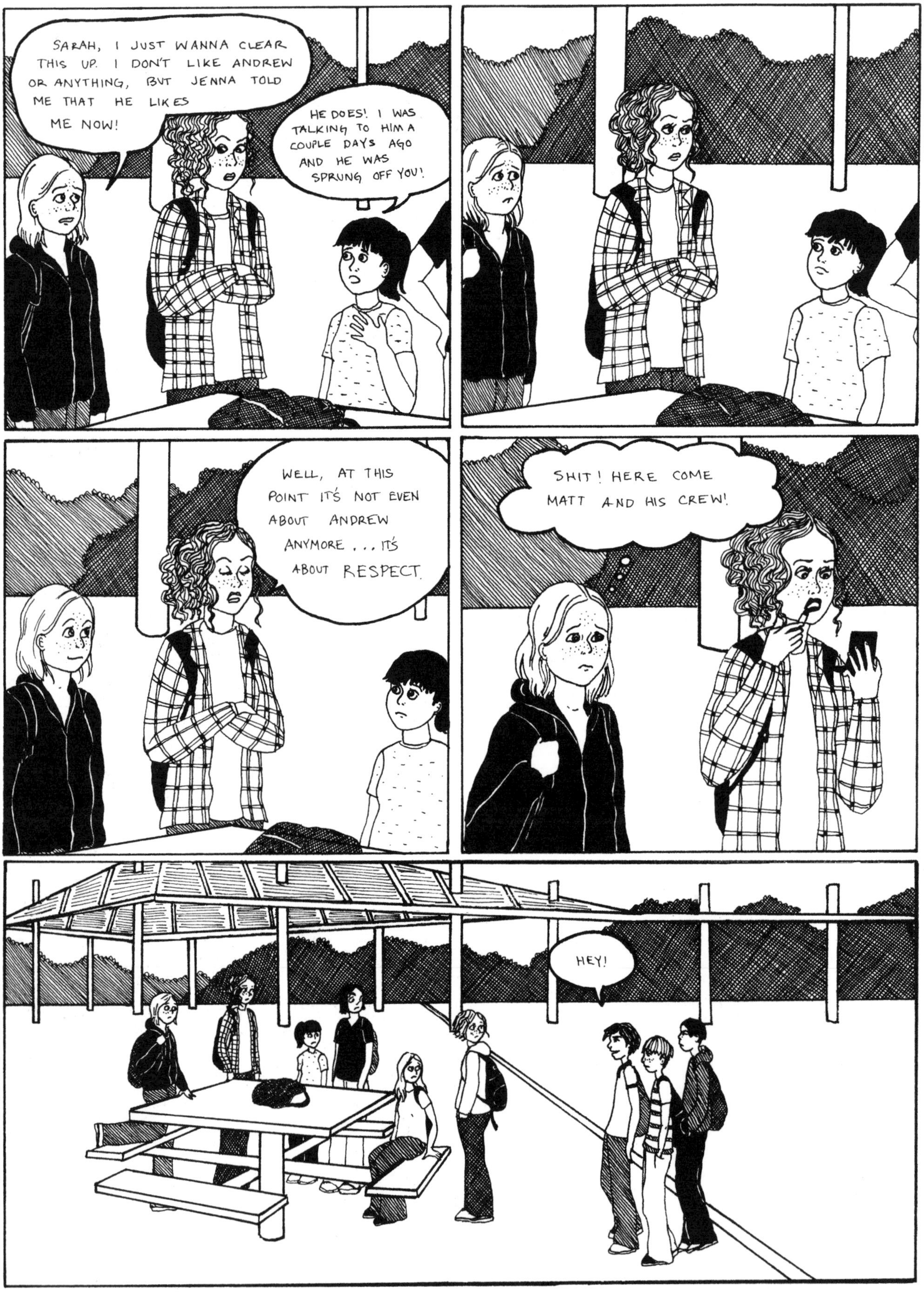
SARAH, I JUST WANNA CLEAR THIS UP. I DON'T LIKE ANDREW OR ANYTHING, BUT JENNA TOLD ME THAT HE LIKES ME NOW!
HE DOES! I WAS TALKING TO HIM A COUPLE DAYS AGO AND HE WAS SPRUNG OFF YOU!
WELL, AT THIS POINT IT'S NOT EVEN ABOUT ANDREW ANYMORE . . . IT'S ABOUT RESPECT.
SHIT! HERE COME MATT AND HIS CREW!
HEY!

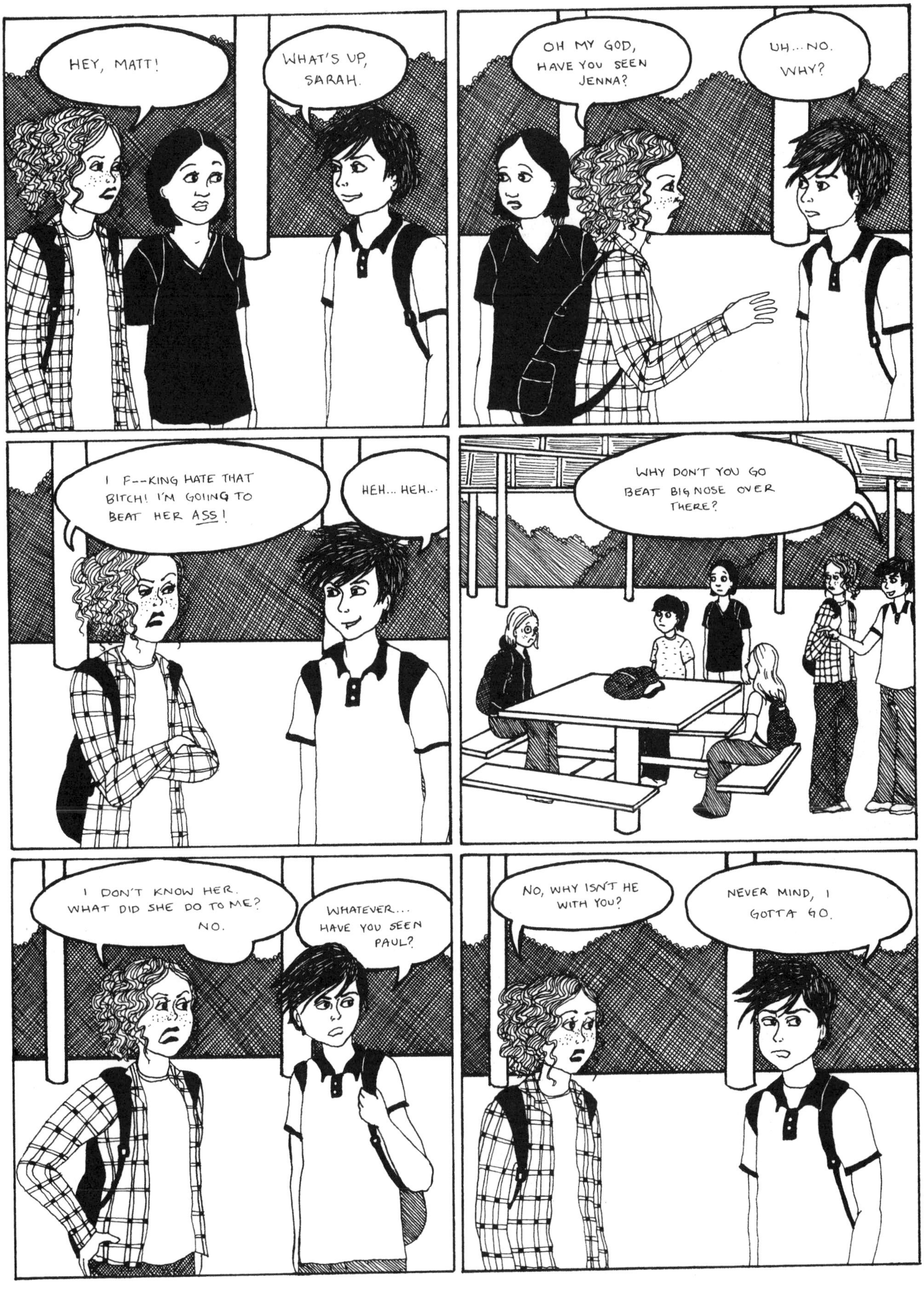
HEY, MATT!
WHAT'S UP, SARAH.
OH MY GOD, HAVE YOU SEEN JENNA?
UH... NO. WHY?
I F--KING HATE THAT BITCH! I'M GOING TO BEAT HER ASS!
HEH... HEH...
WHY DON'T YOU GO BEAT BIG NOSE OVER THERE?
I DON'T KNOW HER. WHAT DID SHE DO TO ME?
WHATEVER... HAVE YOU SEEN PAUL?
NO.
NO, WHY ISN'T HE WITH YOU?
NEVER MIND, I GOTTA GO.

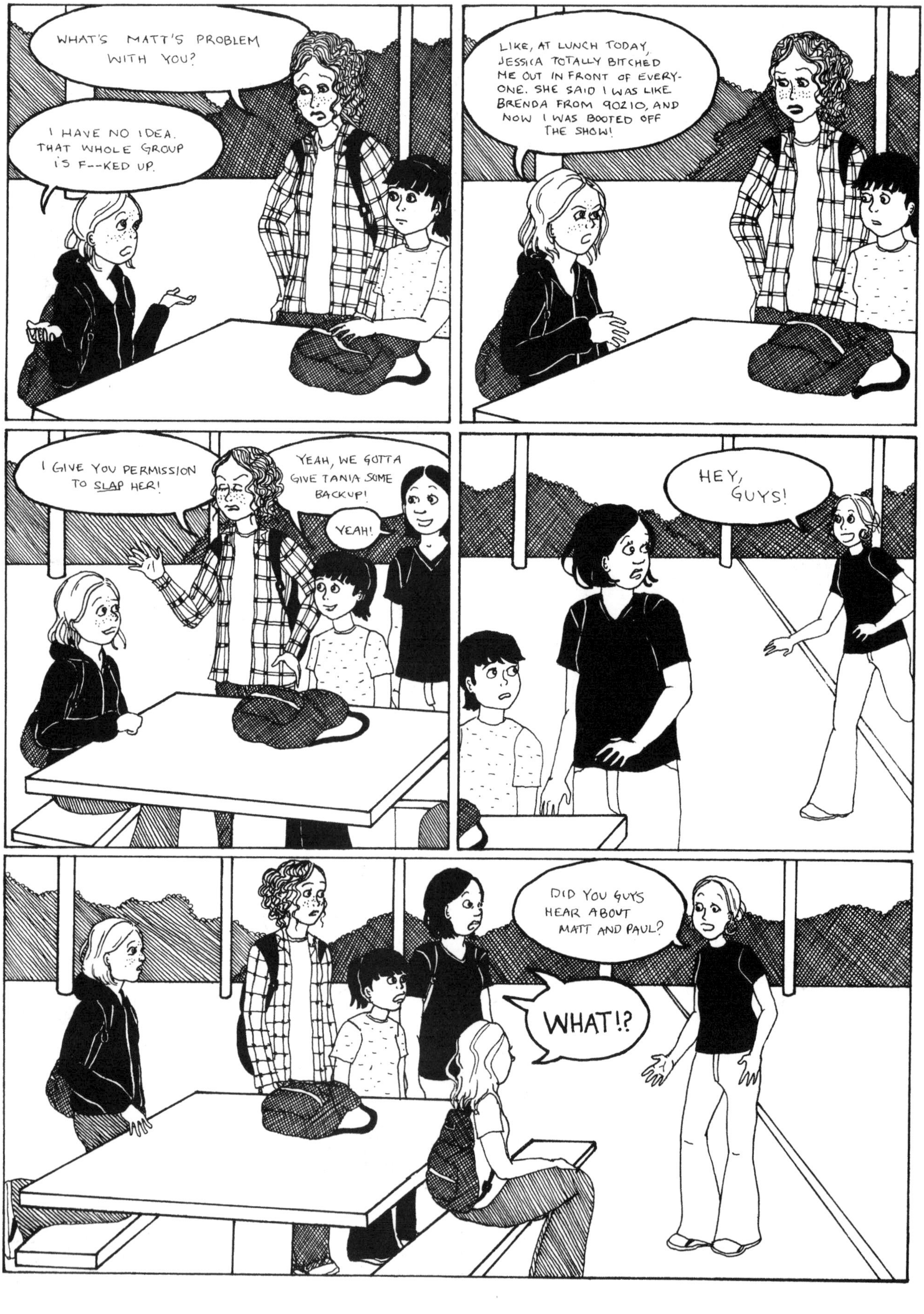
WHAT'S MATT'S PROBLEM WITH YOU?
I HAVE NO IDEA. THAT WHOLE GROUP IS F--KED UP.
LIKE, AT LUNCH TODAY, JESSICA TOTALLY BITCHED ME OUT IN FRONT OF EVERY-ONE. SHE SAID I WAS LIKE BRENDA FROM 90210, AND NOW I WAS BOOTED OFF THE SHOW!
I GIVE YOU PERMISSION TO SLAP HER!
YEAH, WE GOTTA GIVE TANIA SOME BACKUP!
YEAH!
HEY, GUYS!
DID YOU GUYS HEAR ABOUT MATT AND PAUL?
WHAT!?

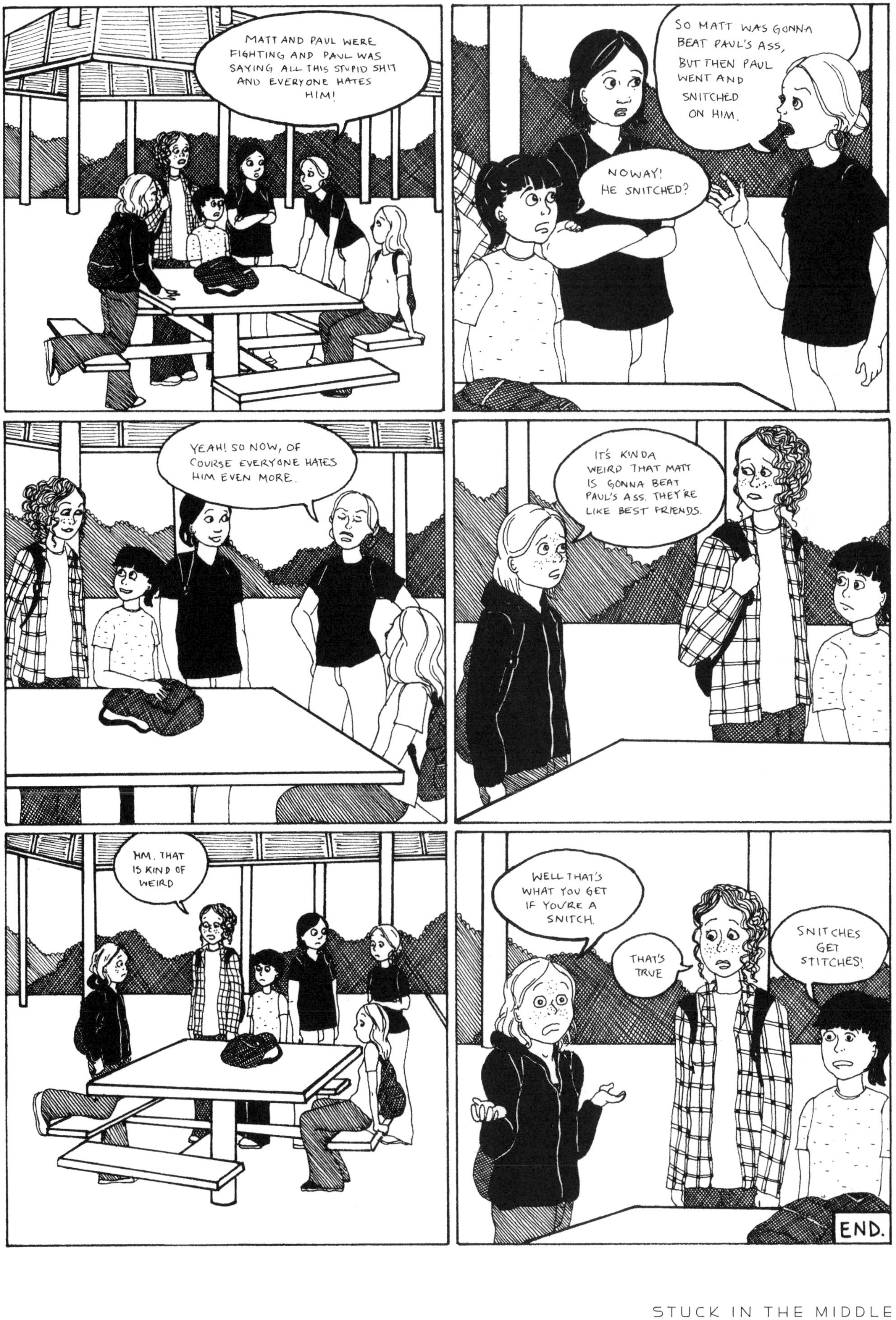
MATT AND PAUL WERE FIGHTING AND PAUL WAS SAYING ALL THIS STUPID SHIT AND EVERYONE HATES HIM!
SO MATT WAS GONNA BEAT PAUL'S ASS, BUT THEN PAUL WENT AND SNITCHED ON HIM.
NOWAY! HE SNITCHED?
YEAH! SO NOW, OF COURSE EVERYONE HATES HIM EVEN MORE.
IT'S KINDA WEIRD THAT MATT IS GONNA BEAT PAUL'S ASS. THEY'RE LIKE BEST FRIENDS.
HM. THAT IS KIND OF WEIRD
WELL THAT'S WHAT YOU GET IF YOU'RE A SNITCH.
THAT'S TRUE
SNITCHES GET STITCHES!
END.

ERIC ENRIGHT

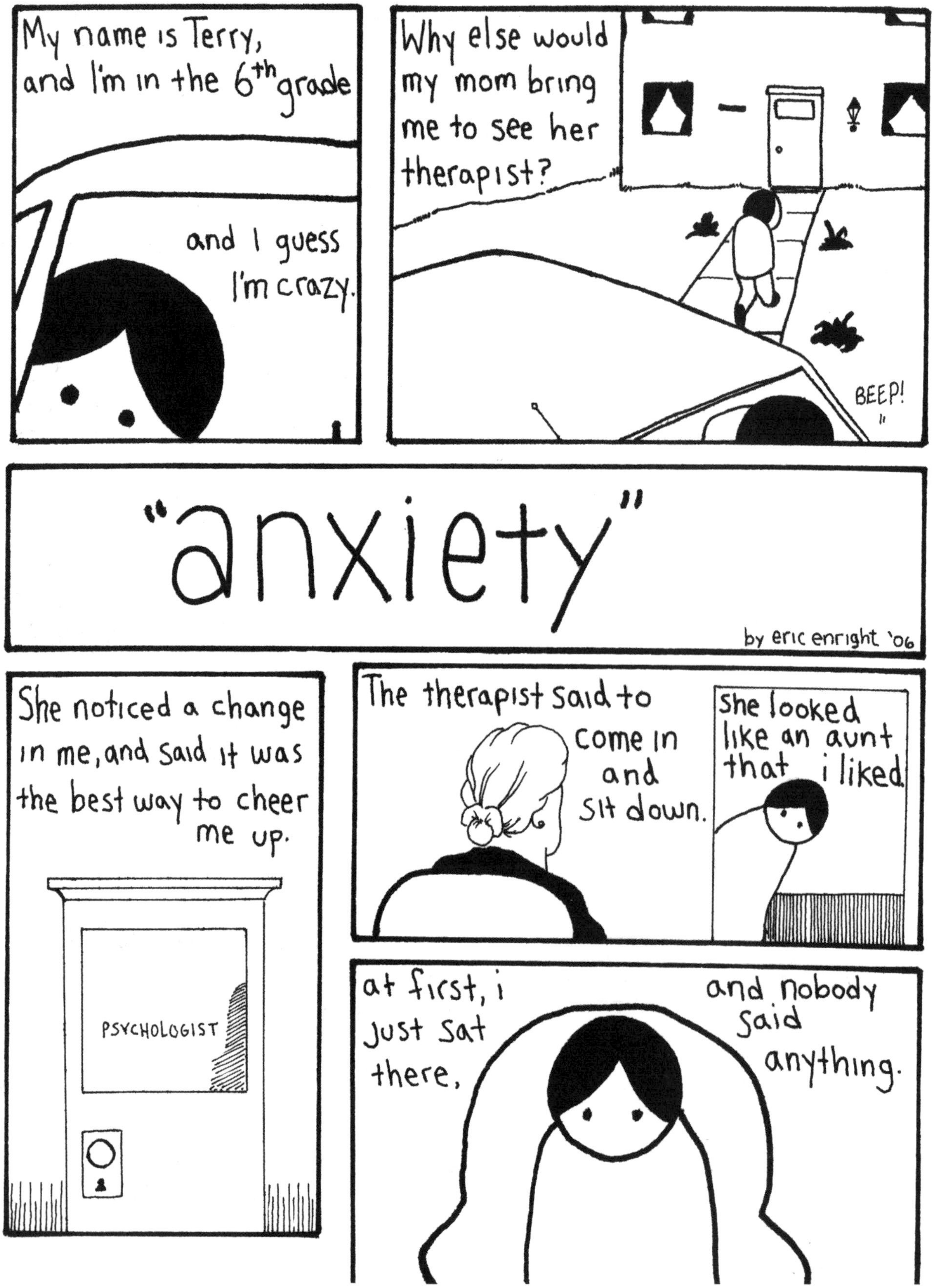
My name is Terry, and I'm in the 6th grade
and I guess I'm crazy.
Why else would my mom bring me to see her therapist?
BEEP!
"anxiety"
by eric enright '06
She noticed a change in me, and said it was the best way to cheer me up.
PSYCHOLOGIST
The therapist said to come in and sit down.
She looked like an aunt that i liked.
at first, i just sat there,
and nobody said anything.

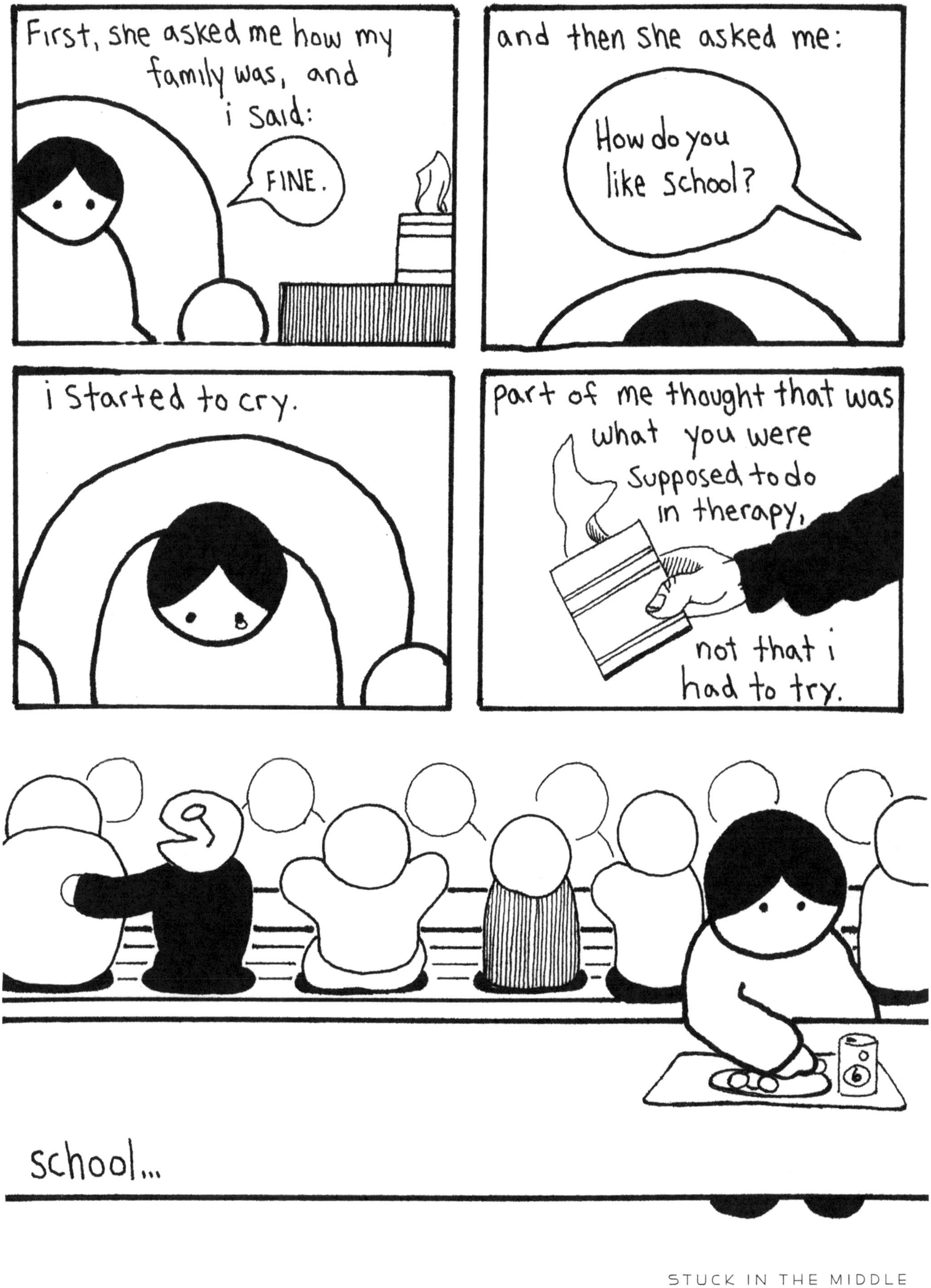
First, she asked me how my family was, and i said:
FINE.
and then she asked me:
How do you like school?
i started to cry.
part of me thought that was what you were supposed to do in therapy,
not that i had to try.
school...

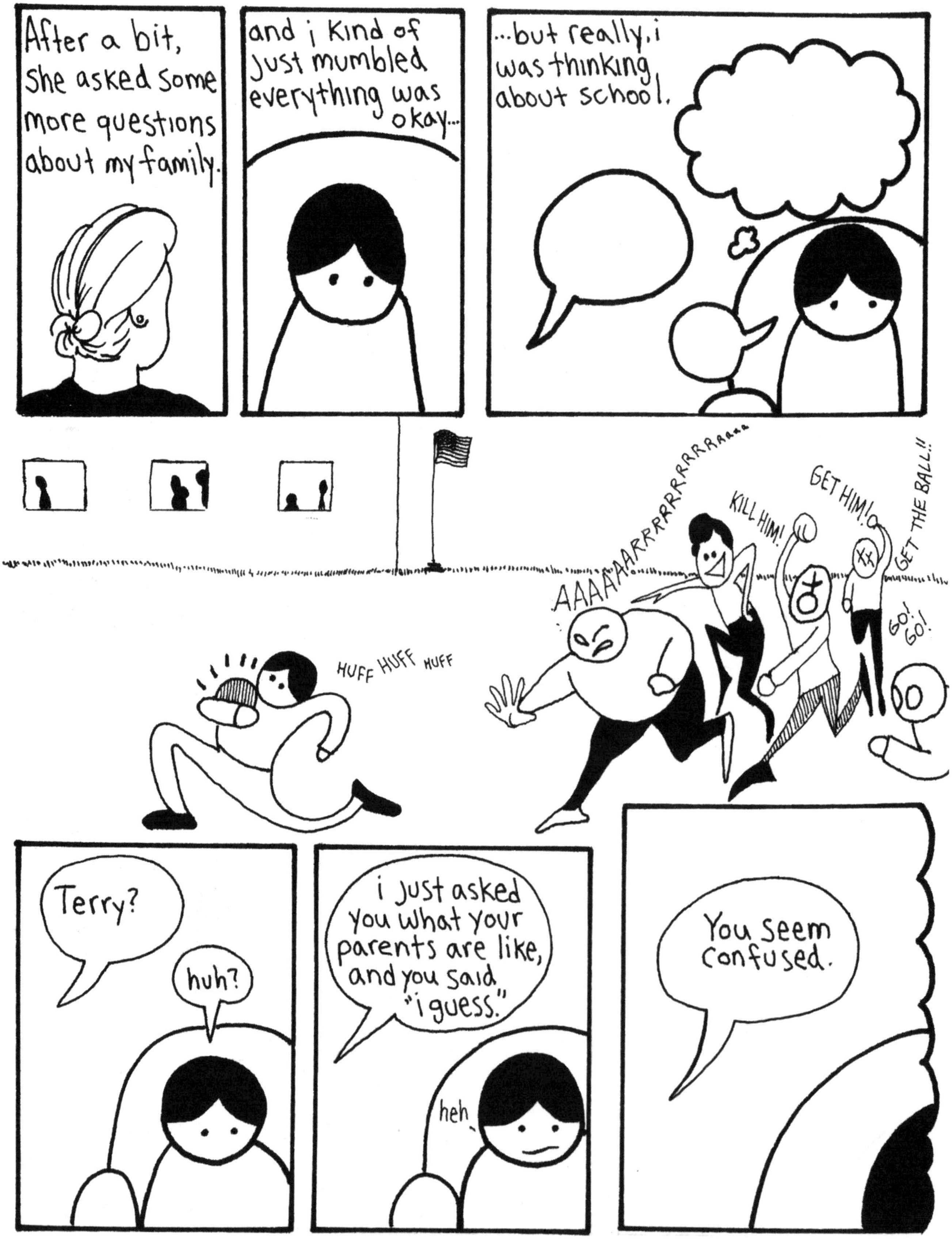
After a bit, she asked some more questions about my family.
and i kind of just mumbled everything was okay...
...but really, i was thinking about school.
AAAAAARRRRRRRRRRRRRaaaa
KILL HIM!
GET HIM!
GET THE BALL!!
GO! GO!
HUFF HUFF HUFF
Terry?
huh?
i just asked you what your parents are like, and you said, "i guess."
heh.
You seem confused.

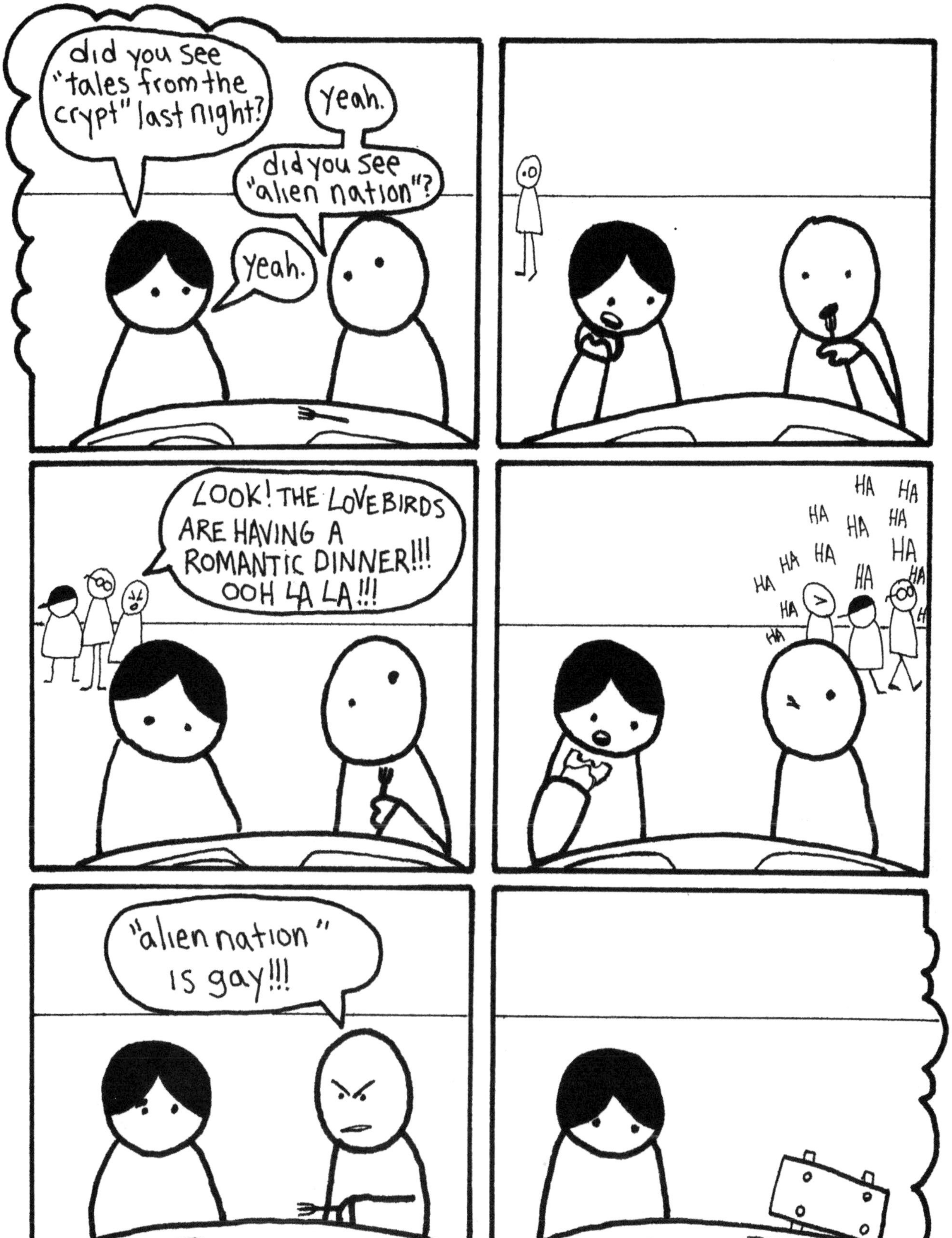
did you see "tales from the crypt" last night?
yeah.
did you see "alien nation"?
yeah.
LOOK! THE LOVEBIRDS ARE HAVING A ROMANTIC DINNER!!! OOH LA LA!!!
HA HA HA HA HA HA HA HA HA HA HA HA HA HA HA HA
"alien nation" is gay!!!

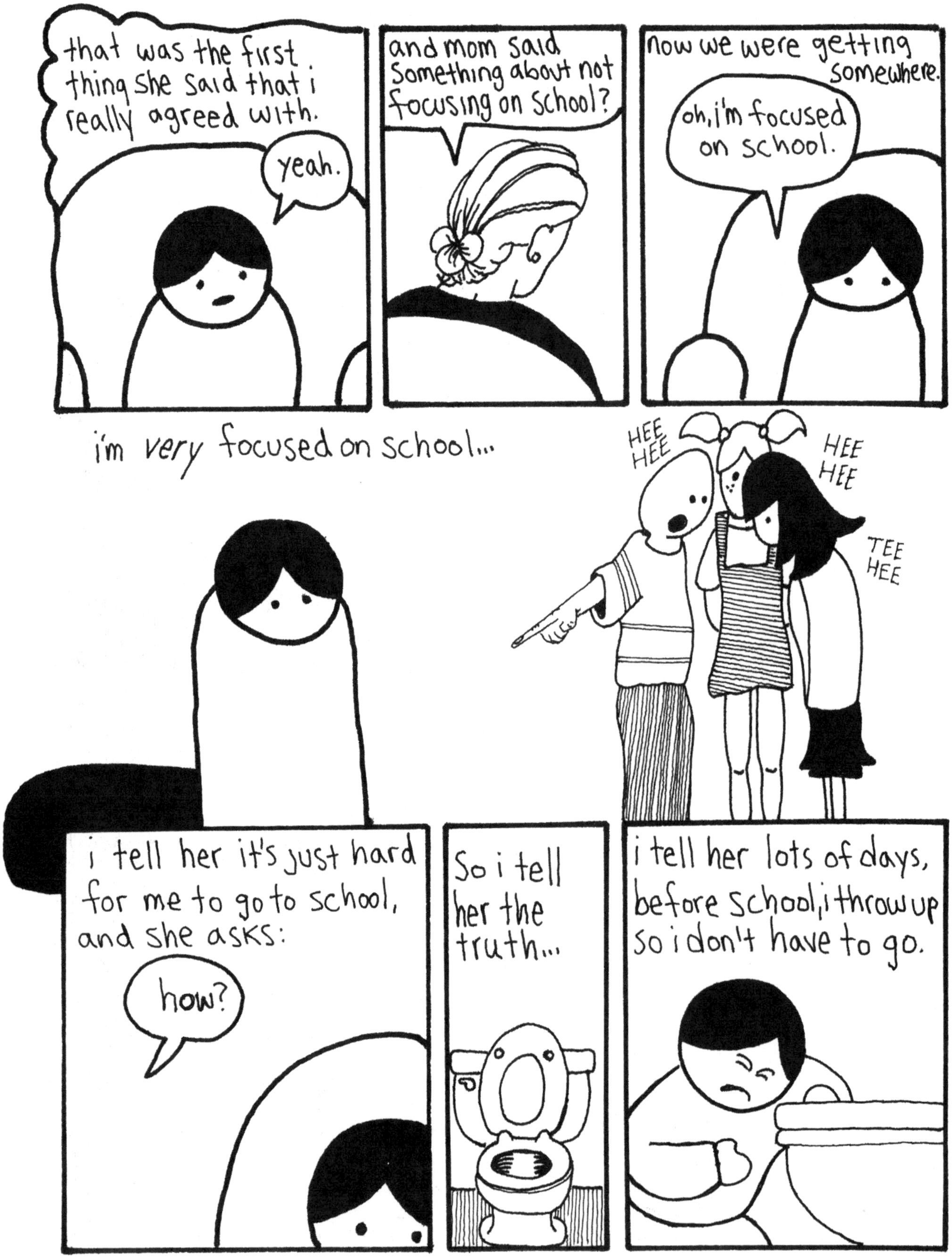
that was the first thing she said that i really agreed with.
yeah.
and mom said something about not focusing on school?
now we were getting somewhere.
oh, i'm focused on school.
i'm *very* focused on school...
HEE HEE
HEE HEE
TEE HEE
i tell her it's just hard for me to go to school, and she asks:
how?
So i tell her the truth...
i tell her lots of days, before school, i throw up so i don't have to go.

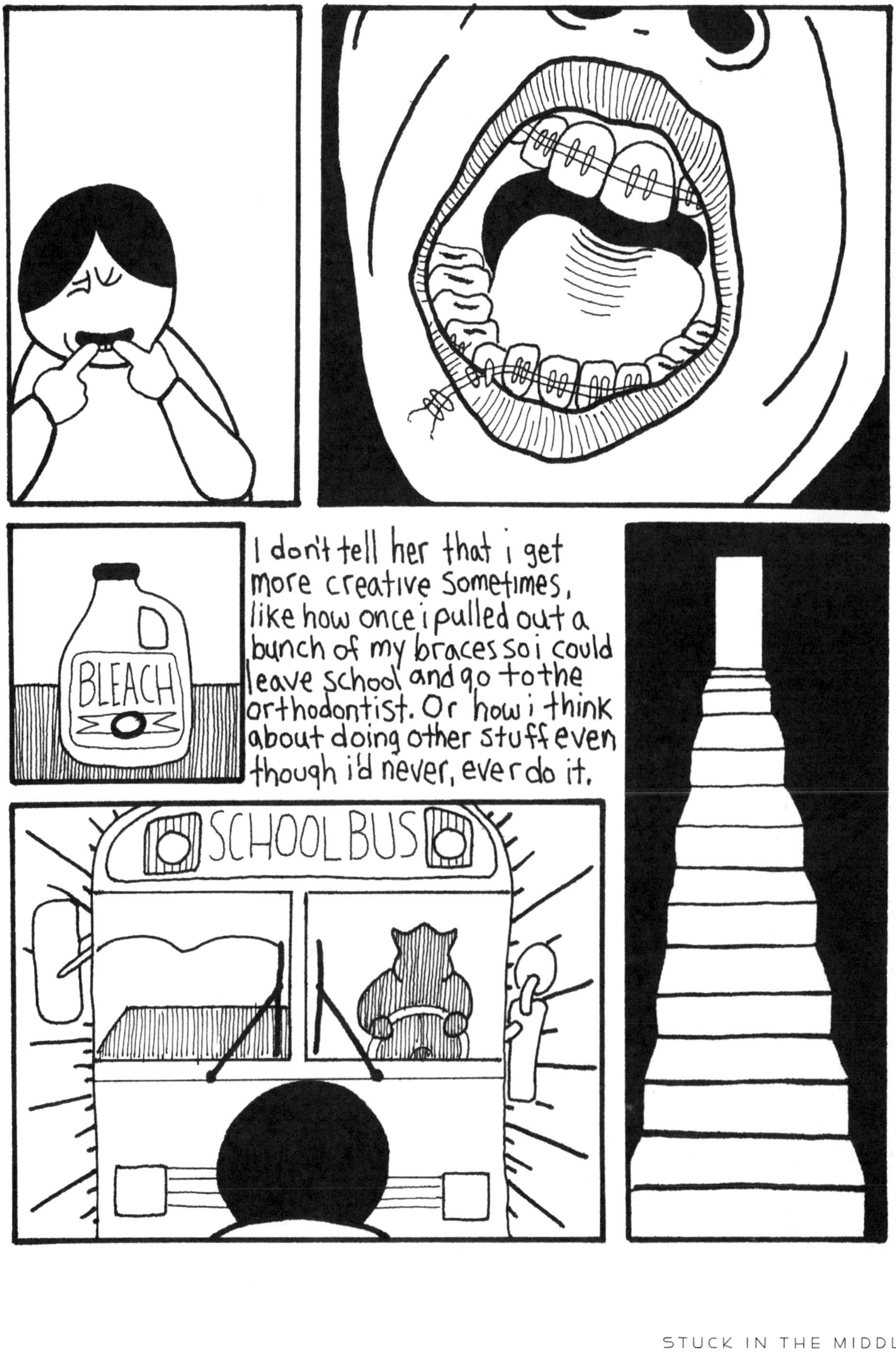
BLEACH
I don't tell her that i get more creative Sometimes, like how once i pulled out a bunch of my braces so i could leave school and go to the orthodontist. Or how i think about doing other stuff even though i'd never, ever do it.
SCHOOL BUS

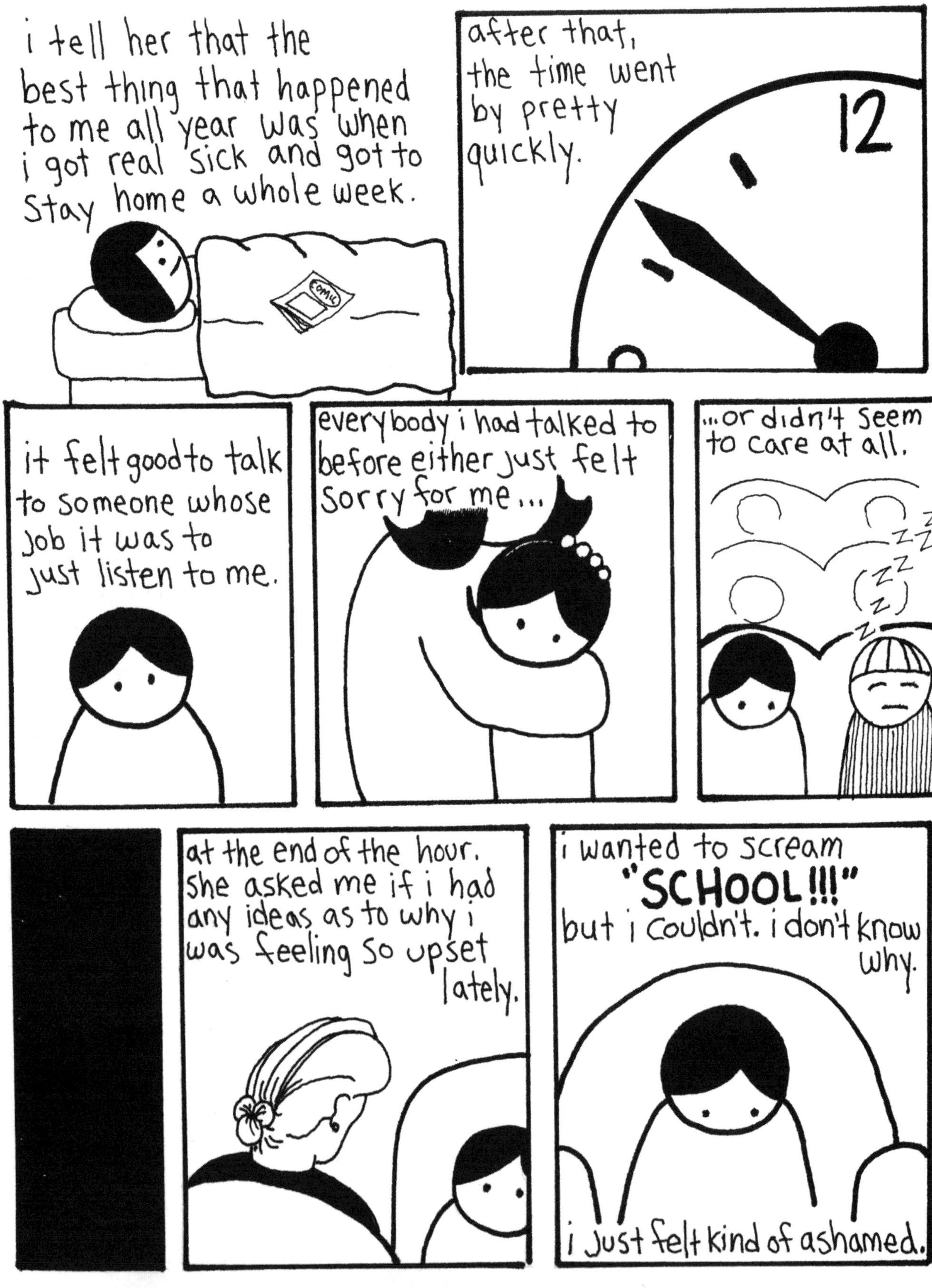
i tell her that the best thing that happened to me all year was when i got real sick and got to stay home a whole week.
COMIC
after that, the time went by pretty quickly.
12
it felt good to talk to someone whose job it was to just listen to me.
everybody i had talked to before either just felt sorry for me...
...or didn't seem to care at all.
z z z
at the end of the hour. she asked me if i had any ideas as to why i was feeling so upset lately.
i wanted to scream
"SCHOOL!!!"
but i couldn't. i don't know why.
i just felt kind of ashamed.

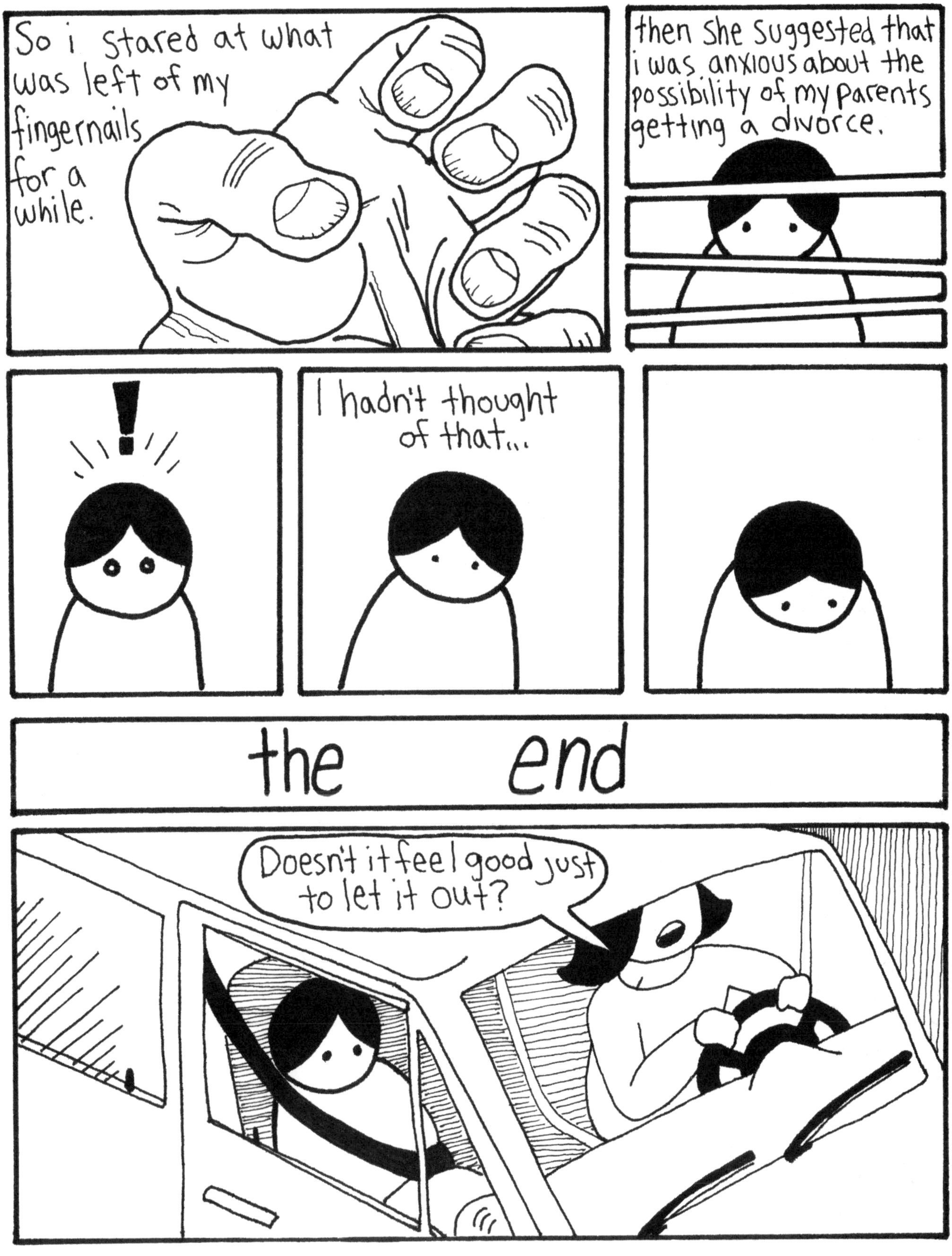
So i stared at what was left of my fingernails for a while.
then she suggested that i was anxious about the possibility of my parents getting a divorce.
!
I hadn't thought of that...
the end
Doesn't it feel good just to let it out?

ARIEL SCHRAG

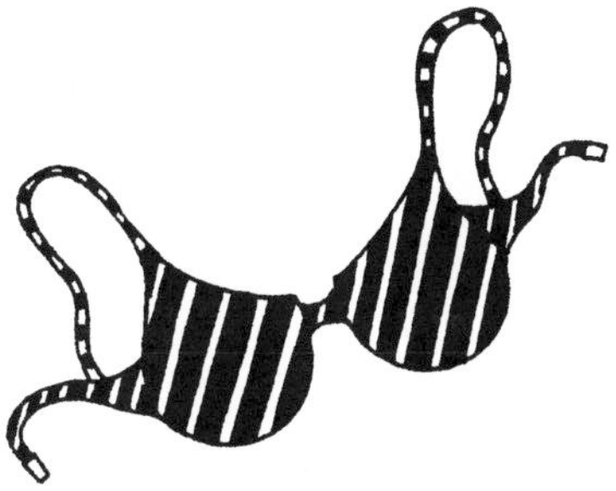

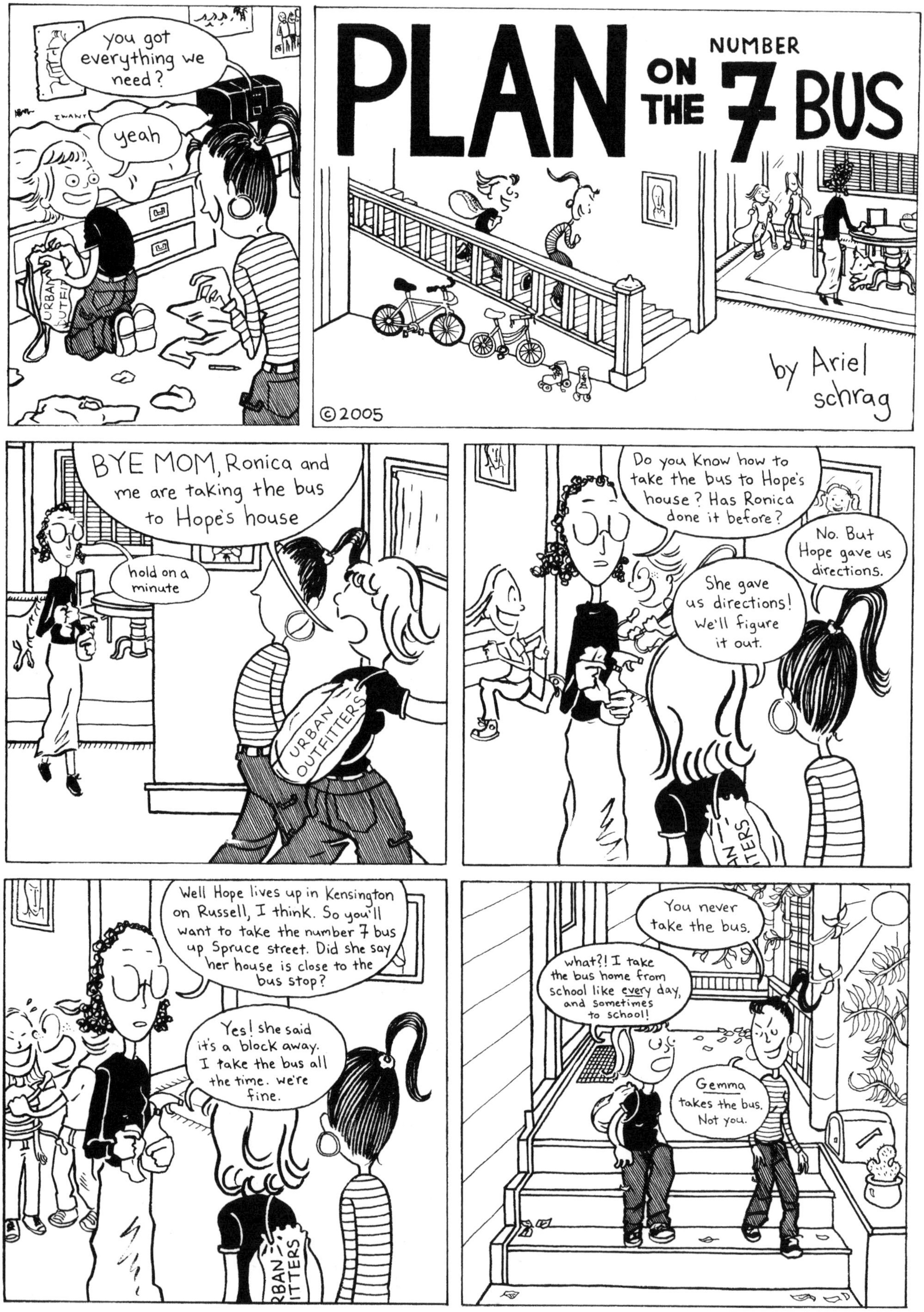
you got everything we need?
yeah
PLAN ON THE NUMBER 7 BUS
by Ariel schrag
©2005
BYE MOM, Ronica and me are taking the bus to Hope's house
hold on a minute
Do you know how to take the bus to Hope's house? Has Ronica done it before?
No. But Hope gave us directions.
She gave us directions! We'll figure it out.
Well Hope lives up in Kensington on Russell, I think. So you'll want to take the number 7 bus up Spruce street. Did she say her house is close to the bus stop?
Yes! she said it's a block away. I take the bus all the time. we're fine.
You never take the bus.
what?! I take the bus home from school like every day, and sometimes to school!
Gemma takes the bus. Not you.

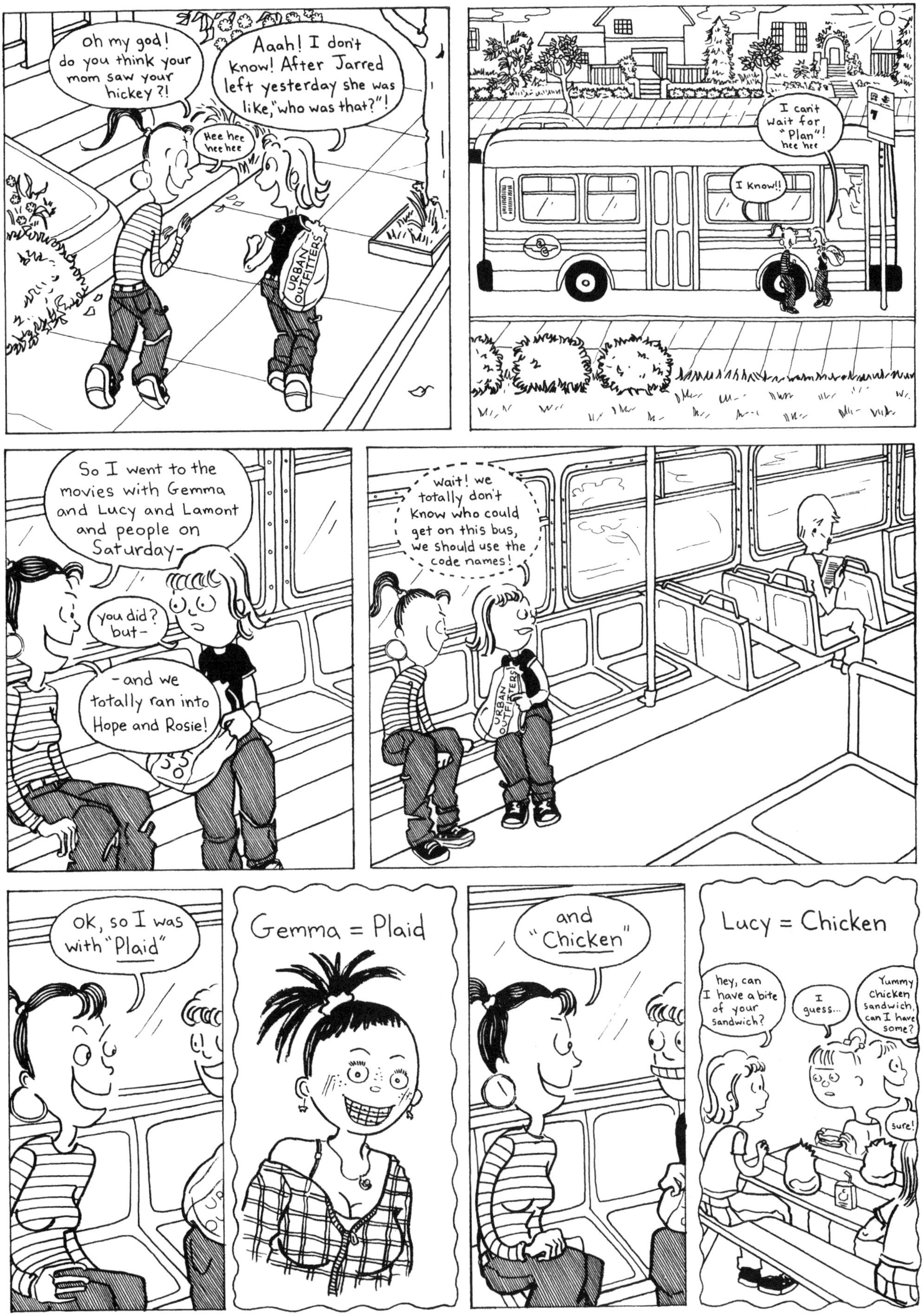

oh my god! do you think your mom saw your hickey ?!
Aaah! I don't know! After Jarred left yesterday she was like, "who was that?"!
Hee hee hee hee
URBAN OUTFITTERS
I can't wait for "Plan"! hee hee
I know!!
So I went to the movies with Gemma and Lucy and Lamont and people on Saturday-
you did? but-
-and we totally ran into Hope and Rosie!
wait! we totally don't know who could get on this bus, we should use the code names!
URBAN OUTFITTERS
ok, so I was with "Plaid"
Gemma = Plaid
and "Chicken"
Lucy = Chicken
hey, can I have a bite of your sandwich?
I guess...
Yummy chicken sandwich, can I have some?
sure!

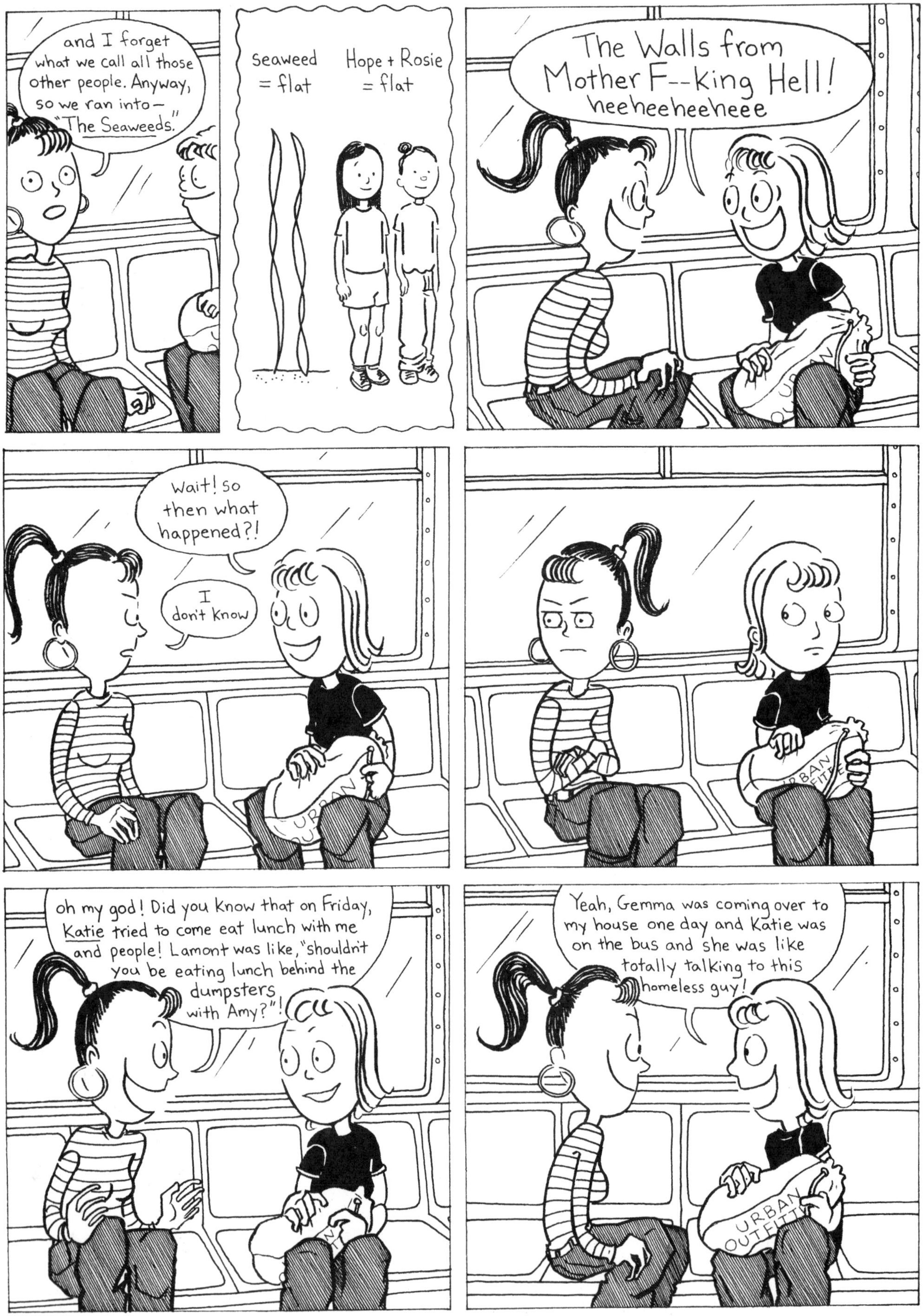
and I forget what we call all those other people. Anyway, so we ran into— "The Seaweeds."
Seaweed = flat
Hope + Rosie = flat
The Walls from Mother F--king Hell! heeheeheeheee
Wait! so then what happened?!
I don't know
oh my god! Did you know that on Friday, Katie tried to come eat lunch with me and people! Lamont was like, "shouldn't you be eating lunch behind the dumpsters with Amy?"!
Yeah, Gemma was coming over to my house one day and Katie was on the bus and she was like totally talking to this homeless guy!

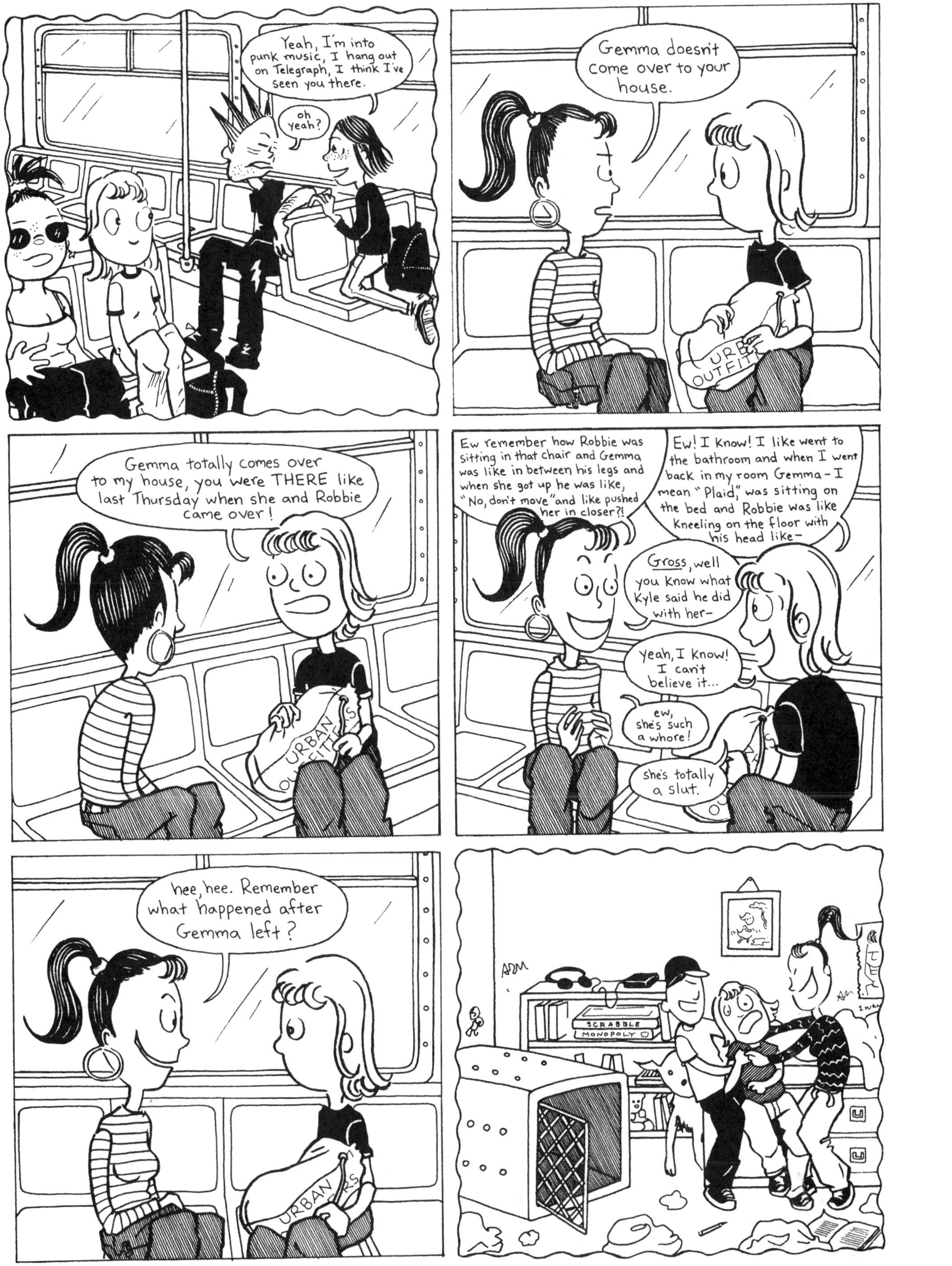
Yeah, I'm into punk music, I hang out on Telegraph, I think I've seen you there.
oh yeah?
Gemma doesn't come over to your house.
Gemma totally comes over to my house, you were THERE like last Thursday when she and Robbie came over!
Ew remember how Robbie was sitting in that chair and Gemma was like in between his legs and when she got up he was like, "No, don't move" and like pushed her in closer?!
Ew! I know! I like went to the bathroom and when I went back in my room Gemma - I mean "Plaid," was sitting on the bed and Robbie was like kneeling on the floor with his head like-
Gross, well you know what Kyle said he did with her-
Yeah, I know! I can't believe it...
ew, she's such a whore!
she's totally a slut.
hee, hee. Remember what happened after Gemma left?
SCRABBLE
MONOPOLY

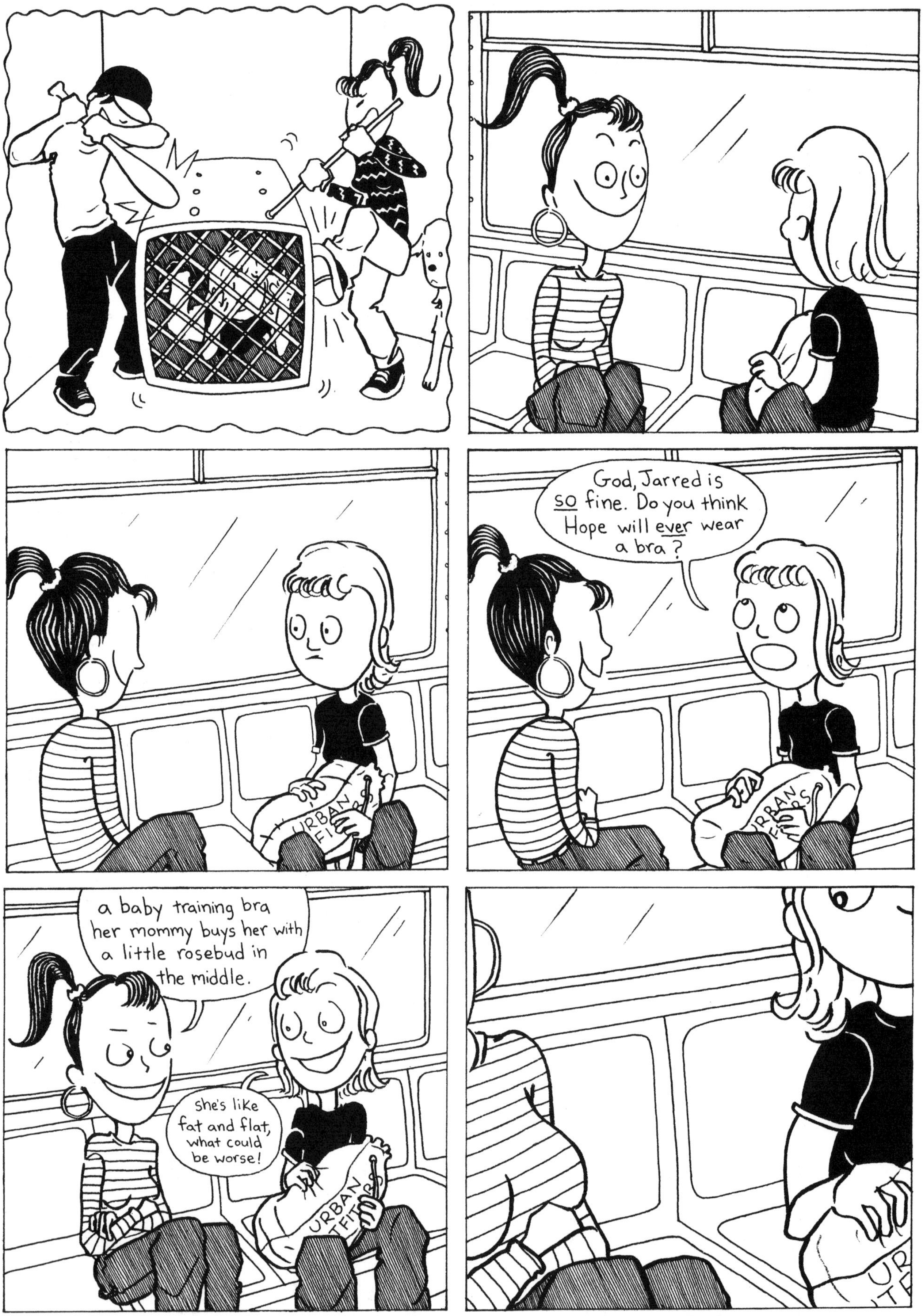
God, Jarred is so fine. Do you think Hope will ever wear a bra?
a baby training bra her mommy buys her with a little rosebud in the middle.
she's like fat and flat, what could be worse!

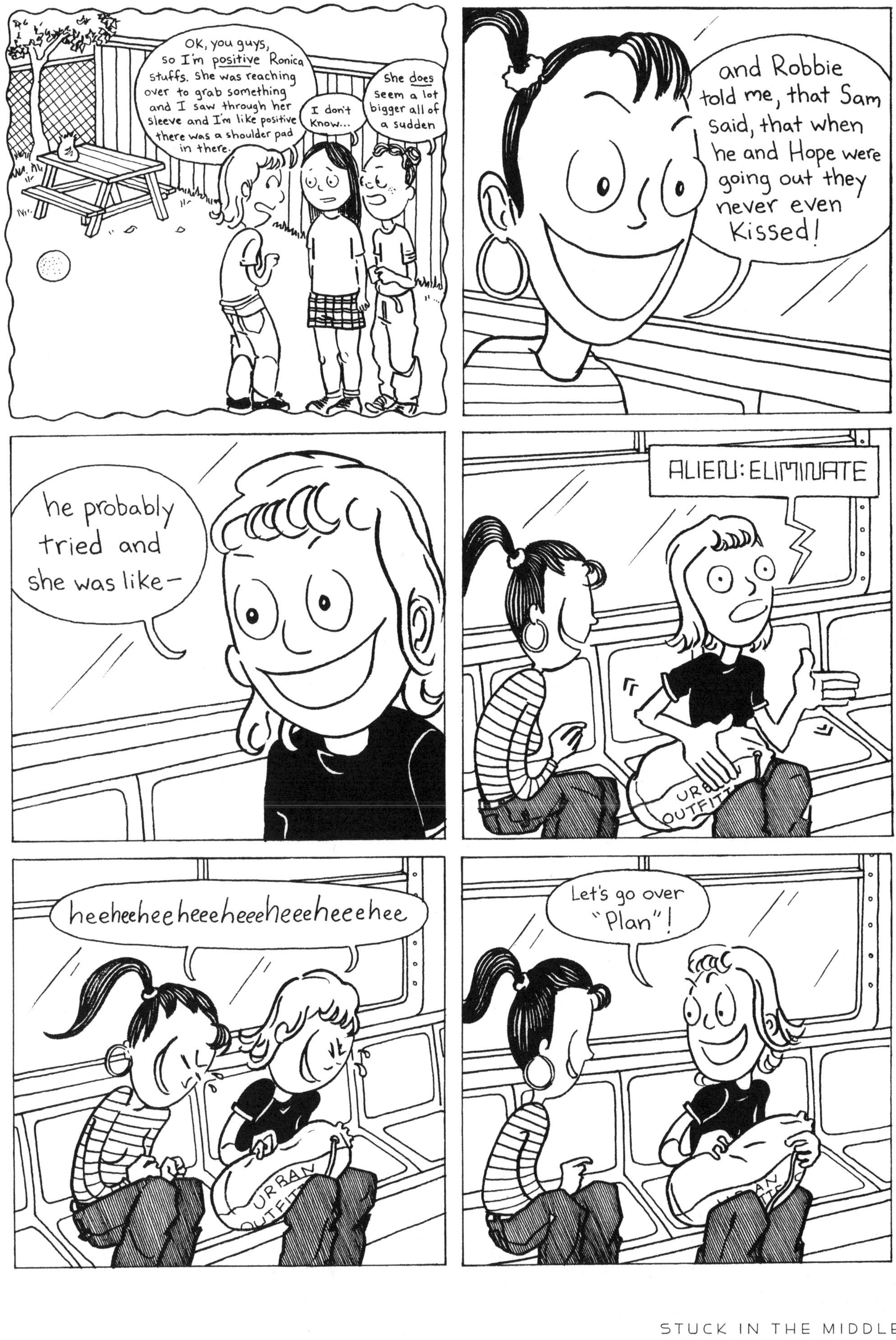
OK, you guys, so I'm positive Ronica stuffs. She was reaching over to grab something and I saw through her sleeve and I'm like positive there was a shoulder pad in there.
I don't Know...
She does seem a lot bigger all of a sudden
and Robbie told me, that Sam said, that when he and Hope were going out they never even Kissed!
he probably tried and she was like–
ALIEN: ELIMINATE
heeheeheeheeeheeeheeeheeehee
Let's go over "Plan"!

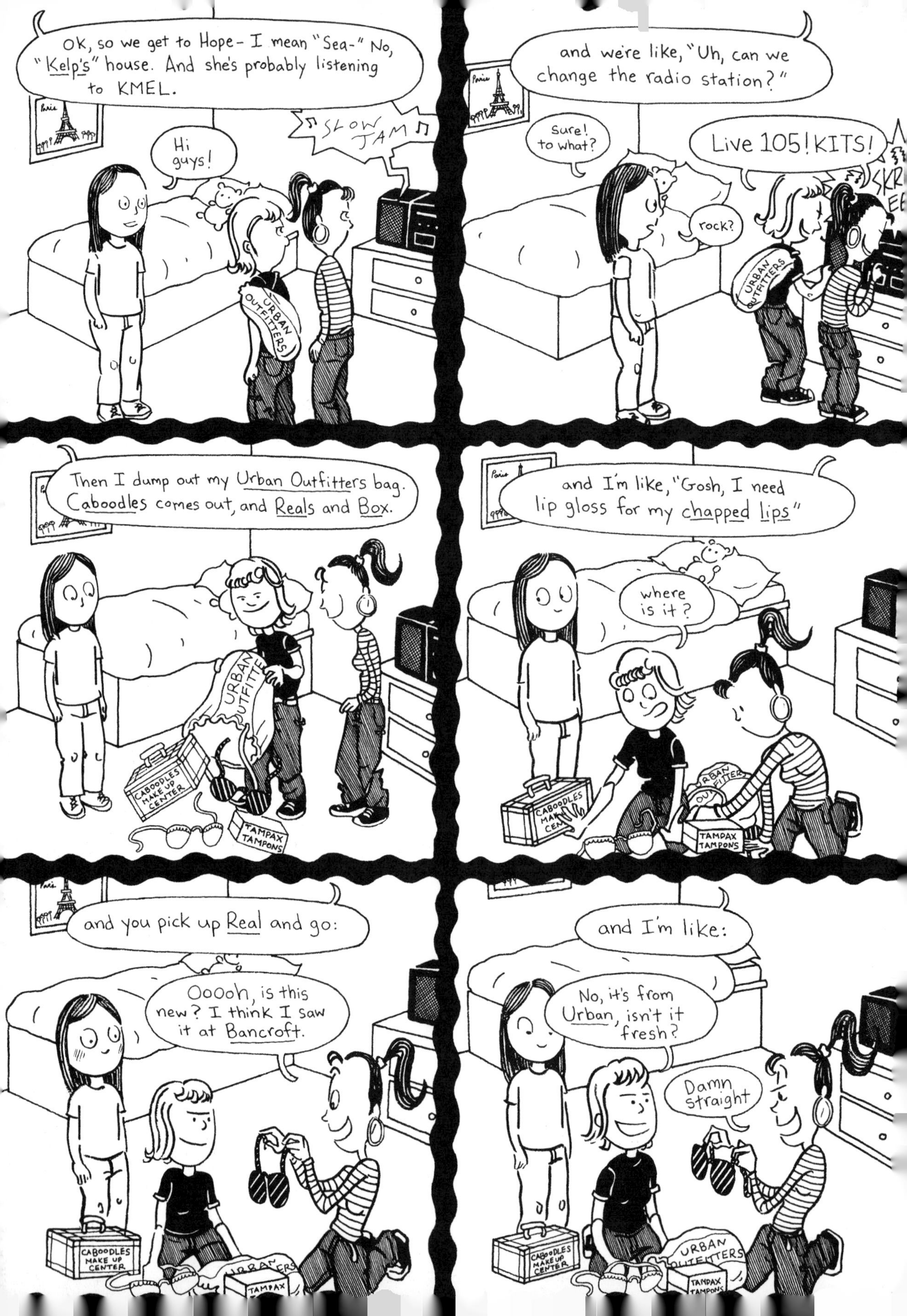
OK, so we get to Hope- I mean "Sea-" No, "Kelp's" house. And she's probably listening to KMEL.
SLOW JAM
Hi guys!
and we're like, "Uh, can we change the radio station?"
Sure! to what?
Live 105! KITS!
rock?
URBAN OUTFITTERS
Then I dump out my Urban Outfitters bag. Caboodles comes out, and Reals and Box.
URBAN OUTFITTERS
CABOODLES MAKE UP CENTER
TAMPAX TAMPONS
and I'm like, "Gosh, I need lip gloss for my chapped lips"
where is it?
and you pick up Real and go:
Ooooh, is this new? I think I saw it at Bancroft.
CABOODLES MAKE UP CENTER
and I'm like:
No, it's from Urban, isn't it fresh?
Damn straight
CABOODLES MAKE UP CENTER
URBAN OUTFITTERS
TAMPAX TAMPONS

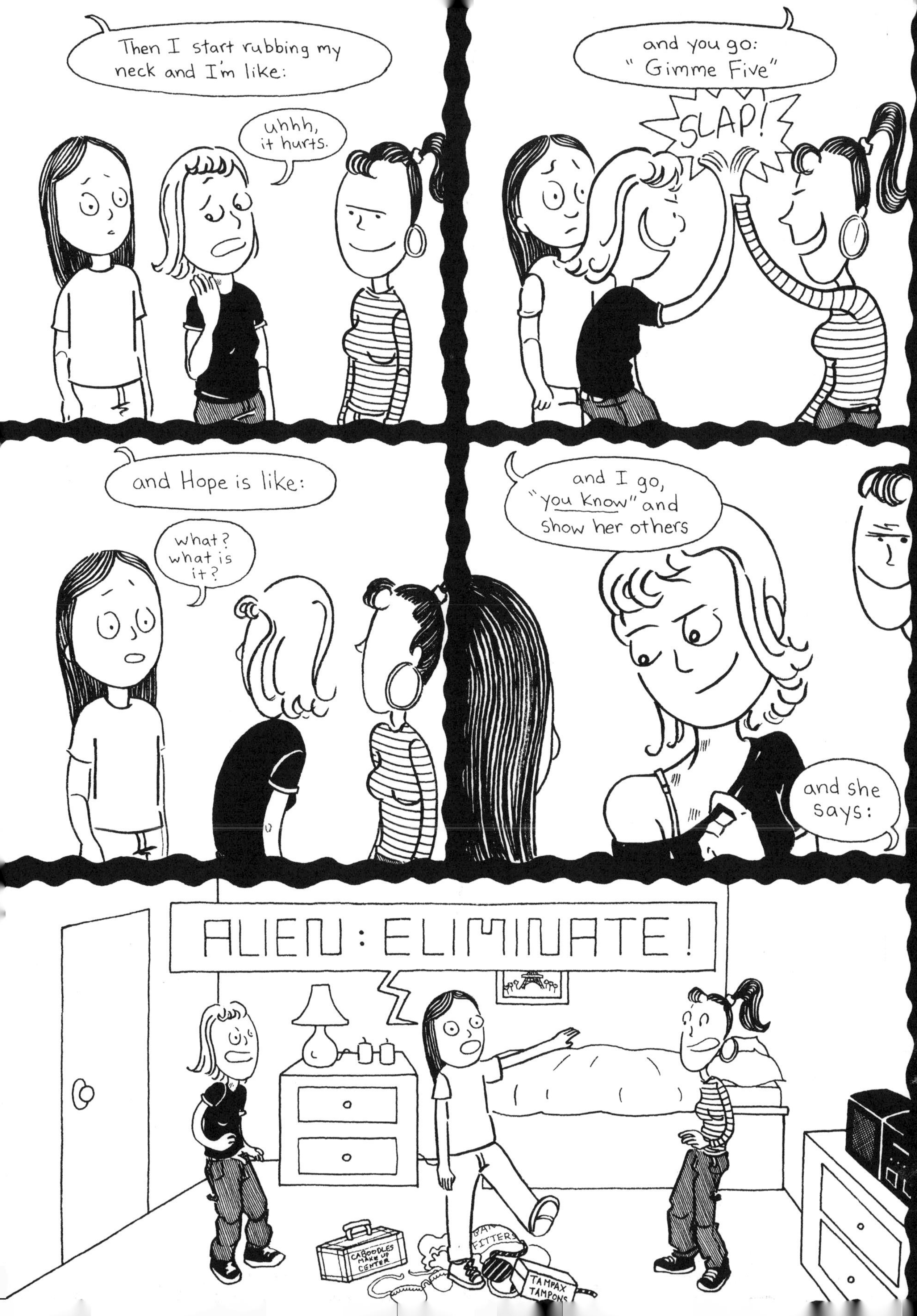
Then I start rubbing my neck and I'm like:
uhhh, it hurts.
and you go: "Gimme Five"
SLAP!
and Hope is like:
what? what is it?
and I go, "you know" and show her others
and she says:
ALIEN : ELIMINATE!
CABOODLES MAKE UP CENTER
TAMPAX TAMPONS

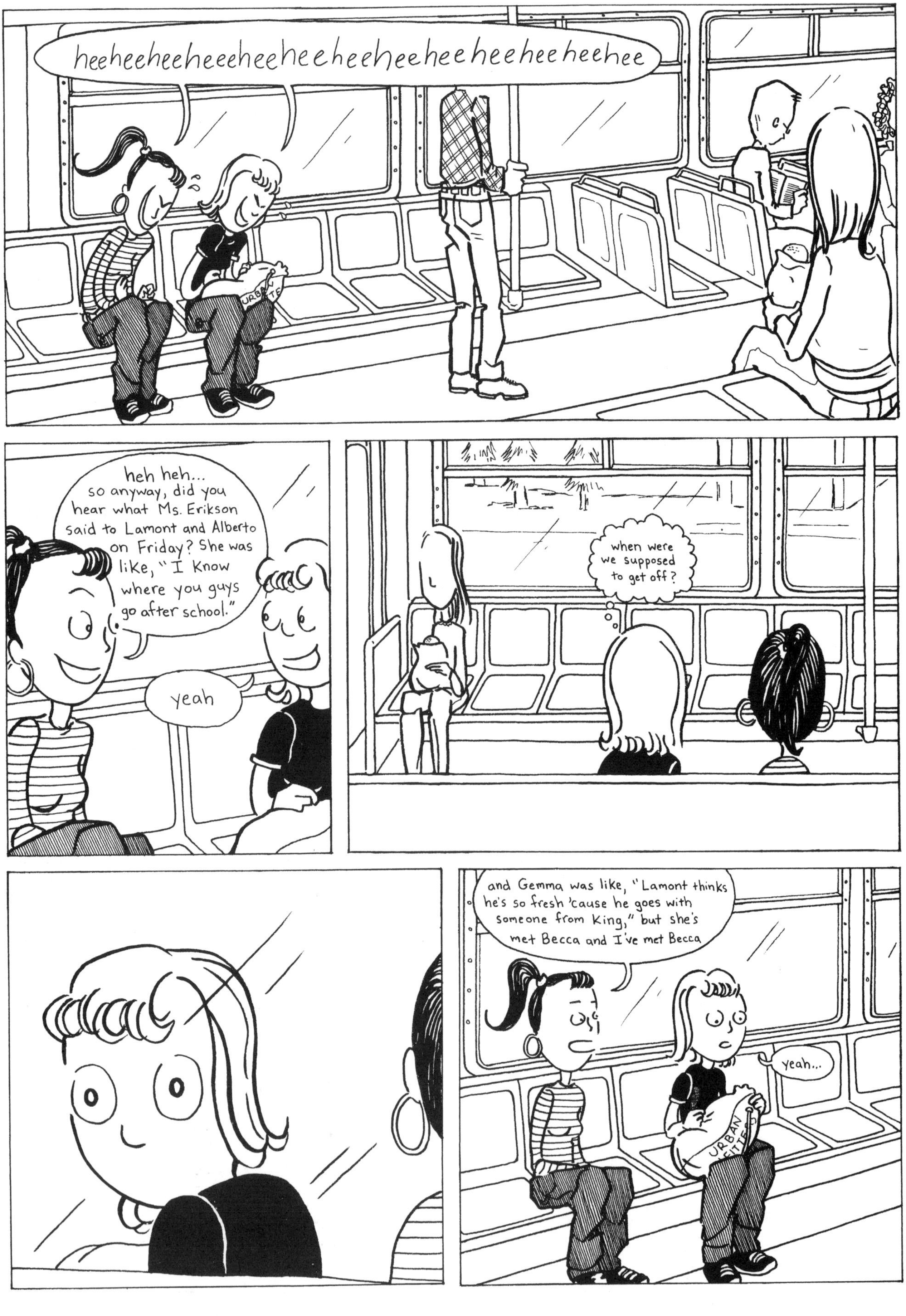
heeheeheeheeeheeheeheeheeheeheeheeheehee
heh heh... so anyway, did you hear what Ms. Erikson said to Lamont and Alberto on Friday? She was like, "I Know where you guys go after school."
yeah
when were we supposed to get off?
and Gemma was like, "Lamont thinks he's so fresh 'cause he goes with someone from King," but she's met Becca and I've met Becca
yeah...

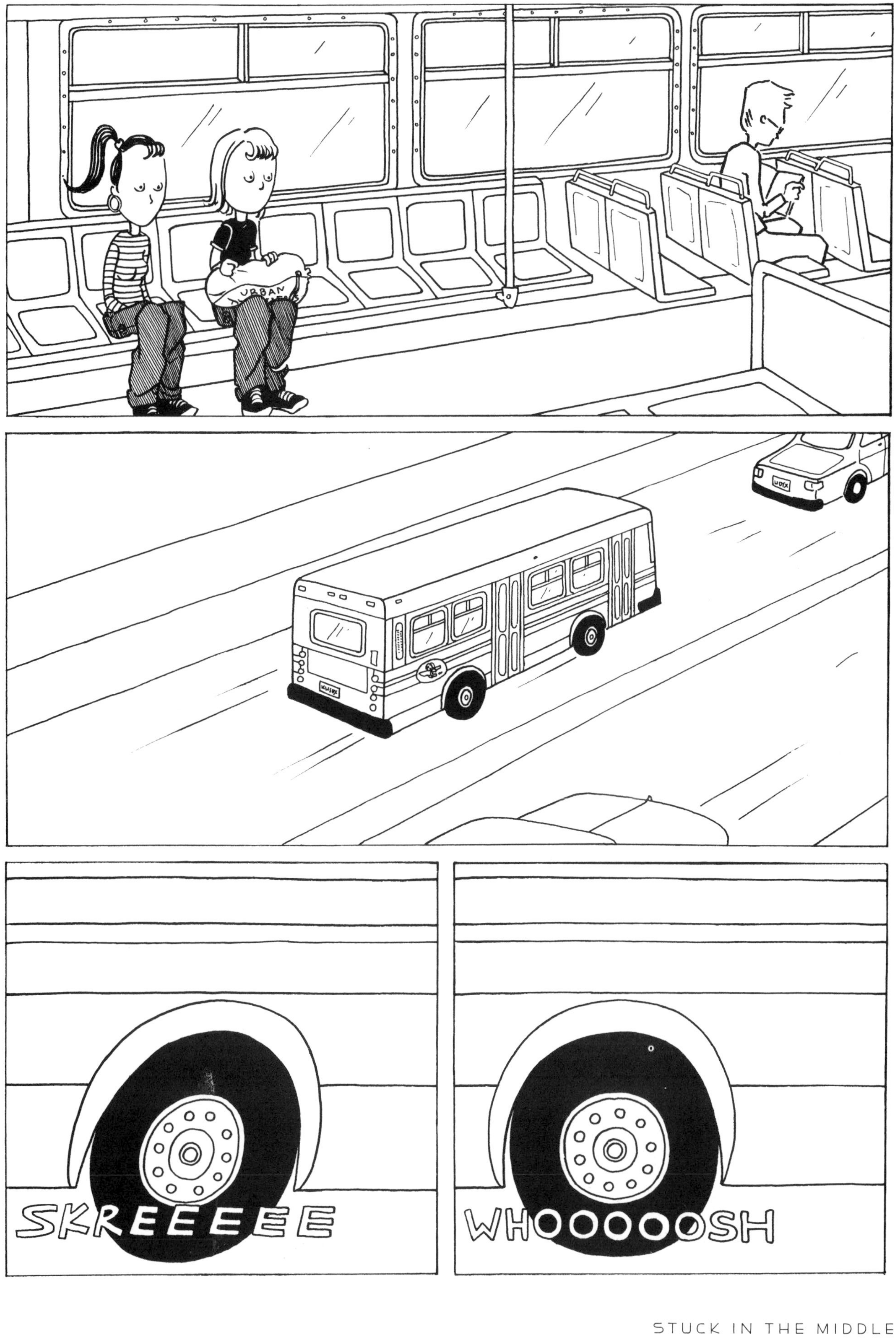
SKREEEEE
WHOOOOOSH

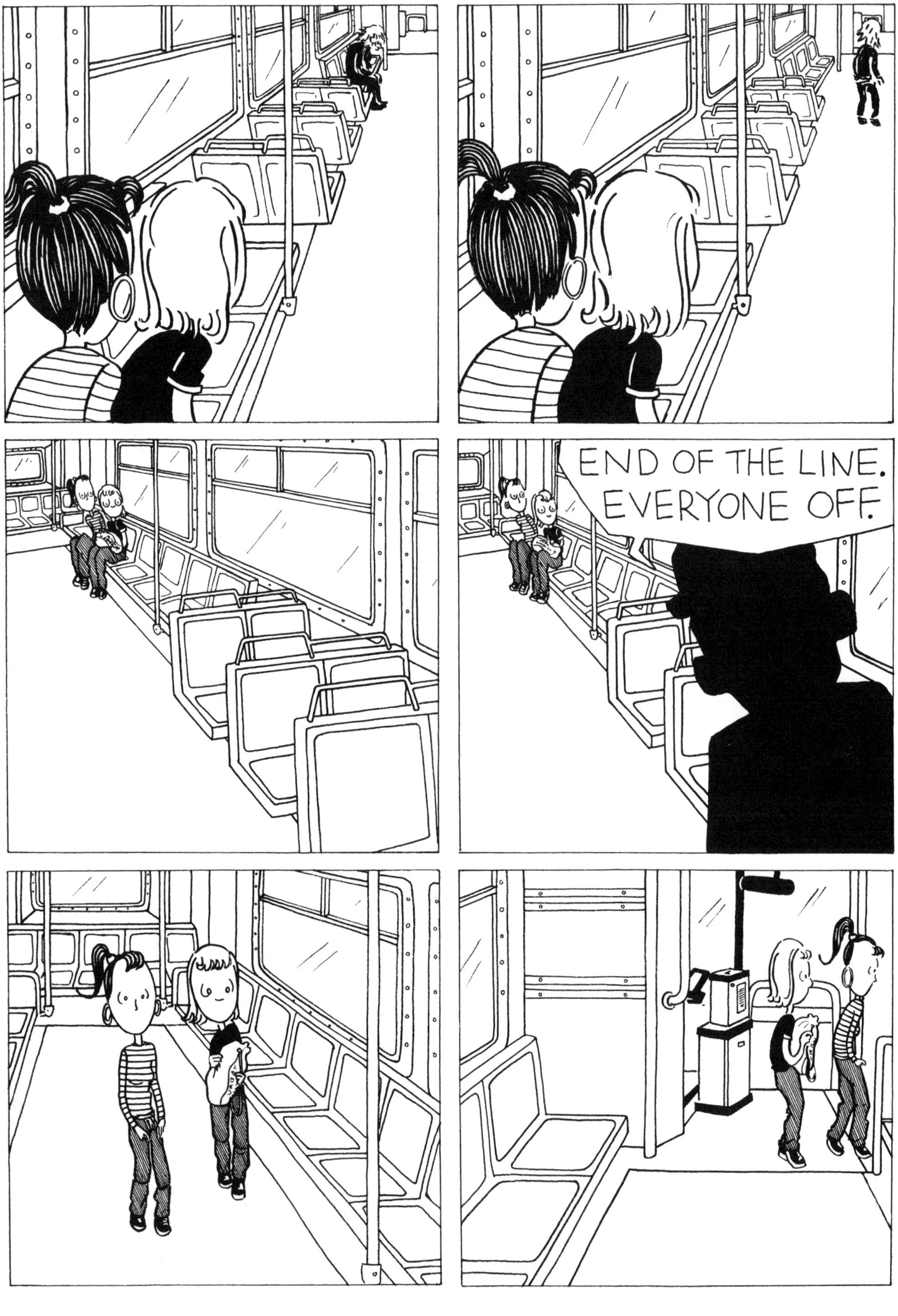
END OF THE LINE. EVERYONE OFF.

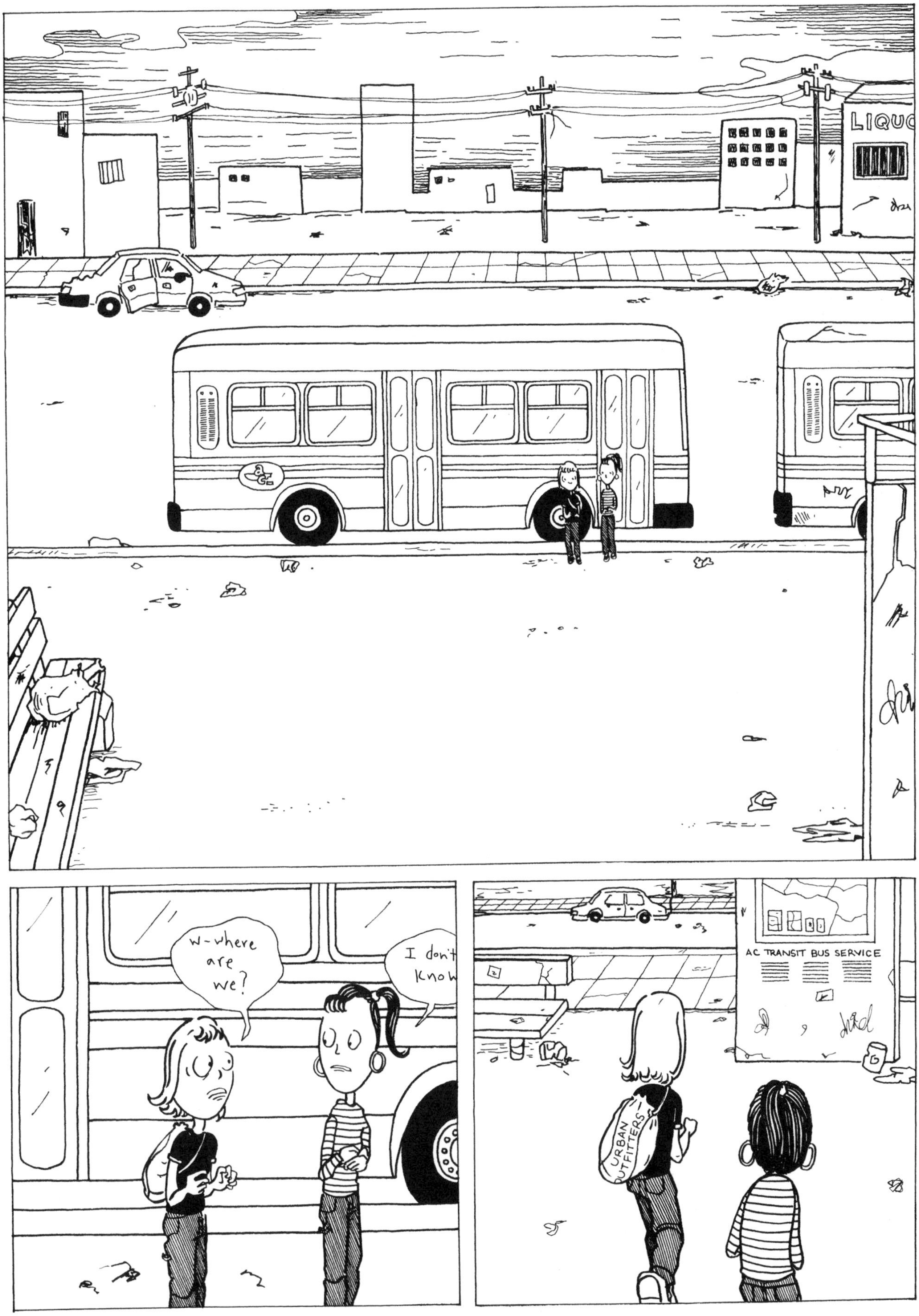
w-where are we?
I don't know
AC TRANSIT BUS SERVICE
URBAN OUTFITTERS

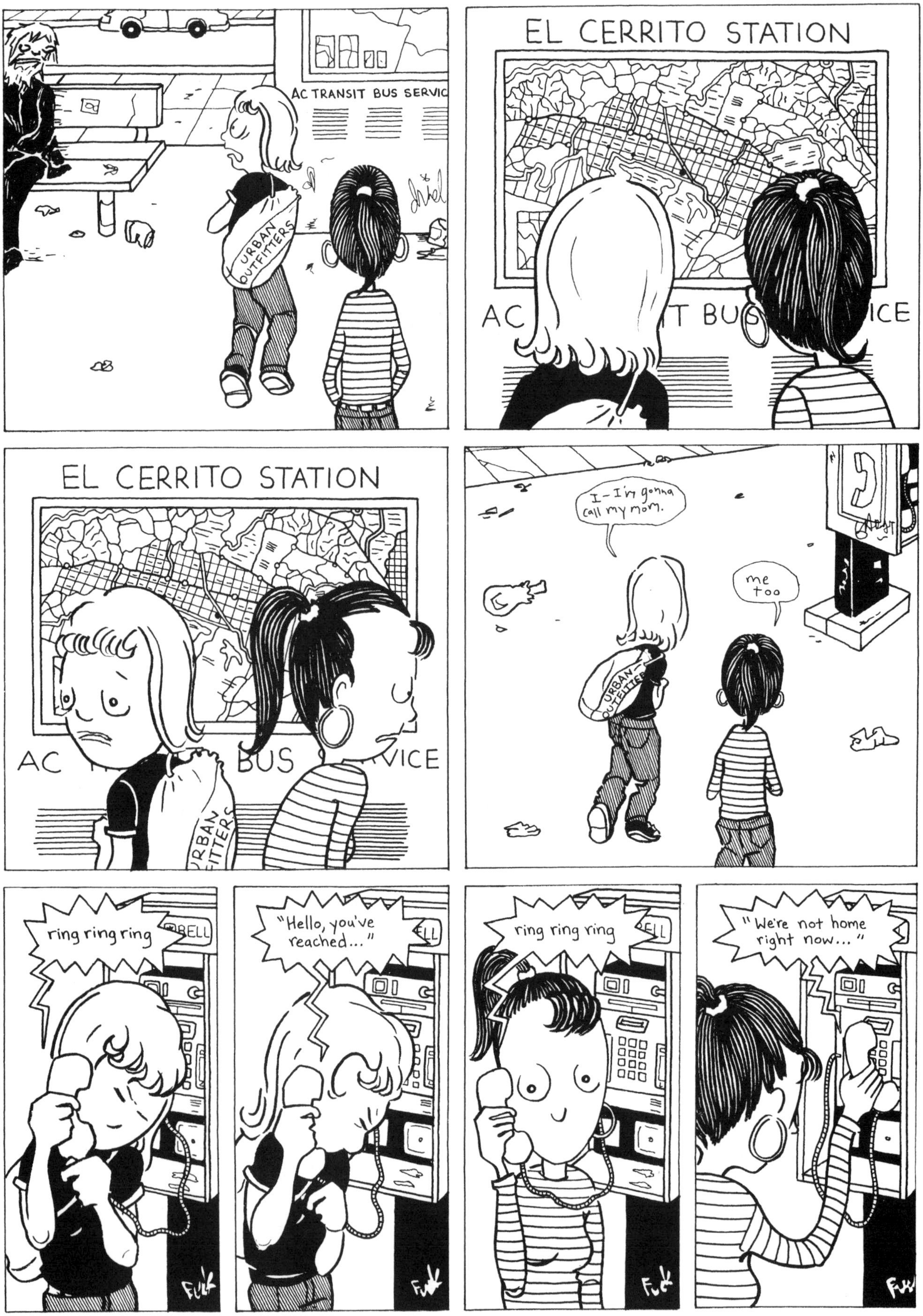
AC TRANSIT BUS SERVIC
URBAN OUTFITTERS
EL CERRITO STATION
EL CERRITO STATION
I- I'm gonna call my mom.
me too
ring ring ring
"Hello, you've reached..."
ring ring ring
"We're not home right now..."

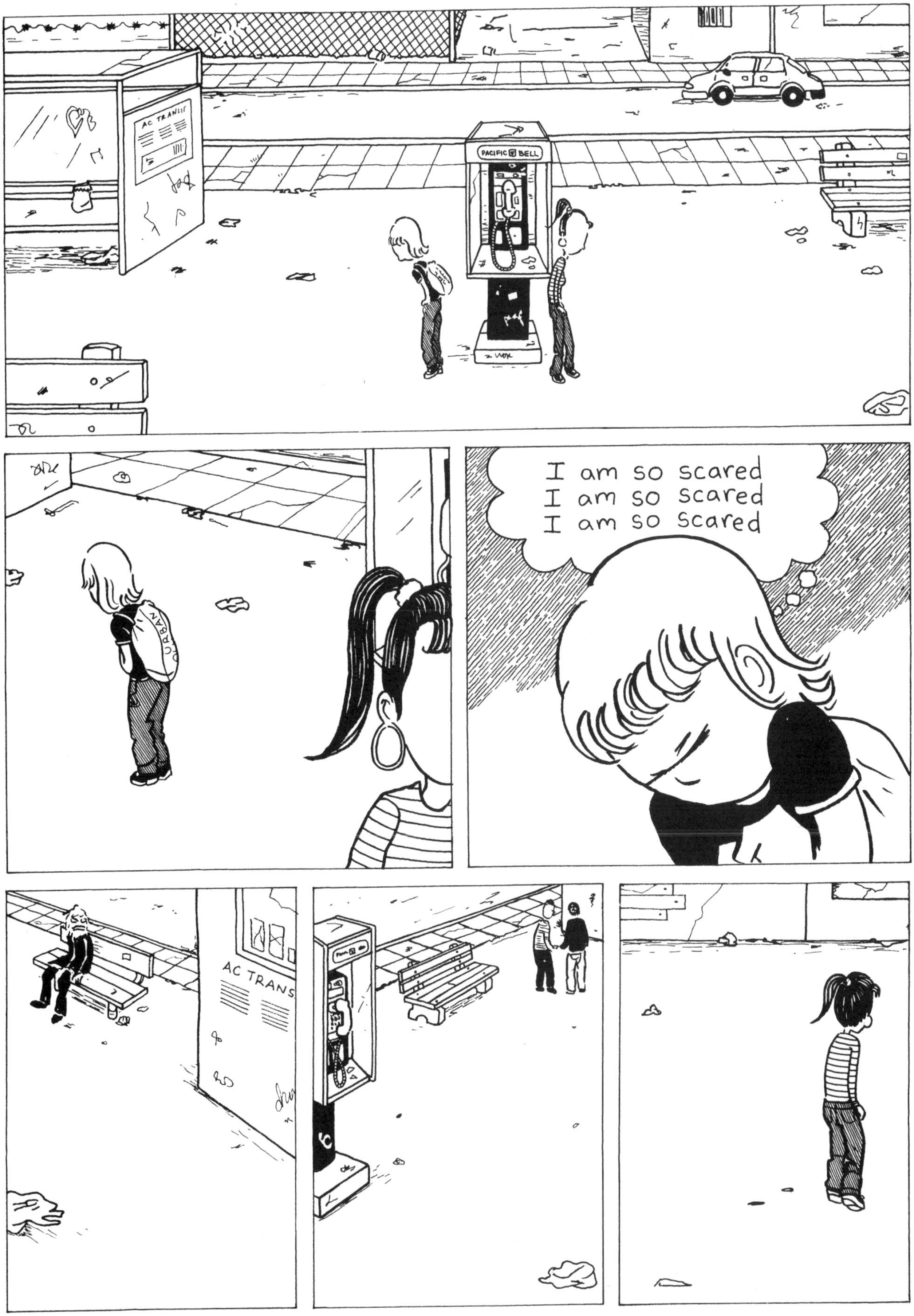
PACIFIC BELL
AC TRANSIT
URBAN
I am so scared
I am so scared
I am so scared
AC TRANS

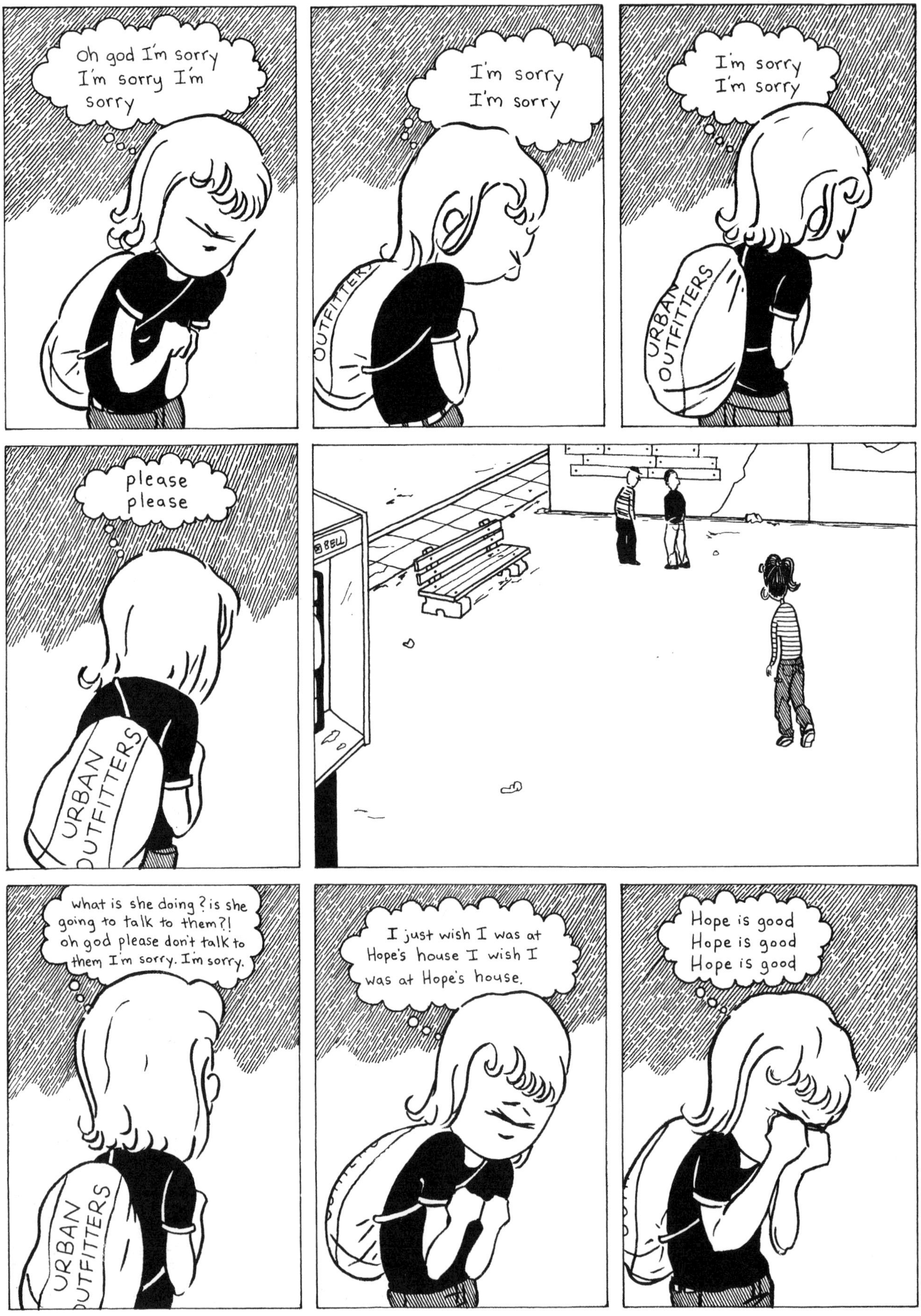
oh god I'm sorry I'm sorry I'm sorry
I'm sorry I'm sorry
OUTFITTERS
I'm sorry I'm sorry
URBAN OUTFITTERS
please please
URBAN OUTFITTERS
BELL
what is she doing? is she going to talk to them?! oh god please don't talk to them I'm sorry. I'm sorry.
URBAN OUTFITTERS
I just wish I was at Hope's house I wish I was at Hope's house.
Hope is good Hope is good Hope is good

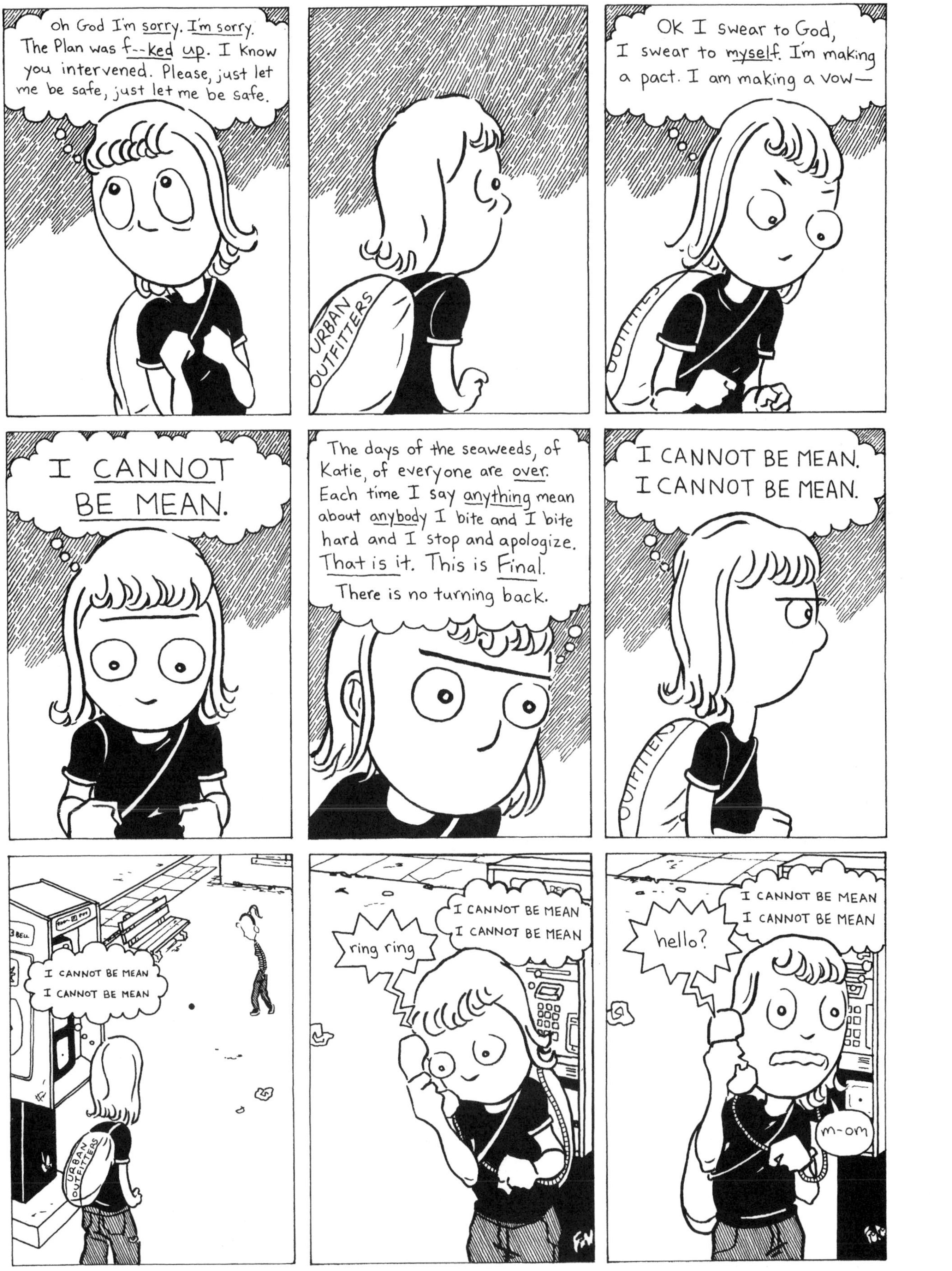
oh God I'm sorry. I'm sorry. The Plan was f--ked up. I know you intervened. Please, just let me be safe, just let me be safe.
URBAN OUTFITTERS
Ok I swear to God, I swear to myself. I'm making a pact. I am making a vow—
I CANNOT BE MEAN.
The days of the seaweeds, of Katie, of everyone are over. Each time I say anything mean about anybody I bite and I bite hard and I stop and apologize. That is it. This is Final. There is no turning back.
I CANNOT BE MEAN. I CANNOT BE MEAN.
I CANNOT BE MEAN
I CANNOT BE MEAN
URBAN OUTFITTERS
ring ring
I CANNOT BE MEAN
I CANNOT BE MEAN
hello?
I CANNOT BE MEAN
I CANNOT BE MEAN
m-om

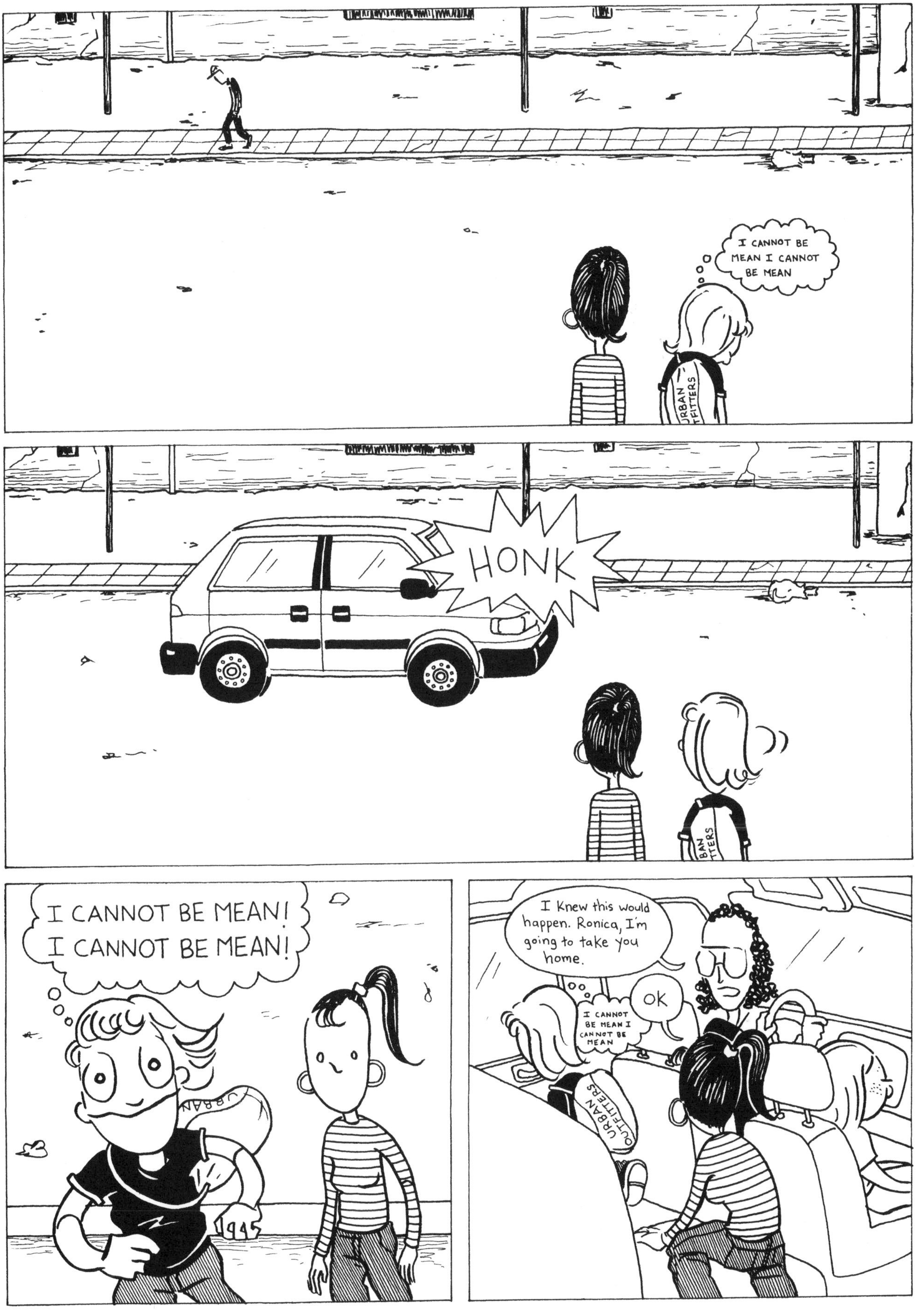
I CANNOT BE MEAN I CANNOT BE MEAN
HONK
I CANNOT BE MEAN! I CANNOT BE MEAN!
I Knew this would happen. Ronica, I'm going to take you home.
I CANNOT BE MEAN I CANNOT BE MEAN
OK
URBAN OUTFITTERS

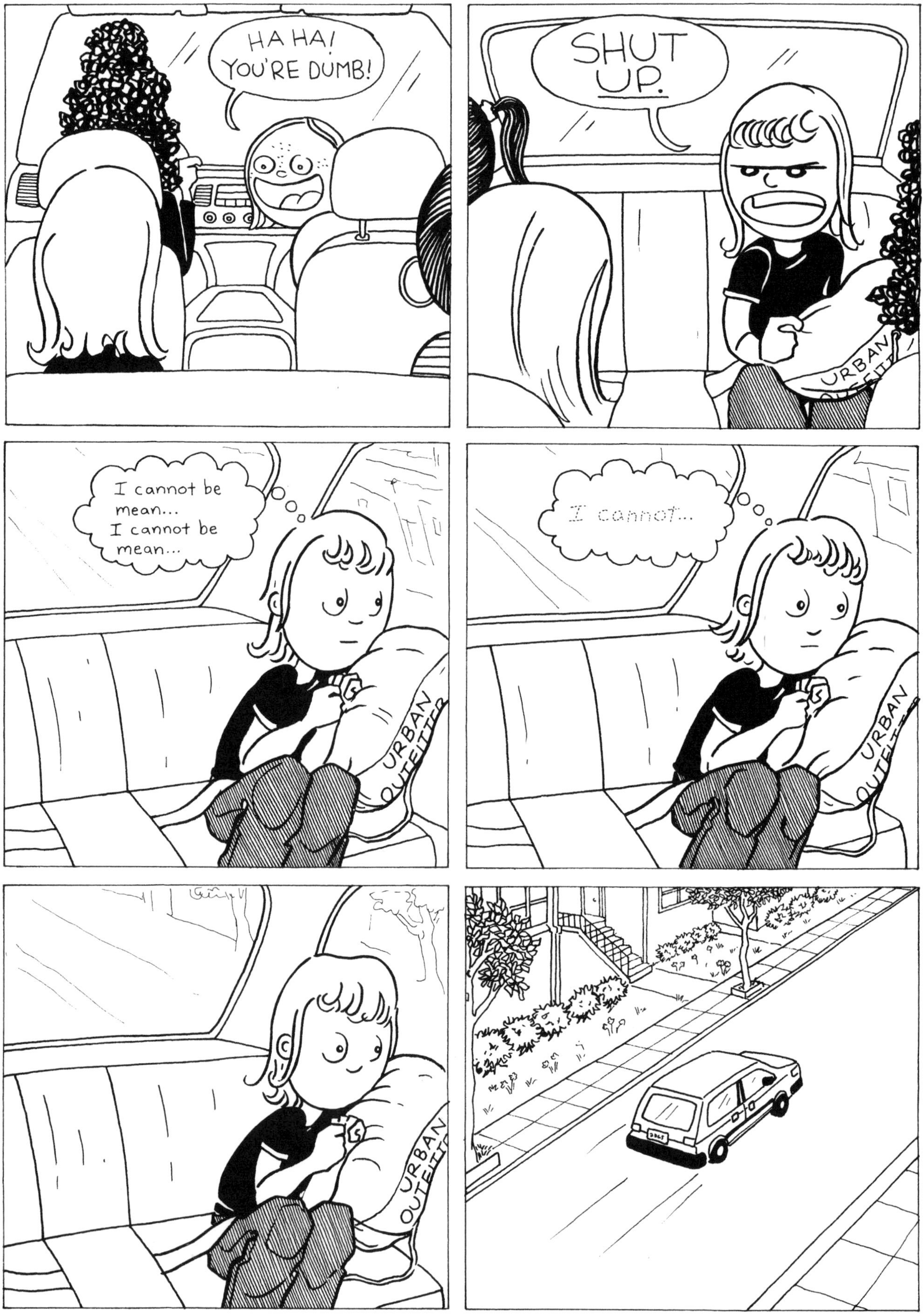
HA HA! YOU'RE DUMB!
SHUT UP.
URBAN OUTFITTER
I cannot be mean... I cannot be mean...
URBAN OUTFITTER
I cannot...
URBAN OUTFITTER
URBAN OUTFITTER

JACE SMITH

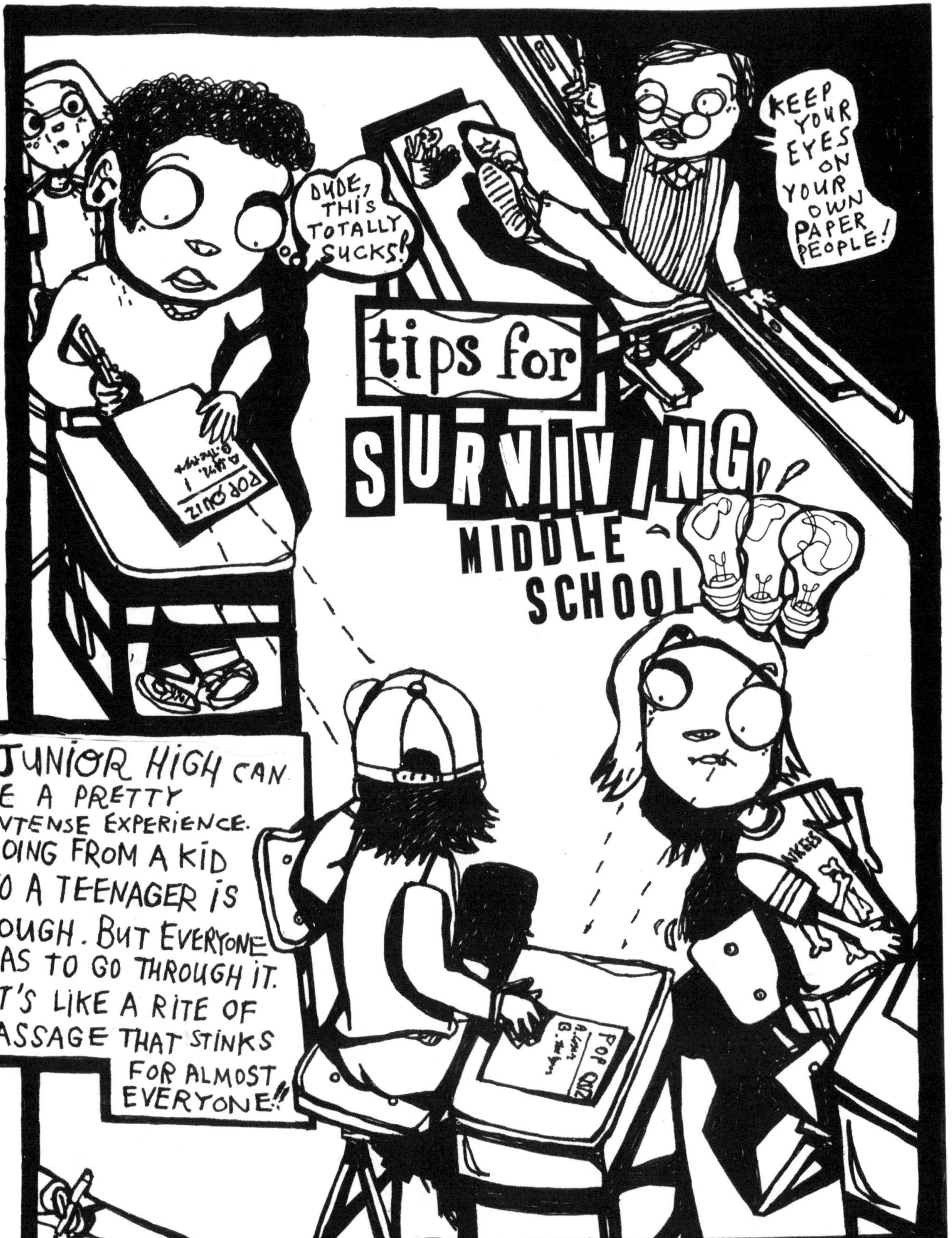
DUDE, THIS TOTALLY SUCKS!
KEEP YOUR EYES ON YOUR OWN PAPER PEOPLE!
tips for
SURVIVING
MIDDLE SCHOOL
POP QUIZ
JUNIOR HIGH CAN BE A PRETTY INTENSE EXPERIENCE. GOING FROM A KID TO A TEENAGER IS ROUGH. BUT EVERYONE HAS TO GO THROUGH IT. IT'S LIKE A RITE OF PASSAGE THAT STINKS FOR ALMOST EVERYONE!!

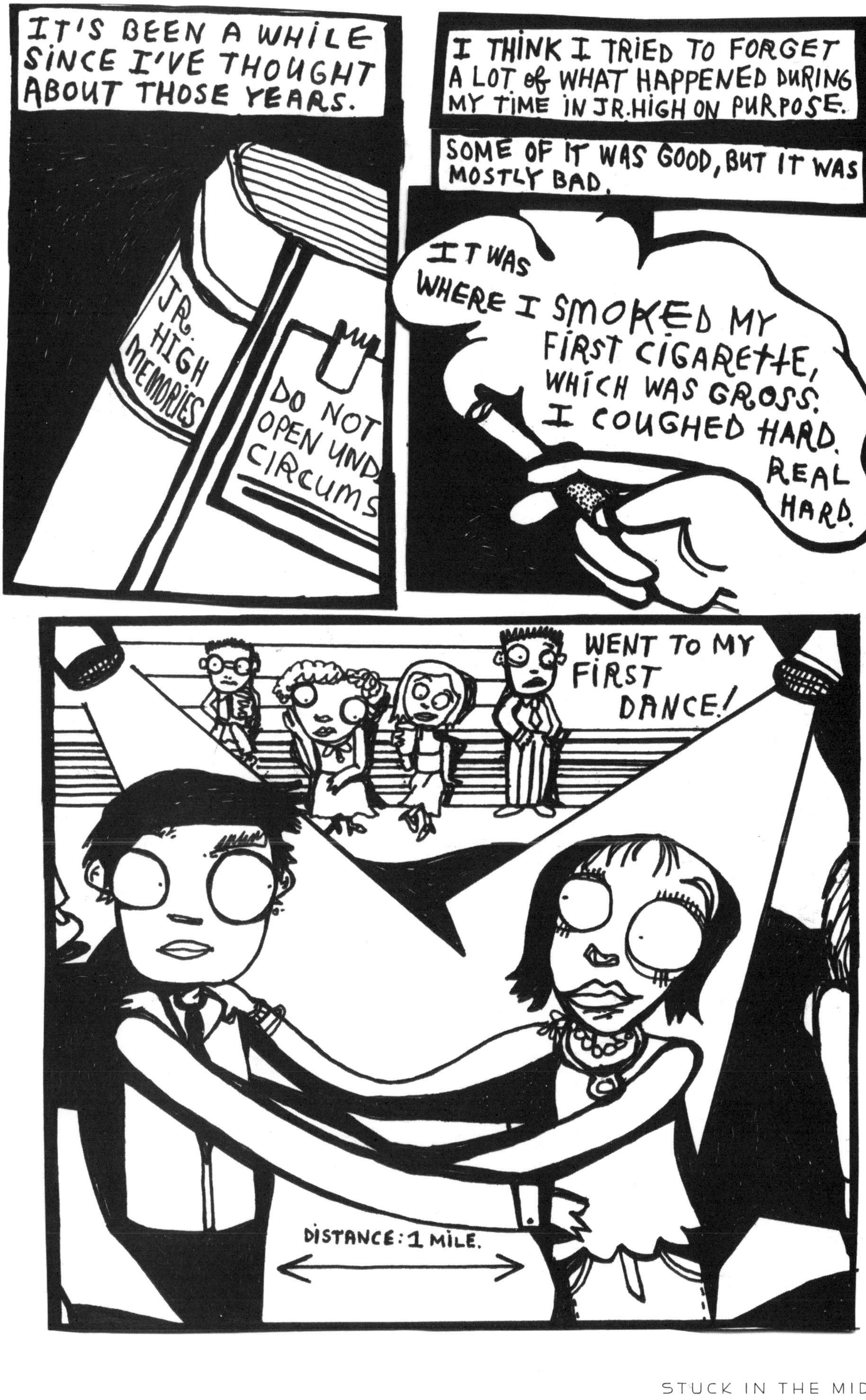
IT'S BEEN A WHILE SINCE I'VE THOUGHT ABOUT THOSE YEARS.
JR. HIGH MEMORIES
DO NOT OPEN UND CIRCUMS
I THINK I TRIED TO FORGET A LOT OF WHAT HAPPENED DURING MY TIME IN JR. HIGH ON PURPOSE.
SOME OF IT WAS GOOD, BUT IT WAS MOSTLY BAD.
IT WAS WHERE I SMOKED MY FIRST CIGARETTE, WHICH WAS GROSS. I COUGHED HARD. REAL HARD.
WENT TO MY FIRST DANCE!
DISTANCE: 1 MILE.

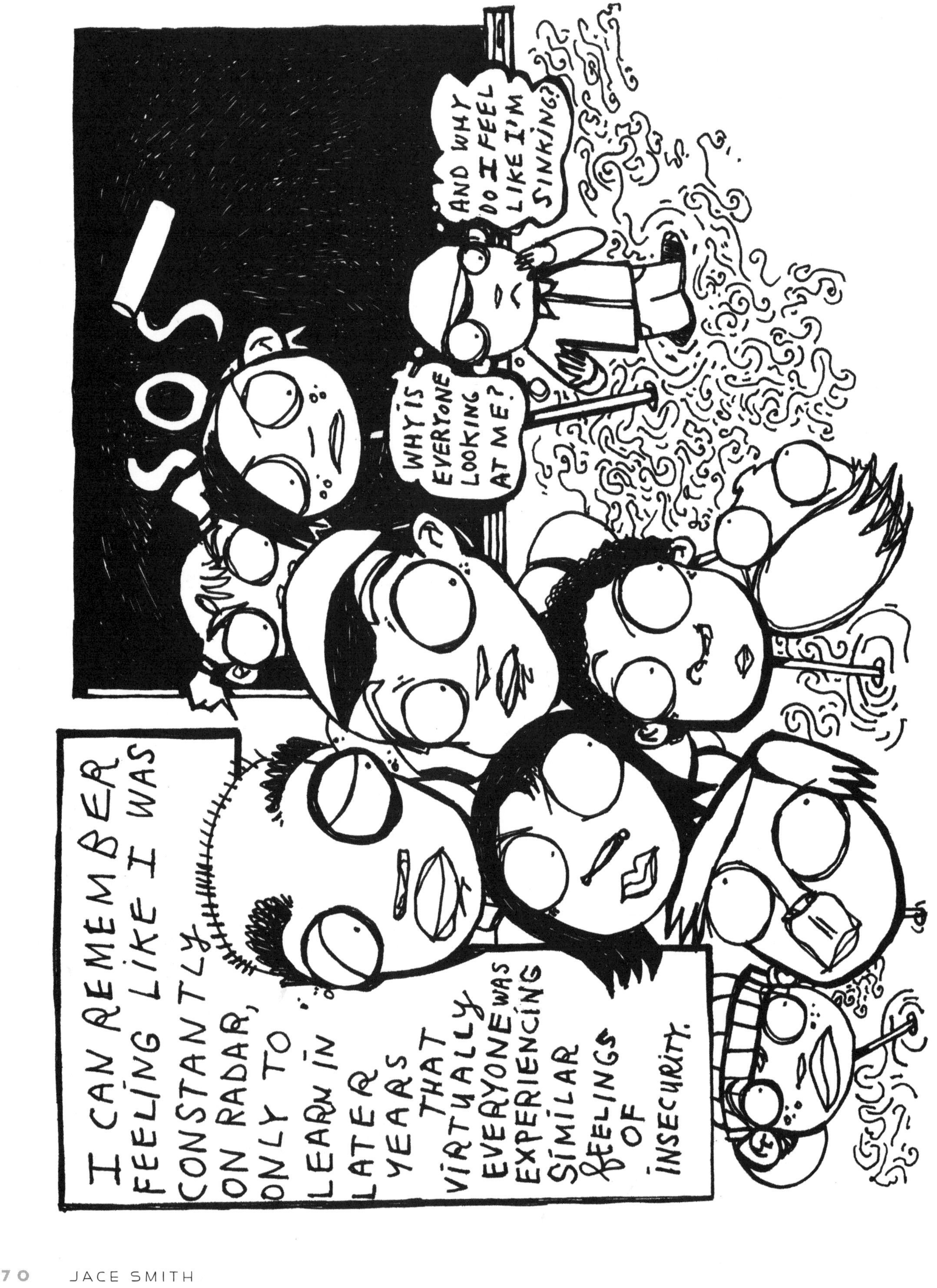
SOS
I CAN REMEMBER FEELING LIKE I WAS CONSTANTLY ON RADAR, ONLY TO LEARN IN LATER YEARS THAT VIRTUALLY EVERYONE WAS EXPERIENCING SIMILAR FEELINGS OF INSECURITY.
WHY IS EVERYONE LOOKING AT ME?
AND WHY DO I FEEL LIKE I'M SINKING?

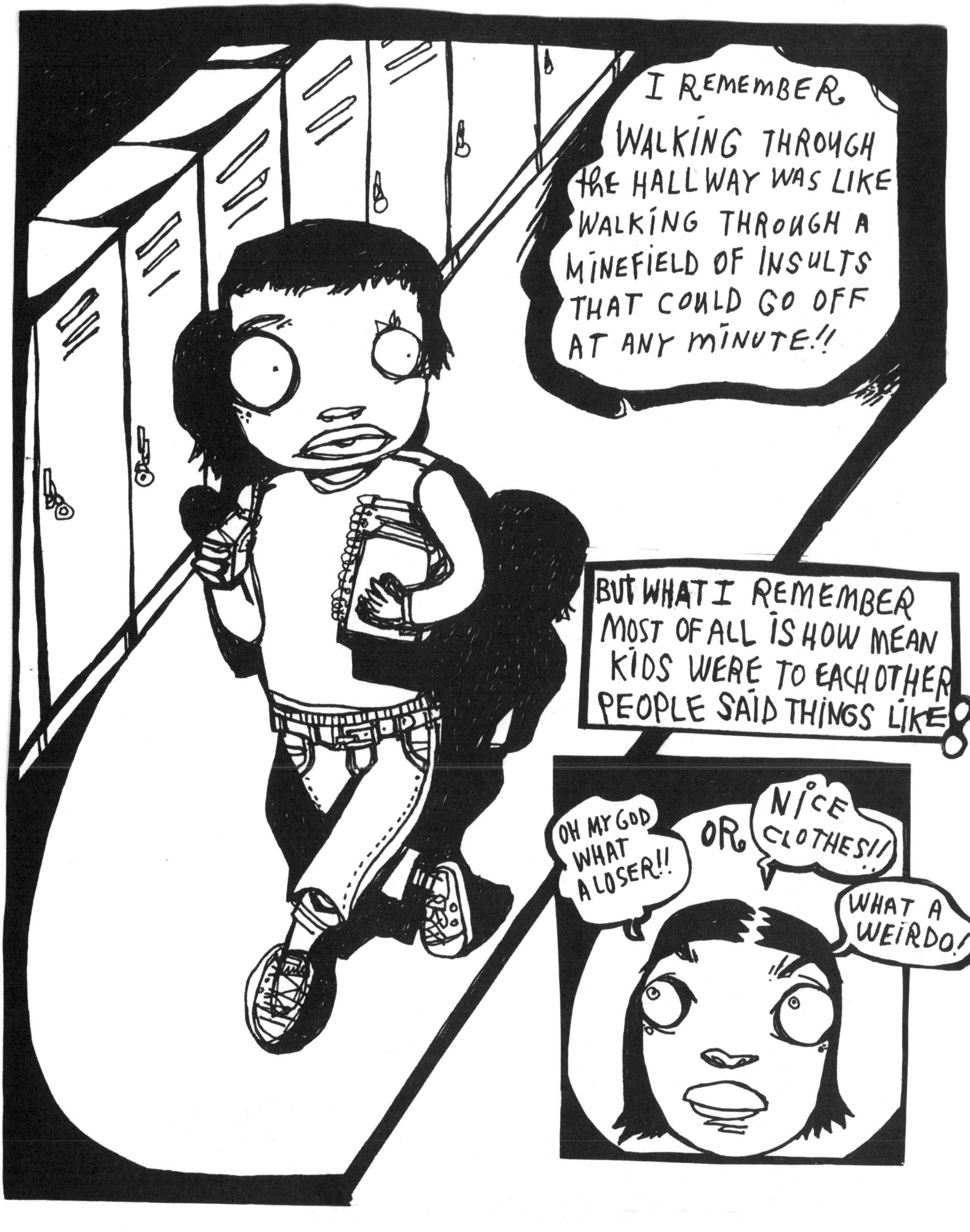
I REMEMBER WALKING THROUGH THE HALLWAY WAS LIKE WALKING THROUGH A MINEFIELD OF INSULTS THAT COULD GO OFF AT ANY MINUTE!!
BUT WHAT I REMEMBER MOST OF ALL IS HOW MEAN KIDS WERE TO EACH OTHER PEOPLE SAID THINGS LIKE:
OH MY GOD WHAT A LOSER!!
OR
NICE CLOTHES!!
WHAT A WEIRDO!

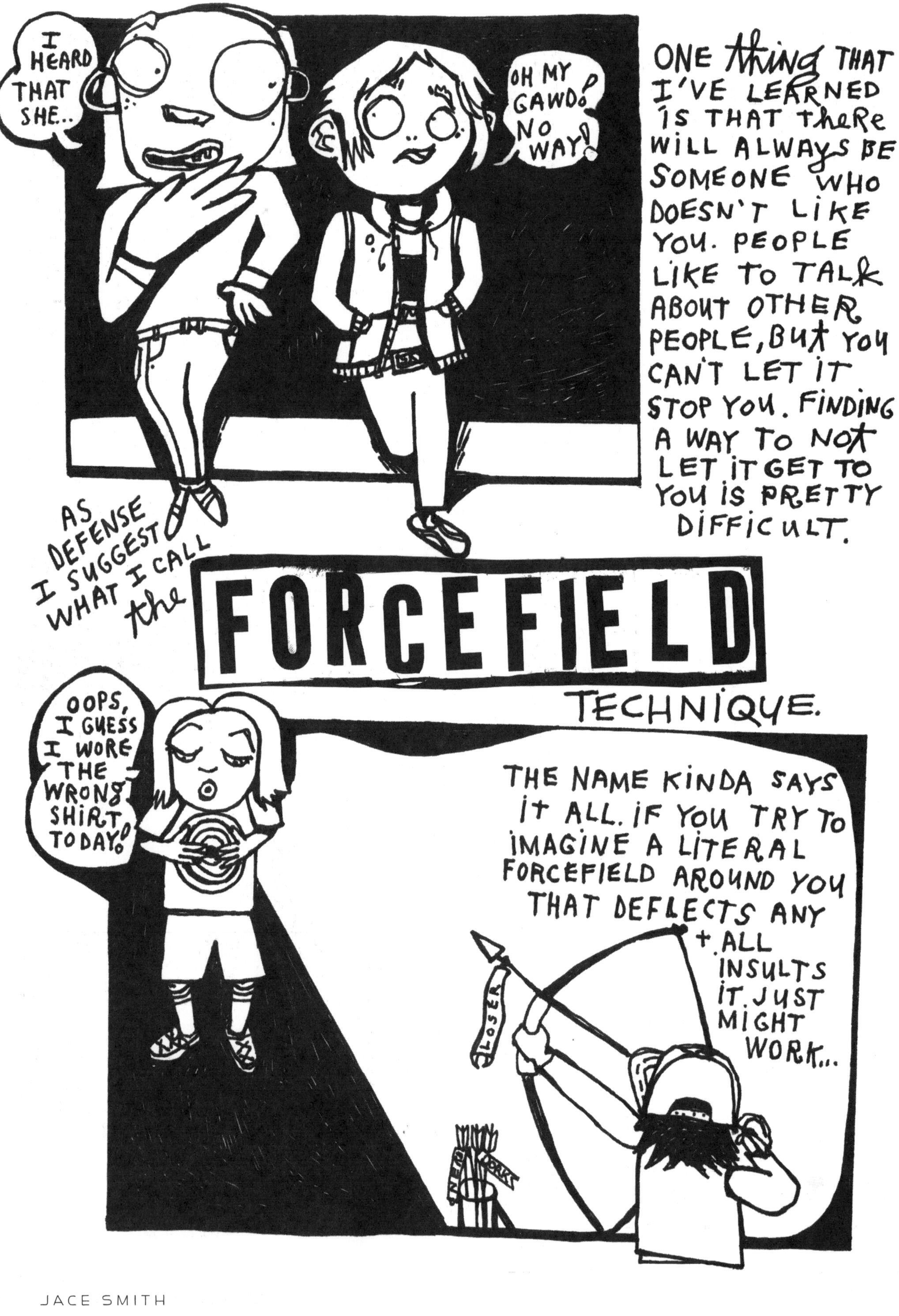
I HEARD THAT SHE...
OH MY GAWD! NO WAY!
ONE thing THAT I'VE LEARNED IS THAT there WILL ALWAYS BE SOMEONE WHO DOESN'T LIKE YOU. PEOPLE LIKE TO TALK ABOUT OTHER PEOPLE, BUT YOU CAN'T LET IT STOP YOU. FINDING A WAY TO NOT LET IT GET TO YOU IS PRETTY DIFFICULT.
AS DEFENSE I SUGGEST WHAT I CALL the
FORCEFIELD
TECHNIQUE.
OOPS, I GUESS I WORE THE WRONG SHIRT TODAY!
THE NAME KINDA SAYS IT ALL. IF YOU TRY TO IMAGINE A LITERAL FORCEFIELD AROUND YOU THAT DEFLECTS ANY + ALL INSULTS IT JUST MIGHT WORK...
LOSER

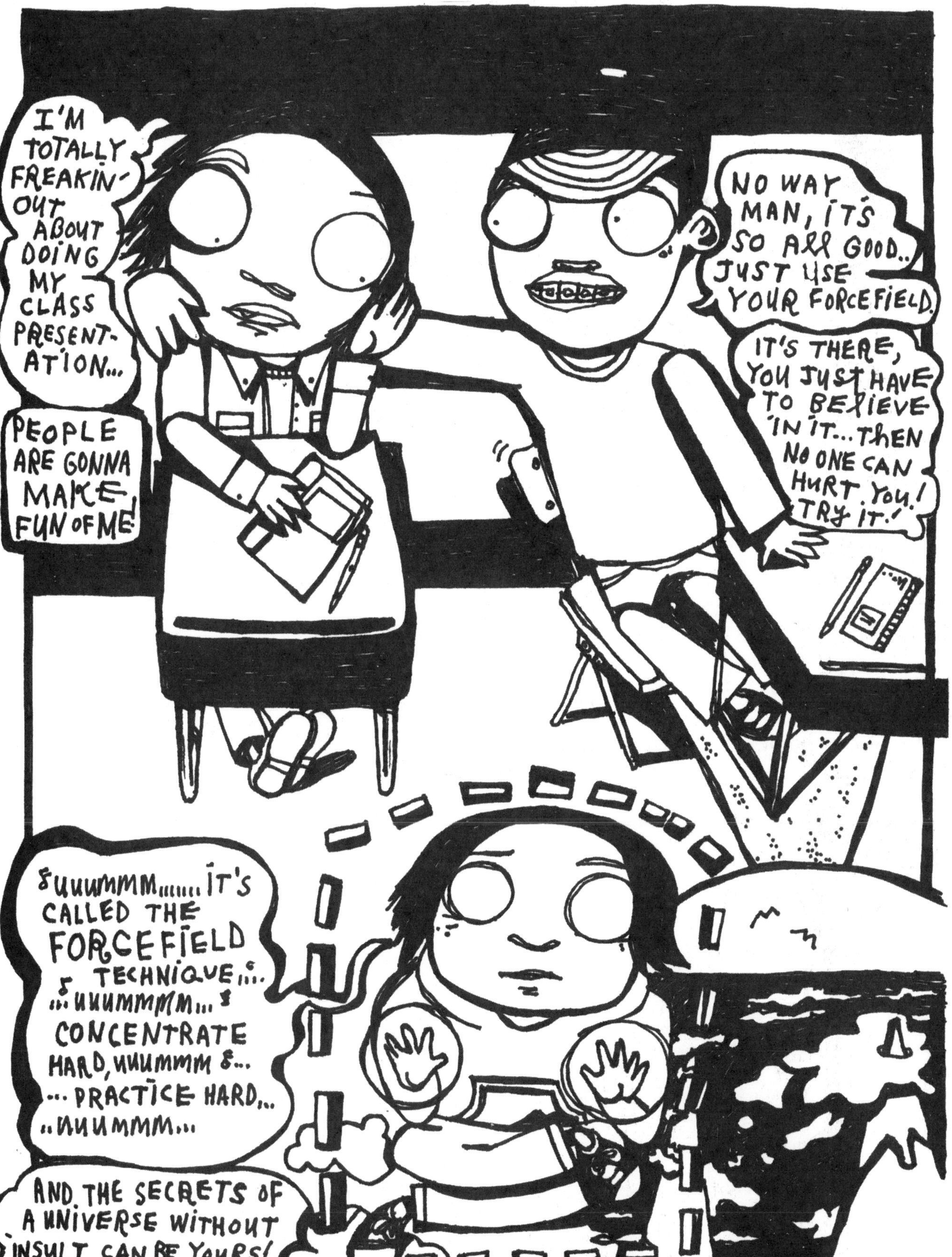
I'M TOTALLY FREAKIN-OUT ABOUT DOING MY CLASS PRESENT-ATION...
PEOPLE ARE GONNA MAKE FUN OF ME!
NO WAY MAN, IT'S SO ALL GOOD.. JUST USE YOUR FORCEFIELD.
IT'S THERE, YOU JUST HAVE TO BELIEVE IN IT... THEN NO ONE CAN HURT YOU! TRY IT!
UUUMMM....... IT'S CALLED THE FORCEFIELD TECHNIQUE..... ...UUUMMMM... CONCENTRATE HARD, UUUMMM ... PRACTICE HARD... ..UUUMMM...
AND THE SECRETS OF A UNIVERSE WITHOUT INSULT CAN BE YOURS!

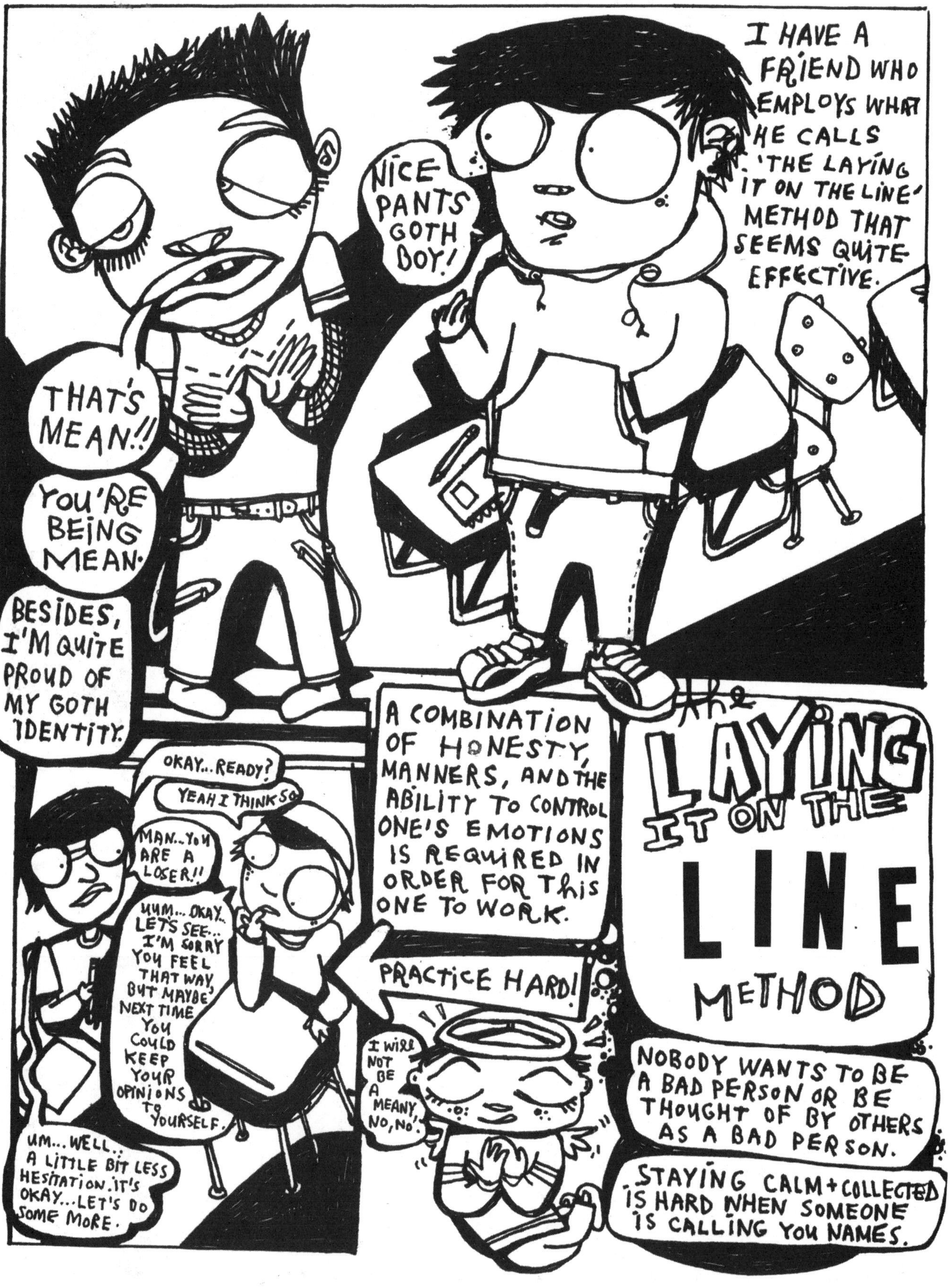
I HAVE A FRIEND WHO EMPLOYS WHAT HE CALLS 'THE LAYING IT ON THE LINE' METHOD THAT SEEMS QUITE EFFECTIVE.
NICE PANTS GOTH BOY!
THAT'S MEAN!!
YOU'RE BEING MEAN.
BESIDES, I'M QUITE PROUD OF MY GOTH IDENTITY.
A COMBINATION OF HONESTY, MANNERS, AND THE ABILITY TO CONTROL ONE'S EMOTIONS IS REQUIRED IN ORDER FOR THIS ONE TO WORK.
THE LAYING IT ON THE LINE METHOD
OKAY... READY?
YEAH I THINK SO
MAN... YOU ARE A LOSER!!
UMM... OKAY.. LET'S SEE... I'M SORRY YOU FEEL THAT WAY BUT MAYBE NEXT TIME YOU COULD KEEP YOUR OPINIONS TO YOURSELF.
UM... WELL.. A LITTLE BIT LESS HESITATION. IT'S OKAY... LET'S DO SOME MORE.
PRACTICE HARD!
I WILL NOT BE A MEANY. NO, NO.
NOBODY WANTS TO BE A BAD PERSON OR BE THOUGHT OF BY OTHERS AS A BAD PERSON.
STAYING CALM + COLLECTED IS HARD WHEN SOMEONE IS CALLING YOU NAMES.

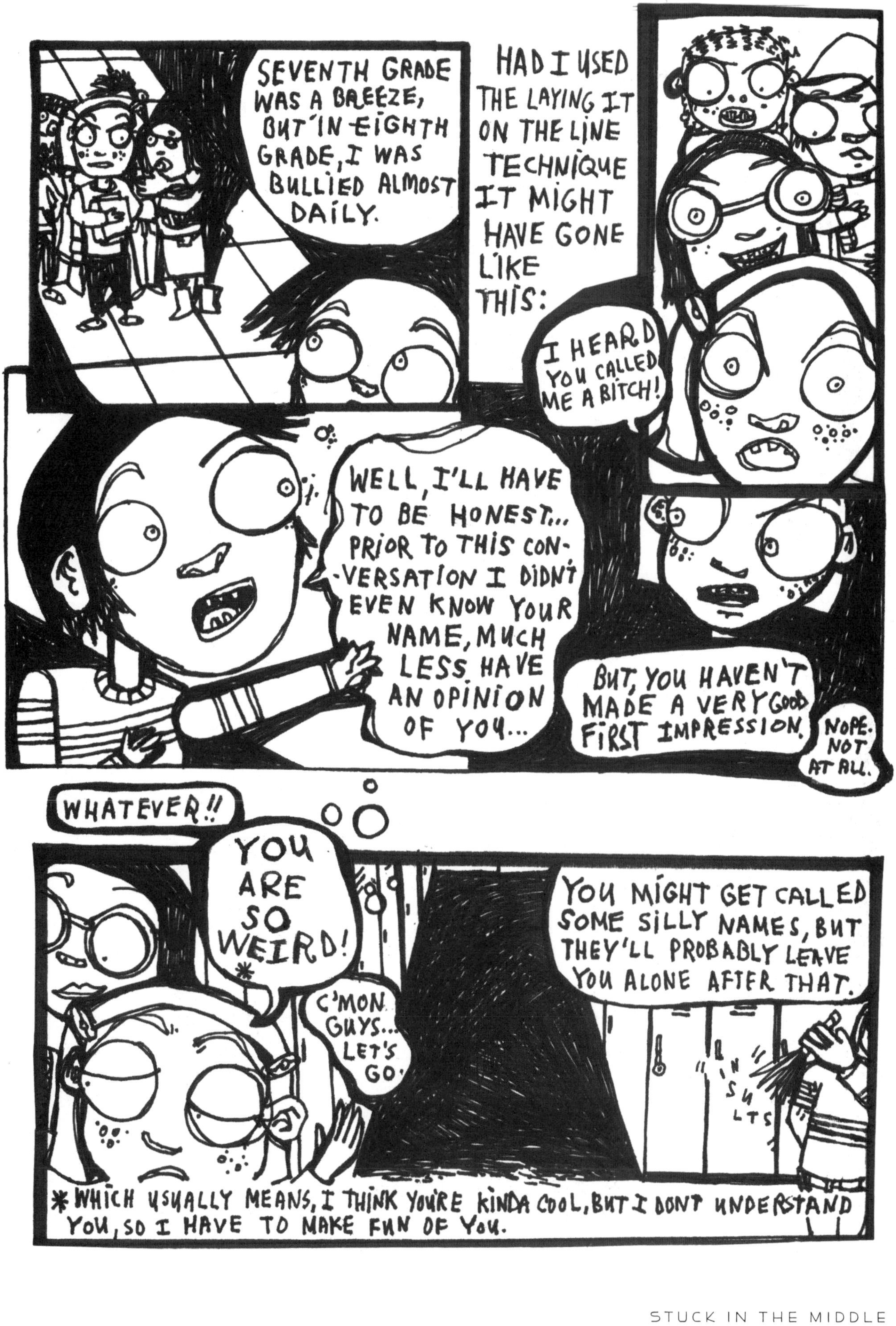
SEVENTH GRADE WAS A BREEZE, BUT IN EIGHTH GRADE, I WAS BULLIED ALMOST DAILY.
HAD I USED THE LAYING IT ON THE LINE TECHNIQUE IT MIGHT HAVE GONE LIKE THIS:
I HEARD YOU CALLED ME A BITCH!
WELL, I'LL HAVE TO BE HONEST... PRIOR TO THIS CON-VERSATION I DIDN'T EVEN KNOW YOUR NAME, MUCH LESS HAVE AN OPINION OF YOU...
BUT, YOU HAVEN'T MADE A VERY GOOD FIRST IMPRESSION.
NOPE. NOT AT ALL.
WHATEVER!!
YOU ARE SO WEIRD! *
C'MON GUYS... LET'S GO.
YOU MIGHT GET CALLED SOME SILLY NAMES, BUT THEY'LL PROBABLY LEAVE YOU ALONE AFTER THAT.
"INSULTS"
* WHICH USUALLY MEANS, I THINK YOU'RE KINDA COOL, BUT I DONT UNDERSTAND YOU, SO I HAVE TO MAKE FUN OF YOU.

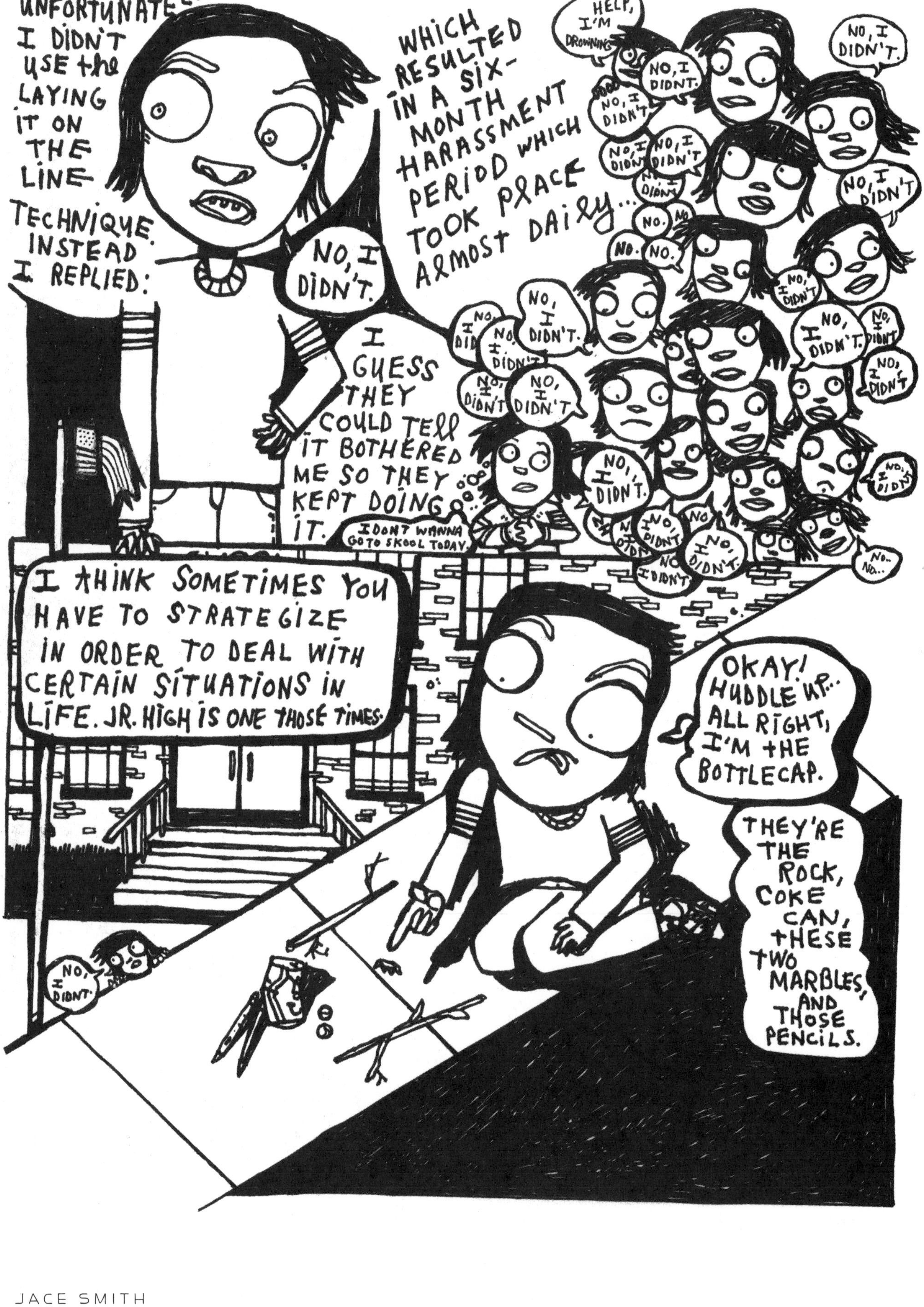
UNFORTUNATELY, I DIDN'T USE the LAYING IT ON THE LINE TECHNIQUE. INSTEAD I REPLIED:
NO, I DIDN'T.
WHICH RESULTED IN A SIX-MONTH HARASSMENT PERIOD WHICH TOOK PLACE ALMOST DAILY...
HELP, I'M DROWNING
NO, I DIDN'T.
NO, I DIDN'T.
NO, I DIDN'T.
NO.
NO.
I GUESS THEY COULD TELL IT BOTHERED ME SO THEY KEPT DOING IT.
I DON'T WANNA GO TO SKOOL TODAY.
I THINK SOMETIMES YOU HAVE TO STRATEGIZE IN ORDER TO DEAL WITH CERTAIN SITUATIONS IN LIFE. JR. HIGH IS ONE THOSE TIMES.
NO, I DIDN'T.
OKAY! HUDDLE UP... ALL RIGHT, I'M THE BOTTLECAP.
THEY'RE THE ROCK, COKE CAN, THESE TWO MARBLES, AND THOSE PENCILS.

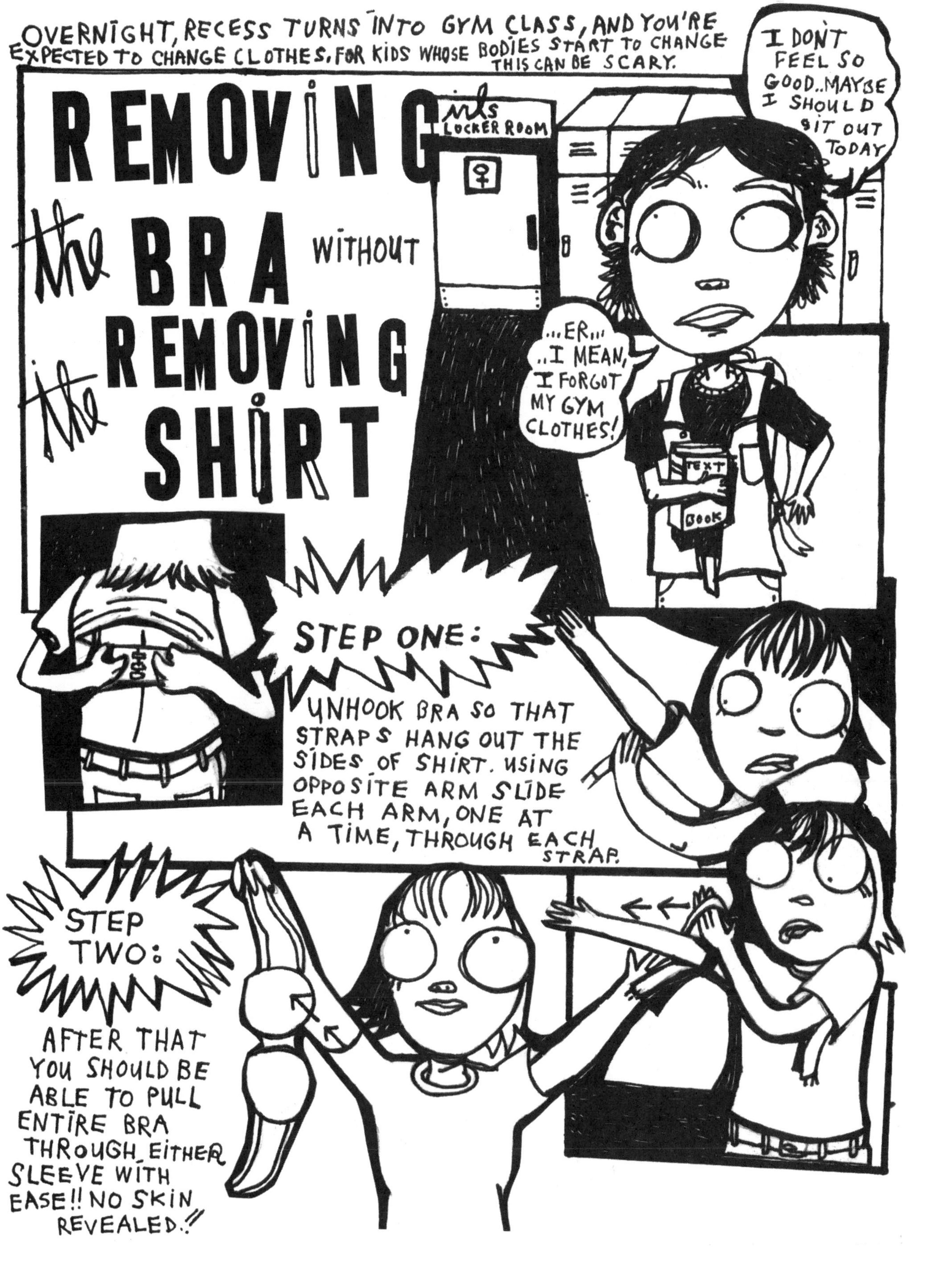
OVERNIGHT, RECESS TURNS INTO GYM CLASS, AND YOU'RE EXPECTED TO CHANGE CLOTHES. FOR KIDS WHOSE BODIES START TO CHANGE THIS CAN BE SCARY.
REMOVING the BRA WITHOUT REMOVING the SHIRT
Girls LOCKER ROOM
I DON'T FEEL SO GOOD..MAYBE I SHOULD SIT OUT TODAY
...ER... ..I MEAN, I FORGOT MY GYM CLOTHES!
TEXT BOOK
STEP ONE:
UNHOOK BRA SO THAT STRAPS HANG OUT THE SIDES OF SHIRT. USING OPPOSITE ARM SLIDE EACH ARM, ONE AT A TIME, THROUGH EACH STRAP.
STEP TWO:
AFTER THAT YOU SHOULD BE ABLE TO PULL ENTIRE BRA THROUGH EITHER SLEEVE WITH EASE!! NO SKIN REVEALED!!

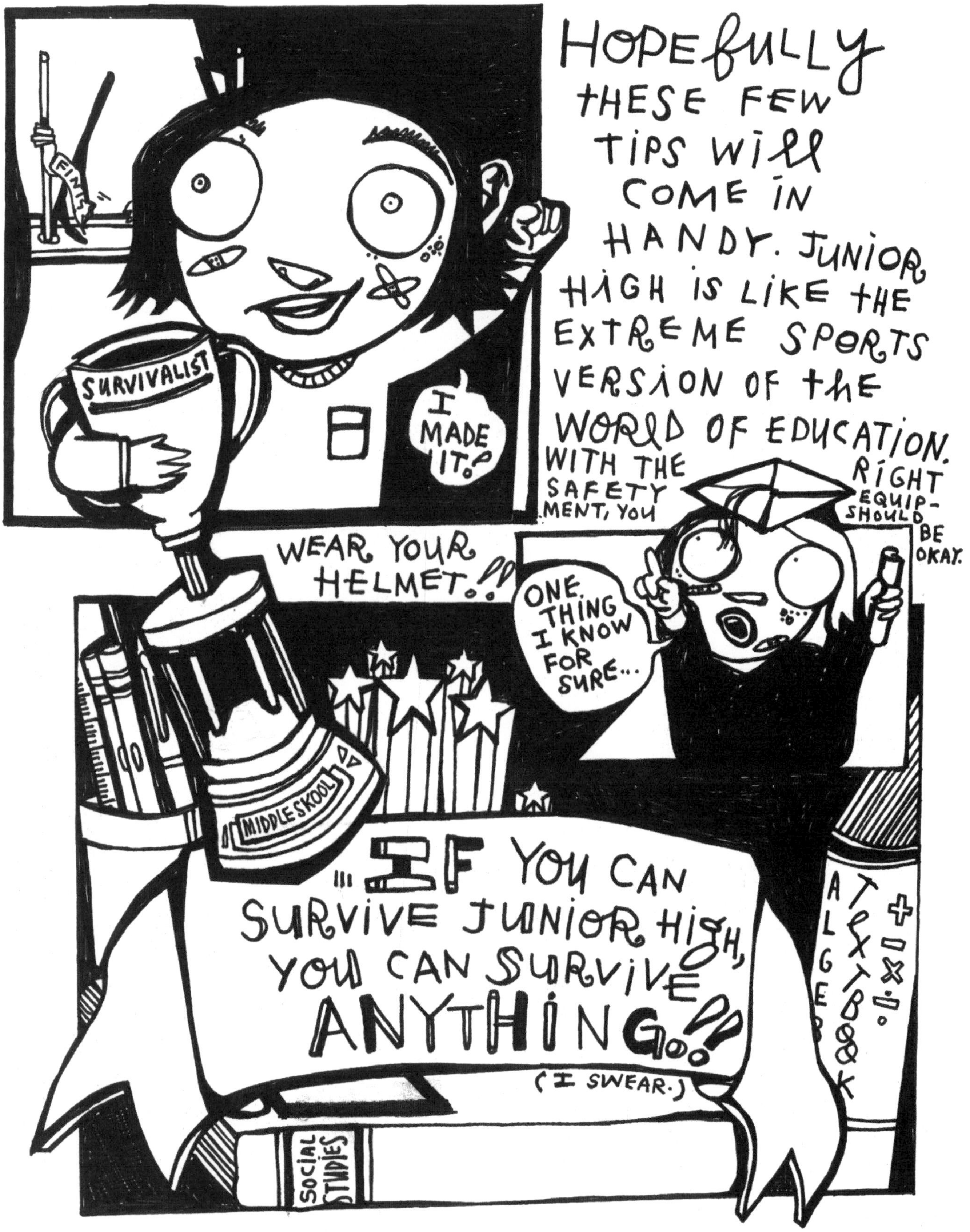
FINIS
SURVIVALIST
I MADE IT!
HOPEfully these few tips will come in HANDY. Junior High is like the extreme sports version of the world of education.
With the right safety equipment, you should be okay.
WEAR YOUR HELMET!!
ONE THING I KNOW FOR SURE...
MIDDLESKOOL
"IF you can survive junior high, you can survive ANYTHING!!
(I swear.)
ALGEBRA TEXTBOOK
SOCIAL STUDIES

DANIEL CLOWES

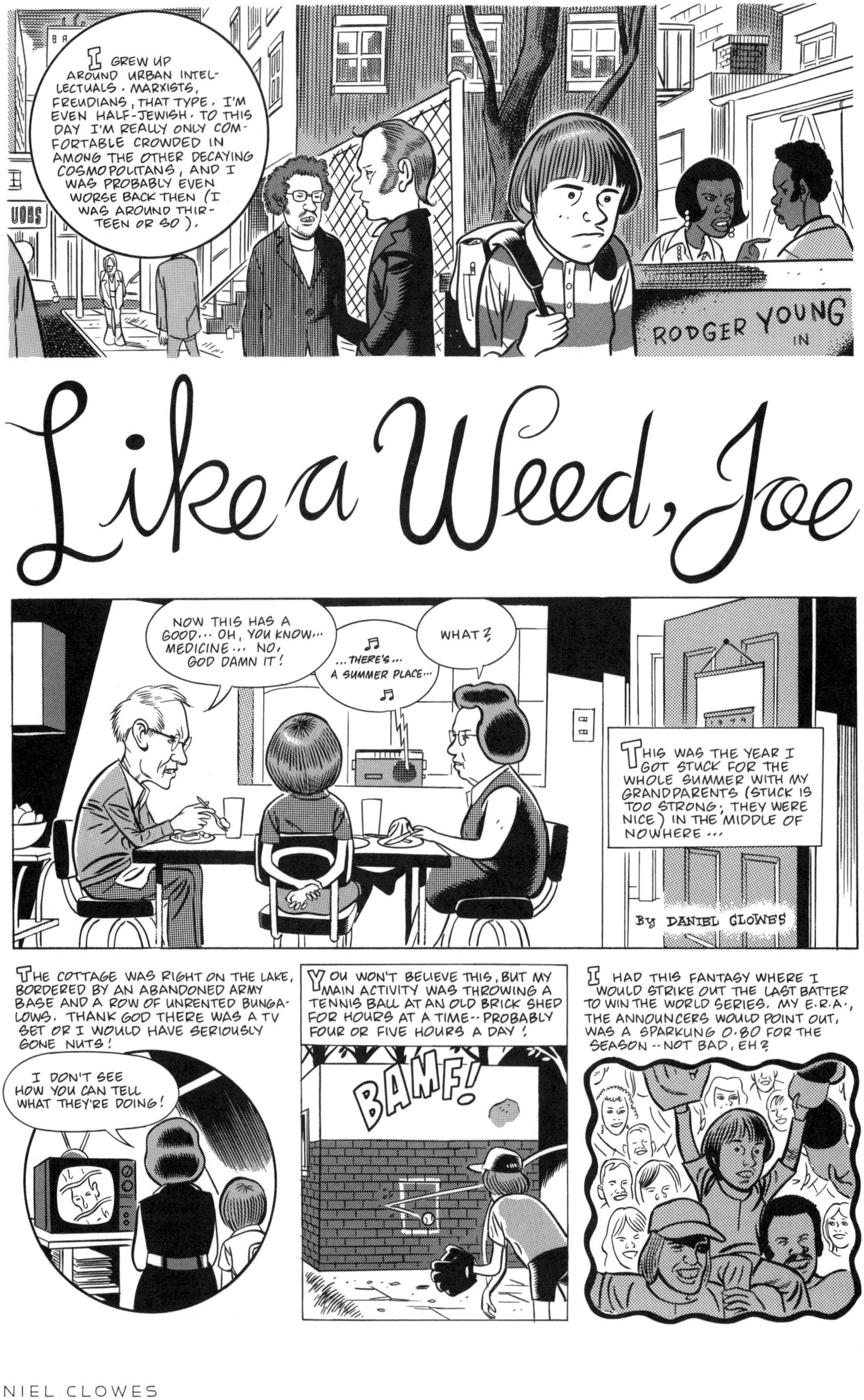

I GREW UP AROUND URBAN INTELLECTUALS. MARXISTS, FREUDIANS, THAT TYPE. I'M EVEN HALF-JEWISH. TO THIS DAY I'M REALLY ONLY COMFORTABLE CROWDED IN AMONG THE OTHER DECAYING COSMOPOLITANS, AND I WAS PROBABLY EVEN WORSE BACK THEN (I WAS AROUND THIRTEEN OR SO).
RODGER YOUNG IN
Like a Weed, Joe
NOW THIS HAS A GOOD... OH, YOU KNOW... MEDICINE... NO, GOD DAMN IT!
...THERE'S... A SUMMER PLACE...
WHAT?
THIS WAS THE YEAR I GOT STUCK FOR THE WHOLE SUMMER WITH MY GRANDPARENTS (STUCK IS TOO STRONG; THEY WERE NICE) IN THE MIDDLE OF NOWHERE...
By DANIEL CLOWES
THE COTTAGE WAS RIGHT ON THE LAKE, BORDERED BY AN ABANDONED ARMY BASE AND A ROW OF UNRENTED BUNGALOWS. THANK GOD THERE WAS A TV SET OR I WOULD HAVE SERIOUSLY GONE NUTS!
I DON'T SEE HOW YOU CAN TELL WHAT THEY'RE DOING!
YOU WON'T BELIEVE THIS, BUT MY MAIN ACTIVITY WAS THROWING A TENNIS BALL AT AN OLD BRICK SHED FOR HOURS AT A TIME-- PROBABLY FOUR OR FIVE HOURS A DAY!
BAMF!
I HAD THIS FANTASY WHERE I WOULD STRIKE OUT THE LAST BATTER TO WIN THE WORLD SERIES. MY E.R.A., THE ANNOUNCERS WOULD POINT OUT, WAS A SPARKLING 0.80 FOR THE SEASON -- NOT BAD, EH?

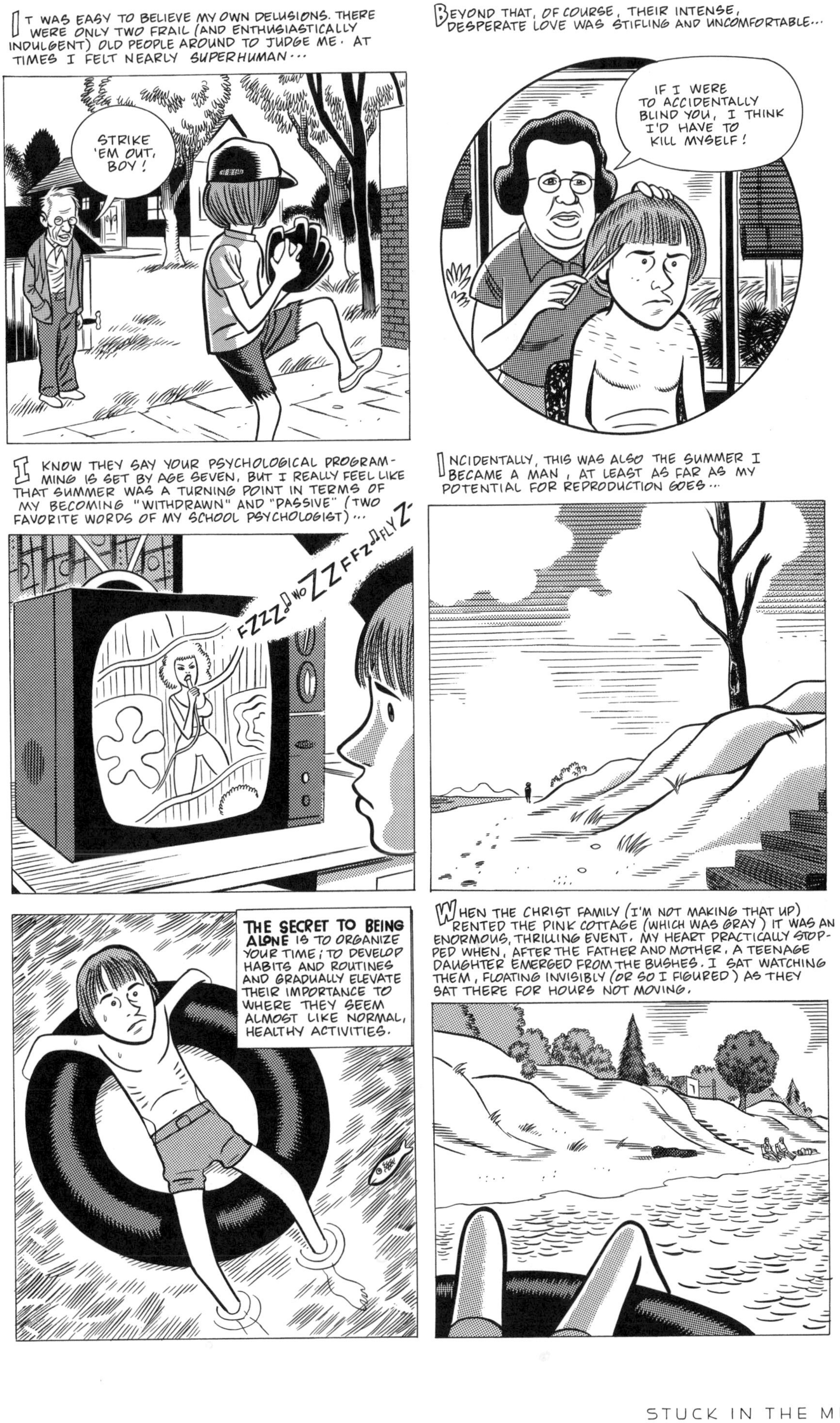
IT WAS EASY TO BELIEVE MY OWN DELUSIONS. THERE WERE ONLY TWO FRAIL (AND ENTHUSIASTICALLY INDULGENT) OLD PEOPLE AROUND TO JUDGE ME. AT TIMES I FELT NEARLY SUPERHUMAN...
STRIKE 'EM OUT, BOY!
BEYOND THAT, OF COURSE, THEIR INTENSE, DESPERATE LOVE WAS STIFLING AND UNCOMFORTABLE...
IF I WERE TO ACCIDENTALLY BLIND YOU, I THINK I'D HAVE TO KILL MYSELF!
I KNOW THEY SAY YOUR PSYCHOLOGICAL PROGRAMMING IS SET BY AGE SEVEN, BUT I REALLY FEEL LIKE THAT SUMMER WAS A TURNING POINT IN TERMS OF MY BECOMING "WITHDRAWN" AND "PASSIVE" (TWO FAVORITE WORDS OF MY SCHOOL PSYCHOLOGIST)...
INCIDENTALLY, THIS WAS ALSO THE SUMMER I BECAME A MAN, AT LEAST AS FAR AS MY POTENTIAL FOR REPRODUCTION GOES...
THE SECRET TO BEING ALONE IS TO ORGANIZE YOUR TIME; TO DEVELOP HABITS AND ROUTINES AND GRADUALLY ELEVATE THEIR IMPORTANCE TO WHERE THEY SEEM ALMOST LIKE NORMAL, HEALTHY ACTIVITIES.
WHEN THE CHRIST FAMILY (I'M NOT MAKING THAT UP) RENTED THE PINK COTTAGE (WHICH WAS GRAY) IT WAS AN ENORMOUS, THRILLING EVENT. MY HEART PRACTICALLY STOPPED WHEN, AFTER THE FATHER AND MOTHER, A TEENAGE DAUGHTER EMERGED FROM THE BUSHES. I SAT WATCHING THEM, FLOATING INVISIBLY (OR SO I FIGURED) AS THEY SAT THERE FOR HOURS NOT MOVING.

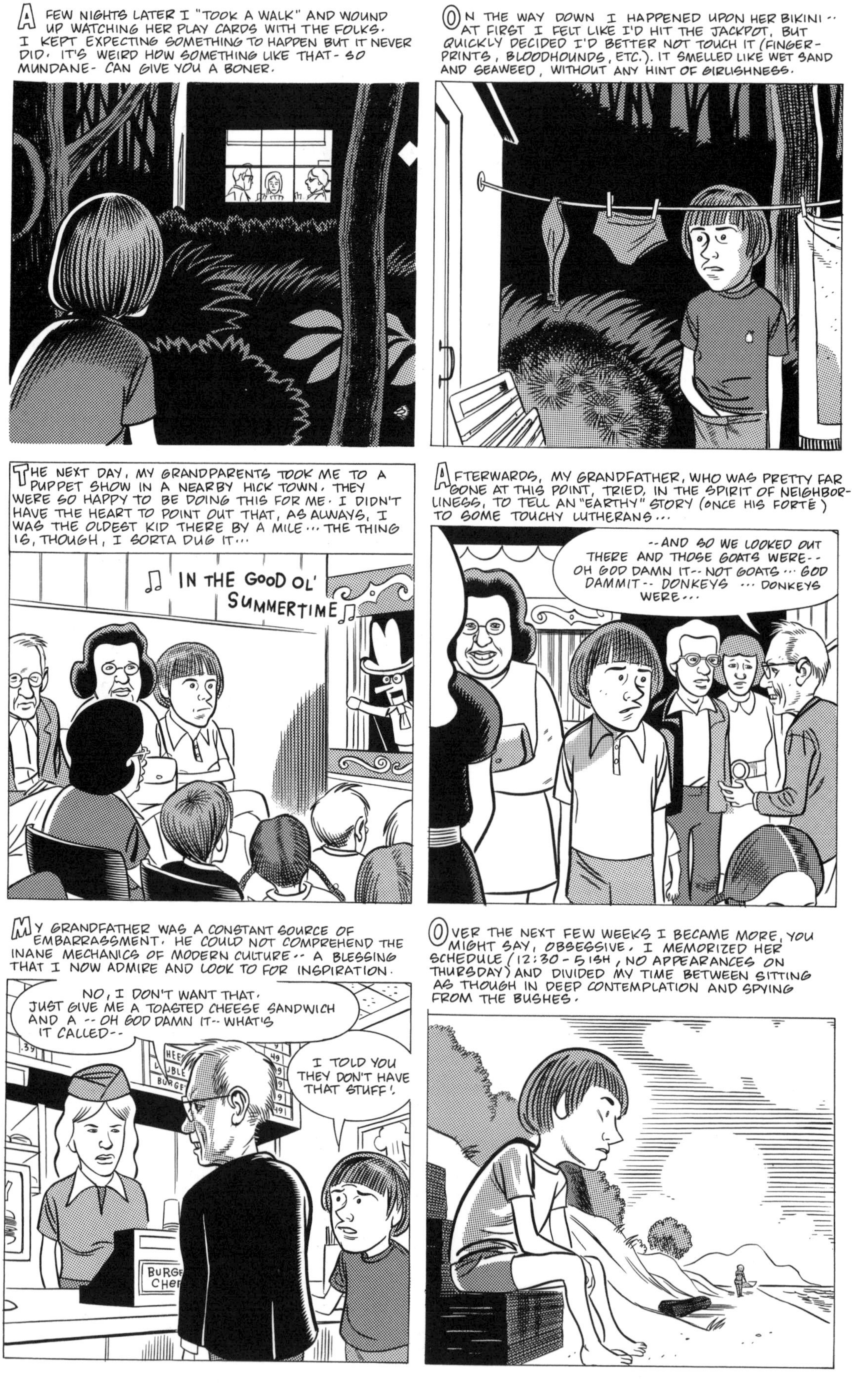
A FEW NIGHTS LATER I "TOOK A WALK" AND WOUND UP WATCHING HER PLAY CARDS WITH THE FOLKS. I KEPT EXPECTING SOMETHING TO HAPPEN BUT IT NEVER DID. IT'S WEIRD HOW SOMETHING LIKE THAT- SO MUNDANE- CAN GIVE YOU A BONER.
ON THE WAY DOWN I HAPPENED UPON HER BIKINI.. AT FIRST I FELT LIKE I'D HIT THE JACKPOT, BUT QUICKLY DECIDED I'D BETTER NOT TOUCH IT (FINGER-PRINTS, BLOODHOUNDS, ETC.). IT SMELLED LIKE WET SAND AND SEAWEED, WITHOUT ANY HINT OF GIRLISHNESS.
THE NEXT DAY, MY GRANDPARENTS TOOK ME TO A PUPPET SHOW IN A NEARBY HICK TOWN. THEY WERE SO HAPPY TO BE DOING THIS FOR ME. I DIDN'T HAVE THE HEART TO POINT OUT THAT, AS ALWAYS, I WAS THE OLDEST KID THERE BY A MILE... THE THING IS, THOUGH, I SORTA DUG IT...
♫ IN THE GOOD OL' SUMMERTIME ♫
AFTERWARDS, MY GRANDFATHER, WHO WAS PRETTY FAR GONE AT THIS POINT, TRIED, IN THE SPIRIT OF NEIGHBOR-LINESS, TO TELL AN "EARTHY" STORY (ONCE HIS FORTÉ) TO SOME TOUCHY LUTHERANS...
--AND SO WE LOOKED OUT THERE AND THOSE GOATS WERE-- OH GOD DAMN IT-- NOT GOATS... GOD DAMMIT-- DONKEYS ... DONKEYS WERE...
MY GRANDFATHER WAS A CONSTANT SOURCE OF EMBARRASSMENT. HE COULD NOT COMPREHEND THE INANE MECHANICS OF MODERN CULTURE-- A BLESSING THAT I NOW ADMIRE AND LOOK TO FOR INSPIRATION.
NO, I DON'T WANT THAT. JUST GIVE ME A TOASTED CHEESE SANDWICH AND A -- OH GOD DAMN IT-- WHAT'S IT CALLED--
I TOLD YOU THEY DON'T HAVE THAT STUFF!
OVER THE NEXT FEW WEEKS I BECAME MORE, YOU MIGHT SAY, OBSESSIVE. I MEMORIZED HER SCHEDULE (12:30 - 5ISH, NO APPEARANCES ON THURSDAY) AND DIVIDED MY TIME BETWEEN SITTING AS THOUGH IN DEEP CONTEMPLATION AND SPYING FROM THE BUSHES.

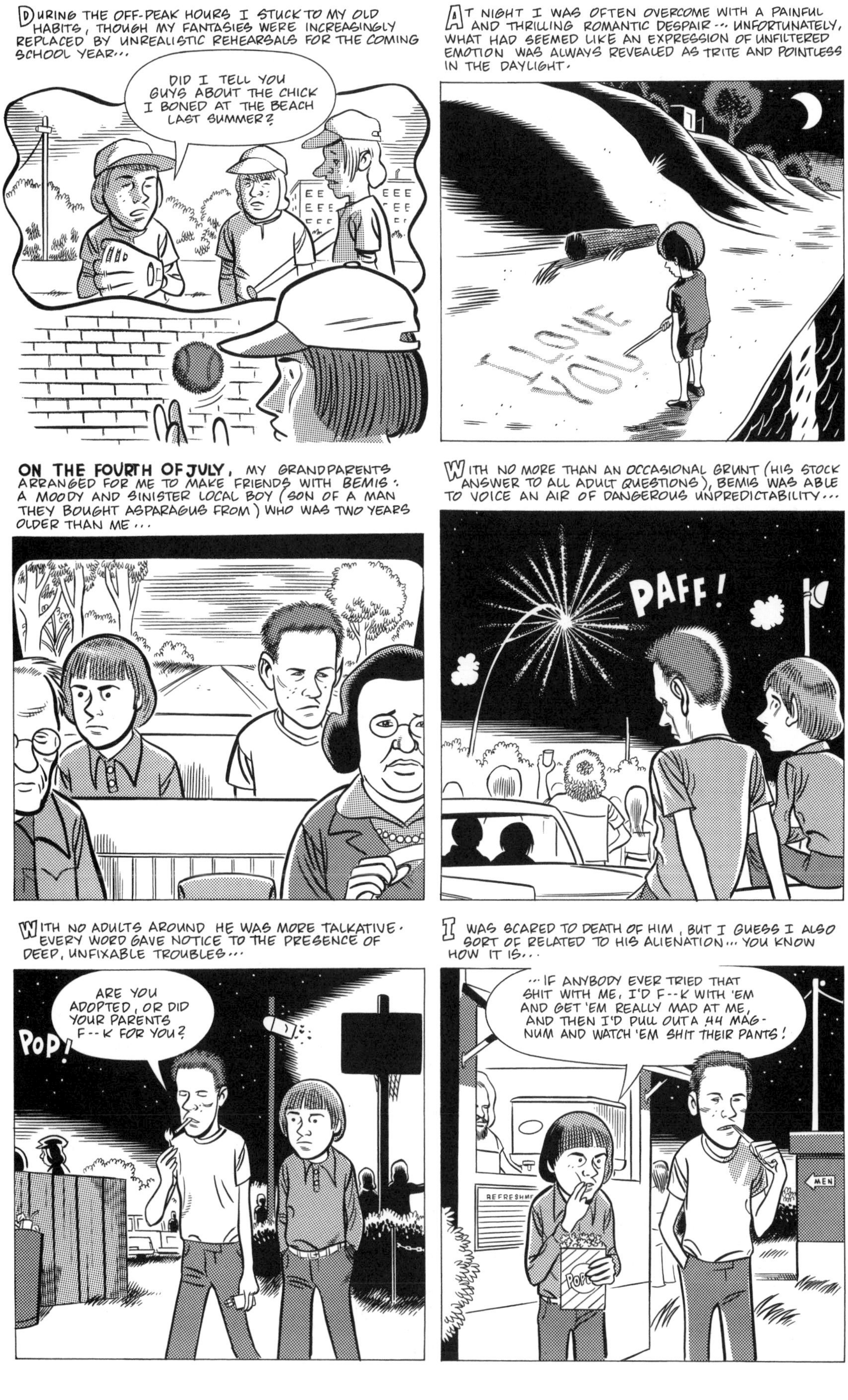
DURING THE OFF-PEAK HOURS I STUCK TO MY OLD HABITS, THOUGH MY FANTASIES WERE INCREASINGLY REPLACED BY UNREALISTIC REHEARSALS FOR THE COMING SCHOOL YEAR...
DID I TELL YOU GUYS ABOUT THE CHICK I BONED AT THE BEACH LAST SUMMER?
AT NIGHT I WAS OFTEN OVERCOME WITH A PAINFUL AND THRILLING ROMANTIC DESPAIR -- UNFORTUNATELY, WHAT HAD SEEMED LIKE AN EXPRESSION OF UNFILTERED EMOTION WAS ALWAYS REVEALED AS TRITE AND POINTLESS IN THE DAYLIGHT.
I LOVE YOU
ON THE FOURTH OF JULY, MY GRANDPARENTS ARRANGED FOR ME TO MAKE FRIENDS WITH BEMIS: A MOODY AND SINISTER LOCAL BOY (SON OF A MAN THEY BOUGHT ASPARAGUS FROM) WHO WAS TWO YEARS OLDER THAN ME...
WITH NO MORE THAN AN OCCASIONAL GRUNT (HIS STOCK ANSWER TO ALL ADULT QUESTIONS), BEMIS WAS ABLE TO VOICE AN AIR OF DANGEROUS UNPREDICTABILITY...
PAFF!
WITH NO ADULTS AROUND HE WAS MORE TALKATIVE. EVERY WORD GAVE NOTICE TO THE PRESENCE OF DEEP, UNFIXABLE TROUBLES...
POP!
ARE YOU ADOPTED, OR DID YOUR PARENTS F--K FOR YOU?
I WAS SCARED TO DEATH OF HIM, BUT I GUESS I ALSO SORT OF RELATED TO HIS ALIENATION... YOU KNOW HOW IT IS...
...IF ANYBODY EVER TRIED THAT SHIT WITH ME, I'D F--K WITH 'EM AND GET 'EM REALLY MAD AT ME, AND THEN I'D PULL OUT A 44 MAG-NUM AND WATCH 'EM SHIT THEIR PANTS!
REFRESHME
MEN
POP

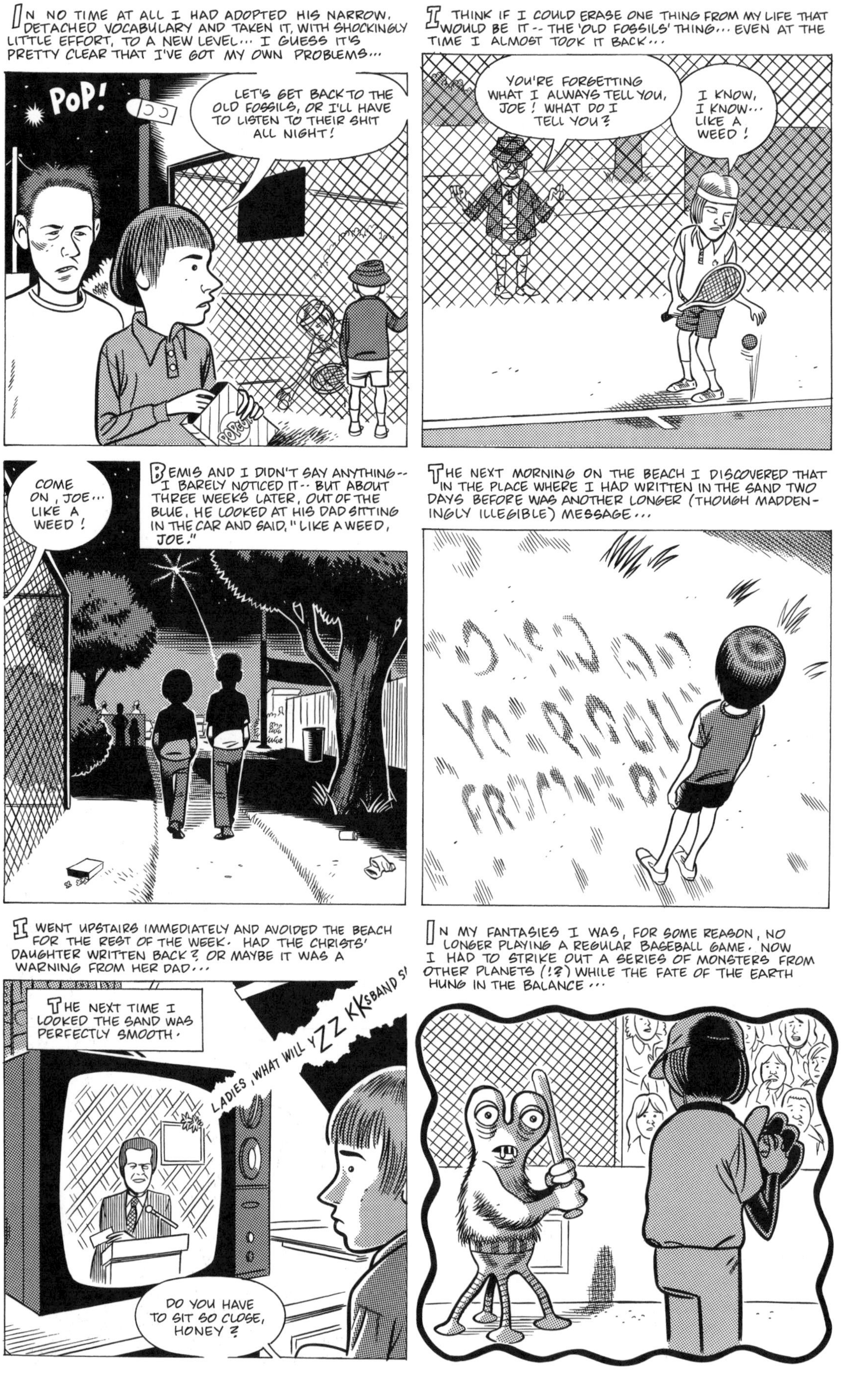
IN NO TIME AT ALL I HAD ADOPTED HIS NARROW, DETACHED VOCABULARY AND TAKEN IT, WITH SHOCKINGLY LITTLE EFFORT, TO A NEW LEVEL... I GUESS IT'S PRETTY CLEAR THAT I'VE GOT MY OWN PROBLEMS...
POP!
LET'S GET BACK TO THE OLD FOSSILS, OR I'LL HAVE TO LISTEN TO THEIR SHIT ALL NIGHT!
I THINK IF I COULD ERASE ONE THING FROM MY LIFE THAT WOULD BE IT -- THE 'OLD FOSSILS' THING... EVEN AT THE TIME I ALMOST TOOK IT BACK...
YOU'RE FORGETTING WHAT I ALWAYS TELL YOU, JOE! WHAT DO I TELL YOU?
I KNOW, I KNOW... LIKE A WEED!
COME ON, JOE... LIKE A WEED!
BEMIS AND I DIDN'T SAY ANYTHING-- I BARELY NOTICED IT-- BUT ABOUT THREE WEEKS LATER, OUT OF THE BLUE, HE LOOKED AT HIS DAD SITTING IN THE CAR AND SAID, "LIKE A WEED, JOE."
THE NEXT MORNING ON THE BEACH I DISCOVERED THAT IN THE PLACE WHERE I HAD WRITTEN IN THE SAND TWO DAYS BEFORE WAS ANOTHER LONGER (THOUGH MADDENINGLY ILLEGIBLE) MESSAGE...
I WENT UPSTAIRS IMMEDIATELY AND AVOIDED THE BEACH FOR THE REST OF THE WEEK. HAD THE CHRISTS' DAUGHTER WRITTEN BACK? OR MAYBE IT WAS A WARNING FROM HER DAD...
THE NEXT TIME I LOOKED THE SAND WAS PERFECTLY SMOOTH.
LADIES, WHAT WILL YZZ KKSBAND S!
DO YOU HAVE TO SIT SO CLOSE, HONEY?
IN MY FANTASIES I WAS, FOR SOME REASON, NO LONGER PLAYING A REGULAR BASEBALL GAME. NOW I HAD TO STRIKE OUT A SERIES OF MONSTERS FROM OTHER PLANETS (!?) WHILE THE FATE OF THE EARTH HUNG IN THE BALANCE...

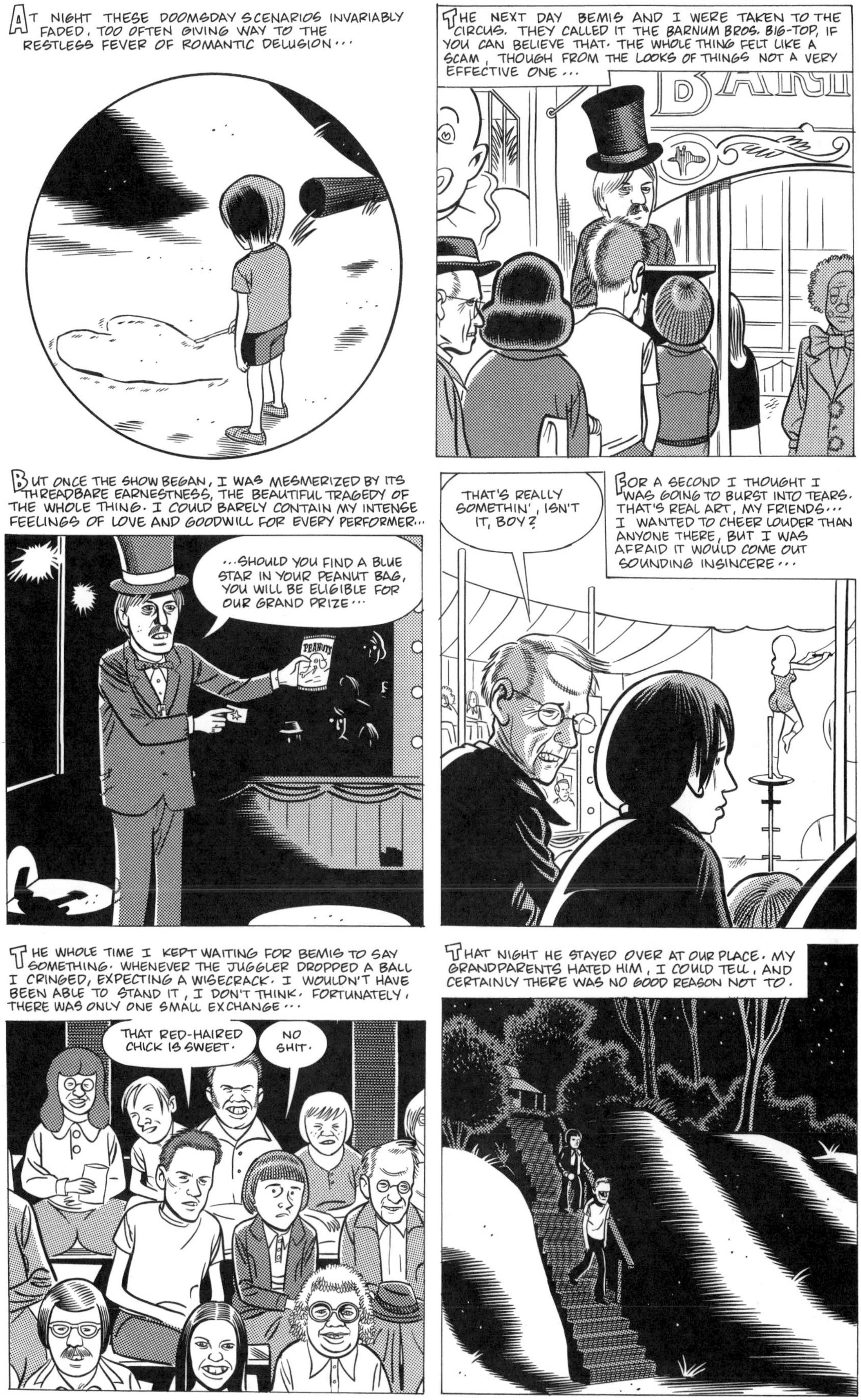
AT NIGHT THESE DOOMSDAY SCENARIOS INVARIABLY FADED, TOO OFTEN GIVING WAY TO THE RESTLESS FEVER OF ROMANTIC DELUSION...
THE NEXT DAY BEMIS AND I WERE TAKEN TO THE CIRCUS. THEY CALLED IT THE BARNUM BROS. BIG-TOP, IF YOU CAN BELIEVE THAT. THE WHOLE THING FELT LIKE A SCAM, THOUGH FROM THE LOOKS OF THINGS NOT A VERY EFFECTIVE ONE...
BUT ONCE THE SHOW BEGAN, I WAS MESMERIZED BY ITS THREADBARE EARNESTNESS, THE BEAUTIFUL TRAGEDY OF THE WHOLE THING. I COULD BARELY CONTAIN MY INTENSE FEELINGS OF LOVE AND GOODWILL FOR EVERY PERFORMER...
...SHOULD YOU FIND A BLUE STAR IN YOUR PEANUT BAG, YOU WILL BE ELIGIBLE FOR OUR GRAND PRIZE...
PEANUTS
THAT'S REALLY SOMETHIN', ISN'T IT, BOY?
FOR A SECOND I THOUGHT I WAS GOING TO BURST INTO TEARS. THAT'S REAL ART, MY FRIENDS... I WANTED TO CHEER LOUDER THAN ANYONE THERE, BUT I WAS AFRAID IT WOULD COME OUT SOUNDING INSINCERE...
THE WHOLE TIME I KEPT WAITING FOR BEMIS TO SAY SOMETHING. WHENEVER THE JUGGLER DROPPED A BALL I CRINGED, EXPECTING A WISECRACK. I WOULDN'T HAVE BEEN ABLE TO STAND IT, I DON'T THINK. FORTUNATELY, THERE WAS ONLY ONE SMALL EXCHANGE...
THAT RED-HAIRED CHICK IS SWEET.
NO SHIT.
THAT NIGHT HE STAYED OVER AT OUR PLACE. MY GRANDPARENTS HATED HIM, I COULD TELL, AND CERTAINLY THERE WAS NO GOOD REASON NOT TO.

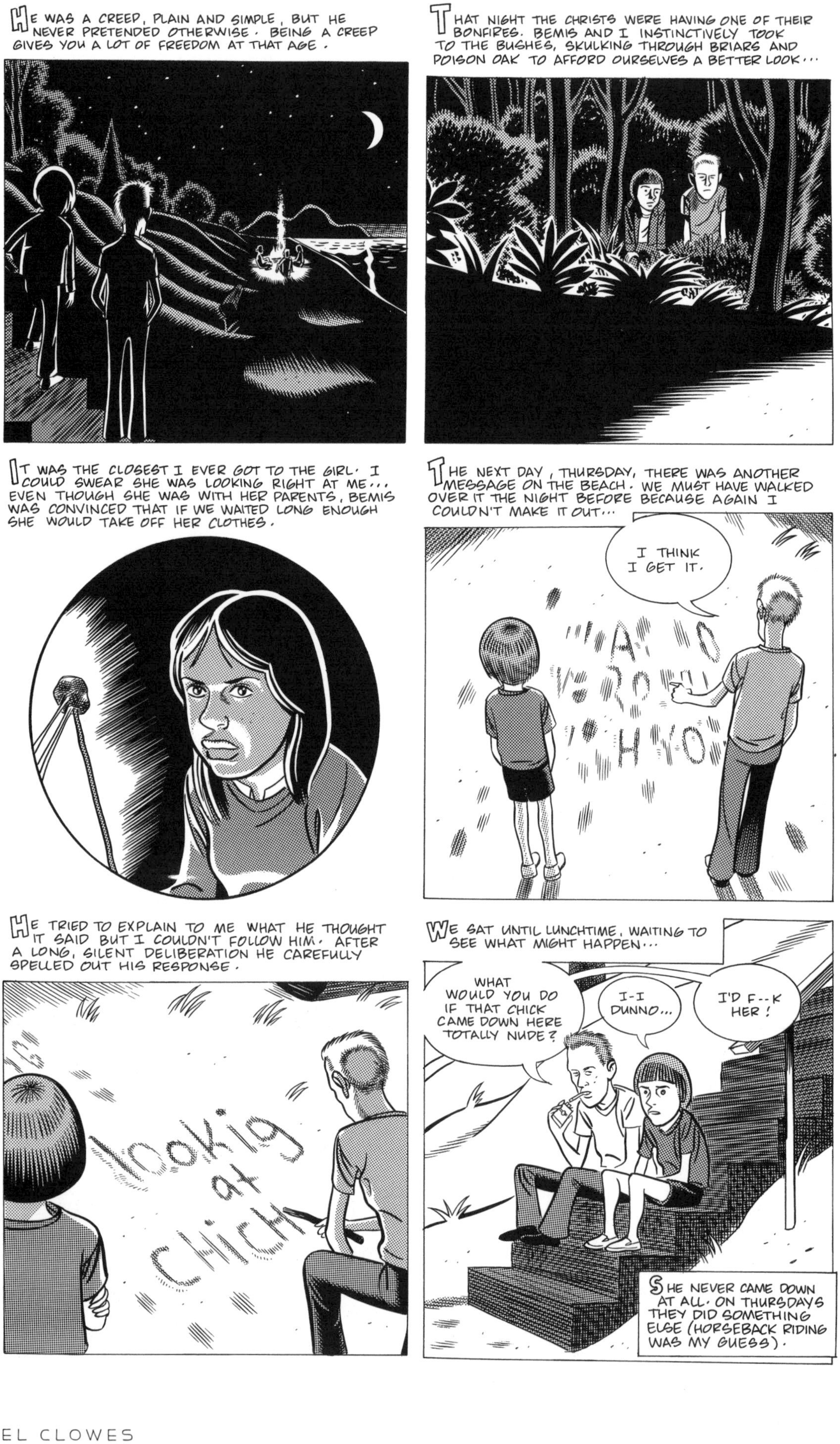
HE WAS A CREEP, PLAIN AND SIMPLE, BUT HE NEVER PRETENDED OTHERWISE. BEING A CREEP GIVES YOU A LOT OF FREEDOM AT THAT AGE.
THAT NIGHT THE CHRISTS WERE HAVING ONE OF THEIR BONFIRES. BEMIS AND I INSTINCTIVELY TOOK TO THE BUSHES, SKULKING THROUGH BRIARS AND POISON OAK TO AFFORD OURSELVES A BETTER LOOK...
IT WAS THE CLOSEST I EVER GOT TO THE GIRL. I COULD SWEAR SHE WAS LOOKING RIGHT AT ME... EVEN THOUGH SHE WAS WITH HER PARENTS, BEMIS WAS CONVINCED THAT IF WE WAITED LONG ENOUGH SHE WOULD TAKE OFF HER CLOTHES.
THE NEXT DAY, THURSDAY, THERE WAS ANOTHER MESSAGE ON THE BEACH. WE MUST HAVE WALKED OVER IT THE NIGHT BEFORE BECAUSE AGAIN I COULDN'T MAKE IT OUT...
I THINK I GET IT.
HE TRIED TO EXPLAIN TO ME WHAT HE THOUGHT IT SAID BUT I COULDN'T FOLLOW HIM. AFTER A LONG, SILENT DELIBERATION HE CAREFULLY SPELLED OUT HIS RESPONSE.
lookig at Chick
WE SAT UNTIL LUNCHTIME, WAITING TO SEE WHAT MIGHT HAPPEN...
WHAT WOULD YOU DO IF THAT CHICK CAME DOWN HERE TOTALLY NUDE?
I-I DUNNO...
I'D F--K HER!
SHE NEVER CAME DOWN AT ALL. ON THURSDAYS THEY DID SOMETHING ELSE (HORSEBACK RIDING WAS MY GUESS).

BEMIS GOT ALL WORKED UP TALKING ABOUT HOW HE LIKED TO GO HUNTING WITH HIS "TWELVE GAUGE" AND BLOW AWAY SQUIRRELS AND STUFF. HE BEGAN THROWING ROCKS AT SEAGULLS. HE THREW LIKE A GIRL AND I FELT THANKFUL THAT AT LEAST MY OLD MAN HAD TAUGHT ME THAT MUCH ...

I FIGURED HERE'S MY CHANCE TO SHOW HIM UP. I HONESTLY DIDN'T EVEN THINK ABOUT WHAT I WAS DOING UNTIL MY THIRD SHOT CONNECTED.

FLAP
FLAP
FLAP

I JUST STOOD THERE FOR A TERRIBLE MOMENT BEFORE BEMIS FINISHED HIM OFF. I GUESS IT WAS AN ACT OF COMPASSION ON HIS PART, AS UNLIKELY AS THAT SEEMS.

WE BETTER BOOK.

LATER, HE WANTED TO GO BY THE CHRIST-GIRL'S BEACH HOUSE AND SNOOP AROUND. THIS MADE ME NERVOUS SO I STAYED ON THE BEACH. AFTER A WHILE HE CAME DOWN AND WE WALKED BACK TO MY GRANDPARENTS' HOUSE WITHOUT A WORD.

JUST AS HE WAS ABOUT TO GET INTO HIS FATHER'S CAR, BEMIS REACHED INTO HIS POCKET AND, LIKE A MAGICIAN, PULLED OUT A PAIR OF STOLEN BIKINI PANTIES (OR WHATEVER THEY'RE CALLED).

TONIGHT I'M GOING TO BEAT OFF INTO THIS.

AFTER DARK I SET OUT TO ERASE BEMIS' ENIGMATIC INSCRIPTION AND TO SOMEHOW ALTER THE CRIME SCENE SO AS TO DIVERT SUSPICION AWAY FROM MYSELF, BUT MY GRANDFATHER STOOD IN THE WAY.

AT THE TIME I REALLY COULDN'T SEE WHAT WAS THE BIG DEAL ABOUT THE MOON AND THE STARS, BUT THE OLD GUY GOT SO CHOKED UP OVER IT ALL THAT I DECIDED I DIDN'T DARE RISK DISAPPOINTING HIM BY CARRYING OUT MY LITTLE PLAN...

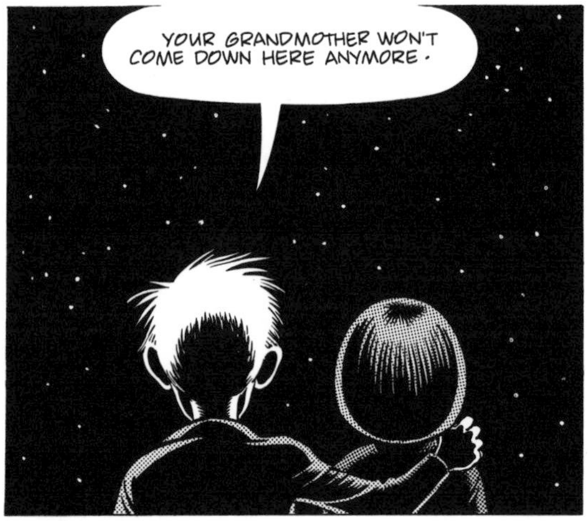
YOUR GRANDMOTHER WON'T COME DOWN HERE ANYMORE.

THE NEXT MORNING THERE WAS ANOTHER MESSAGE ON THE BEACH. IT COULDN'T HAVE BEEN THERE VERY LONG BUT IT HAD BEEN TRAMPLED AND WINDBLOWN LIKE THE OTHERS AND WAS JUST AS IMPOSSIBLE TO READ...

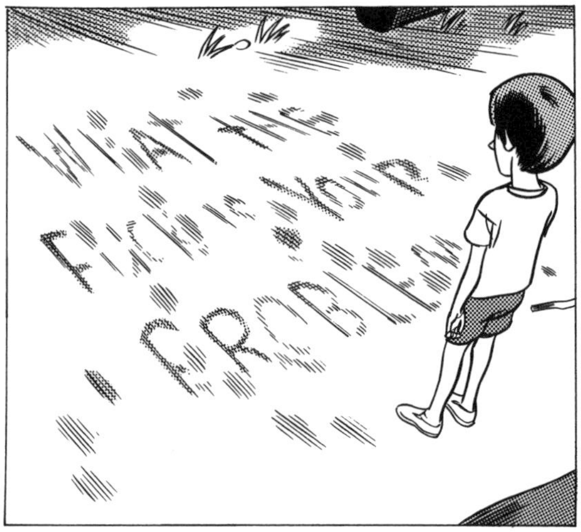
WHAT THE

LATER THAT AFTERNOON SHE LEFT FOR GOOD. UNLIKE MOST RENTERS, THE CHRISTS WERE IMMACULATE AND LEFT NO SIGN WHATSOEVER THAT THEY HAD BEEN THERE.

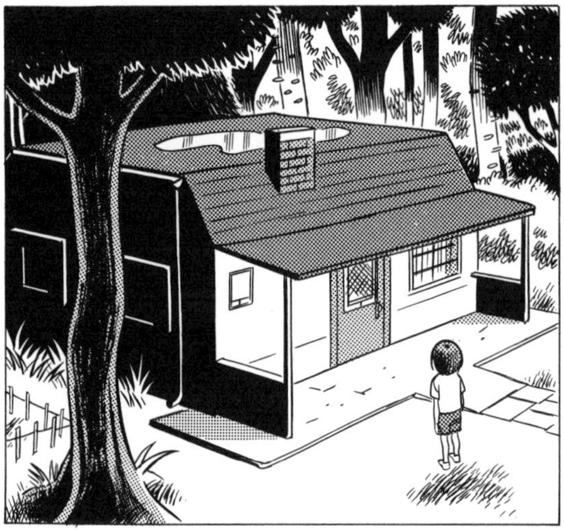

I WAS ABLE TO DULL THE PAIN OF NEVER EVEN KNOWING HER FIRST NAME BY FALLING BACK INTO MY OLD HABITS. YEARS LATER I NAMED HER KATHY AND WAS ABLE TO CONVINCE MYSELF AND OTHERS THAT SHE WAS THE FIRST GIRL I EVER KISSED.

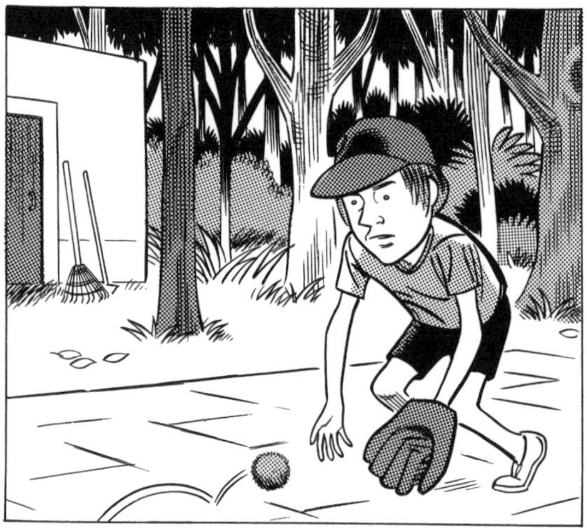

I SAW A LOT OF BEMIS UNTIL HE GOT A JOB AT THE CANNERY TO PAY FOR SOME FANCY DIRT BIKE THAT HE WOULDN'T SHUT UP ABOUT, BUT THAT'S ANOTHER STORY.

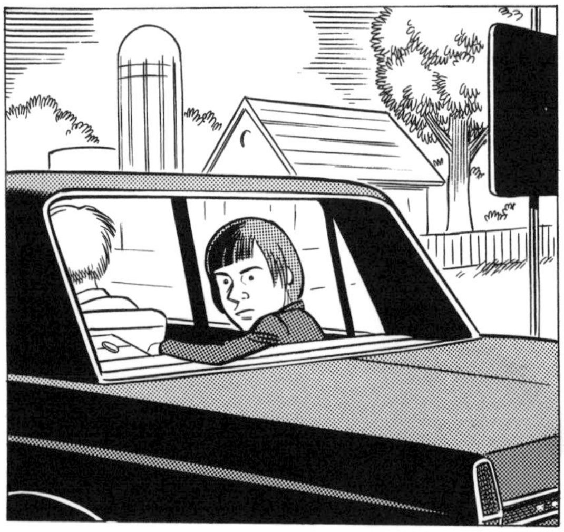

AT THE END OF THE SUMMER IT WAS DECIDED THAT I SHOULD KEEP ON LIVING WITH MY GRANDPARENTS. WE MOVED BACK TO THE CITY (MY GRANDFATHER NEEDED SURGERY) AND I WENT TO A NEW SCHOOL WHERE I STRUGGLED TO BE THOUGHT OF AS SOMEONE WHO HOUSED A VITAL AND COMPLICATED INNER WORLD.

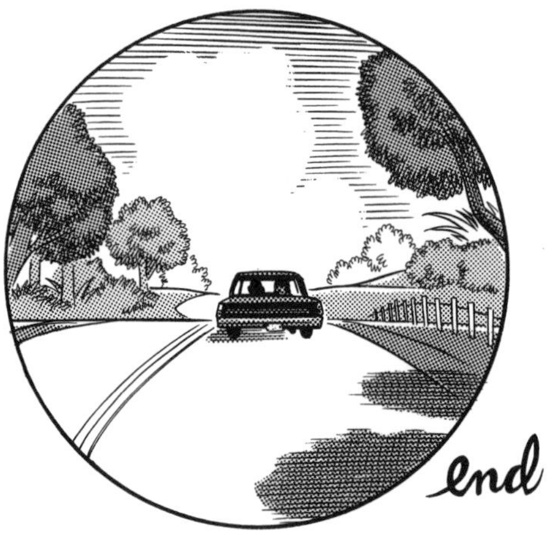
end

COLE JOHNSON

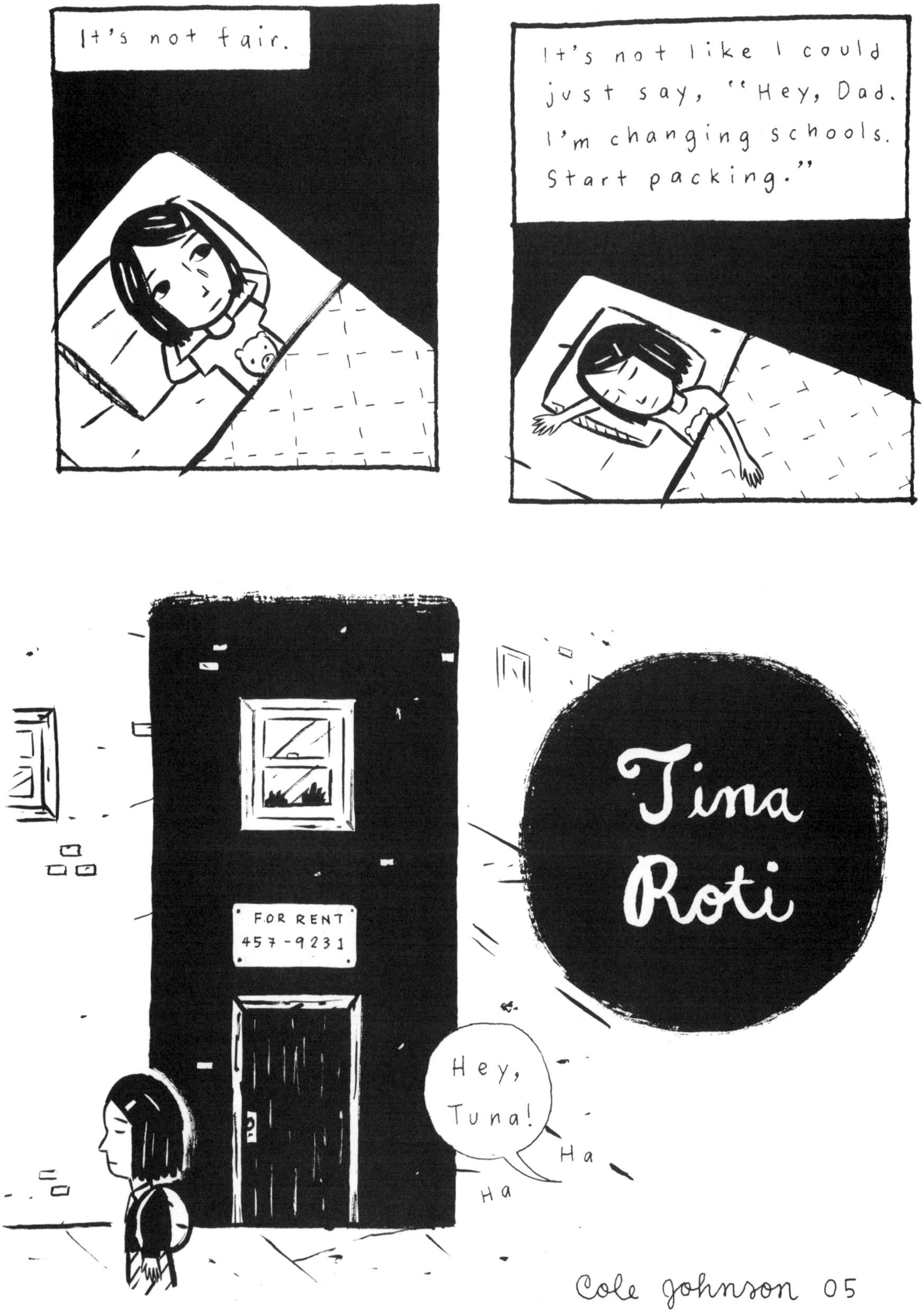
It's not fair.
It's not like I could just say, "Hey, Dad. I'm changing schools. Start packing."
Tina Roti
FOR RENT
457-9231
Hey, Tuna!
Ha
Ha
Cole Johnson 05

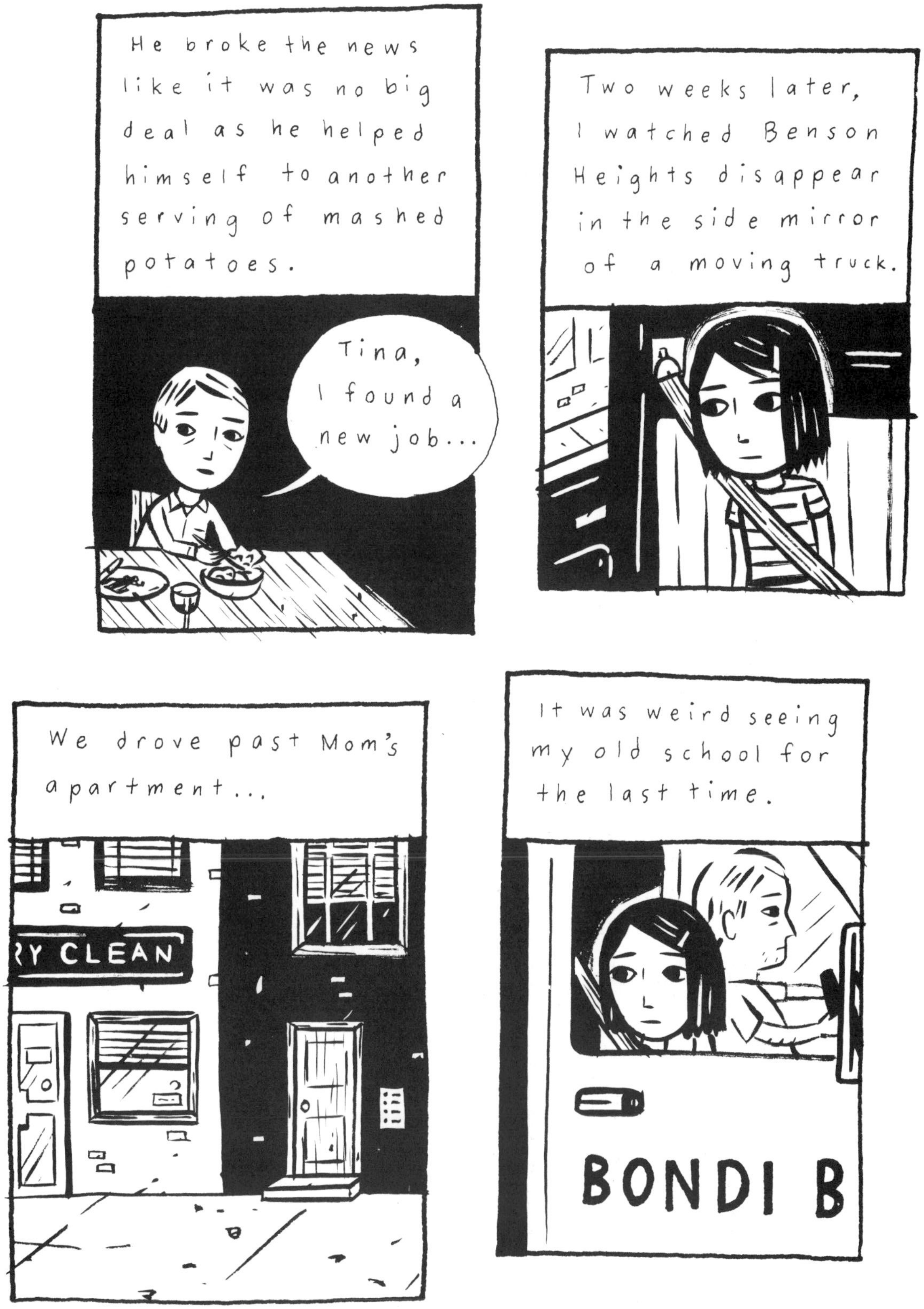
He broke the news like it was no big deal as he helped himself to another serving of mashed potatoes.
Tina, I found a new job...
Two weeks later, I watched Benson Heights disappear in the side mirror of a moving truck.
We drove past Mom's apartment...
RY CLEAN
It was weird seeing my old school for the last time.
BONDI B

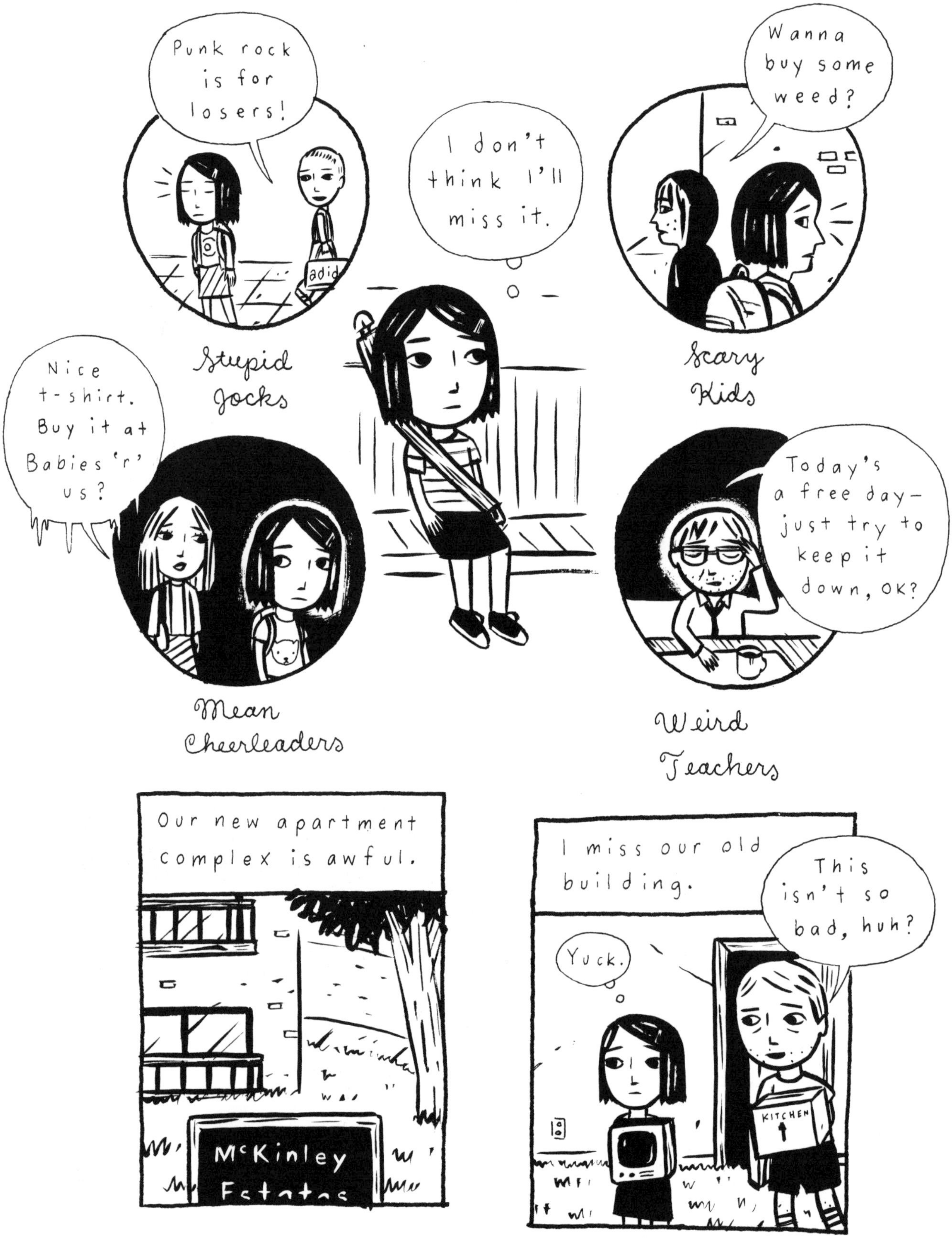
Punk rock is for losers!
adid
Stupid Jocks
I don't think I'll miss it.
Wanna buy some weed?
Scary Kids
Nice t-shirt. Buy it at Babies 'r' us?
Mean Cheerleaders
Today's a free day- just try to keep it down, OK?
Weird Teachers
Our new apartment complex is awful.
McKinley
I miss our old building.
This isn't so bad, huh?
Yuck.
KITCHEN

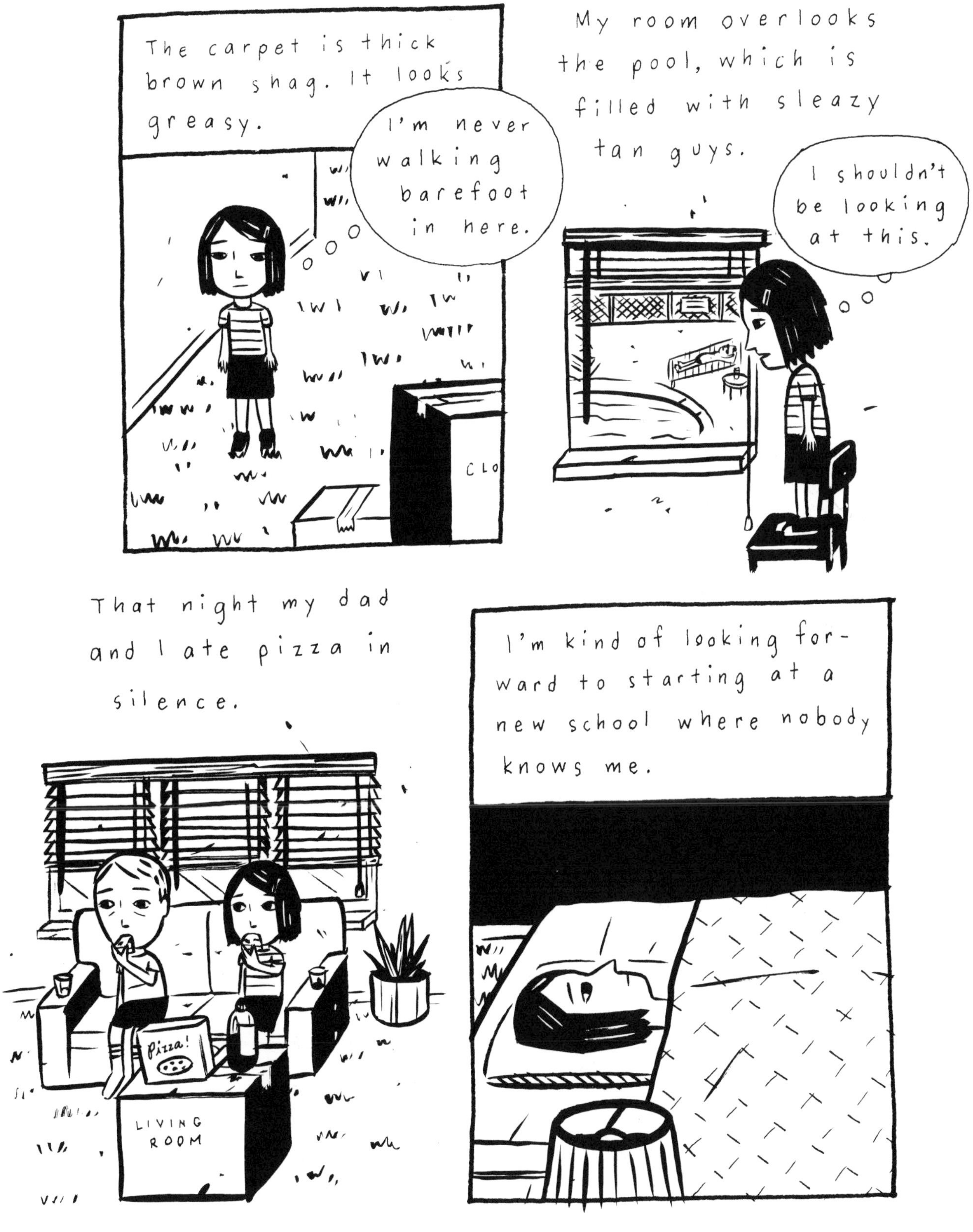
The carpet is thick brown shag. It looks greasy.
I'm never walking barefoot in here.
CLO
My room overlooks the pool, which is filled with sleazy tan guys.
I shouldn't be looking at this.
That night my dad and I ate pizza in silence.
Pizza!
LIVING ROOM
I'm kind of looking for-ward to starting at a new school where nobody knows me.

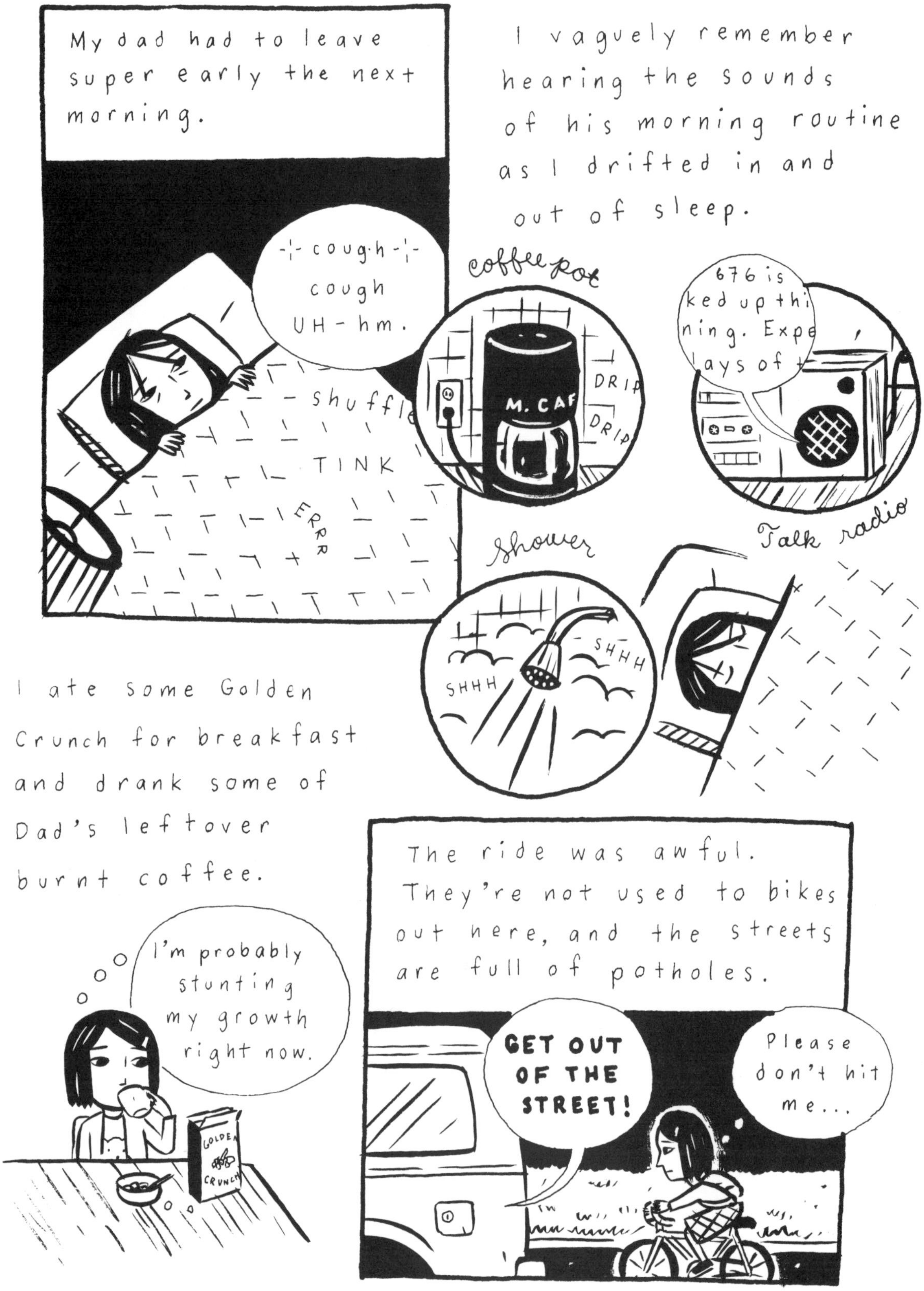
My dad had to leave super early the next morning.
-¦- cough -¦- cough UH-hm.
shuffle
TINK
ERRR
I vaguely remember hearing the sounds of his morning routine as I drifted in and out of sleep.
coffee pot
M. CAF
DRIP
DRIP
676 is
ked up thi
ning. Expe
lays of
Talk radio
Shower
SHHH
SHHH
I ate some Golden Crunch for breakfast and drank some of Dad's leftover burnt coffee.
I'm probably stunting my growth right now.
GOLDEN CRUNCH
The ride was awful. They're not used to bikes out here, and the streets are full of potholes.
GET OUT OF THE STREET!
Please don't hit me...

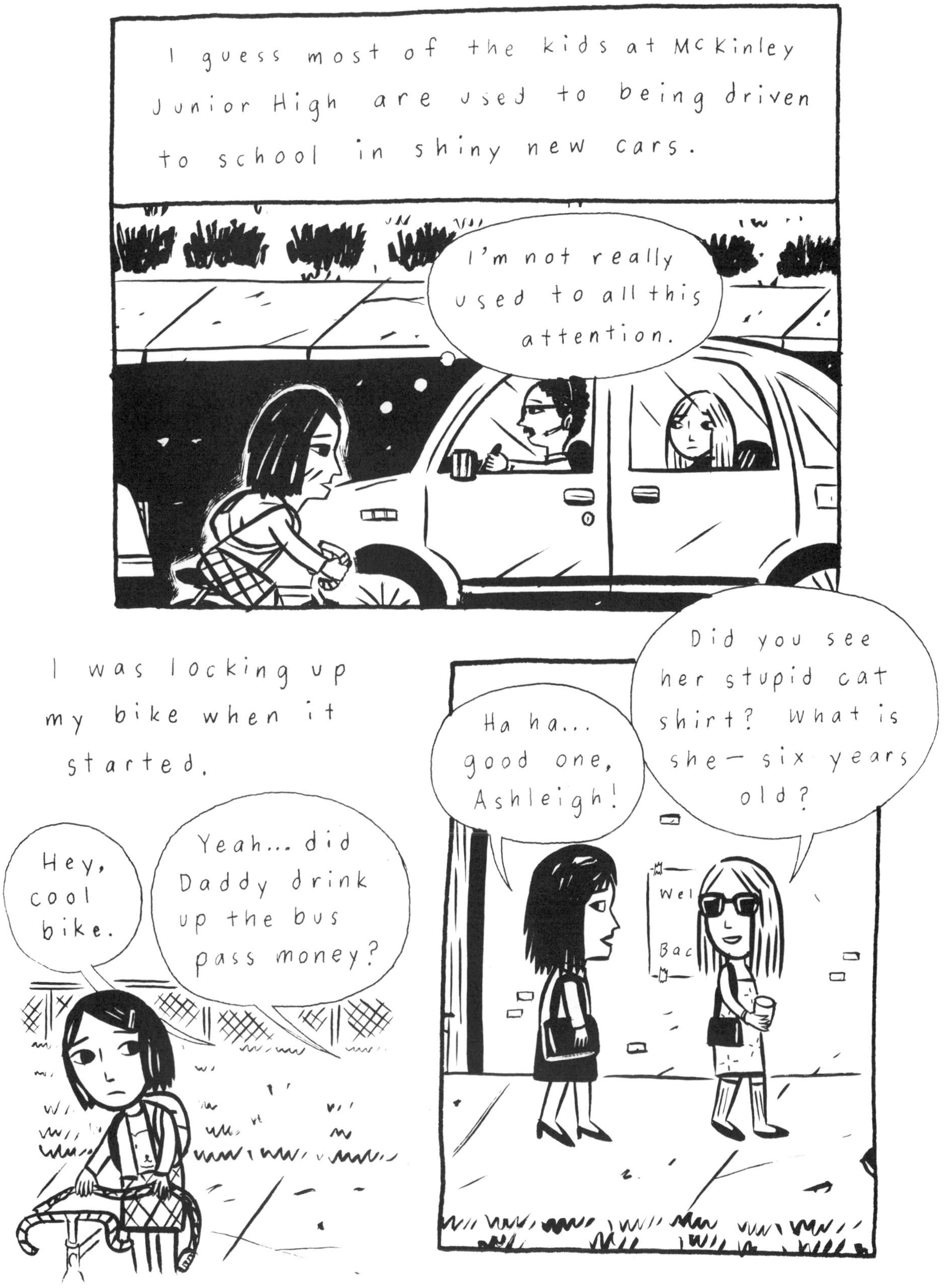
I guess most of the kids at McKinley Junior High are used to being driven to school in shiny new cars.
I'm not really used to all this attention.
I was locking up my bike when it started.
Hey, cool bike.
Yeah... did Daddy drink up the bus pass money?
Did you see her stupid cat shirt? What is she— six years old?
Ha ha... good one, Ashleigh!
Wel
Bac

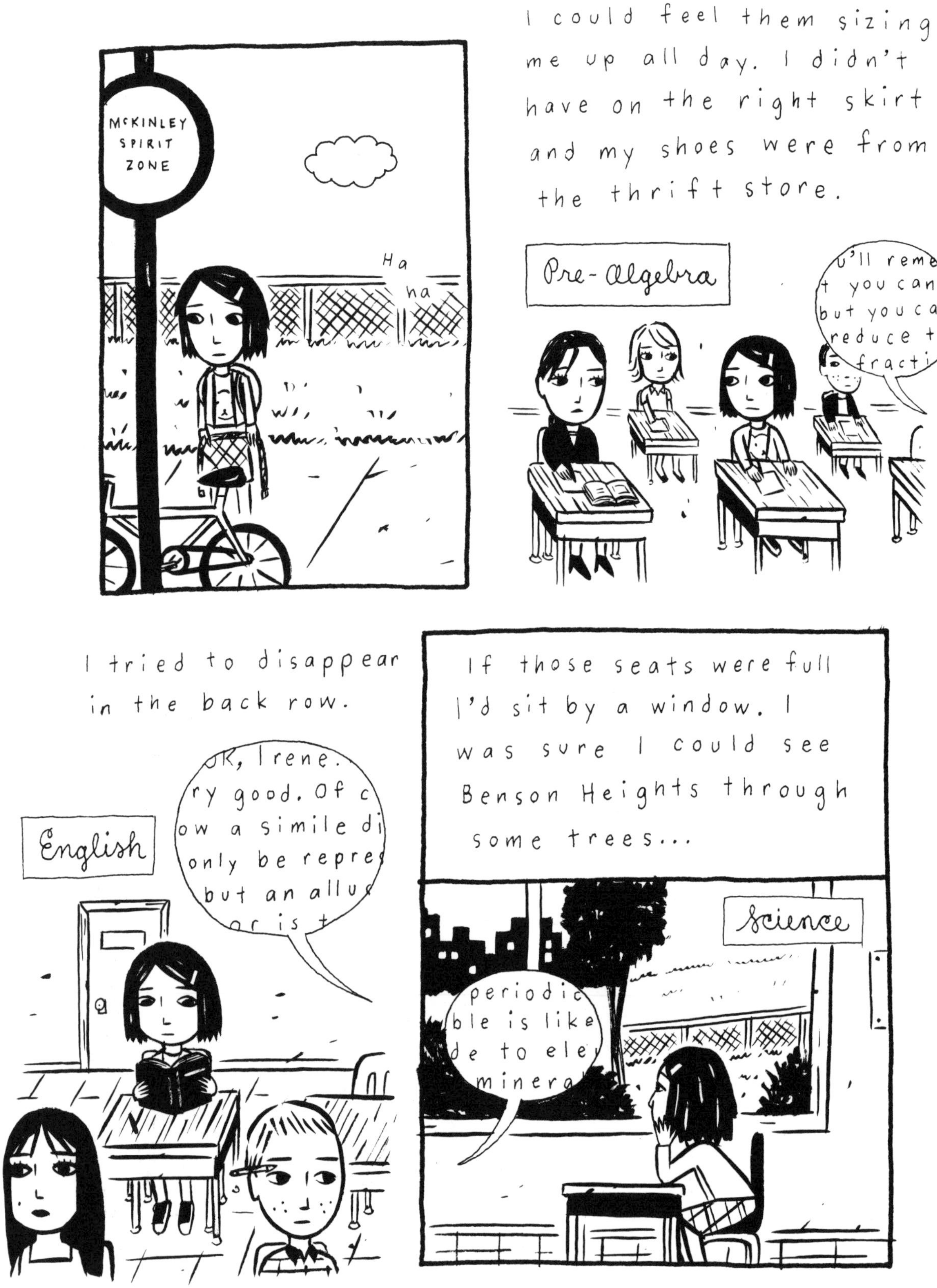
McKINLEY SPIRIT ZONE
Ha ha
I could feel them sizing me up all day. I didn't have on the right skirt and my shoes were from the thrift store.
Pre-Algebra
'll reme t you can' but you can reduce th fracti
I tried to disappear in the back row.
English
OK, Irene. ry good. Of c ow a simile di only be repre but an allu or is t
If those seats were full I'd sit by a window. I was sure I could see Benson Heights through some trees...
Science
periodic ble is like de to ele minera

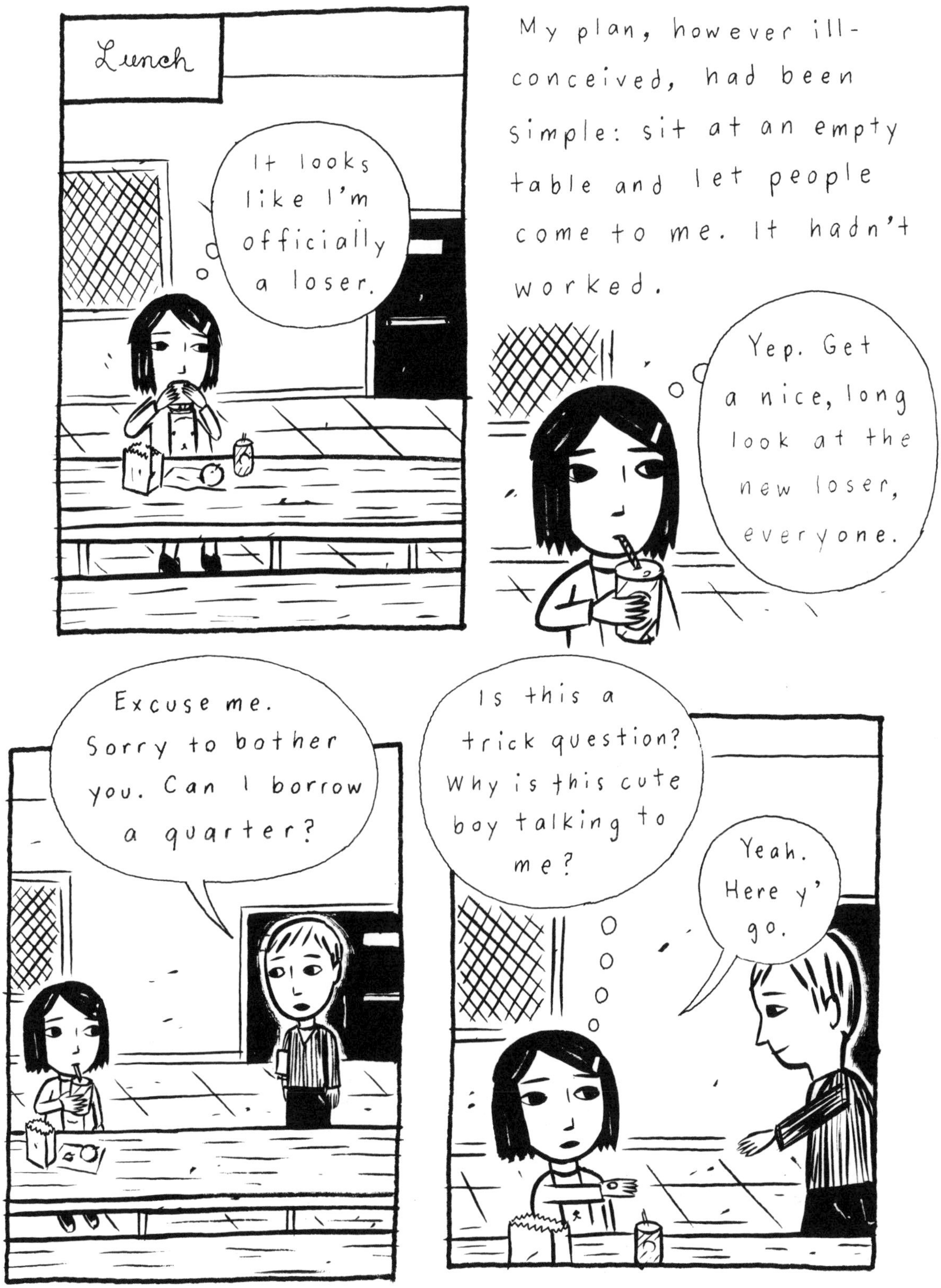
Lunch
It looks like I'm officially a loser.
My plan, however ill-conceived, had been simple: sit at an empty table and let people come to me. It hadn't worked.
Yep. Get a nice, long look at the new loser, everyone.
Excuse me. Sorry to bother you. Can I borrow a quarter?
Is this a trick question? Why is this cute boy talking to me?
Yeah. Here y' go.

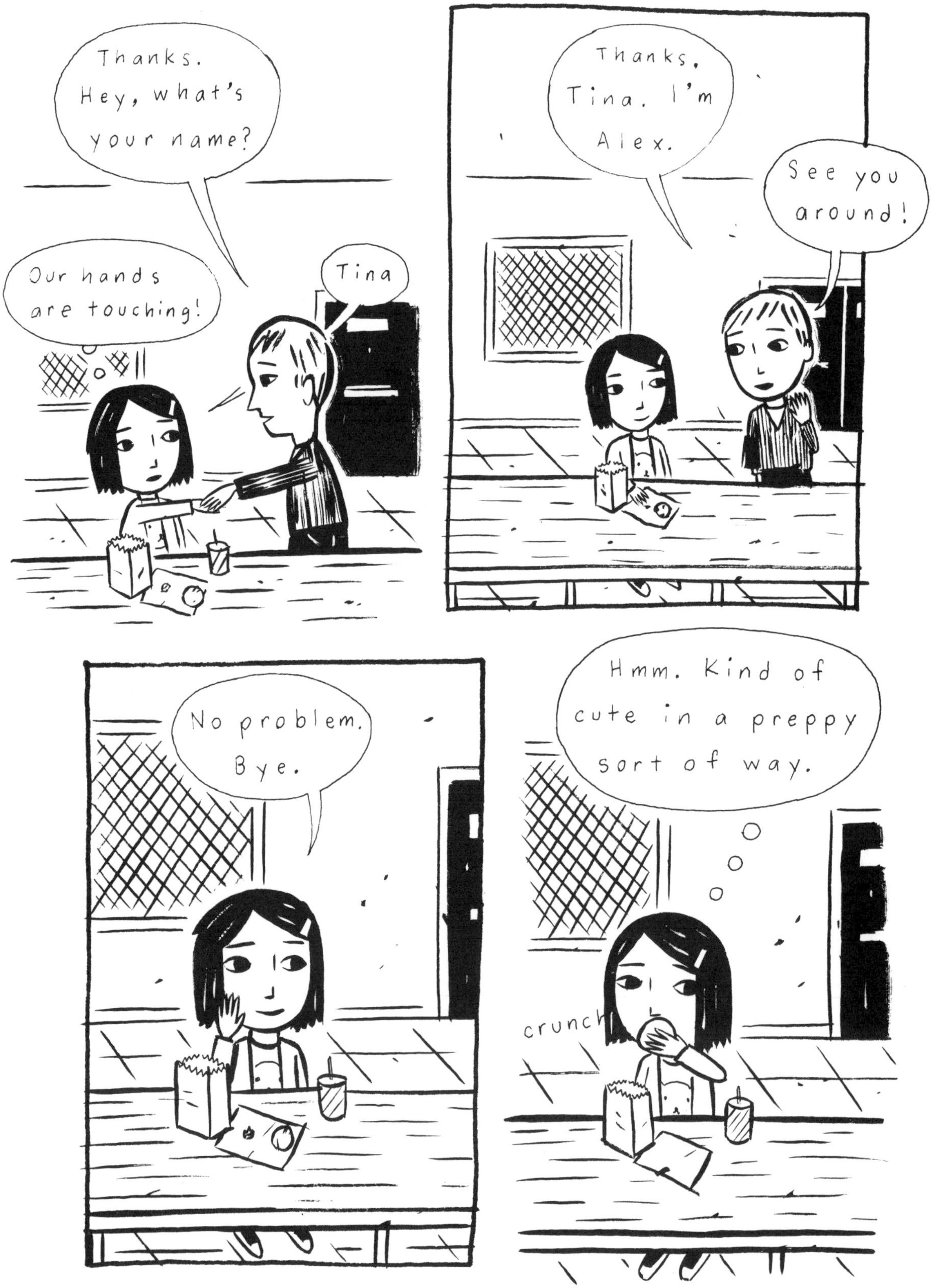
Thanks. Hey, what's your name?
Our hands are touching!
Tina
Thanks, Tina. I'm Alex.
See you around!
No problem. Bye.
Hmm. Kind of cute in a preppy sort of way.
crunch

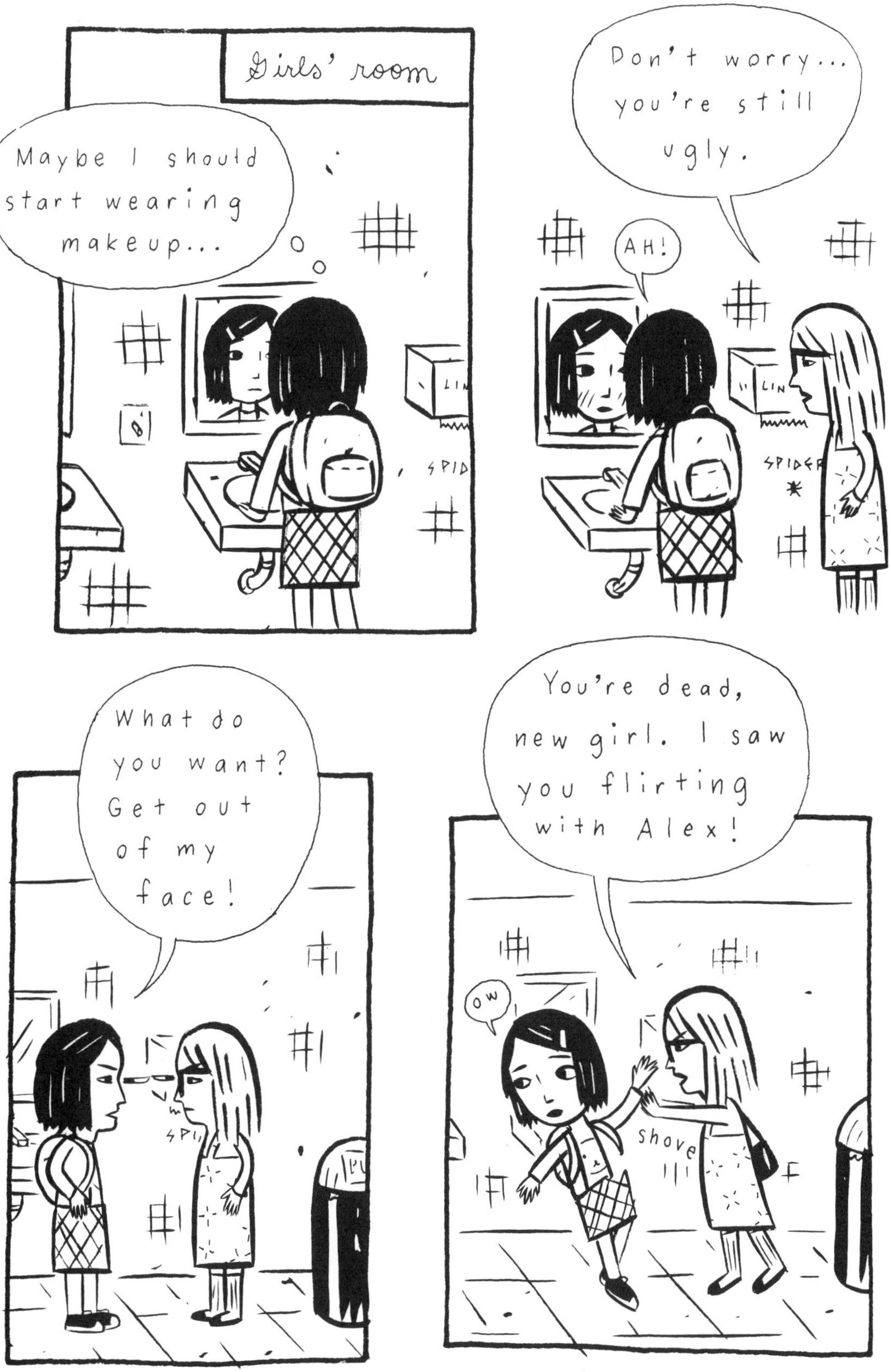
Girls' room
Maybe I should start wearing makeup...
Don't worry... you're still ugly.
AH!
SPIDER
What do you want? Get out of my face!
You're dead, new girl. I saw you flirting with Alex!
OW
Shove

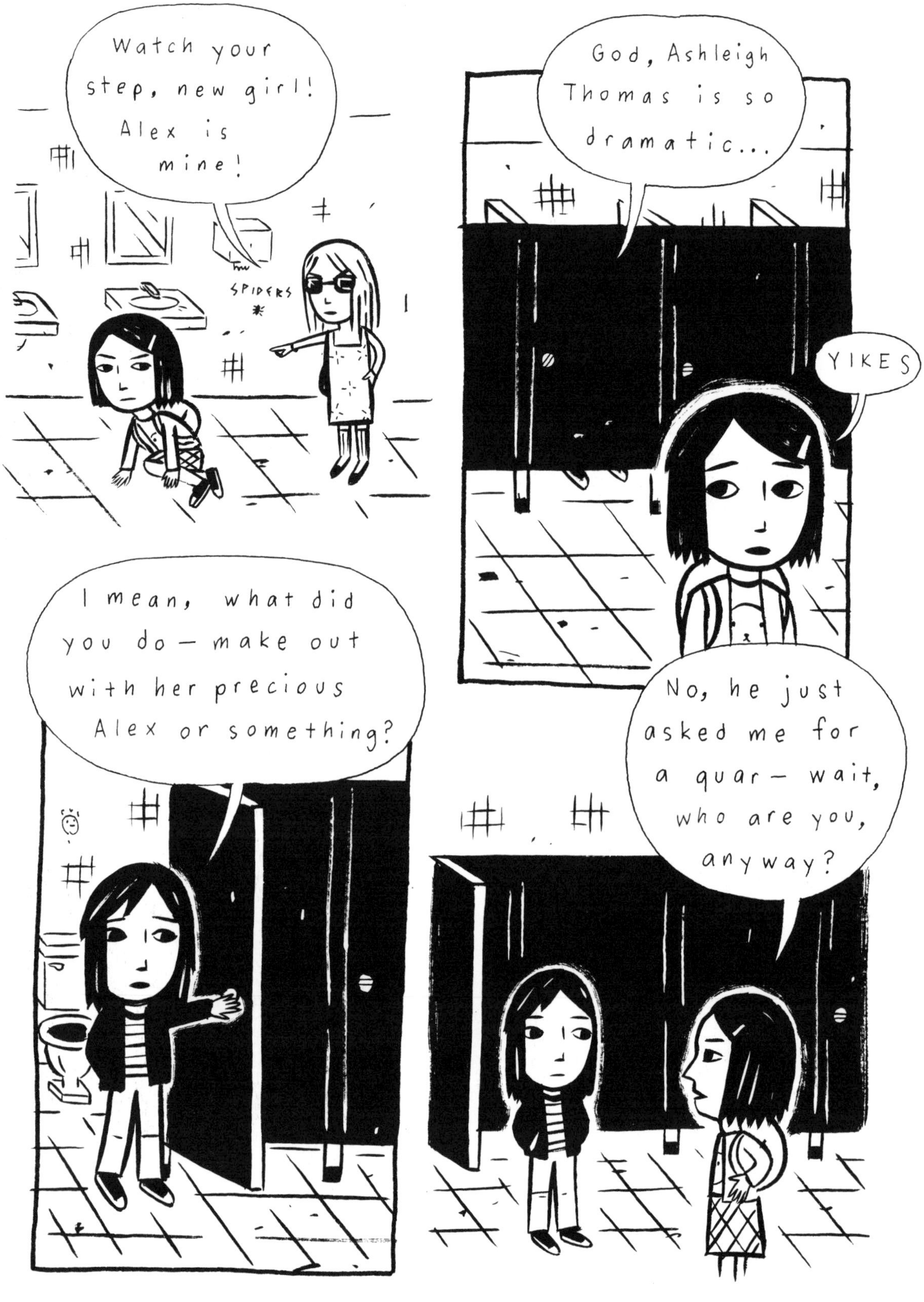
Watch your step, new girl! Alex is mine!
SPIDERS
God, Ashleigh Thomas is so dramatic...
YIKES
I mean, what did you do—make out with her precious Alex or something?
No, he just asked me for a quar—wait, who are you, anyway?

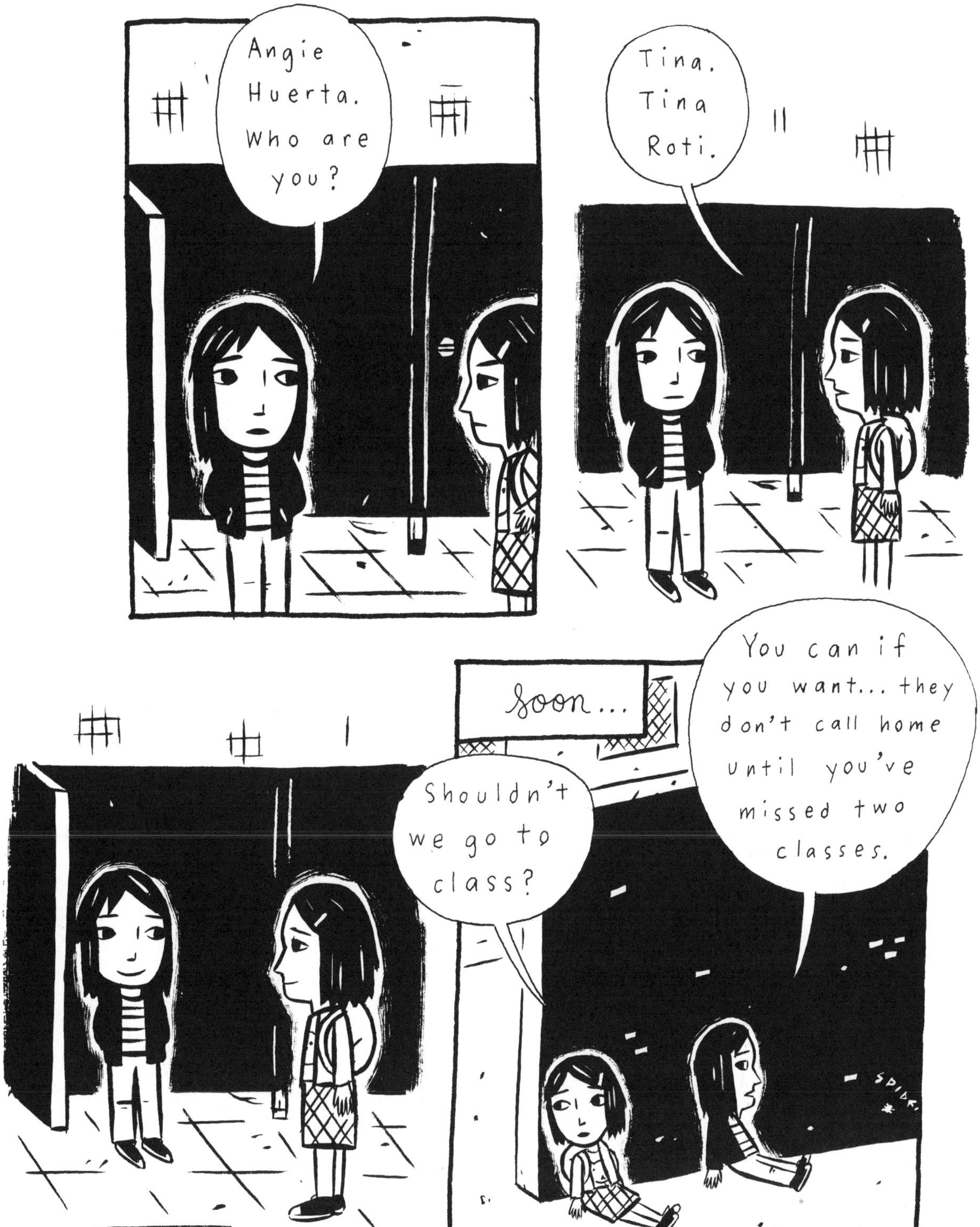
Angie Huerta. Who are you?
Tina. Tina Roti.
Soon...
Shouldn't we go to class?
You can if you want... they don't call home until you've missed two classes.

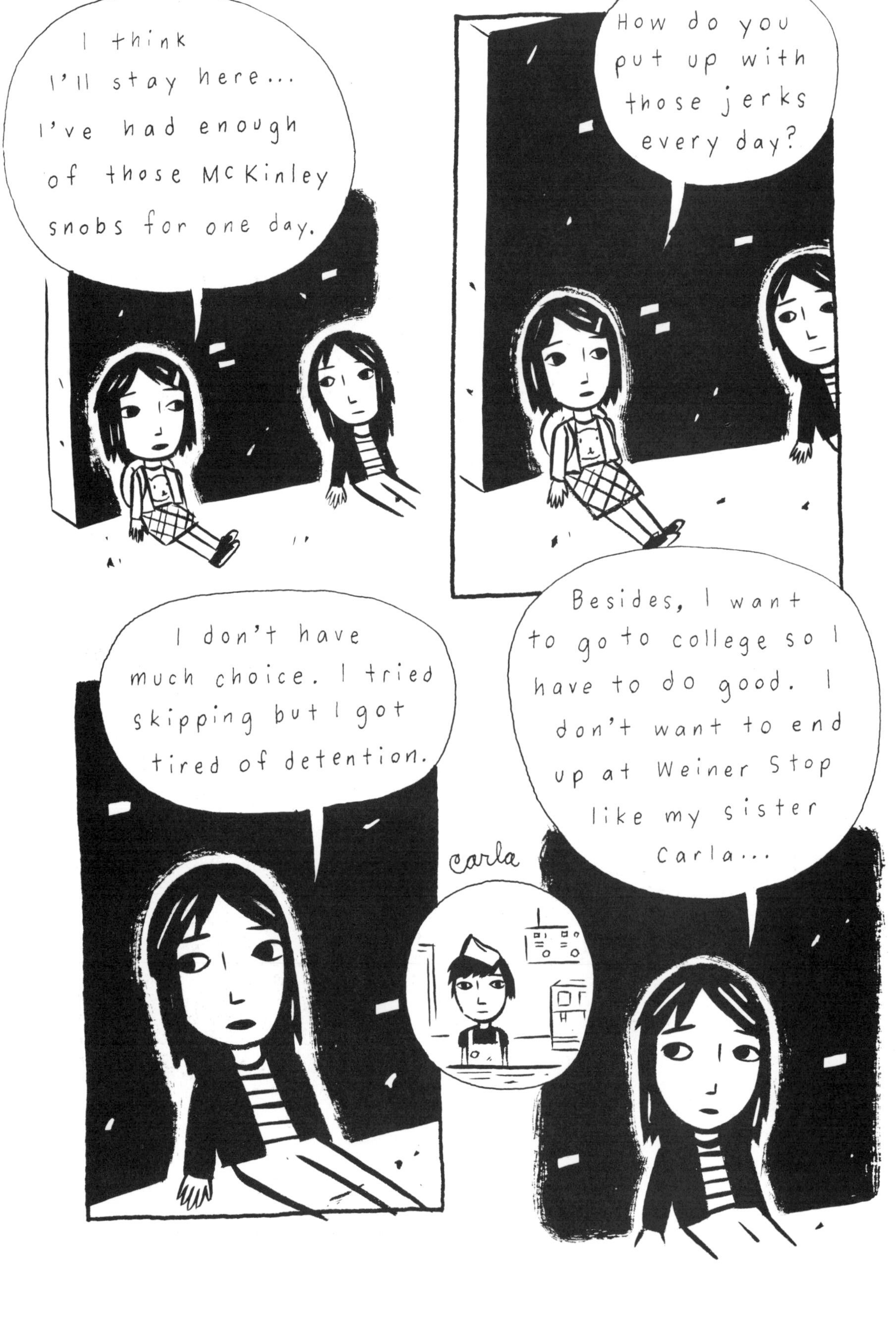
I think I'll stay here... I've had enough of those McKinley snobs for one day.
How do you put up with those jerks every day?
I don't have much choice. I tried skipping but I got tired of detention.
Besides, I want to go to college so I have to do good. I don't want to end up at Weiner Stop like my sister Carla...
carla

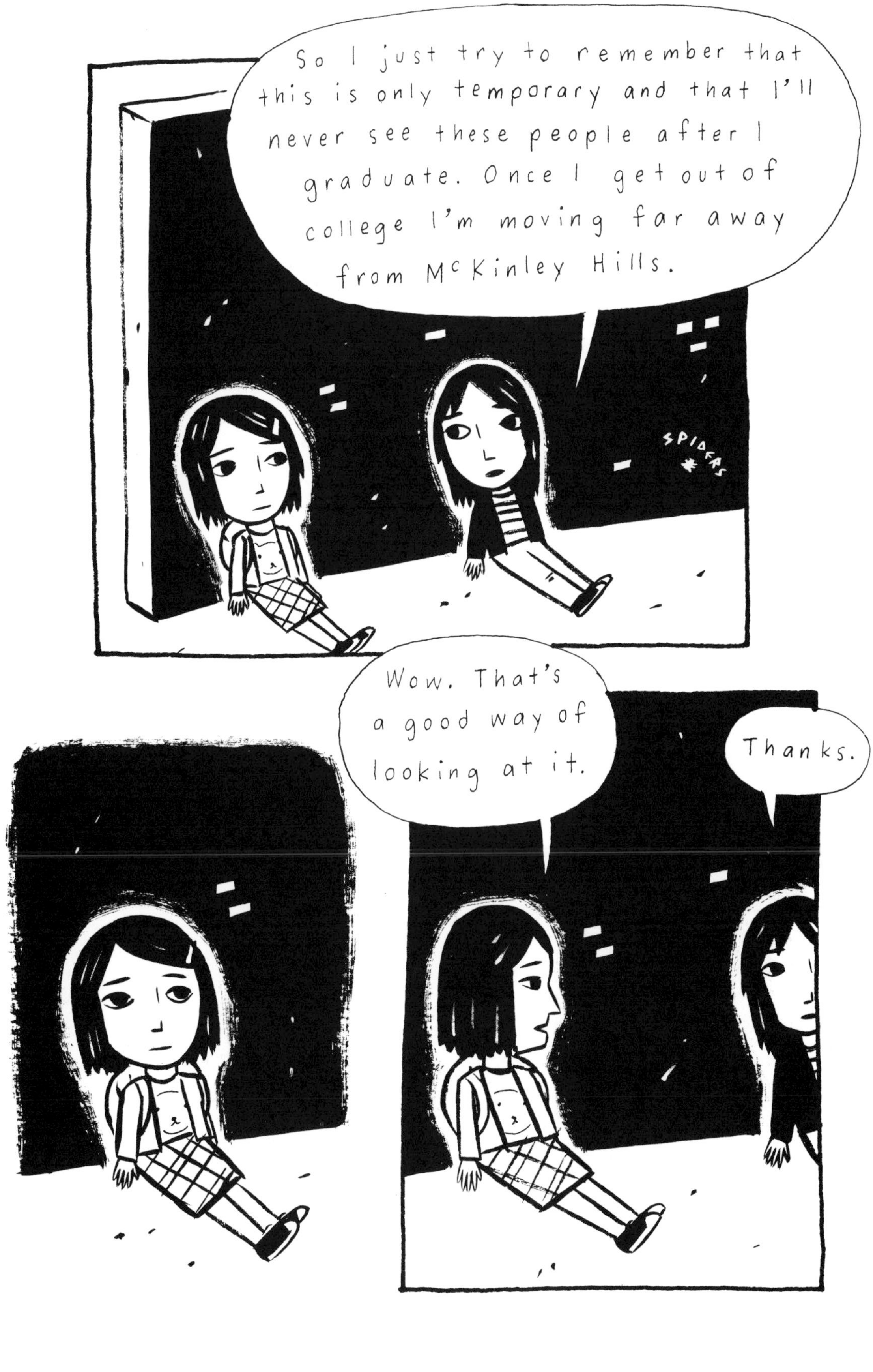
So I just try to remember that this is only temporary and that I'll never see these people after I graduate. Once I get out of college I'm moving far away from McKinley Hills.
SPIDERS
Wow. That's a good way of looking at it.
Thanks.

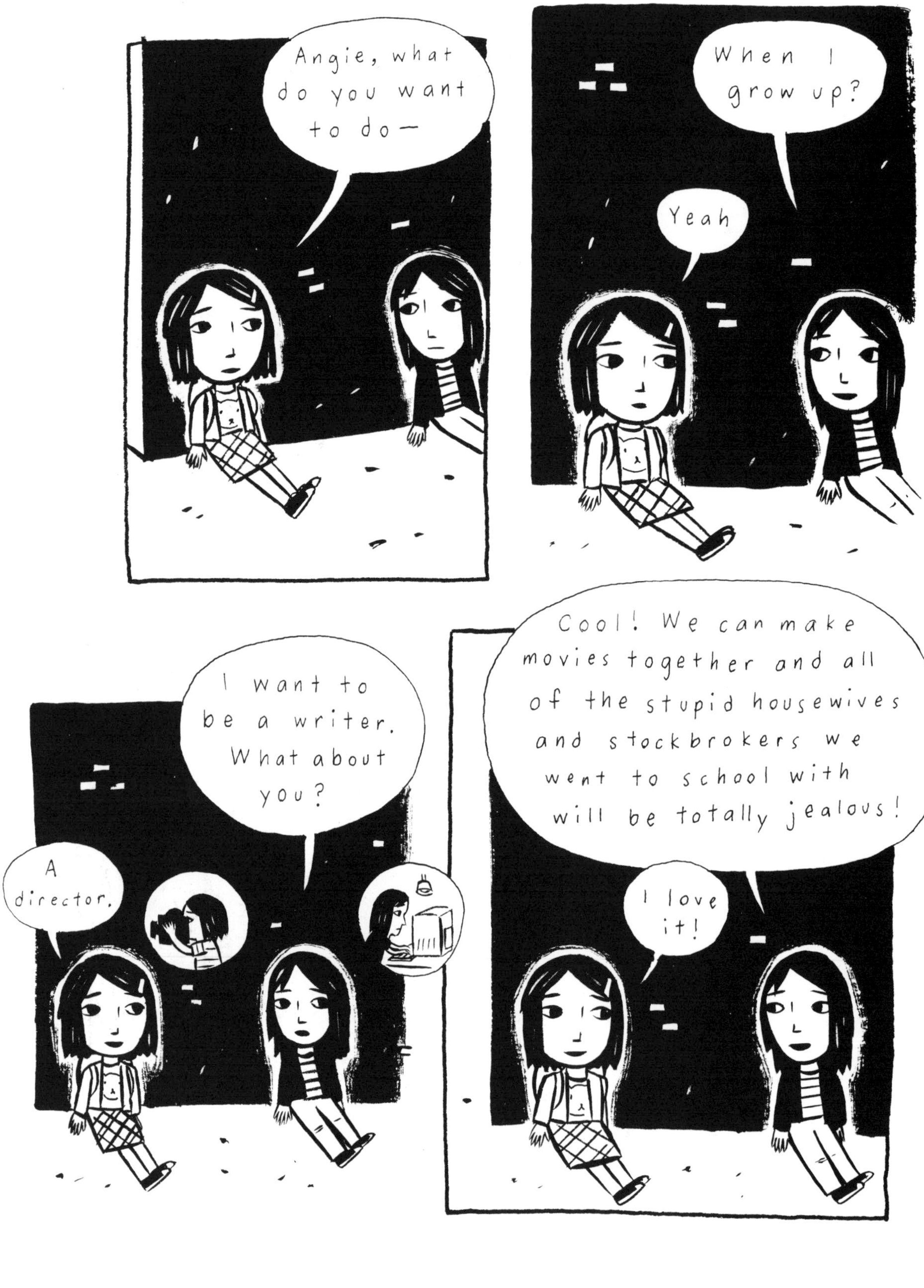

Angie, what do you want to do—
When I grow up?
Yeah
I want to be a writer. What about you?
A director.
Cool! We can make movies together and all of the stupid housewives and stockbrokers we went to school with will be totally jealous!
I love it!

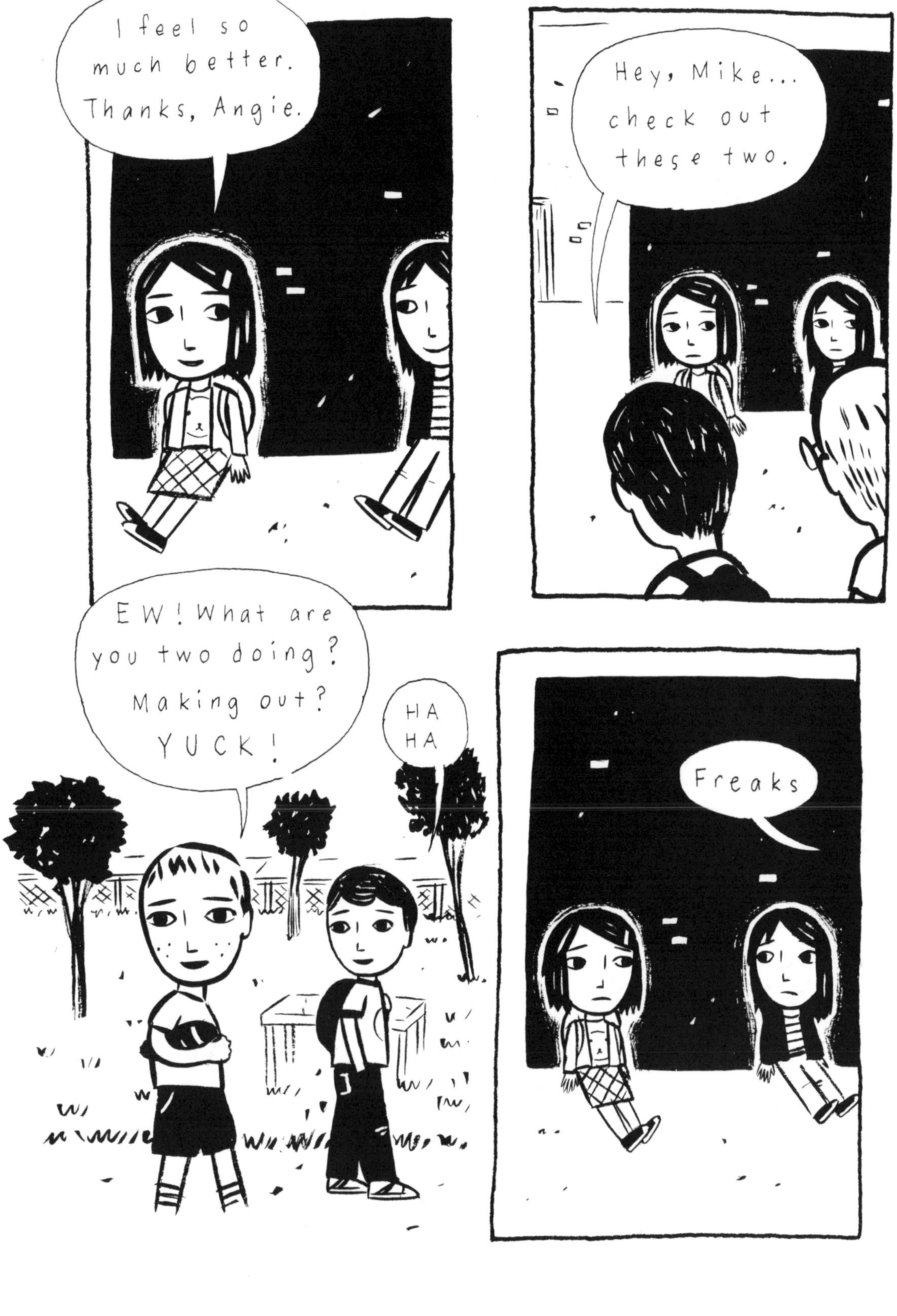
I feel so much better. Thanks, Angie.
Hey, Mike... check out these two.
EW! What are you two doing? Making out? YUCK!
HA HA
Freaks

NICK ELIOPULOS

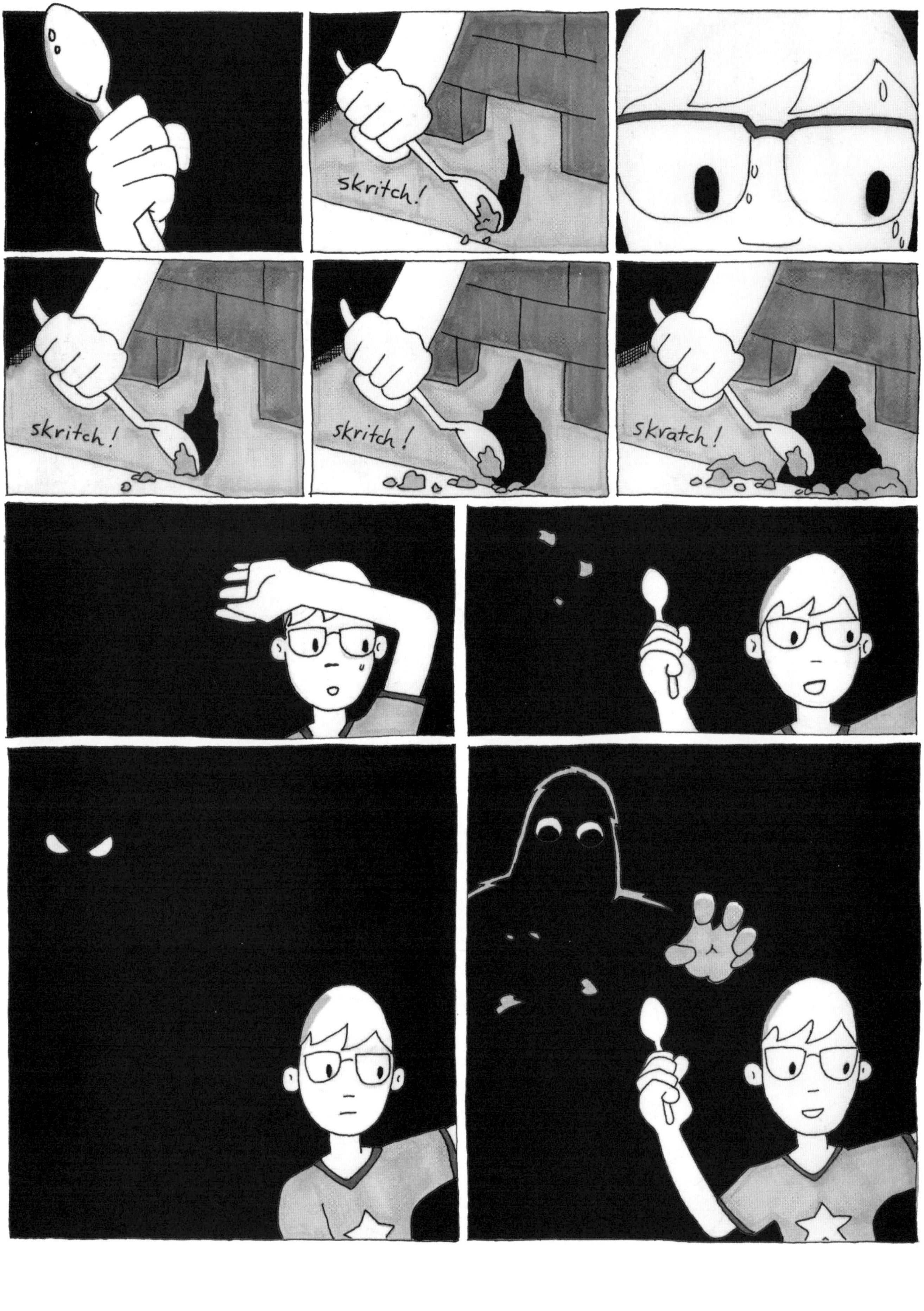
skritch!
skritch!
skritch!
skratch!

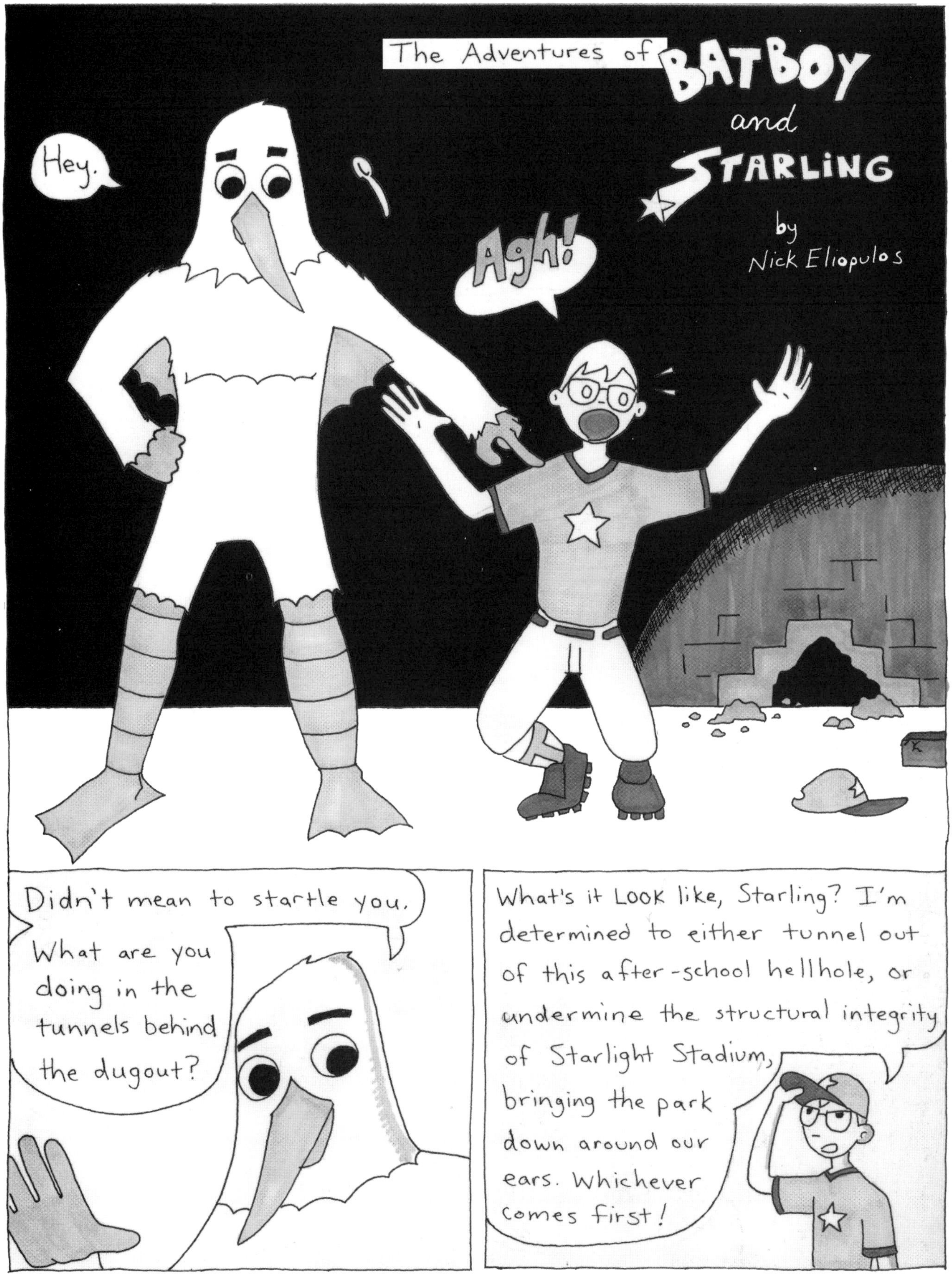
The Adventures of
BATBOY
and
STARLING
by
Nick Eliopulos
Hey.
Agh!
Didn't mean to startle you.
What are you doing in the tunnels behind the dugout?
What's it LOOK like, Starling? I'm determined to either tunnel out of this after-school hellhole, or undermine the structural integrity of Starlight Stadium,
bringing the park down around our ears. Whichever comes first!

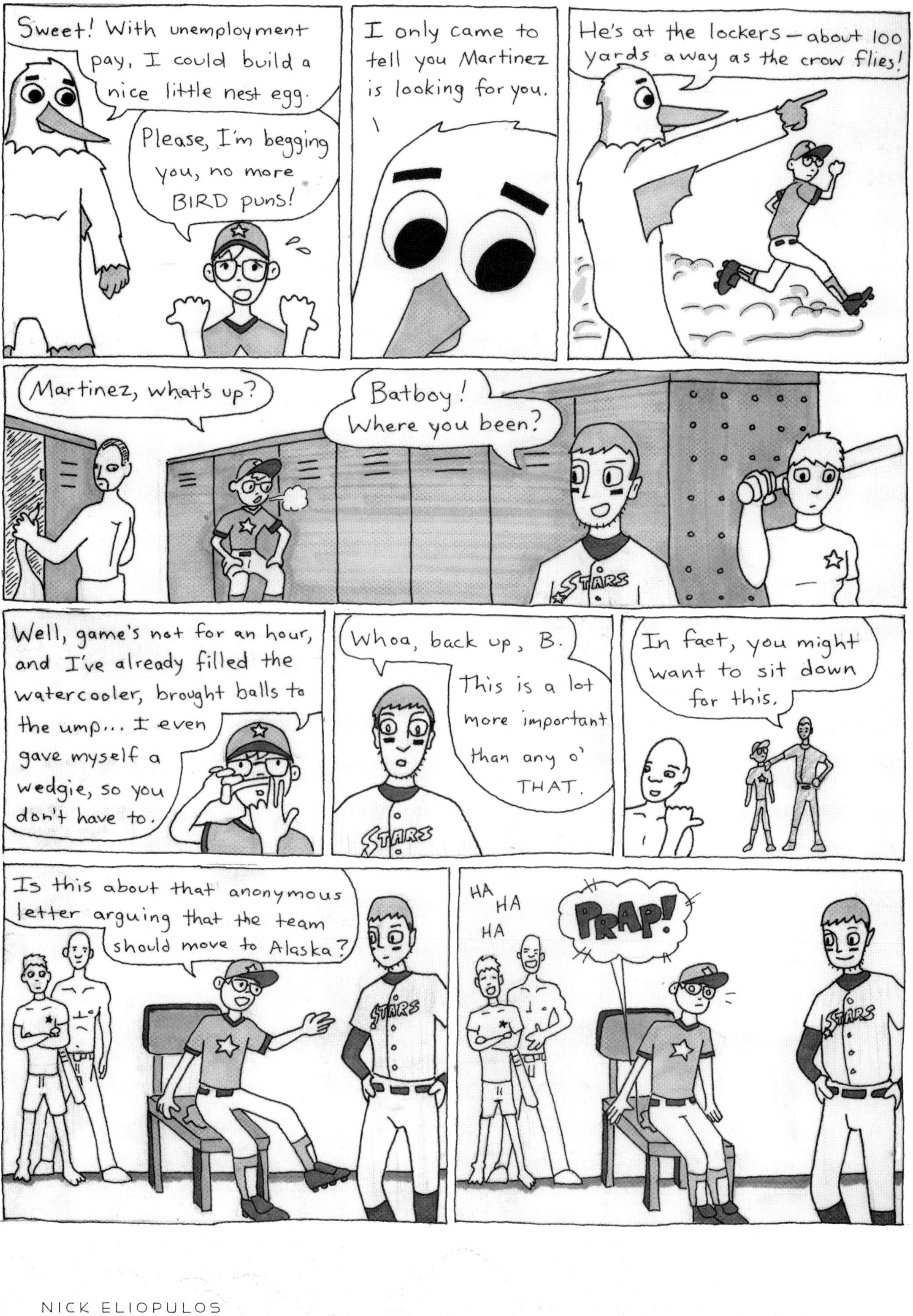
Sweet! With unemployment pay, I could build a nice little nest egg.
Please, I'm begging you, no more BIRD puns!
I only came to tell you Martinez is looking for you.
He's at the lockers—about 100 yards away as the crow flies!
Martinez, what's up?
Batboy! Where you been?
Well, game's not for an hour, and I've already filled the watercooler, brought balls to the ump... I even gave myself a wedgie, so you don't have to.
Whoa, back up, B.
This is a lot more important than any o' THAT.
In fact, you might want to sit down for this.
Is this about that anonymous letter arguing that the team should move to Alaska?
HA
HA
HA
PRAP!

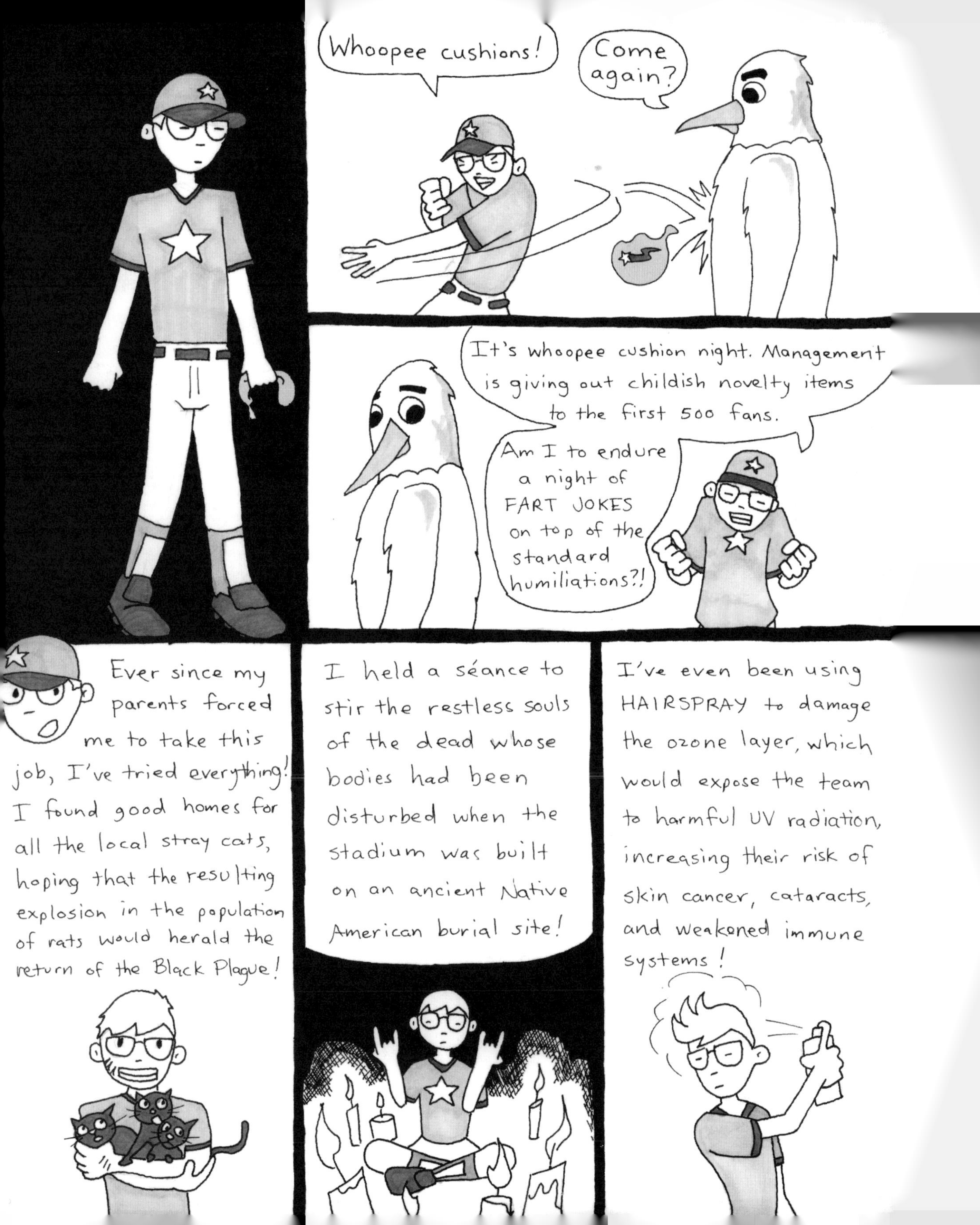

Whoopee cushions!
Come again?
It's whoopee cushion night. Management is giving out childish novelty items to the first 500 fans.
Am I to endure a night of FART JOKES on top of the standard humiliations?!
Ever since my parents forced me to take this job, I've tried everything! I found good homes for all the local stray cats, hoping that the resulting explosion in the population of rats would herald the return of the Black Plague!
I held a séance to stir the restless souls of the dead whose bodies had been disturbed when the stadium was built on an ancient Native American burial site!
I've even been using HAIRSPRAY to damage the ozone layer, which would expose the team to harmful UV radiation, increasing their risk of skin cancer, cataracts, and weakened immune systems!

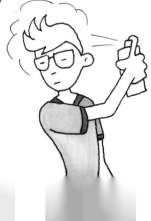

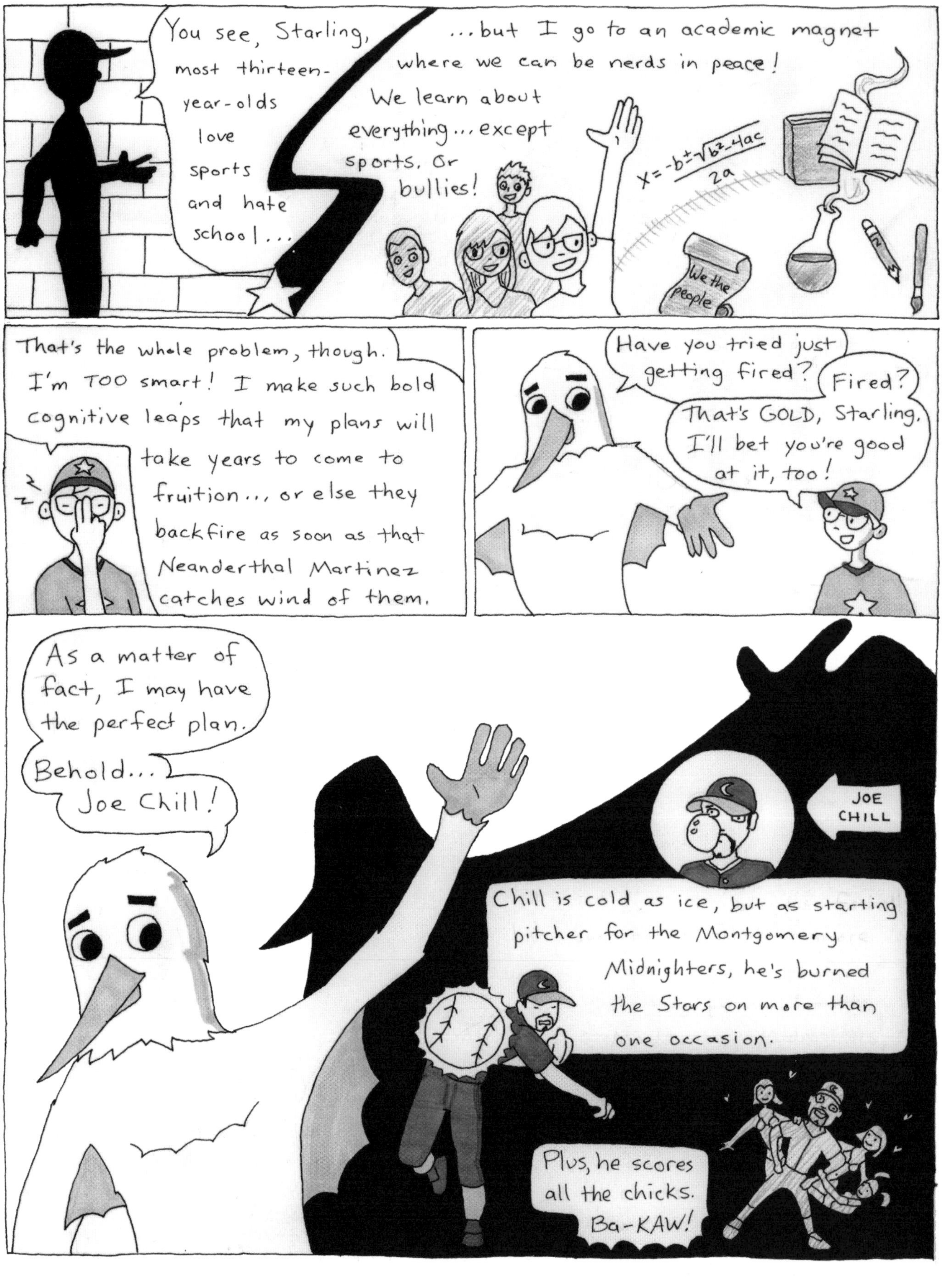
You see, Starling, most thirteen-year-olds love sports and hate school...
...but I go to an academic magnet where we can be nerds in peace!
We learn about everything... except sports. Or bullies!
$x = \frac{-b \pm \sqrt{b^2 - 4ac}}{2a}$
We the people
That's the whole problem, though. I'm TOO smart! I make such bold cognitive leaps that my plans will take years to come to fruition... or else they backfire as soon as that Neanderthal Martinez catches wind of them.
Have you tried just getting fired?
Fired?
That's GOLD, Starling. I'll bet you're good at it, too!
As a matter of fact, I may have the perfect plan.
Behold... Joe Chill!
JOE CHILL
Chill is cold as ice, but as starting pitcher for the Montgomery Midnighters, he's burned the Stars on more than one occasion.
Plus, he scores all the chicks. Ba-KAW!

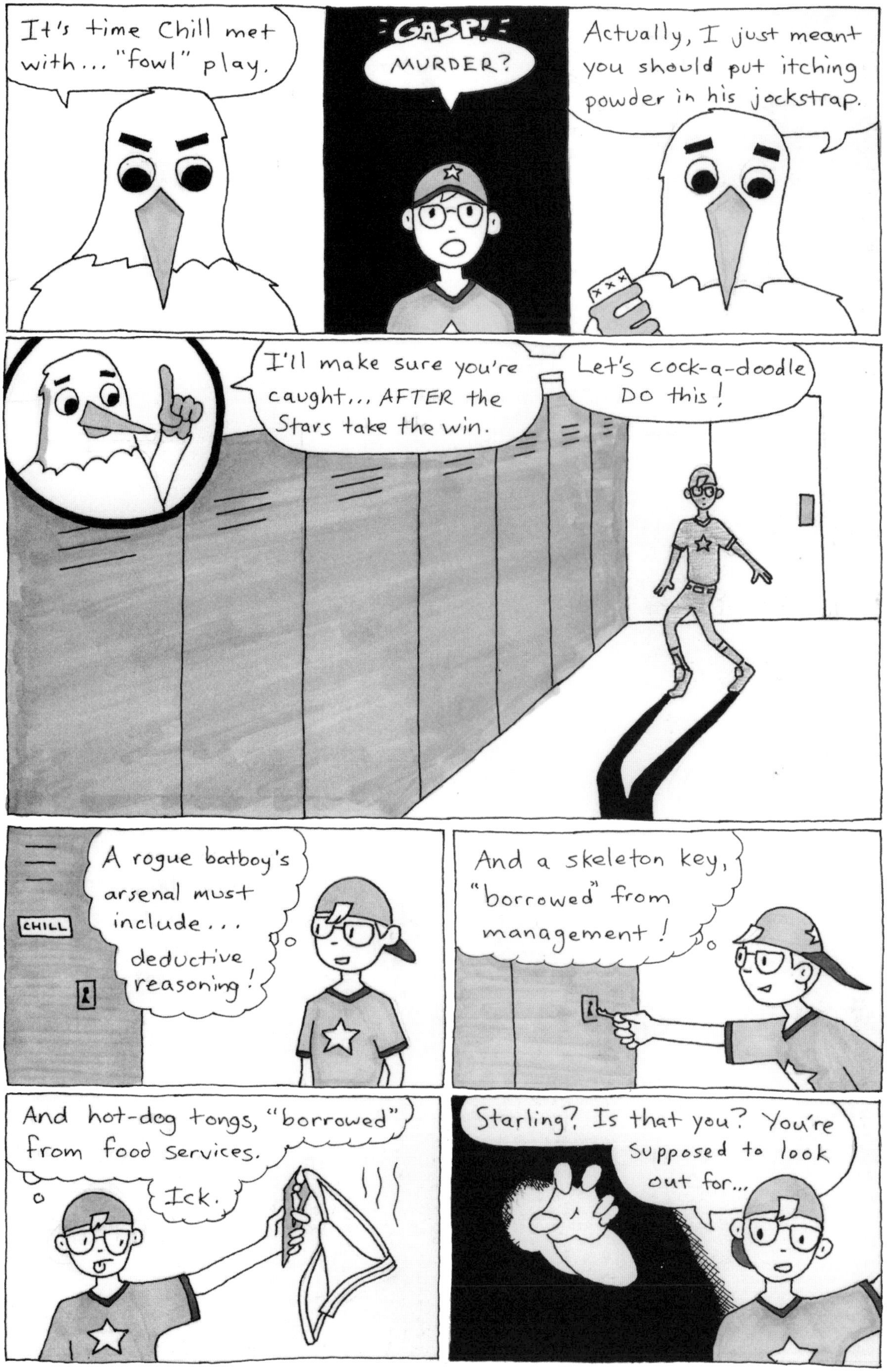
It's time Chill met with... "fowl" play.
GASP!
MURDER?
Actually, I just meant you should put itching powder in his jockstrap.
I'll make sure you're caught... AFTER the Stars take the win.
Let's cock-a-doodle DO this!
A rogue batboy's arsenal must include... deductive reasoning!
CHILL
And a skeleton key, "borrowed" from management!
And hot-dog tongs, "borrowed" from food services.
Ick.
Starling? Is that you? You're supposed to look out for...

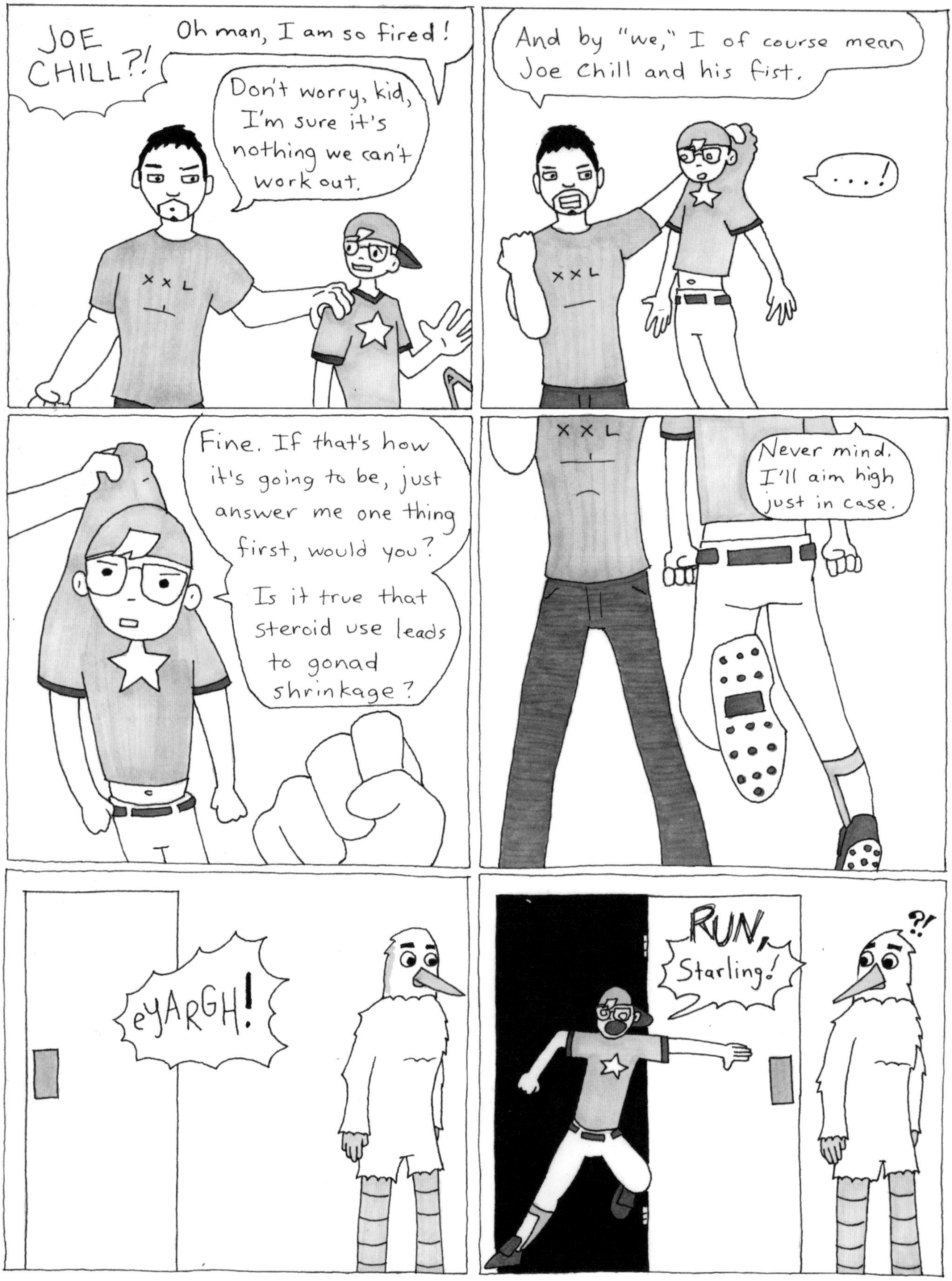
JOE CHILL?!
Oh man, I am so fired!
Don't worry, kid, I'm sure it's nothing we can't work out.
And by "we," I of course mean Joe Chill and his fist.
. . . !
Fine. If that's how it's going to be, just answer me one thing first, would you?
Is it true that steroid use leads to gonad shrinkage?
Never mind. I'll aim high just in case.
eYARGH!
RUN, Starling!
?!

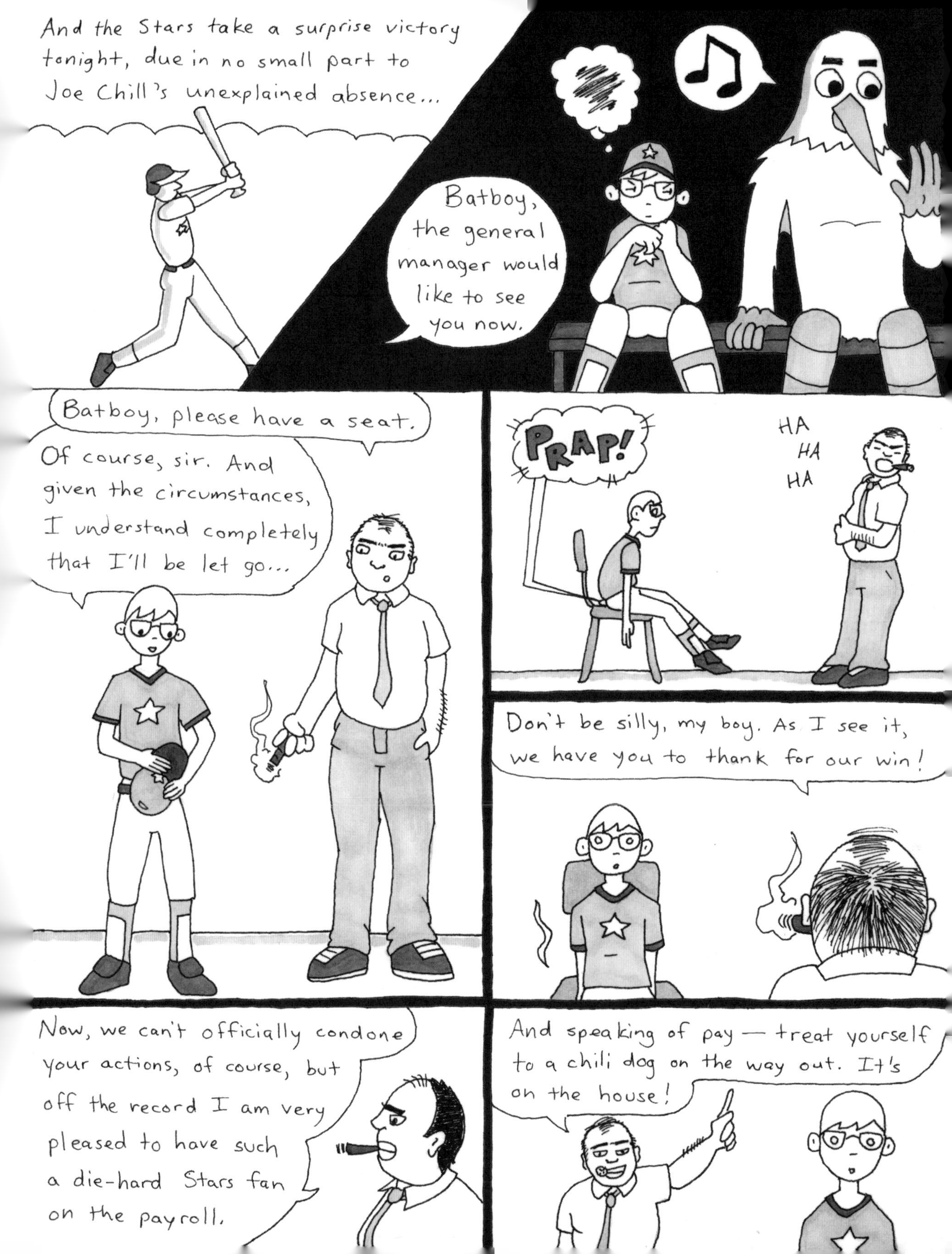
And the Stars take a surprise victory tonight, due in no small part to Joe Chill's unexplained absence...
Batboy, the general manager would like to see you now.
Batboy, please have a seat.
Of course, sir. And given the circumstances, I understand completely that I'll be let go...
PRAP!
HA HA HA
Don't be silly, my boy. As I see it, we have you to thank for our win!
Now, we can't officially condone your actions, of course, but off the record I am very pleased to have such a die-hard Stars fan on the payroll.
And speaking of pay — treat yourself to a chili dog on the way out. It's on the house!

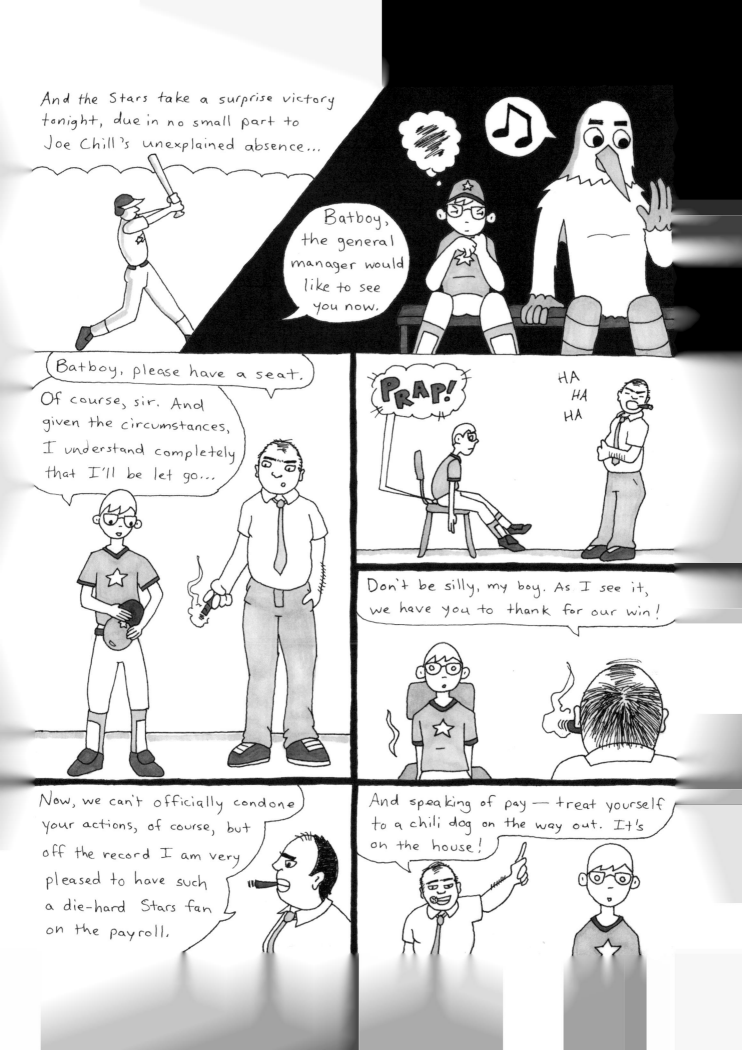

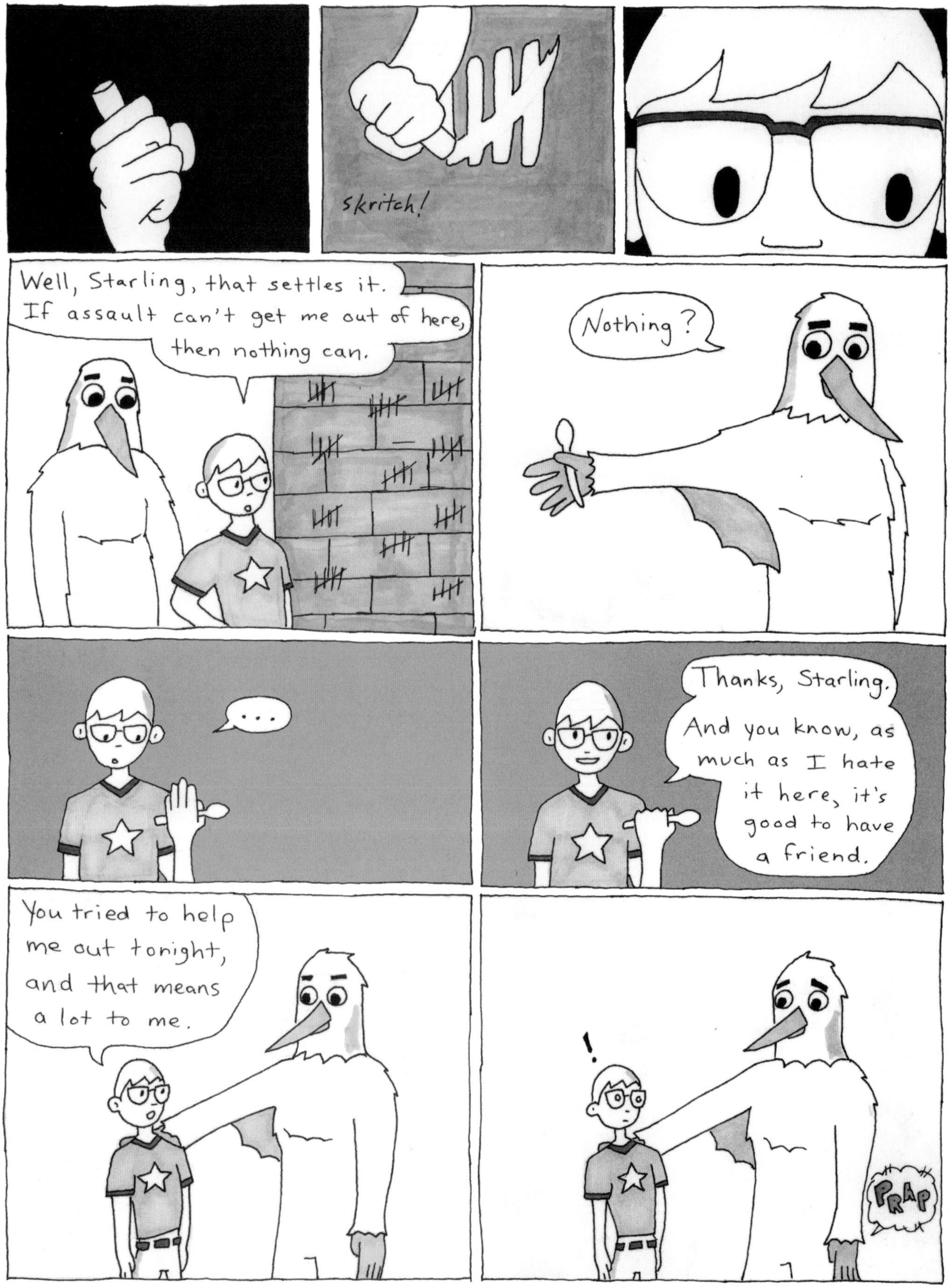
skritch!
Well, Starling, that settles it. If assault can't get me out of here, then nothing can.
Nothing?
. . .
Thanks, Starling.
And you know, as much as I hate it here, it's good to have a friend.
You tried to help me out tonight, and that means a lot to me.
!
PRAP

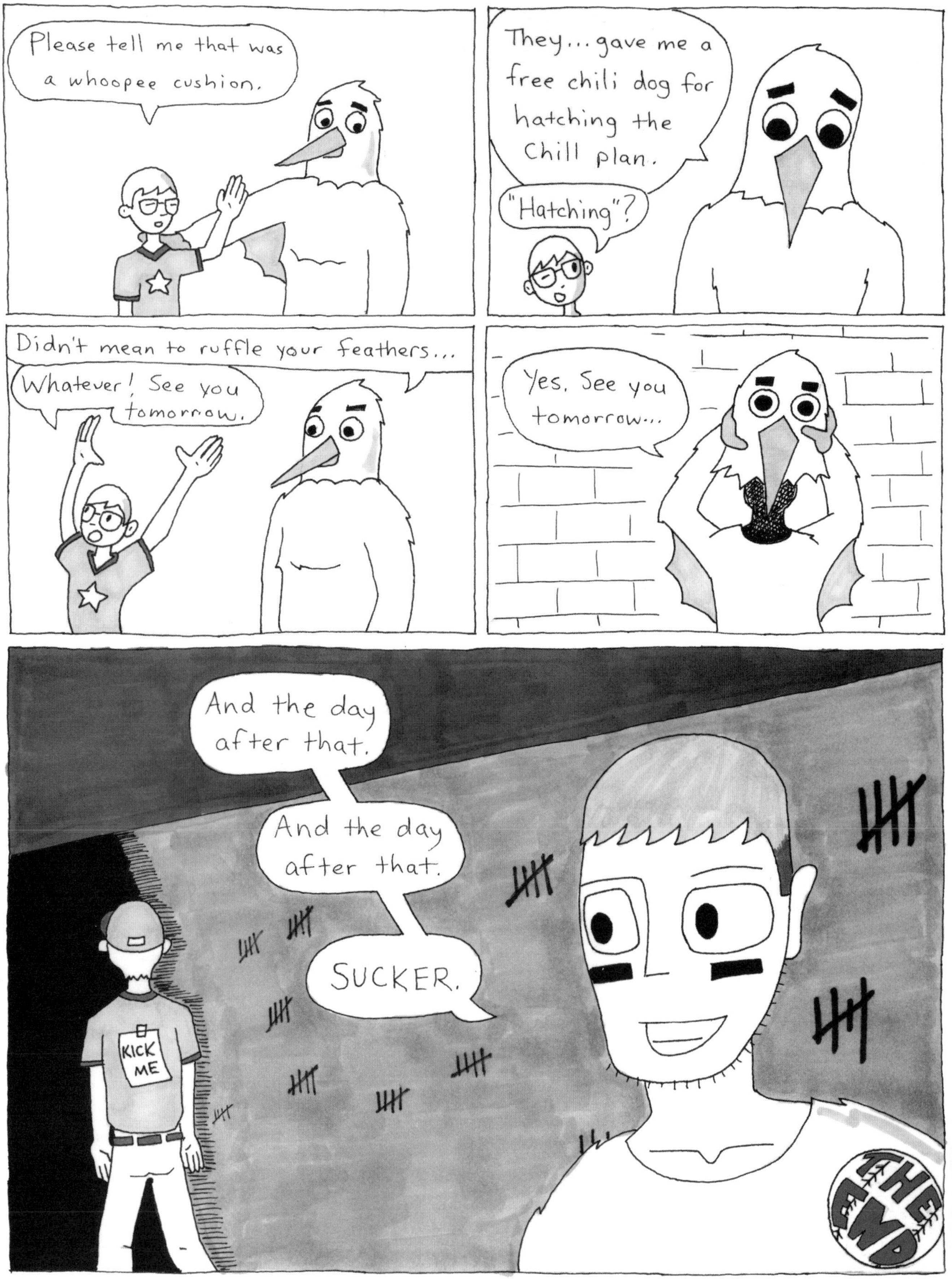
Please tell me that was a whoopee cushion.
They... gave me a free chili dog for hatching the Chill plan.
"Hatching"?
Didn't mean to ruffle your feathers...
Whatever! See you tomorrow.
Yes. See you tomorrow...
And the day after that.
And the day after that.
SUCKER.
KICK ME
THE END

GABRIELLE BELL

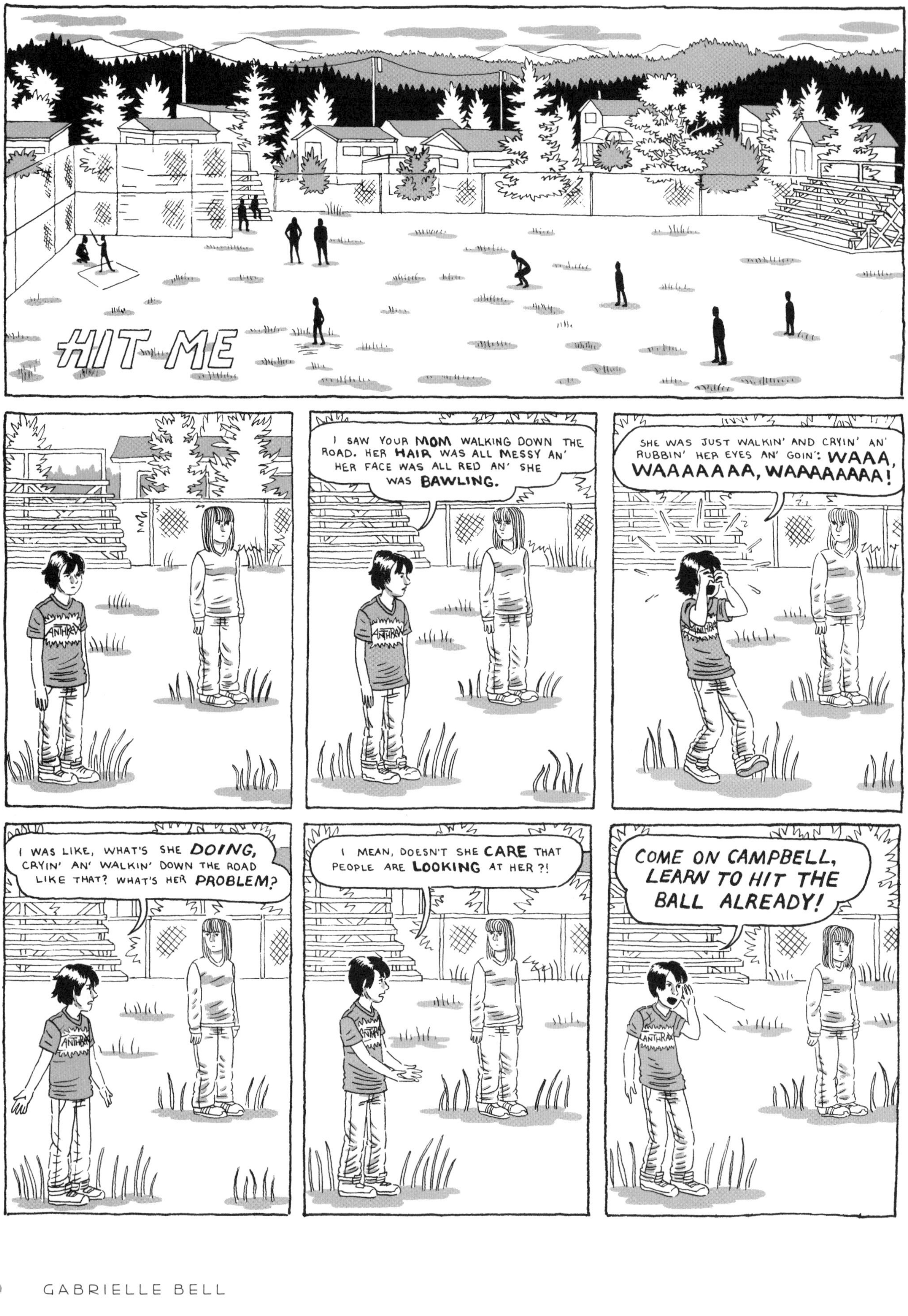
HIT ME
I SAW YOUR MOM WALKING DOWN THE ROAD. HER HAIR WAS ALL MESSY AN' HER FACE WAS ALL RED AN' SHE WAS BAWLING.
SHE WAS JUST WALKIN' AND CRYIN' AN' RUBBIN' HER EYES AN' GOIN': WAAA, WAAAAAAA, WAAAAAAAA!
I WAS LIKE, WHAT'S SHE DOING, CRYIN' AN' WALKIN' DOWN THE ROAD LIKE THAT? WHAT'S HER PROBLEM?
I MEAN, DOESN'T SHE CARE THAT PEOPLE ARE LOOKING AT HER?!
COME ON CAMPBELL, LEARN TO HIT THE BALL ALREADY!

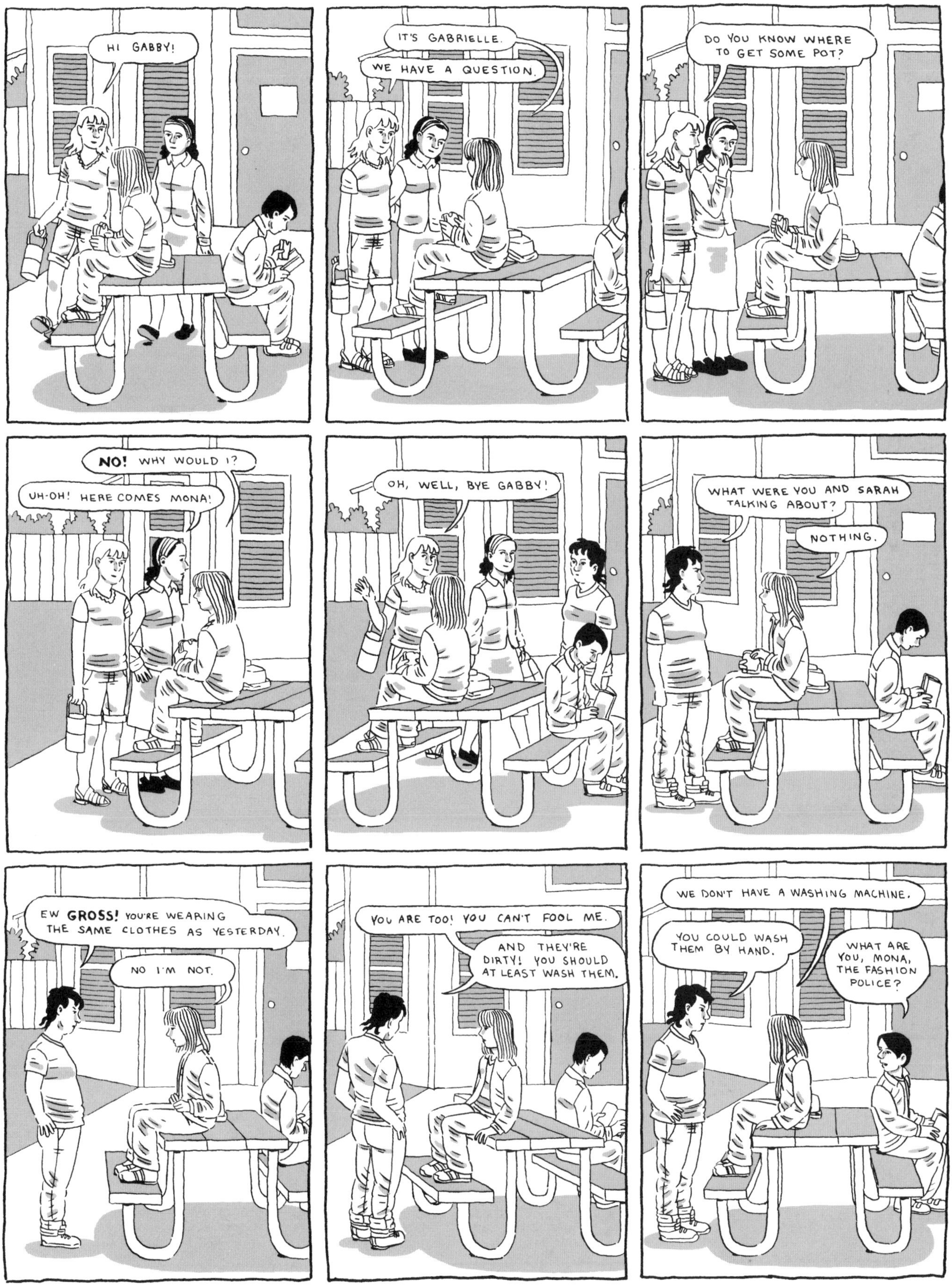
HI GABBY!
IT'S GABRIELLE.
WE HAVE A QUESTION.
DO YOU KNOW WHERE TO GET SOME POT?
UH-OH! HERE COMES MONA!
NO! WHY WOULD I?
OH, WELL, BYE GABBY!
WHAT WERE YOU AND SARAH TALKING ABOUT?
NOTHING.
EW GROSS! YOU'RE WEARING THE SAME CLOTHES AS YESTERDAY.
NO I'M NOT.
YOU ARE TOO! YOU CAN'T FOOL ME.
AND THEY'RE DIRTY! YOU SHOULD AT LEAST WASH THEM.
WE DON'T HAVE A WASHING MACHINE.
YOU COULD WASH THEM BY HAND.
WHAT ARE YOU, MONA, THE FASHION POLICE?

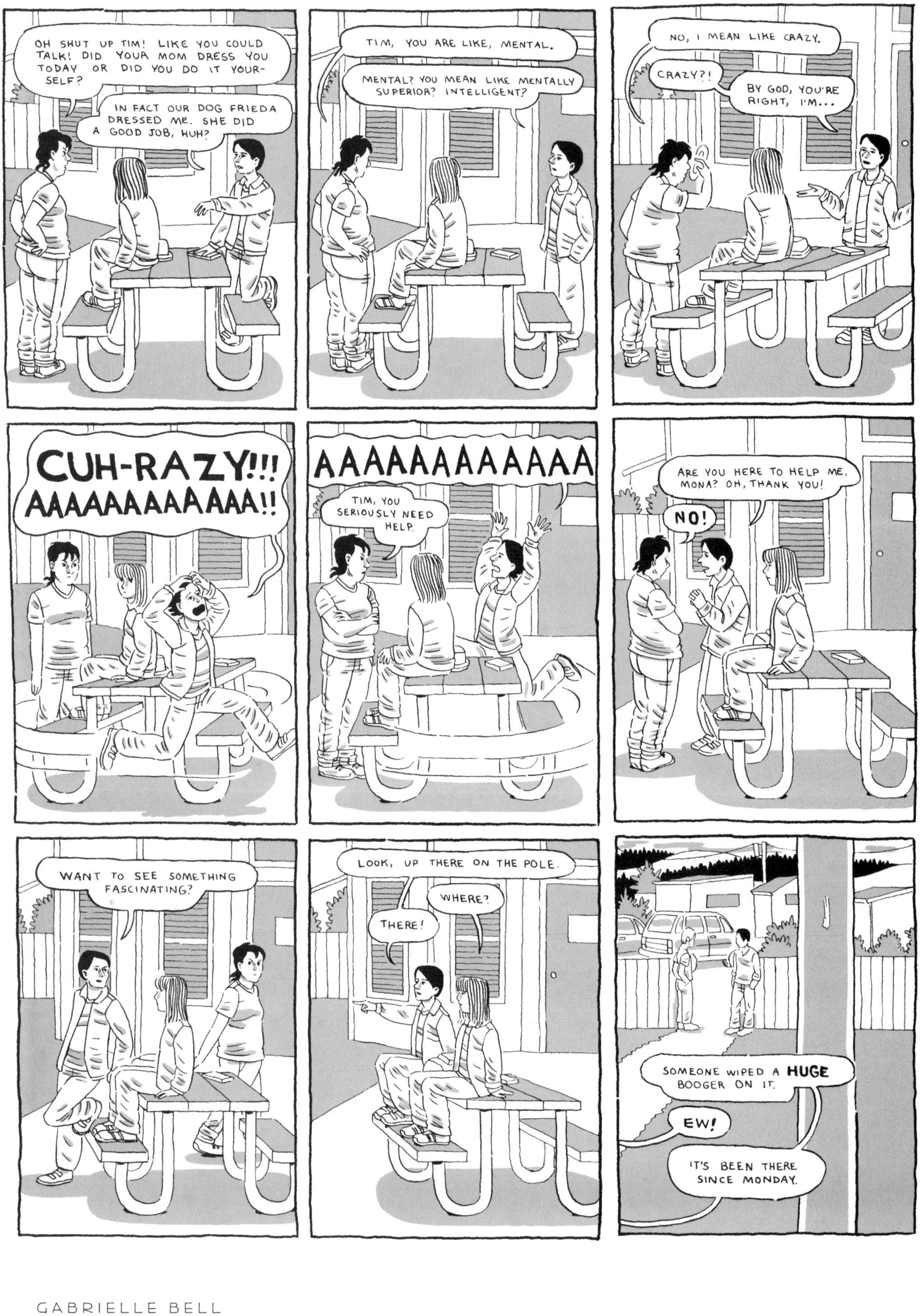

OH SHUT UP TIM! LIKE YOU COULD TALK! DID YOUR MOM DRESS YOU TODAY OR DID YOU DO IT YOURSELF?
IN FACT OUR DOG FRIEDA DRESSED ME. SHE DID A GOOD JOB, HUH?
TIM, YOU ARE LIKE, MENTAL.
MENTAL? YOU MEAN LIKE MENTALLY SUPERIOR? INTELLIGENT?
NO, I MEAN LIKE CRAZY.
CRAZY?!
BY GOD, YOU'RE RIGHT, I'M...
CUH-RAZY!!! AAAAAAAAAAAA!!
AAAAAAAAAAAAA
TIM, YOU SERIOUSLY NEED HELP.
ARE YOU HERE TO HELP ME, MONA? OH, THANK YOU!
NO!
WANT TO SEE SOMETHING FASCINATING?
LOOK, UP THERE ON THE POLE.
WHERE?
THERE!
SOMEONE WIPED A **HUGE** BOOGER ON IT.
EW!
IT'S BEEN THERE SINCE MONDAY.

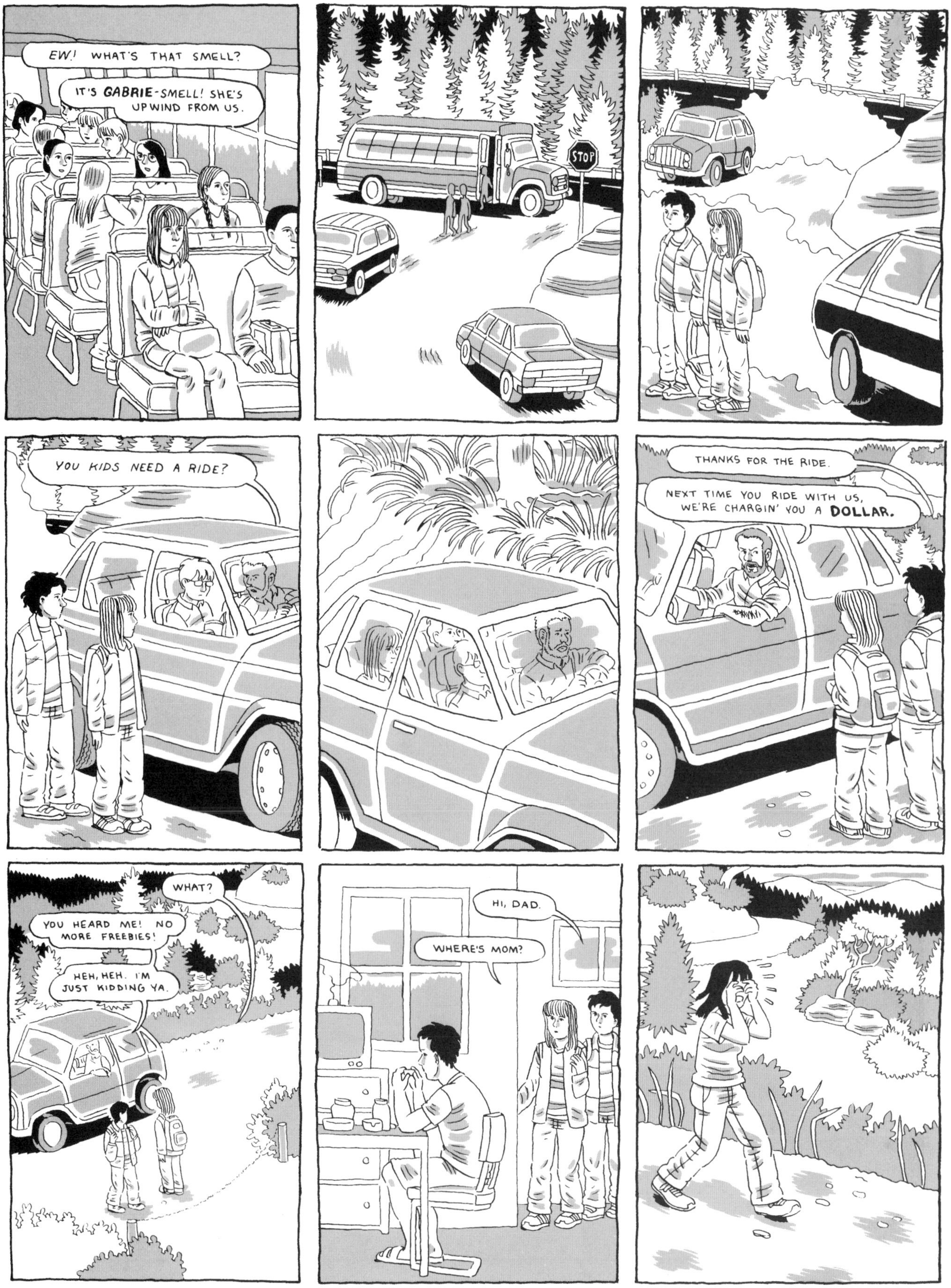
EW! WHAT'S THAT SMELL?
IT'S GABRIE-SMELL! SHE'S UPWIND FROM US.
STOP
YOU KIDS NEED A RIDE?
THANKS FOR THE RIDE.
NEXT TIME YOU RIDE WITH US, WE'RE CHARGIN' YOU A DOLLAR.
WHAT?
YOU HEARD ME! NO MORE FREEBIES!
HEH, HEH. I'M JUST KIDDING YA.
HI, DAD.
WHERE'S MOM?

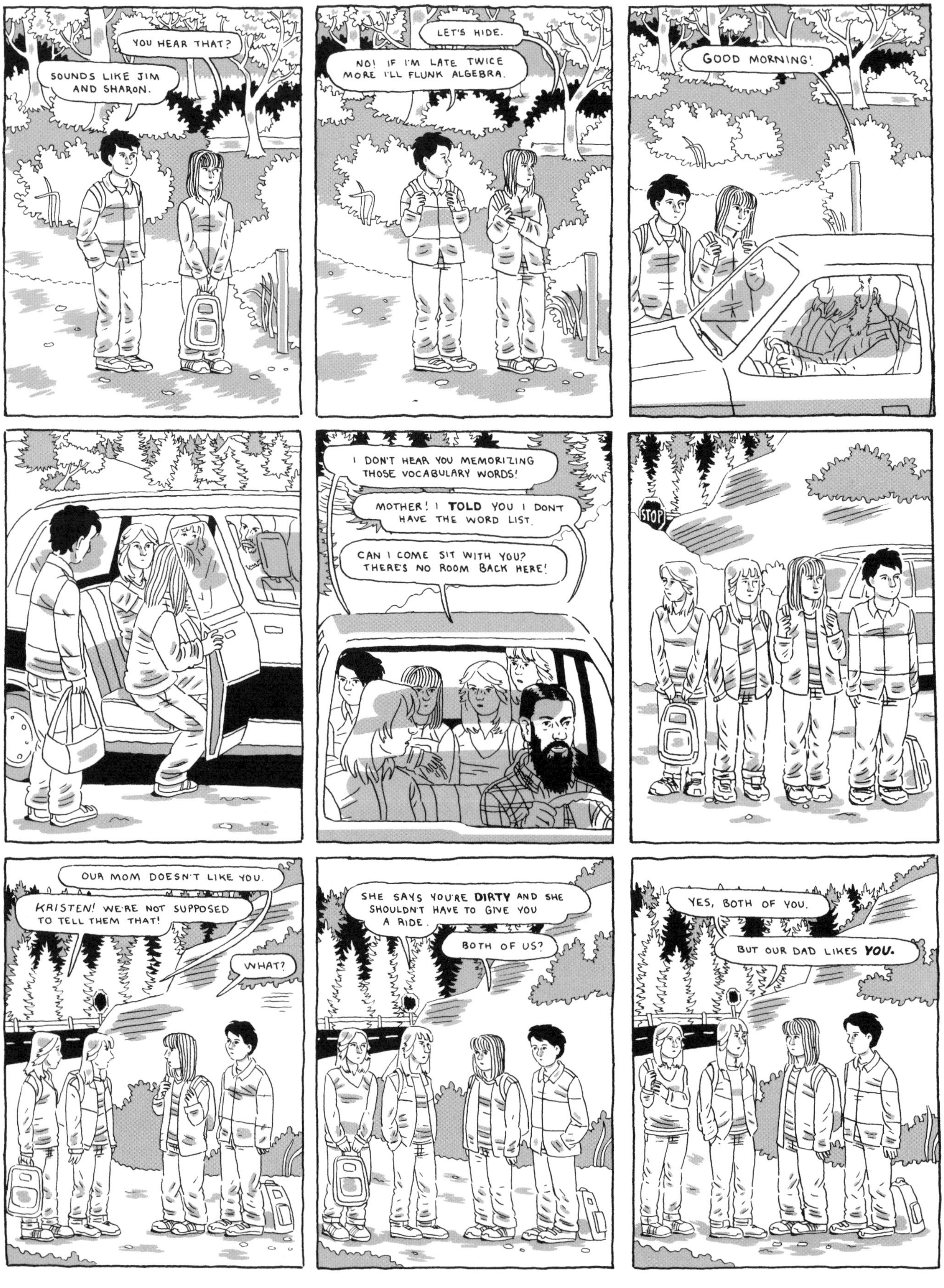
YOU HEAR THAT?
SOUNDS LIKE JIM AND SHARON.
LET'S HIDE.
NO! IF I'M LATE TWICE MORE I'LL FLUNK ALGEBRA.
GOOD MORNING!
I DON'T HEAR YOU MEMORIZING THOSE VOCABULARY WORDS!
MOTHER! I **TOLD** YOU I DON'T HAVE THE WORD LIST.
CAN I COME SIT WITH YOU? THERE'S NO ROOM BACK HERE!
STOP
OUR MOM DOESN'T LIKE YOU.
KRISTEN! WE'RE NOT SUPPOSED TO TELL THEM THAT!
WHAT?
SHE SAYS YOU'RE **DIRTY** AND SHE SHOULDN'T HAVE TO GIVE YOU A RIDE.
BOTH OF US?
YES, BOTH OF YOU.
BUT OUR DAD LIKES **YOU.**

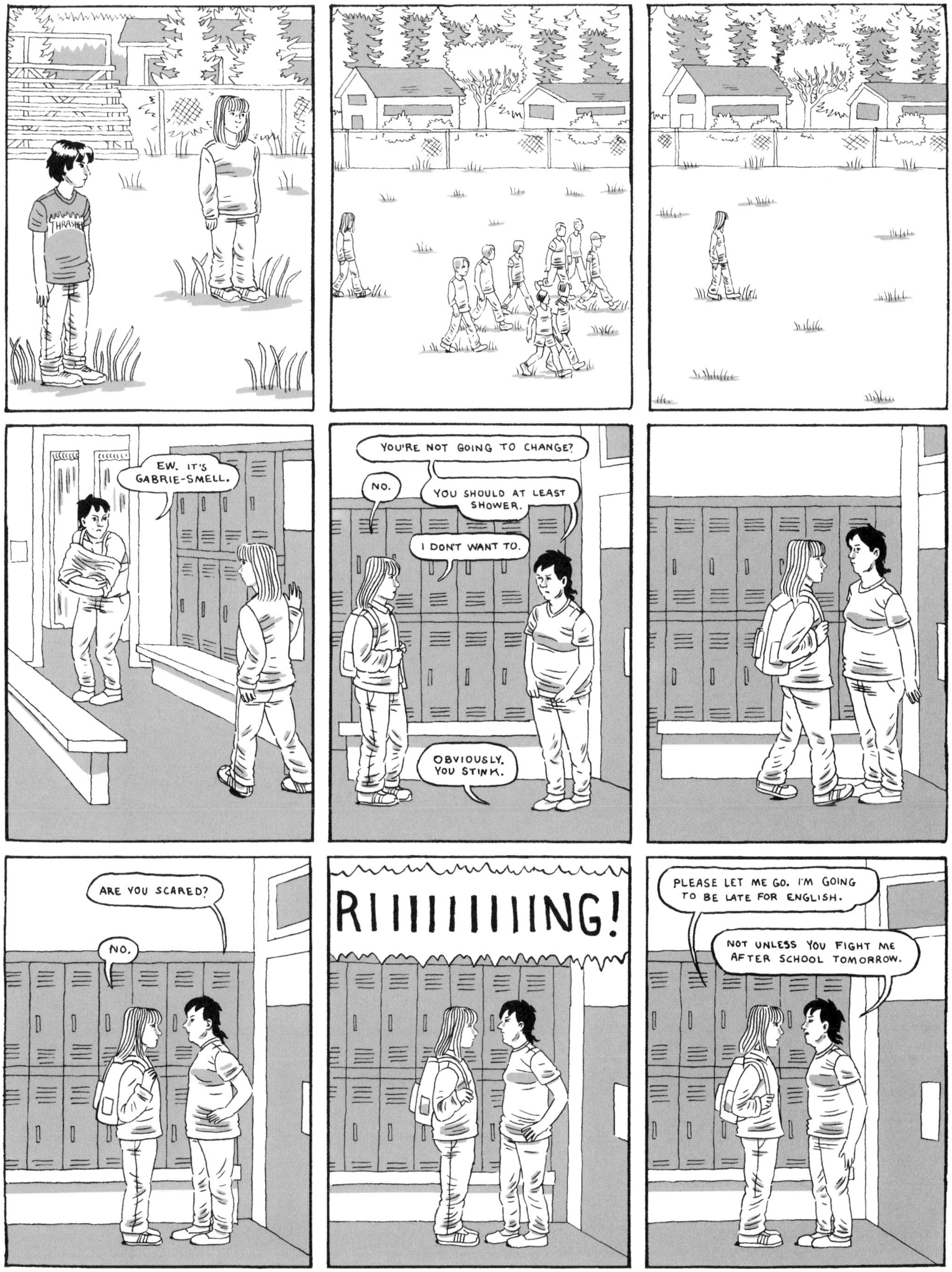
EW. IT'S GABRIE-SMELL.
YOU'RE NOT GOING TO CHANGE?
NO.
YOU SHOULD AT LEAST SHOWER.
I DON'T WANT TO.
OBVIOUSLY. YOU STINK.
ARE YOU SCARED?
NO.
RIIIIIIIING!
PLEASE LET ME GO. I'M GOING TO BE LATE FOR ENGLISH.
NOT UNLESS YOU FIGHT ME AFTER SCHOOL TOMORROW.

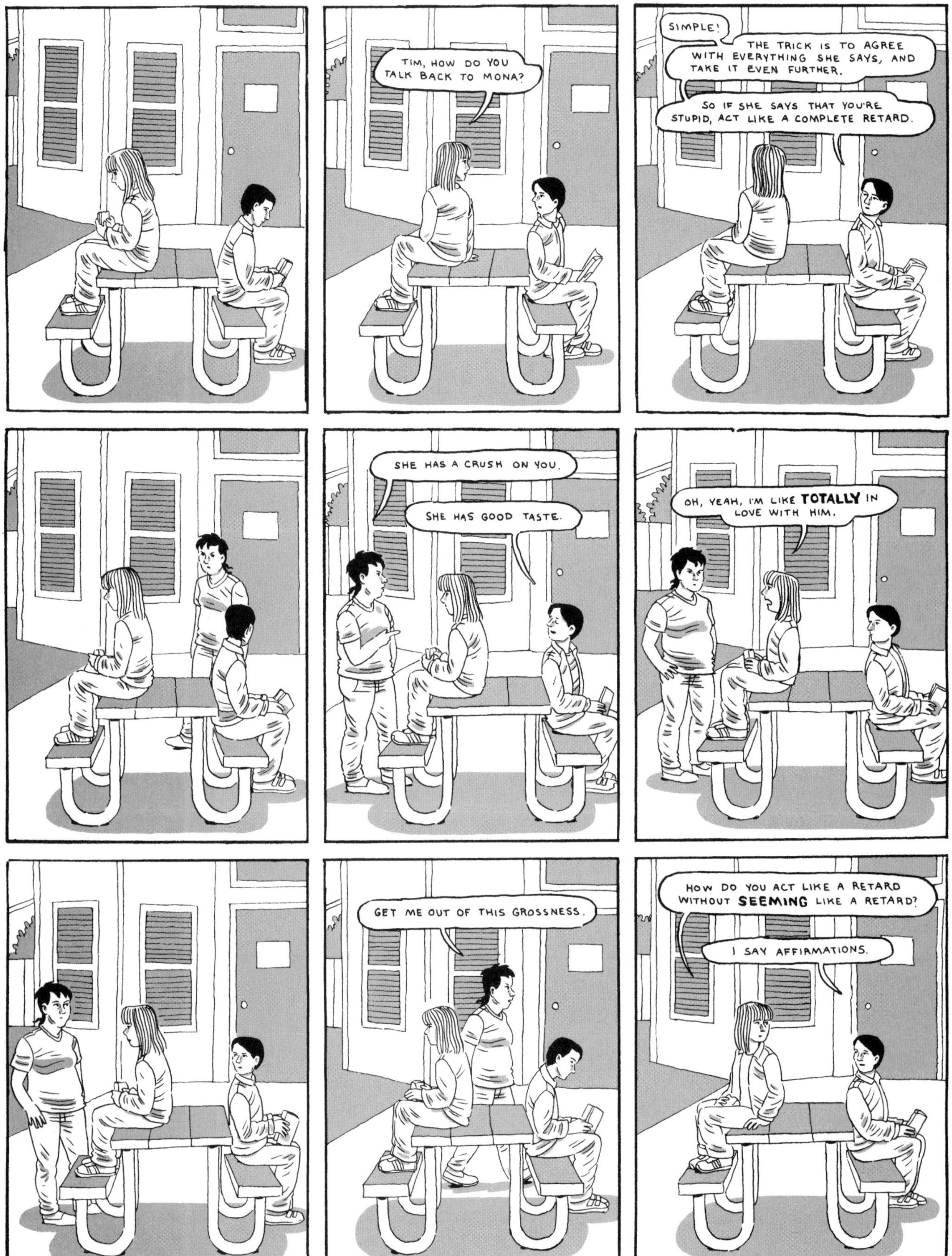
TIM, HOW DO YOU TALK BACK TO MONA?
SIMPLE!
THE TRICK IS TO AGREE WITH EVERYTHING SHE SAYS, AND TAKE IT EVEN FURTHER.
SO IF SHE SAYS THAT YOU'RE STUPID, ACT LIKE A COMPLETE RETARD.
SHE HAS A CRUSH ON YOU.
SHE HAS GOOD TASTE.
OH, YEAH, I'M LIKE **TOTALLY** IN LOVE WITH HIM.
GET ME OUT OF THIS GROSSNESS.
HOW DO YOU ACT LIKE A RETARD WITHOUT **SEEMING** LIKE A RETARD?
I SAY AFFIRMATIONS.

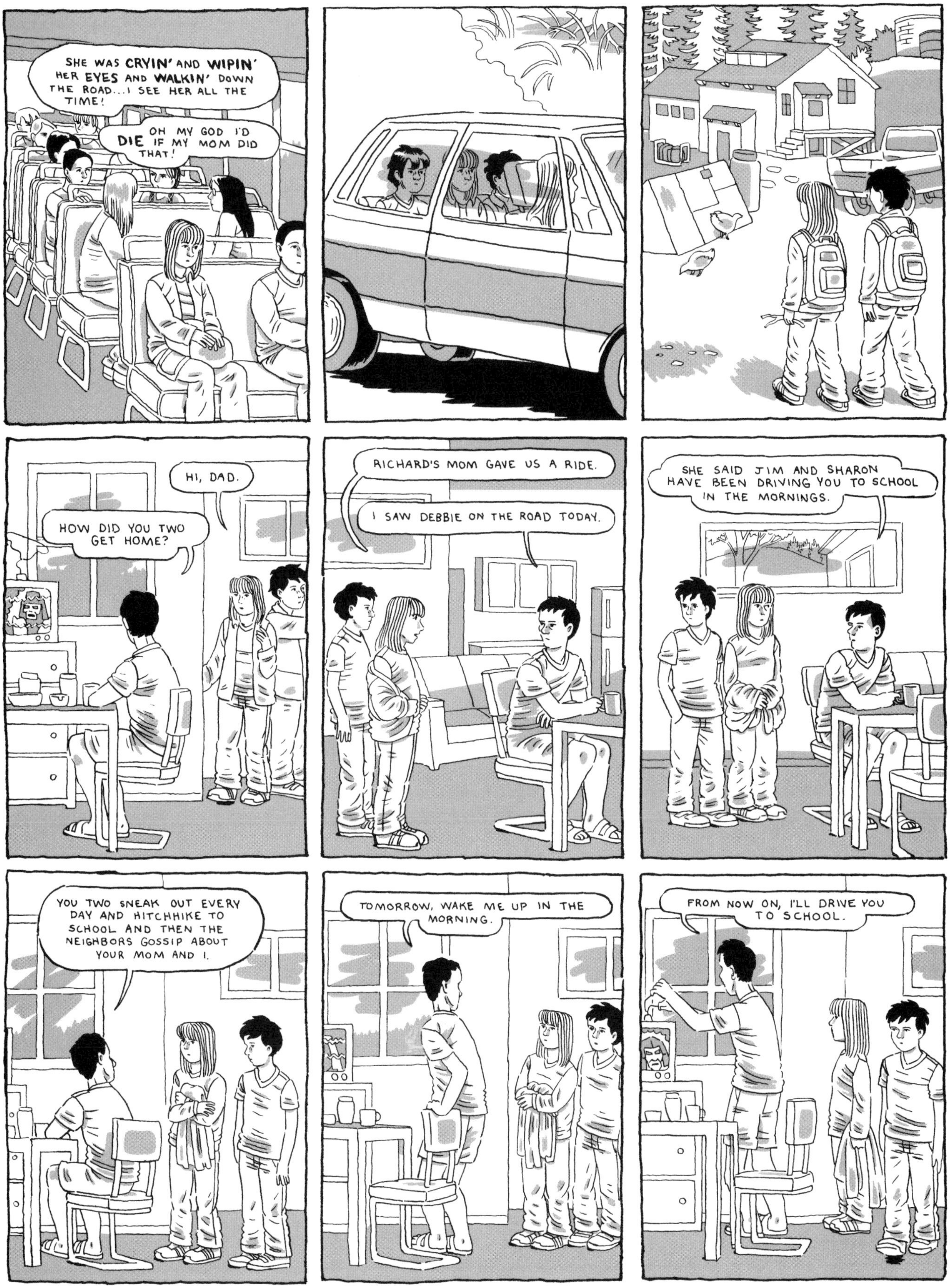
SHE WAS **CRYIN'** AND **WIPIN'** HER **EYES** AND **WALKIN'** DOWN THE ROAD... I SEE HER ALL THE TIME!
OH MY GOD I'D **DIE** IF MY MOM DID THAT!
HI, DAD.
HOW DID YOU TWO GET HOME?
RICHARD'S MOM GAVE US A RIDE.
I SAW DEBBIE ON THE ROAD TODAY.
SHE SAID JIM AND SHARON HAVE BEEN DRIVING YOU TO SCHOOL IN THE MORNINGS.
YOU TWO SNEAK OUT EVERY DAY AND HITCHHIKE TO SCHOOL AND THEN THE NEIGHBORS GOSSIP ABOUT YOUR MOM AND I.
TOMORROW, WAKE ME UP IN THE MORNING.
FROM NOW ON, I'LL DRIVE YOU TO SCHOOL.

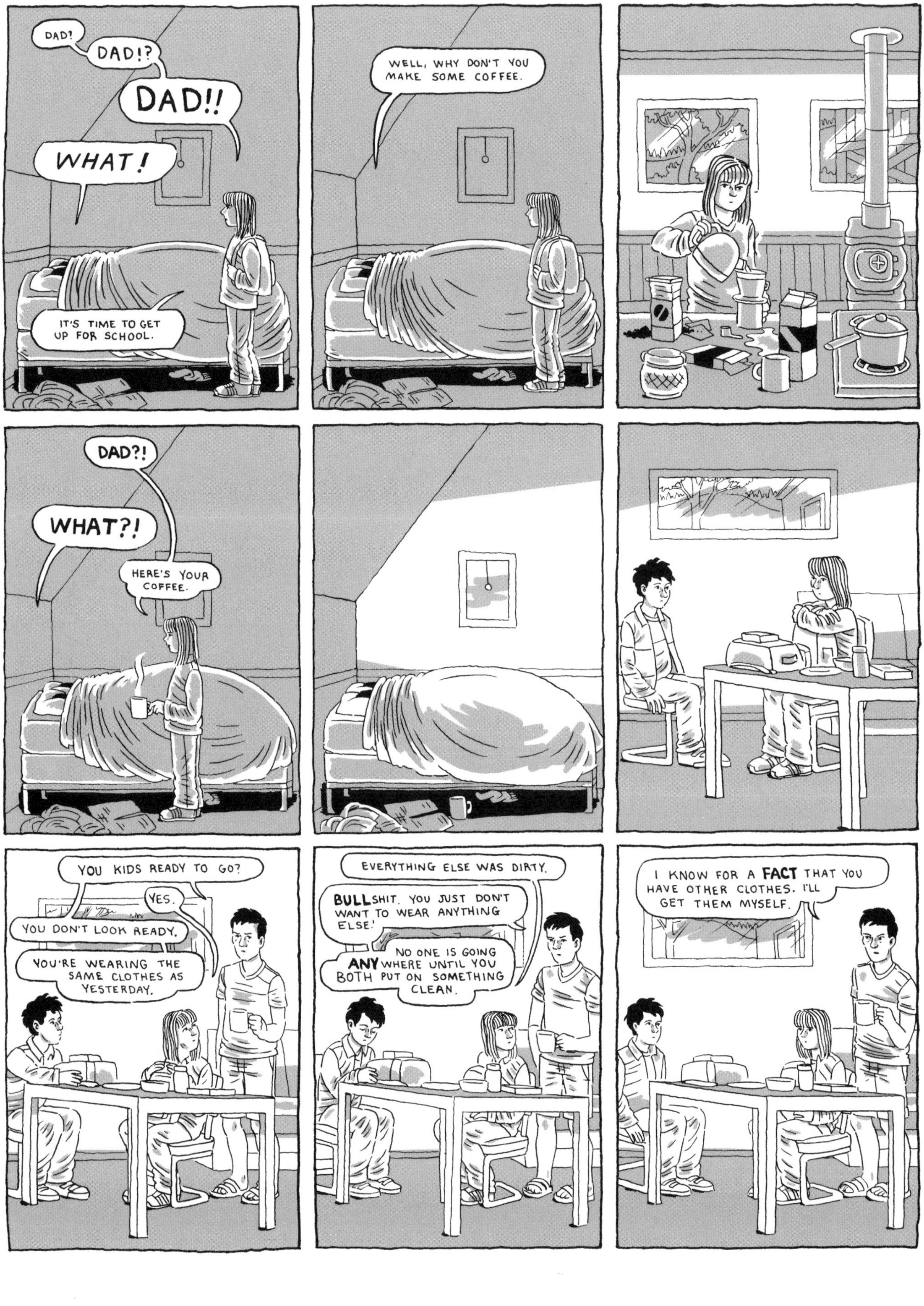
DAD?
DAD!?
DAD!!
WHAT!
IT'S TIME TO GET UP FOR SCHOOL.
WELL, WHY DON'T YOU MAKE SOME COFFEE.
DAD?!
WHAT?!
HERE'S YOUR COFFEE.
YOU KIDS READY TO GO?
YES.
YOU DON'T LOOK READY.
YOU'RE WEARING THE SAME CLOTHES AS YESTERDAY.
EVERYTHING ELSE WAS DIRTY.
BULLSHIT. YOU JUST DON'T WANT TO WEAR ANYTHING ELSE!
NO ONE IS GOING ANYWHERE UNTIL YOU BOTH PUT ON SOMETHING CLEAN.
I KNOW FOR A FACT THAT YOU HAVE OTHER CLOTHES. I'LL GET THEM MYSELF.

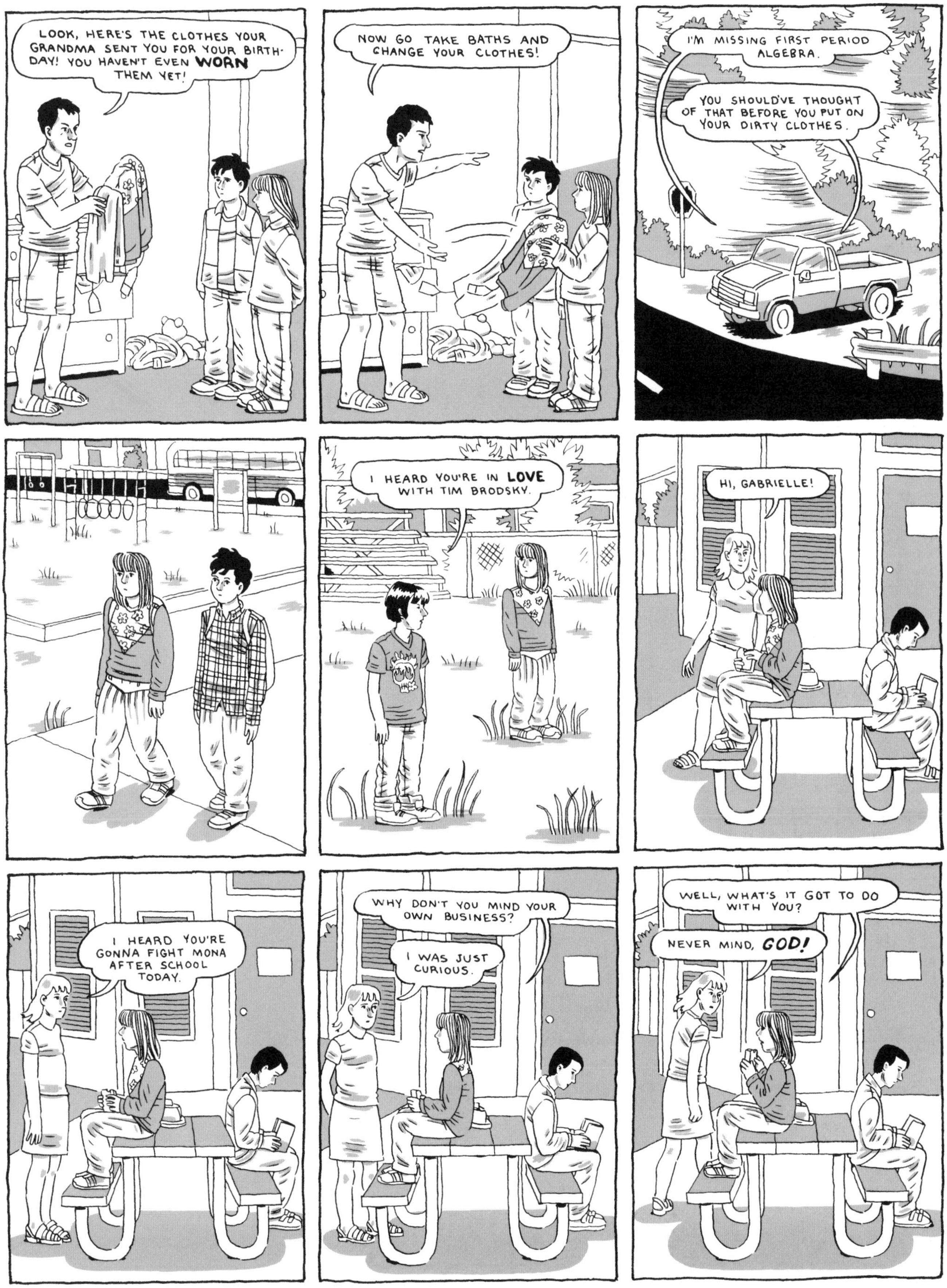
LOOK, HERE'S THE CLOTHES YOUR GRANDMA SENT YOU FOR YOUR BIRTHDAY! YOU HAVEN'T EVEN WORN THEM YET!
NOW GO TAKE BATHS AND CHANGE YOUR CLOTHES!
I'M MISSING FIRST PERIOD ALGEBRA.
YOU SHOULD'VE THOUGHT OF THAT BEFORE YOU PUT ON YOUR DIRTY CLOTHES.
I HEARD YOU'RE IN LOVE WITH TIM BRODSKY.
HI, GABRIELLE!
I HEARD YOU'RE GONNA FIGHT MONA AFTER SCHOOL TODAY.
WHY DON'T YOU MIND YOUR OWN BUSINESS?
I WAS JUST CURIOUS.
WELL, WHAT'S IT GOT TO DO WITH YOU?
NEVER MIND, GOD!

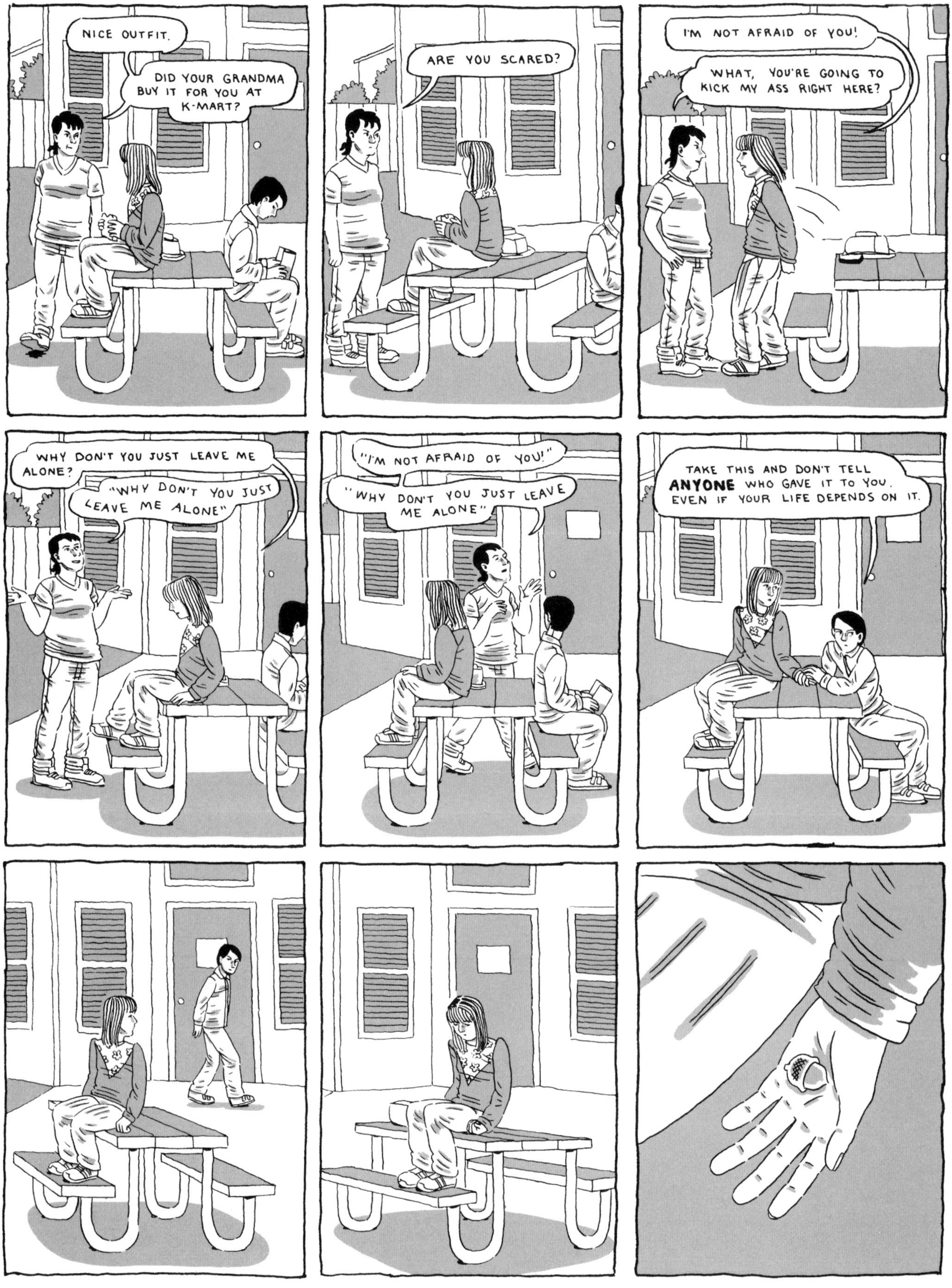
NICE OUTFIT.
DID YOUR GRANDMA BUY IT FOR YOU AT K-MART?
ARE YOU SCARED?
I'M NOT AFRAID OF YOU!
WHAT, YOU'RE GOING TO KICK MY ASS RIGHT HERE?
WHY DON'T YOU JUST LEAVE ME ALONE?
"WHY DON'T YOU JUST LEAVE ME ALONE"
"I'M NOT AFRAID OF YOU!"
"WHY DON'T YOU JUST LEAVE ME ALONE"
TAKE THIS AND DON'T TELL **ANYONE** WHO GAVE IT TO YOU. EVEN IF YOUR LIFE DEPENDS ON IT.

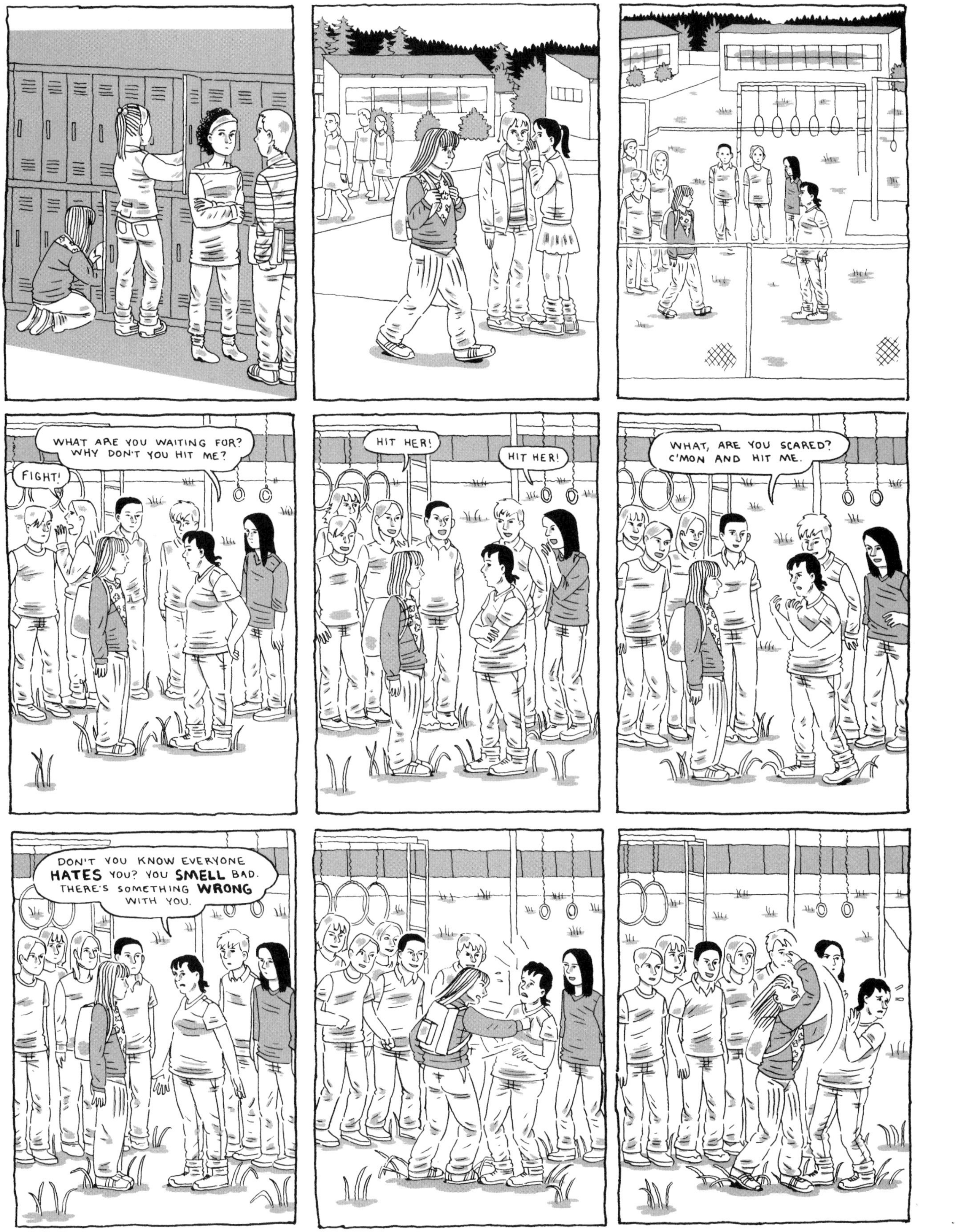
WHAT ARE YOU WAITING FOR? WHY DON'T YOU HIT ME?
FIGHT!
HIT HER!
HIT HER!
WHAT, ARE YOU SCARED? C'MON AND HIT ME.
DON'T YOU KNOW EVERYONE HATES YOU? YOU SMELL BAD. THERE'S SOMETHING WRONG WITH YOU.

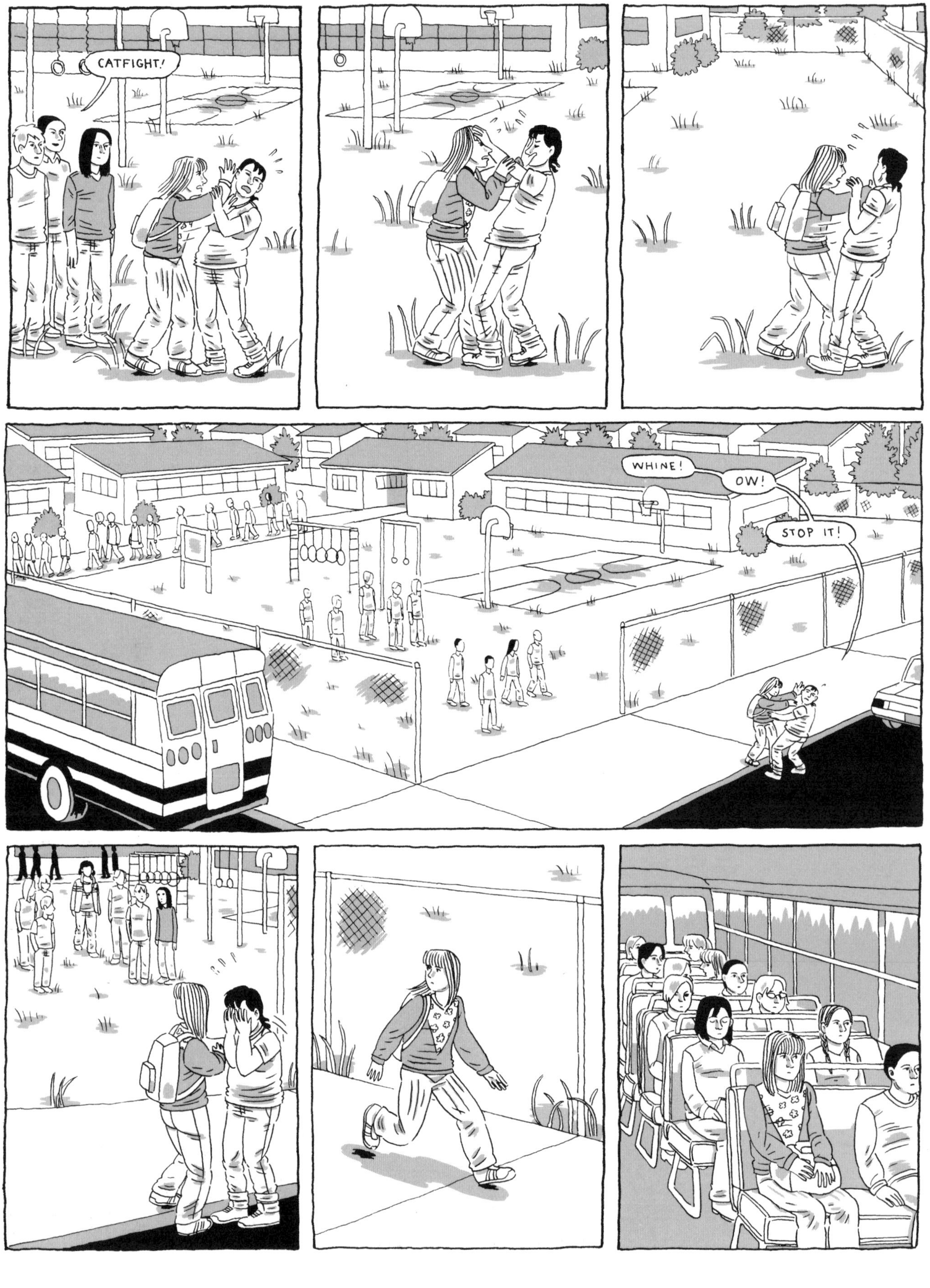
CATFIGHT!
WHINE!
OW!
STOP IT!

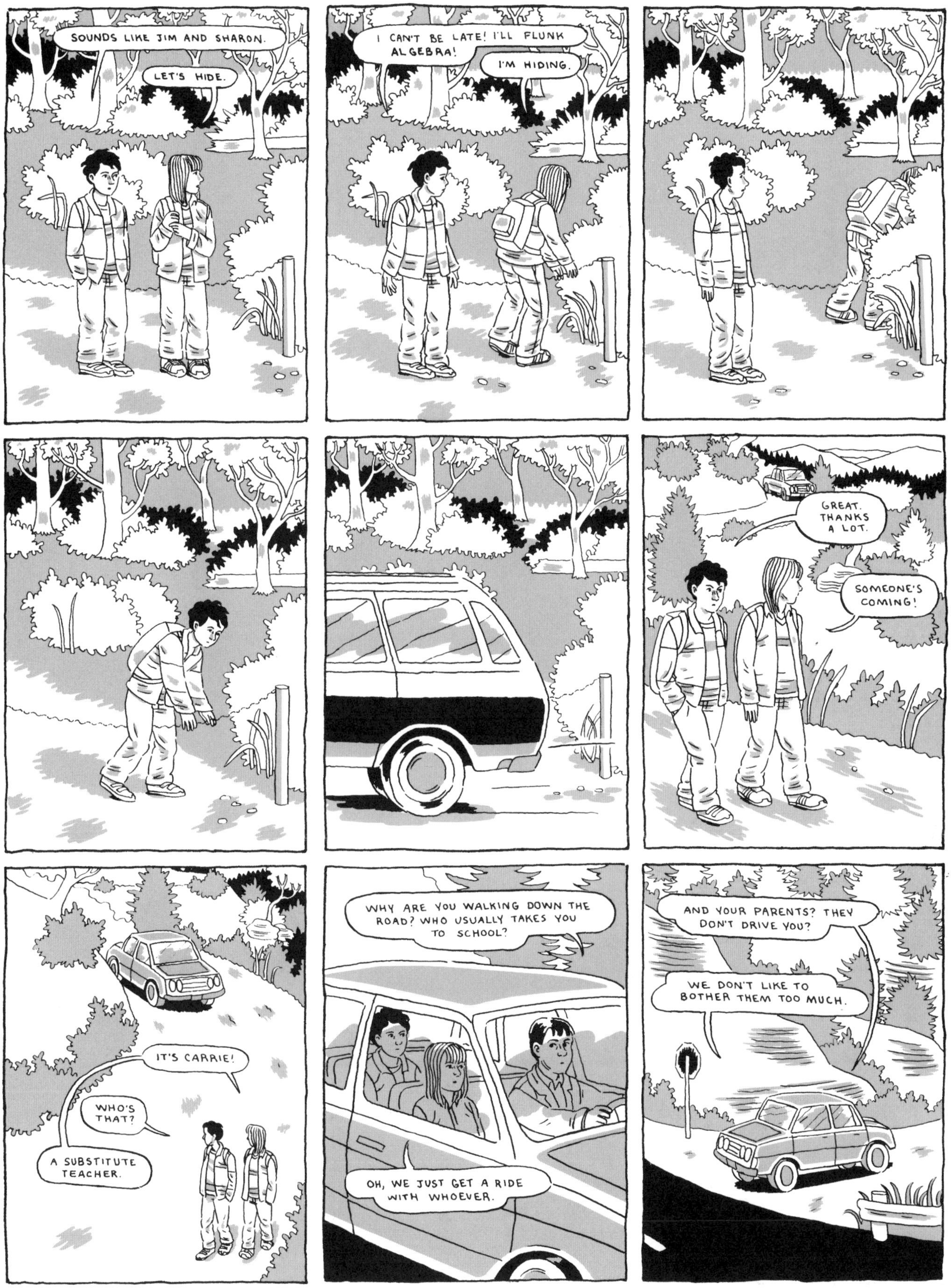
SOUNDS LIKE JIM AND SHARON.
LET'S HIDE.
I CAN'T BE LATE! I'LL FLUNK ALGEBRA!
I'M HIDING.
GREAT. THANKS A LOT.
SOMEONE'S COMING!
IT'S CARRIE!
WHO'S THAT?
A SUBSTITUTE TEACHER.
WHY ARE YOU WALKING DOWN THE ROAD? WHO USUALLY TAKES YOU TO SCHOOL?
OH, WE JUST GET A RIDE WITH WHOEVER.
AND YOUR PARENTS? THEY DON'T DRIVE YOU?
WE DON'T LIKE TO BOTHER THEM TOO MUCH.

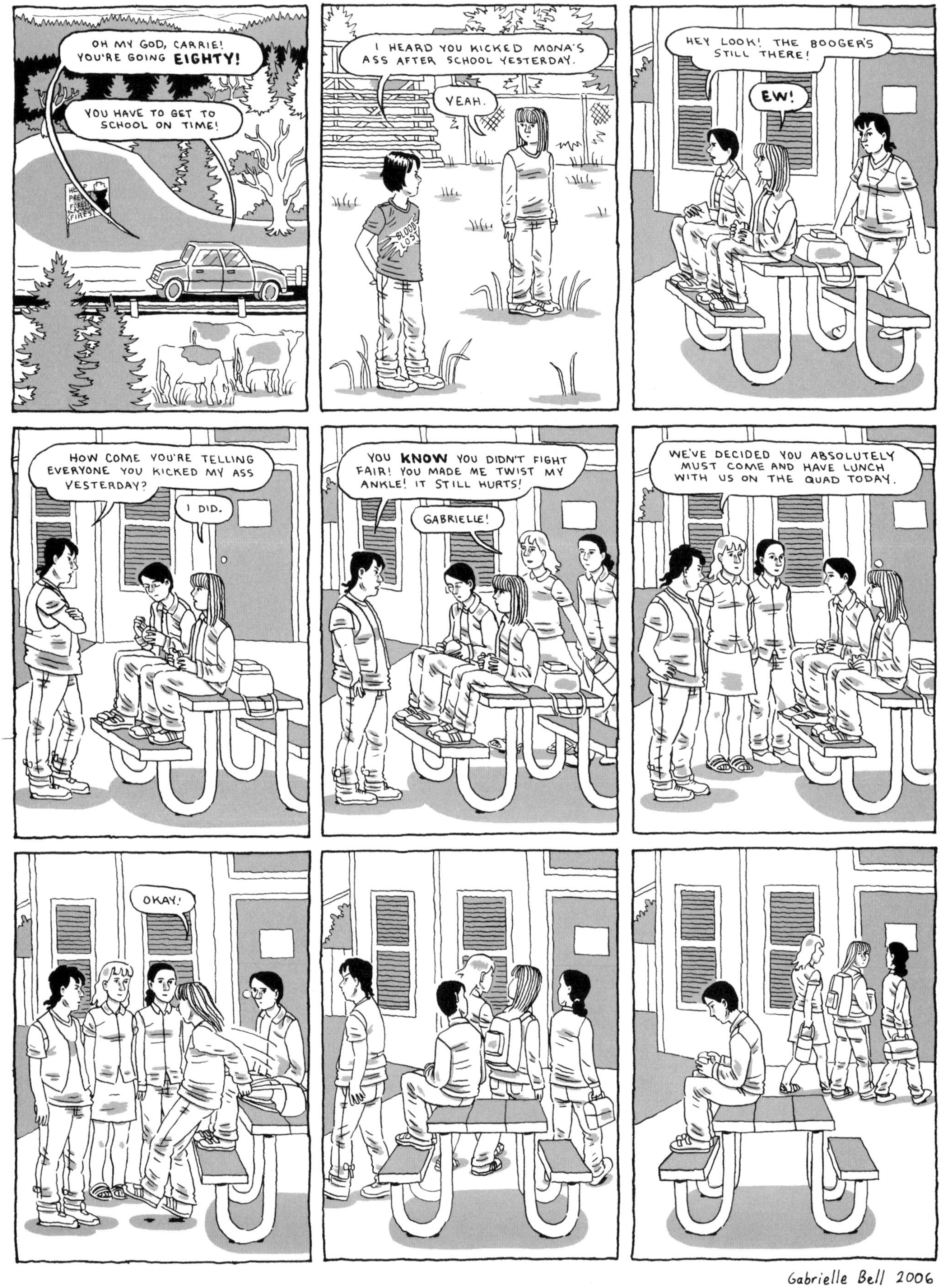
OH MY GOD, CARRIE! YOU'RE GOING EIGHTY!
YOU HAVE TO GET TO SCHOOL ON TIME!
I HEARD YOU KICKED MONA'S ASS AFTER SCHOOL YESTERDAY.
YEAH.
HEY LOOK! THE BOOGER'S STILL THERE!
EW!
HOW COME YOU'RE TELLING EVERYONE YOU KICKED MY ASS YESTERDAY?
I DID.
YOU KNOW YOU DIDN'T FIGHT FAIR! YOU MADE ME TWIST MY ANKLE! IT STILL HURTS!
GABRIELLE!
WE'VE DECIDED YOU ABSOLUTELY MUST COME AND HAVE LUNCH WITH US ON THE QUAD TODAY.
OKAY!
Gabrielle Bell 2006

DASH SHAW

TITLE: "CRATER FACE" AUTHOR: Dash Shaw

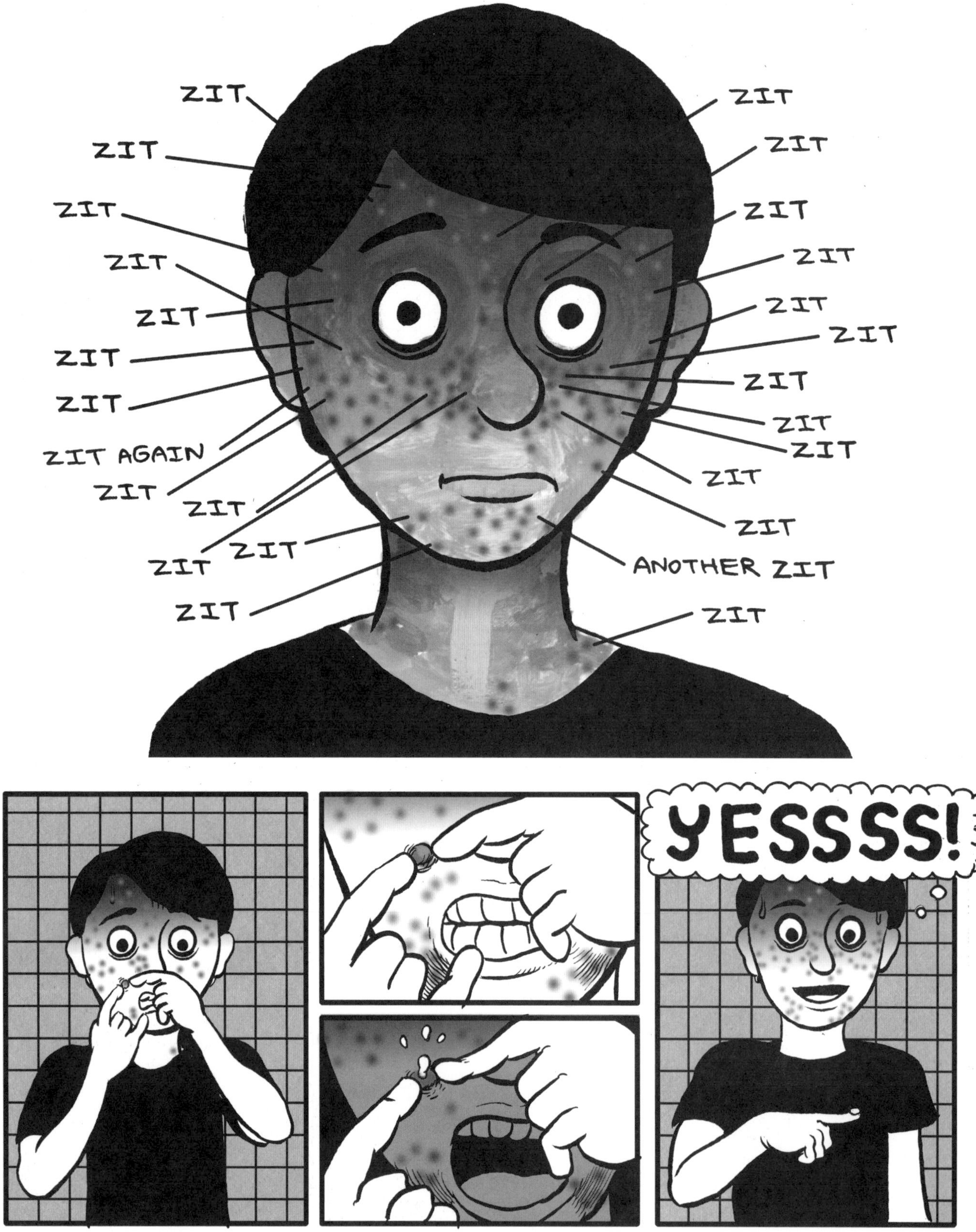

ZIT
ZIT
ZIT
ZIT
ZIT
ZIT
ZIT
ZIT AGAIN
ZIT
ZIT
ZIT
ZIT
ZIT
ZIT
ZIT
ZIT
ZIT
ZIT
ZIT
ZIT
ZIT
ZIT
ZIT
ZIT
ZIT
ANOTHER ZIT
ZIT
YESSSS!

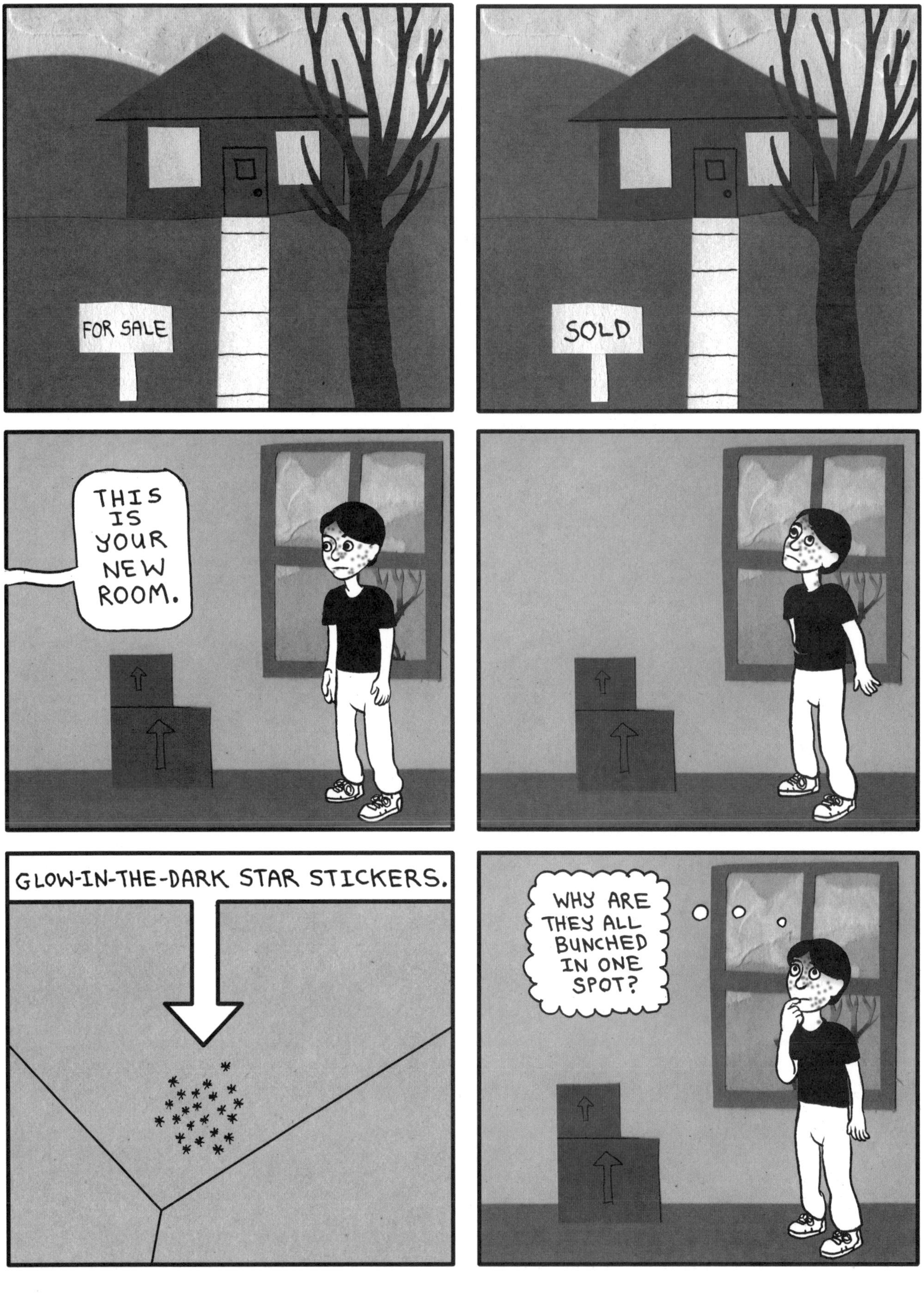
FOR SALE
SOLD
THIS IS YOUR NEW ROOM.
GLOW-IN-THE-DARK STAR STICKERS.
WHY ARE THEY ALL BUNCHED IN ONE SPOT?

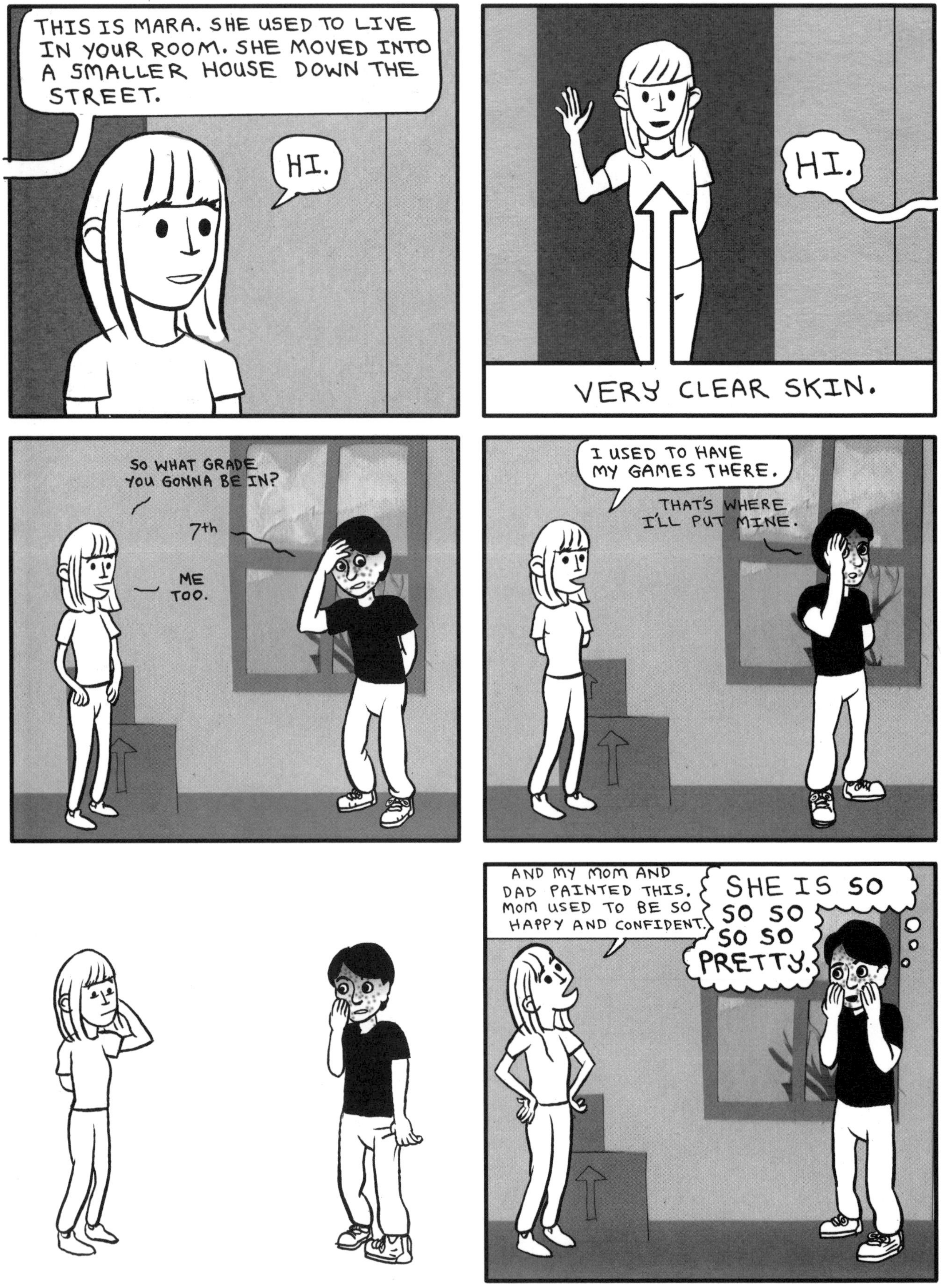

THIS IS MARA. SHE USED TO LIVE IN YOUR ROOM. SHE MOVED INTO A SMALLER HOUSE DOWN THE STREET.
HI.
HI.
VERY CLEAR SKIN.
SO WHAT GRADE YOU GONNA BE IN?
7th
ME TOO.
I USED TO HAVE MY GAMES THERE.
THAT'S WHERE I'LL PUT MINE.
AND MY MOM AND DAD PAINTED THIS. MOM USED TO BE SO HAPPY AND CONFIDENT.
SHE IS SO SO SO SO SO PRETTY.

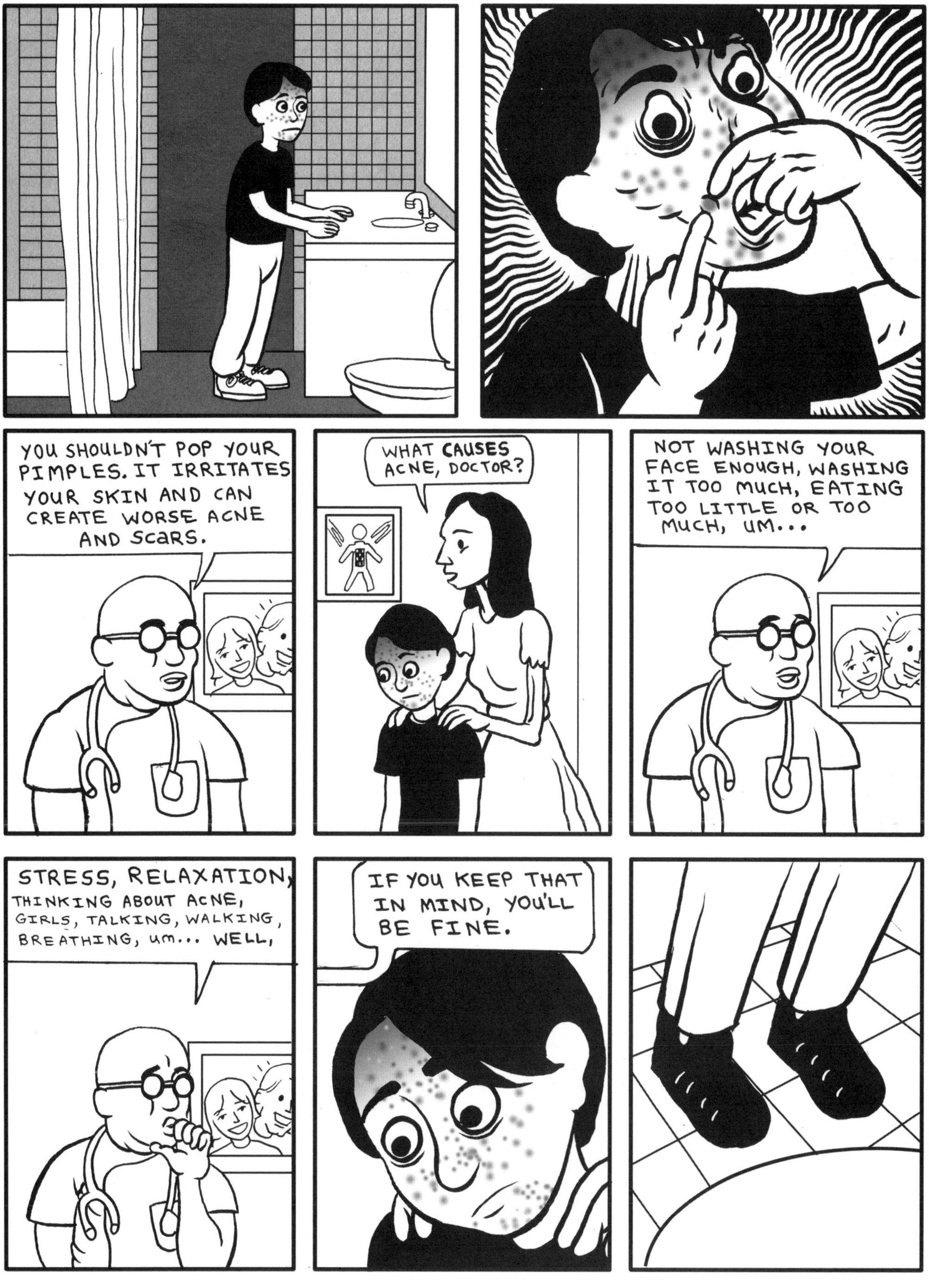
YOU SHOULDN'T POP YOUR PIMPLES. IT IRRITATES YOUR SKIN AND CAN CREATE WORSE ACNE AND SCARS.
WHAT CAUSES ACNE, DOCTOR?
NOT WASHING YOUR FACE ENOUGH, WASHING IT TOO MUCH, EATING TOO LITTLE OR TOO MUCH, UM...
STRESS, RELAXATION, THINKING ABOUT ACNE, GIRLS, TALKING, WALKING, BREATHING, UM... WELL,
IF YOU KEEP THAT IN MIND, YOU'LL BE FINE.

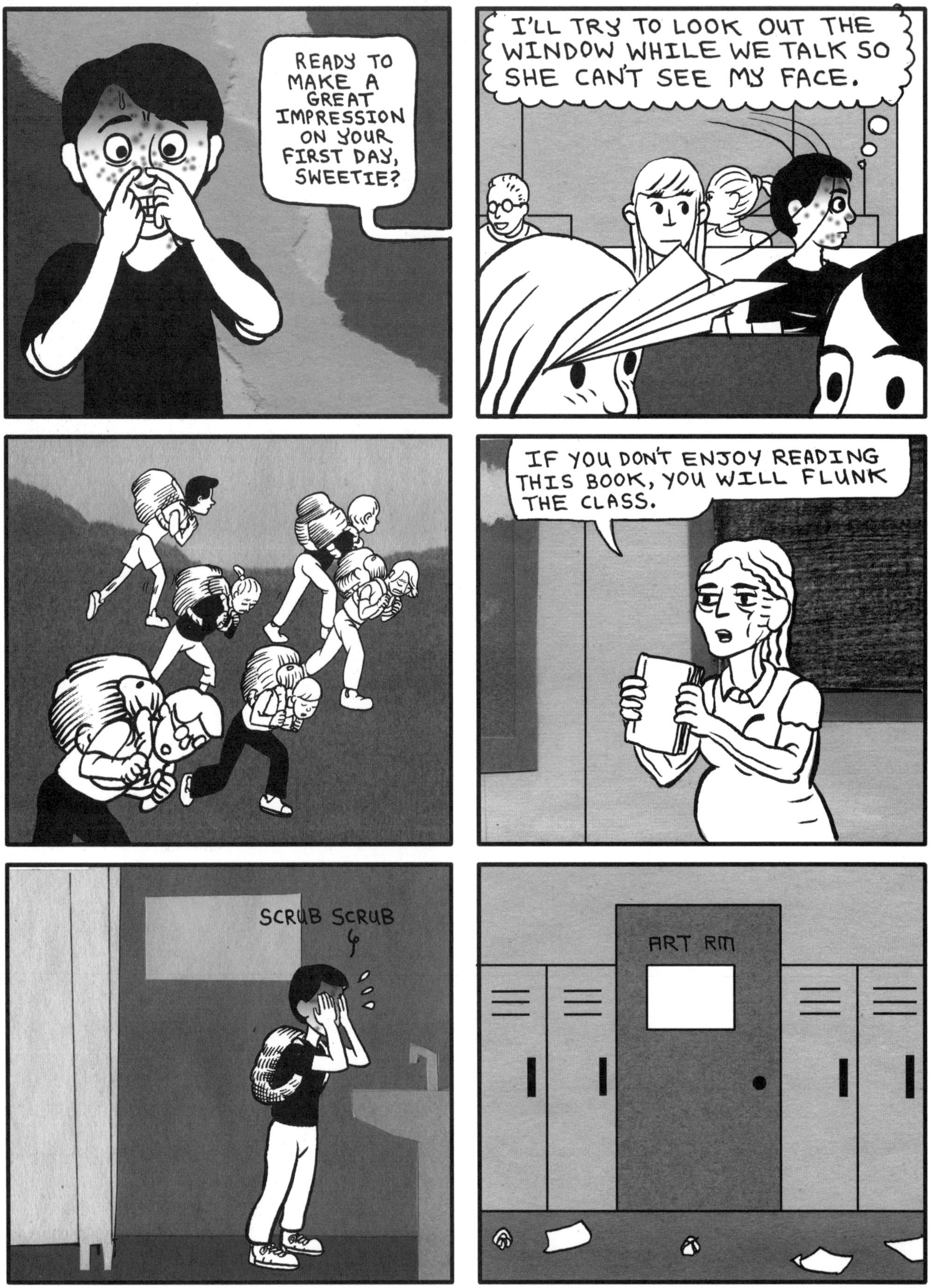
READY TO MAKE A GREAT IMPRESSION ON YOUR FIRST DAY, SWEETIE?
I'LL TRY TO LOOK OUT THE WINDOW WHILE WE TALK SO SHE CAN'T SEE MY FACE.
IF YOU DON'T ENJOY READING THIS BOOK, YOU WILL FLUNK THE CLASS.
SCRUB SCRUB
ART RM

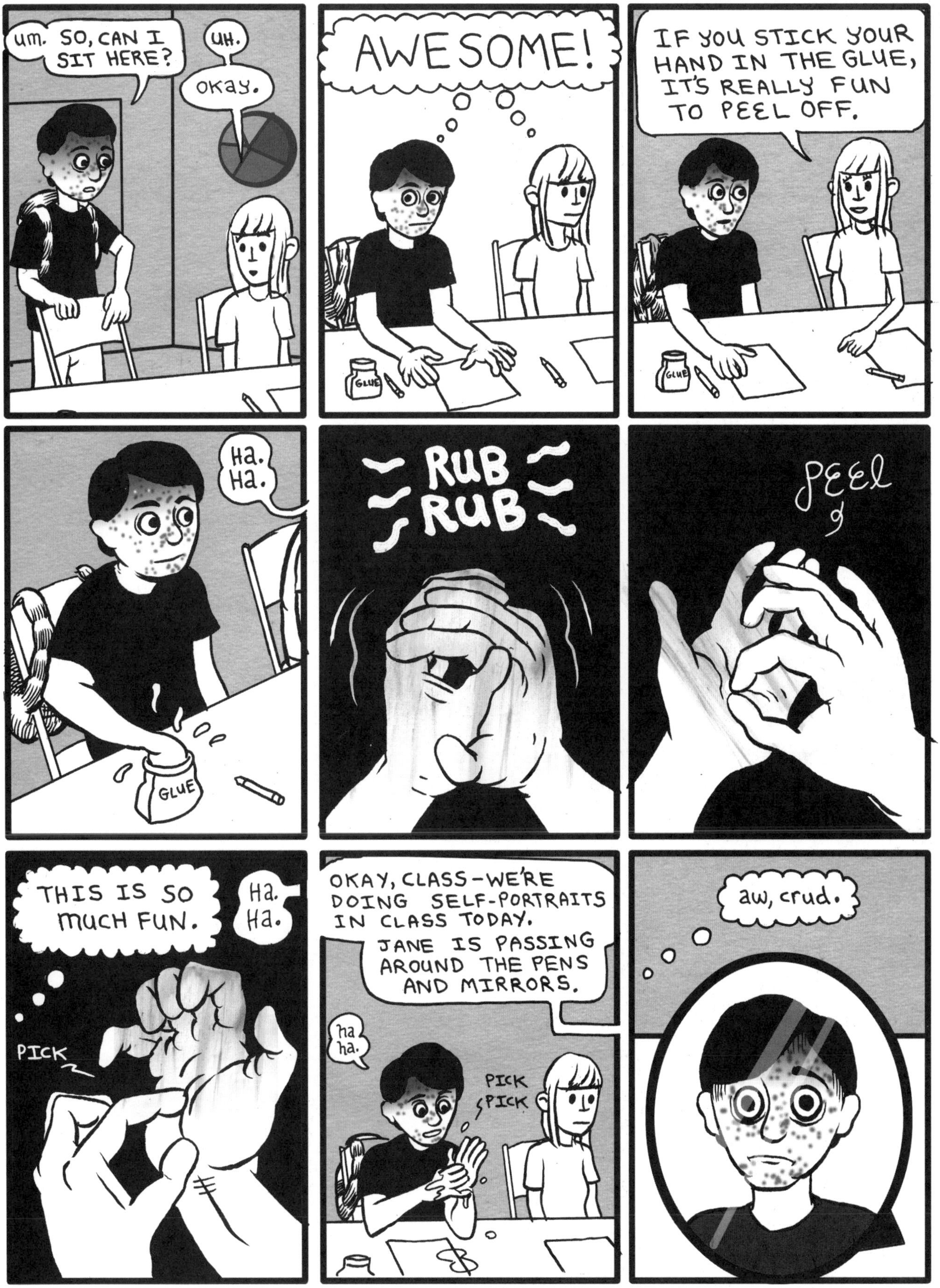
um. SO, CAN I SIT HERE?
UH.
Okay.
AWESOME!
IF YOU STICK YOUR HAND IN THE GLUE, IT'S REALLY FUN TO PEEL OFF.
GLUE
GLUE
Ha. Ha.
GLUE
RUB RUB
PEEL
THIS IS SO much FUN.
Ha. Ha.
PICK
OKAY, CLASS–WE'RE DOING SELF-PORTRAITS IN CLASS TODAY.
JANE IS PASSING AROUND THE PENS AND MIRRORS.
ha ha.
PICK PICK
aw, crud.

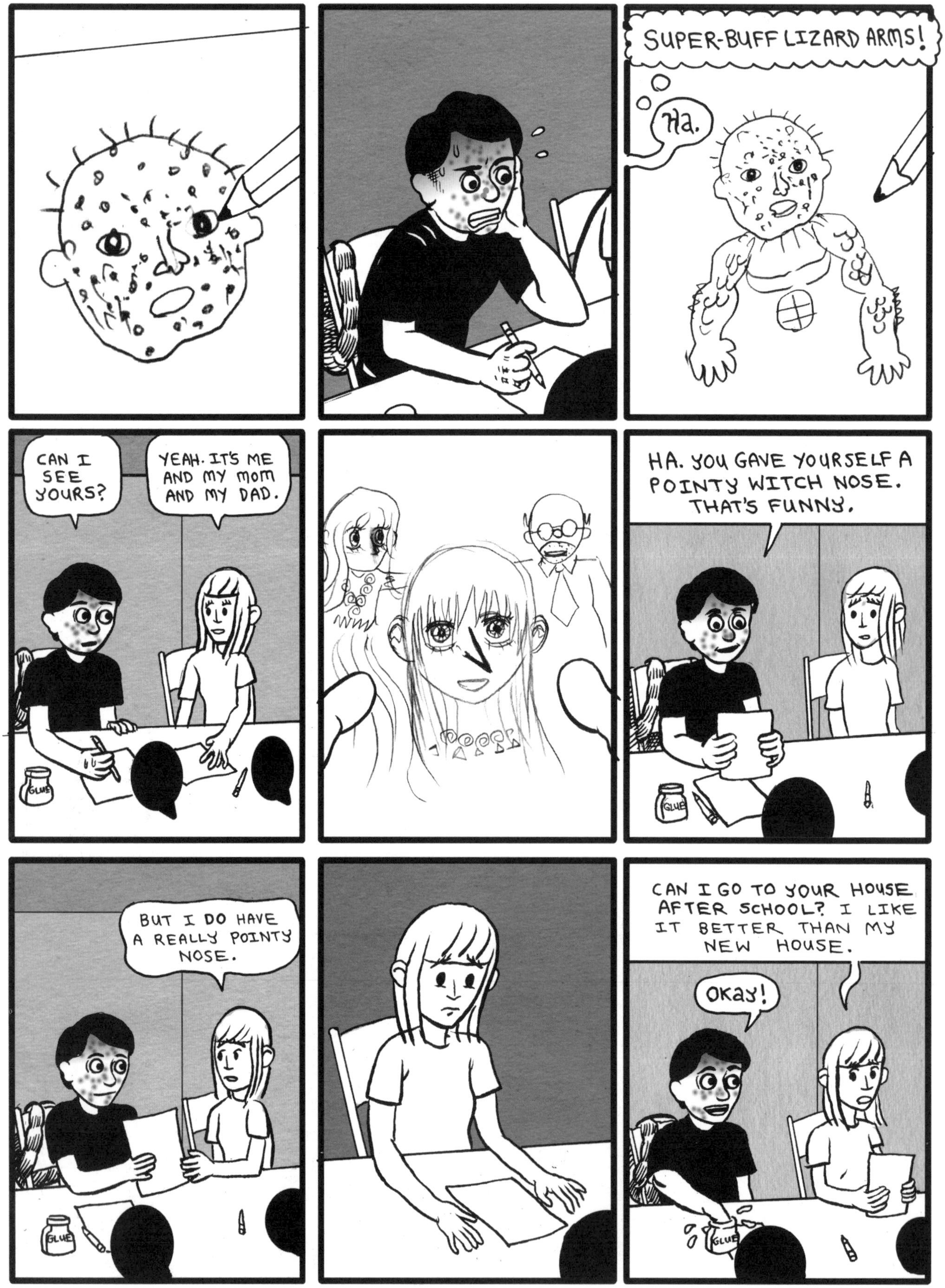
SUPER-BUFF LIZARD ARMS!
HA.
CAN I SEE YOURS?
YEAH. IT'S ME AND MY MOM AND MY DAD.
HA. YOU GAVE YOURSELF A POINTY WITCH NOSE. THAT'S FUNNY.
BUT I DO HAVE A REALLY POINTY NOSE.
CAN I GO TO YOUR HOUSE AFTER SCHOOL? I LIKE IT BETTER THAN MY NEW HOUSE.
OKAY!

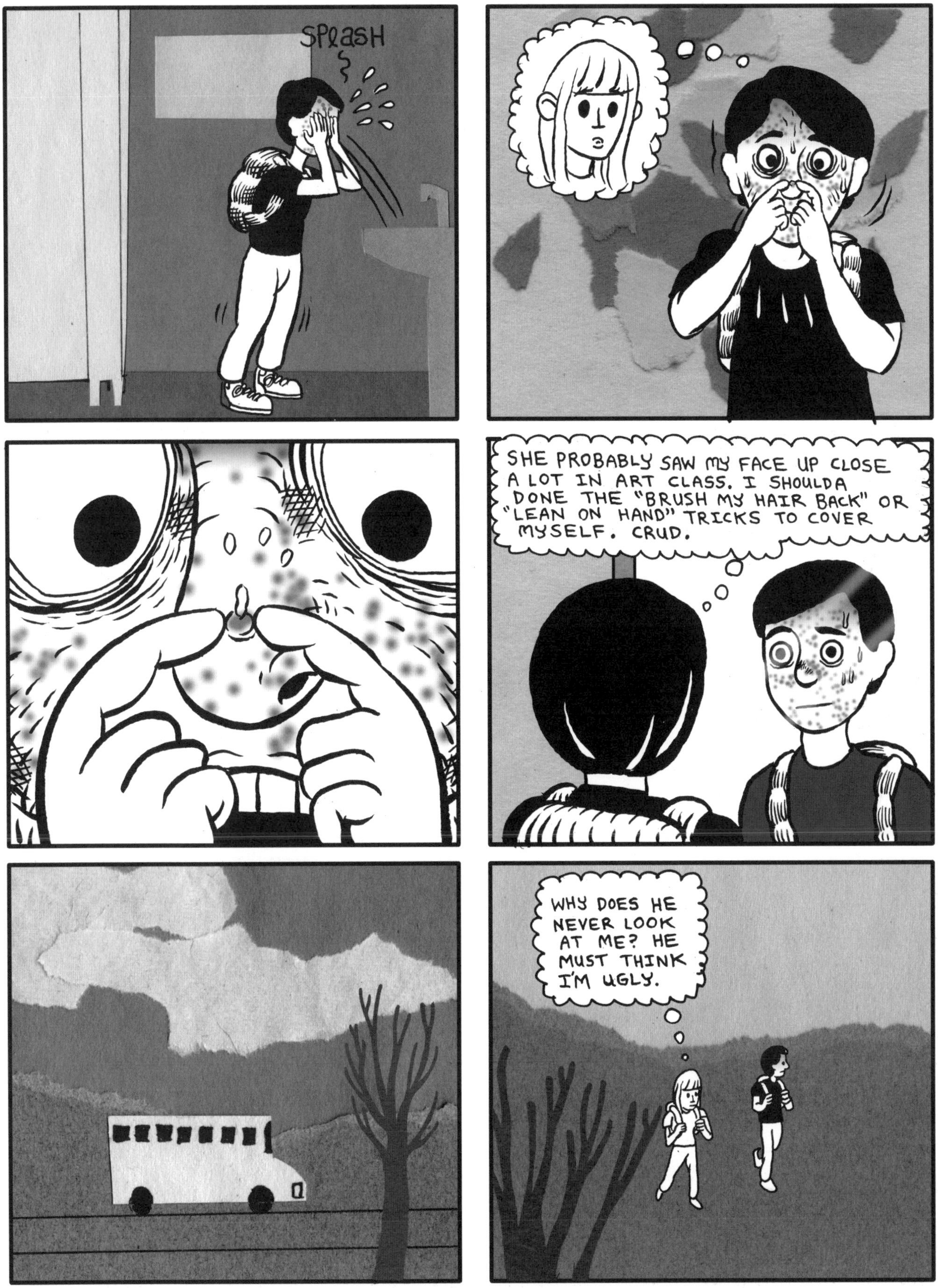
SPLASH
SHE PROBABLY SAW MY FACE UP CLOSE A LOT IN ART CLASS. I SHOULDA DONE THE "BRUSH MY HAIR BACK" OR "LEAN ON HAND" TRICKS TO COVER MYSELF. CRUD.
WHY DOES HE NEVER LOOK AT ME? HE MUST THINK I'M UGLY.

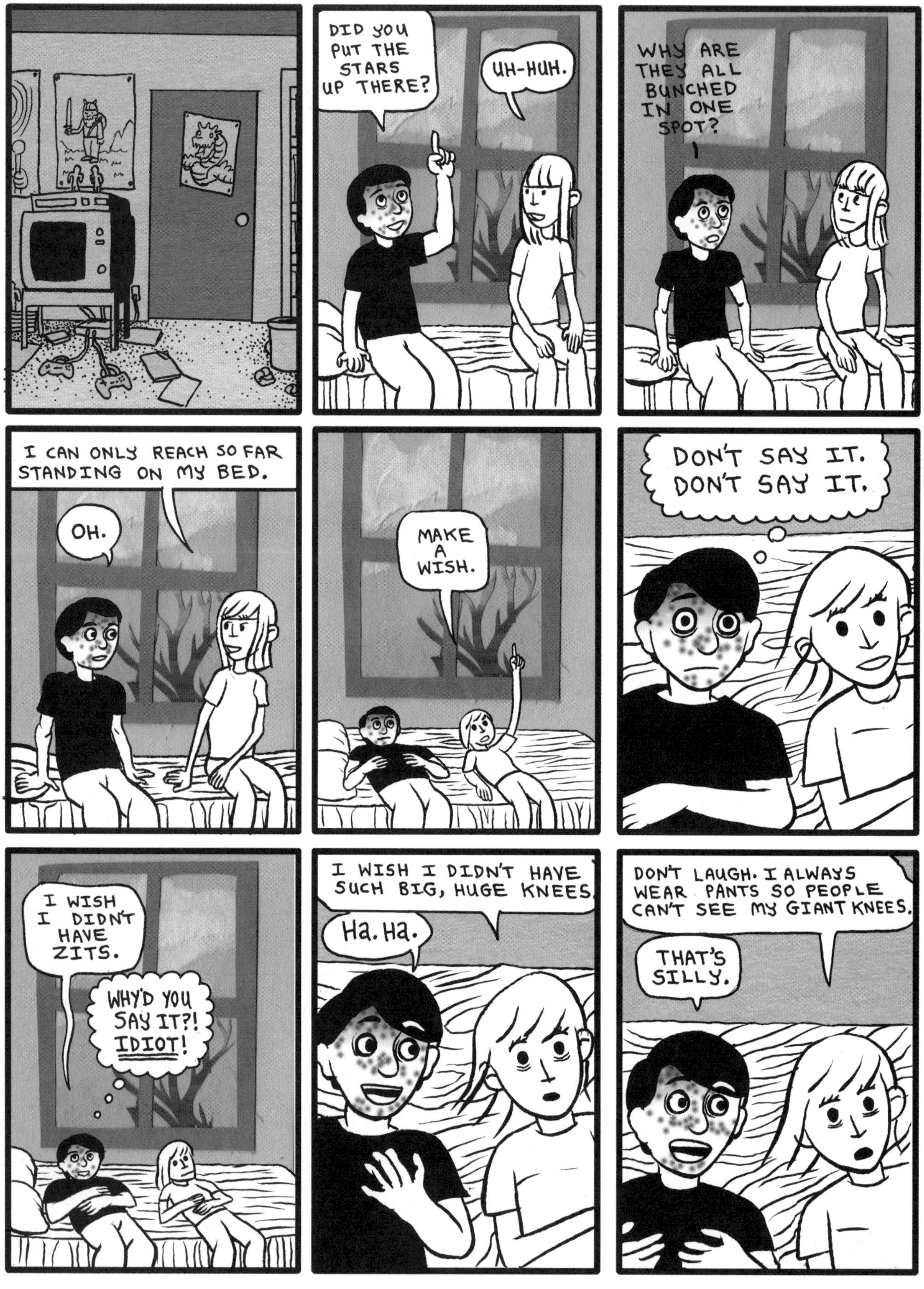
DID YOU PUT THE STARS UP THERE?
UH-HUH.
WHY ARE THEY ALL BUNCHED IN ONE SPOT?
I CAN ONLY REACH SO FAR STANDING ON MY BED.
OH.
MAKE A WISH.
DON'T SAY IT. DON'T SAY IT.
I WISH I DIDN'T HAVE ZITS.
WHY'D YOU SAY IT?! IDIOT!
I WISH I DIDN'T HAVE SUCH BIG, HUGE KNEES.
Ha. Ha.
DON'T LAUGH. I ALWAYS WEAR PANTS SO PEOPLE CAN'T SEE MY GIANT KNEES.
THAT'S SILLY.

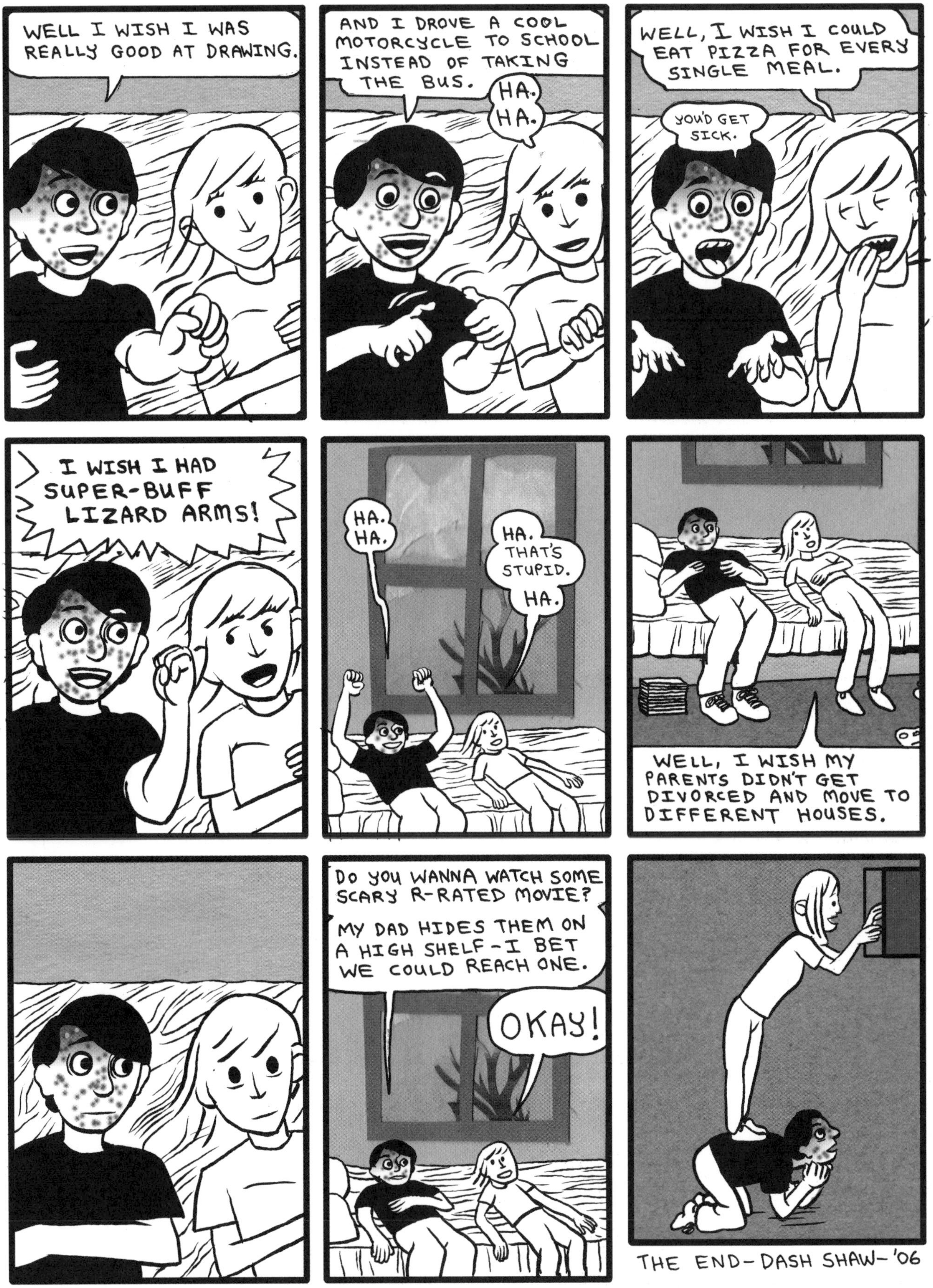
WELL I WISH I WAS REALLY GOOD AT DRAWING.
AND I DROVE A COOL MOTORCYCLE TO SCHOOL INSTEAD OF TAKING THE BUS.
HA. HA.
WELL, I WISH I COULD EAT PIZZA FOR EVERY SINGLE MEAL.
YOU'D GET SICK.
I WISH I HAD SUPER-BUFF LIZARD ARMS!
HA. HA.
HA. THAT'S STUPID. HA.
WELL, I WISH MY PARENTS DIDN'T GET DIVORCED AND MOVE TO DIFFERENT HOUSES.
DO YOU WANNA WATCH SOME SCARY R-RATED MOVIE?
MY DAD HIDES THEM ON A HIGH SHELF - I BET WE COULD REACH ONE.
OKAY!

THE END - DASH SHAW - '06

LAUREN WEINSTEIN

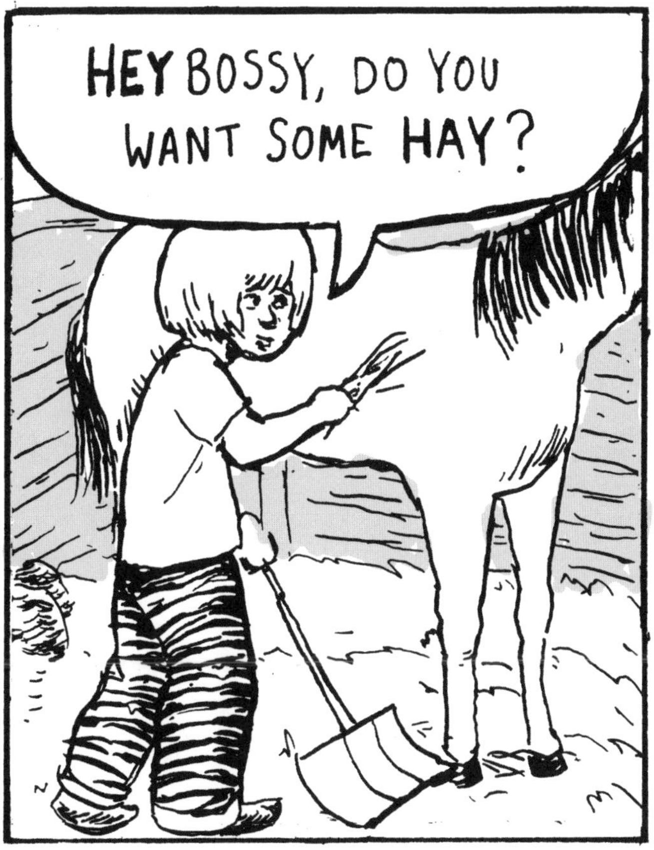
HEY BOSSY, DO YOU WANT SOME HAY?

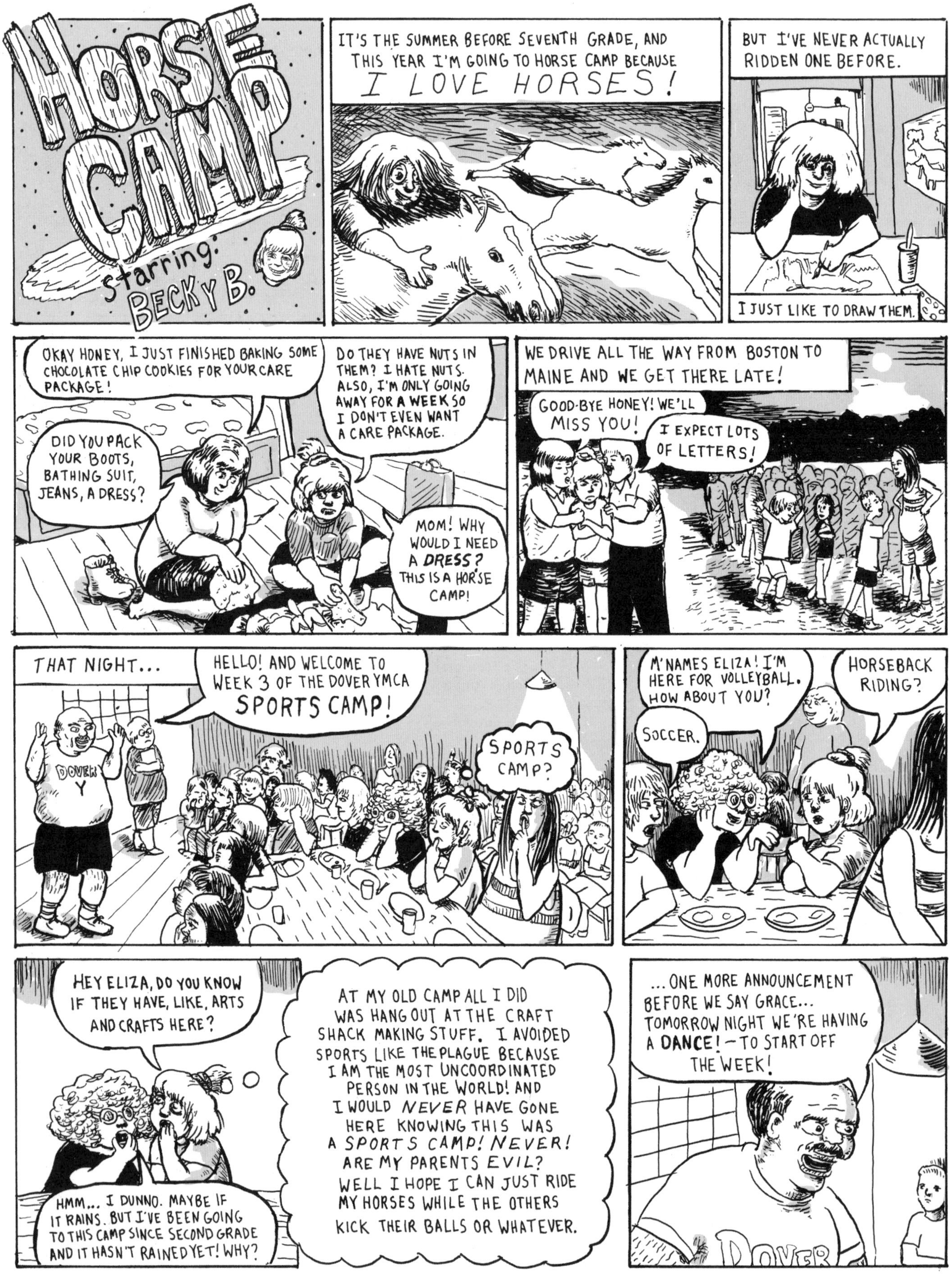
HORSE CAMP
starring: BECKY B.
IT'S THE SUMMER BEFORE SEVENTH GRADE, AND THIS YEAR I'M GOING TO HORSE CAMP BECAUSE I LOVE HORSES!
BUT I'VE NEVER ACTUALLY RIDDEN ONE BEFORE.
I JUST LIKE TO DRAW THEM.
OKAY HONEY, I JUST FINISHED BAKING SOME CHOCOLATE CHIP COOKIES FOR YOUR CARE PACKAGE!
DO THEY HAVE NUTS IN THEM? I HATE NUTS. ALSO, I'M ONLY GOING AWAY FOR A WEEK SO I DON'T EVEN WANT A CARE PACKAGE.
DID YOU PACK YOUR BOOTS, BATHING SUIT, JEANS, A DRESS?
MOM! WHY WOULD I NEED A DRESS? THIS IS A HORSE CAMP!
WE DRIVE ALL THE WAY FROM BOSTON TO MAINE AND WE GET THERE LATE!
GOOD-BYE HONEY! WE'LL MISS YOU!
I EXPECT LOTS OF LETTERS!
THAT NIGHT...
HELLO! AND WELCOME TO WEEK 3 OF THE DOVER YMCA SPORTS CAMP!
DOVER Y
SPORTS CAMP?
M'NAMES ELIZA! I'M HERE FOR VOLLEYBALL. HOW ABOUT YOU?
SOCCER.
HORSEBACK RIDING?
HEY ELIZA, DO YOU KNOW IF THEY HAVE, LIKE, ARTS AND CRAFTS HERE?
HMM... I DUNNO. MAYBE IF IT RAINS. BUT I'VE BEEN GOING TO THIS CAMP SINCE SECOND GRADE AND IT HASN'T RAINED YET! WHY?
AT MY OLD CAMP ALL I DID WAS HANG OUT AT THE CRAFT SHACK MAKING STUFF. I AVOIDED SPORTS LIKE THE PLAGUE BECAUSE I AM THE MOST UNCOORDINATED PERSON IN THE WORLD! AND I WOULD NEVER HAVE GONE HERE KNOWING THIS WAS A SPORTS CAMP! NEVER! ARE MY PARENTS EVIL? WELL I HOPE I CAN JUST RIDE MY HORSES WHILE THE OTHERS KICK THEIR BALLS OR WHATEVER.
...ONE MORE ANNOUNCEMENT BEFORE WE SAY GRACE... TOMORROW NIGHT WE'RE HAVING A DANCE! —TO START OFF THE WEEK!
DOVER

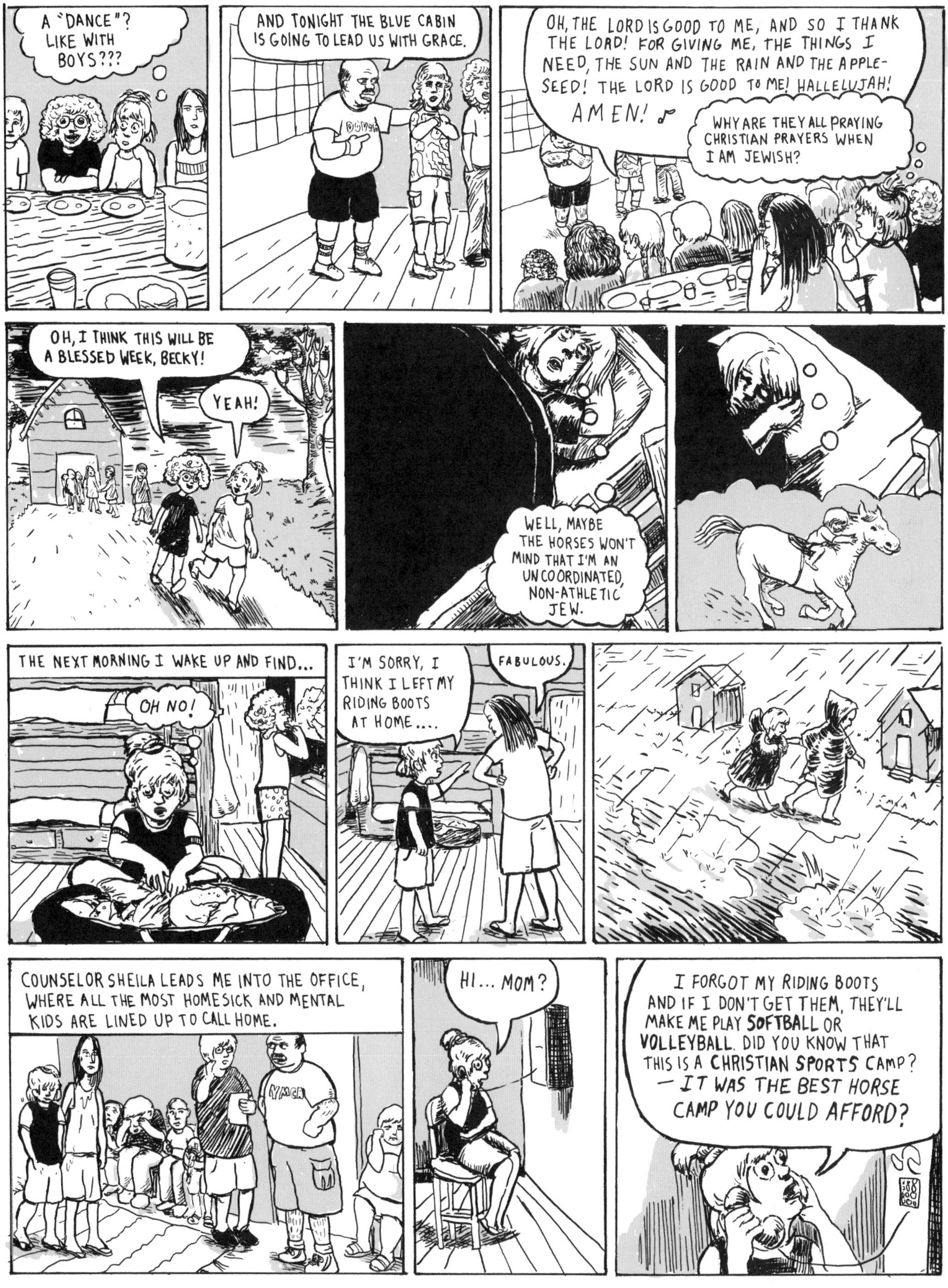
A "DANCE"? LIKE WITH BOYS???
AND TONIGHT THE BLUE CABIN IS GOING TO LEAD US WITH GRACE.
OH, THE LORD IS GOOD TO ME, AND SO I THANK THE LORD! FOR GIVING ME, THE THINGS I NEED, THE SUN AND THE RAIN AND THE APPLE-SEED! THE LORD IS GOOD TO ME! HALLELUJAH! AMEN!
WHY ARE THEY ALL PRAYING CHRISTIAN PRAYERS WHEN I AM JEWISH?
OH, I THINK THIS WILL BE A BLESSED WEEK, BECKY!
YEAH!
WELL, MAYBE THE HORSES WON'T MIND THAT I'M AN UNCOORDINATED, NON-ATHLETIC JEW.
THE NEXT MORNING I WAKE UP AND FIND...
OH NO!
I'M SORRY, I THINK I LEFT MY RIDING BOOTS AT HOME....
FABULOUS.
COUNSELOR SHEILA LEADS ME INTO THE OFFICE, WHERE ALL THE MOST HOMESICK AND MENTAL KIDS ARE LINED UP TO CALL HOME.
YMCA
HI... MOM?
I FORGOT MY RIDING BOOTS AND IF I DON'T GET THEM, THEY'LL MAKE ME PLAY SOFTBALL OR VOLLEYBALL. DID YOU KNOW THAT THIS IS A CHRISTIAN SPORTS CAMP? — IT WAS THE BEST HORSE CAMP YOU COULD AFFORD?

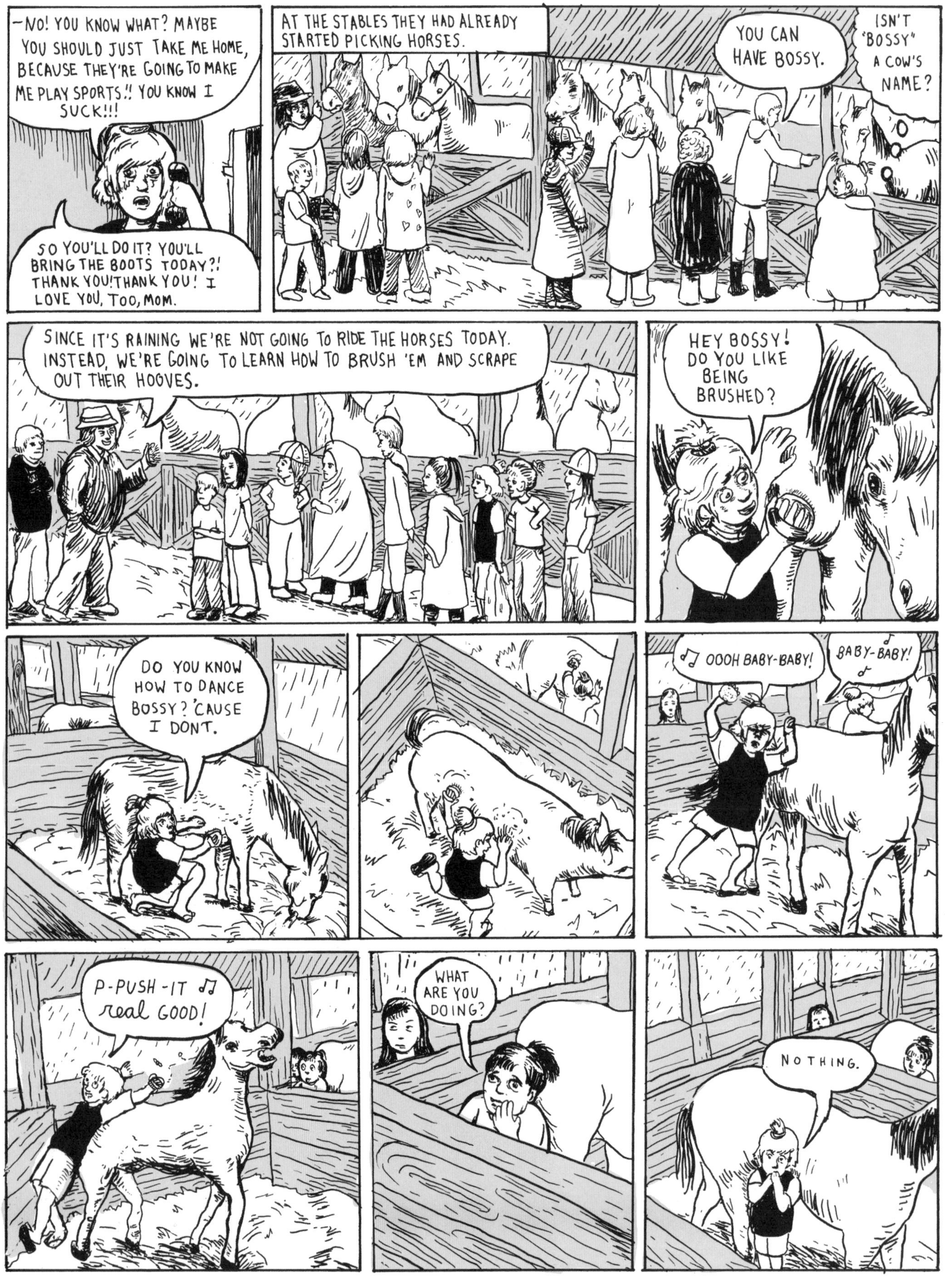

–NO! YOU KNOW WHAT? MAYBE YOU SHOULD JUST TAKE ME HOME, BECAUSE THEY'RE GOING TO MAKE ME PLAY SPORTS!! YOU KNOW I SUCK!!!
SO YOU'LL DO IT? YOU'LL BRING THE BOOTS TODAY?! THANK YOU! THANK YOU! I LOVE YOU, TOO, MOM.
AT THE STABLES THEY HAD ALREADY STARTED PICKING HORSES.
YOU CAN HAVE BOSSY.
ISN'T "BOSSY" A COW'S NAME?
SINCE IT'S RAINING WE'RE NOT GOING TO RIDE THE HORSES TODAY. INSTEAD, WE'RE GOING TO LEARN HOW TO BRUSH 'EM AND SCRAPE OUT THEIR HOOVES.
HEY BOSSY! DO YOU LIKE BEING BRUSHED?
DO YOU KNOW HOW TO DANCE BOSSY? 'CAUSE I DONT.
♫ OOOH BABY-BABY!
BABY-BABY! ♪
P-PUSH-IT ♫ real GOOD!
WHAT ARE YOU DOING?
NOTHING.

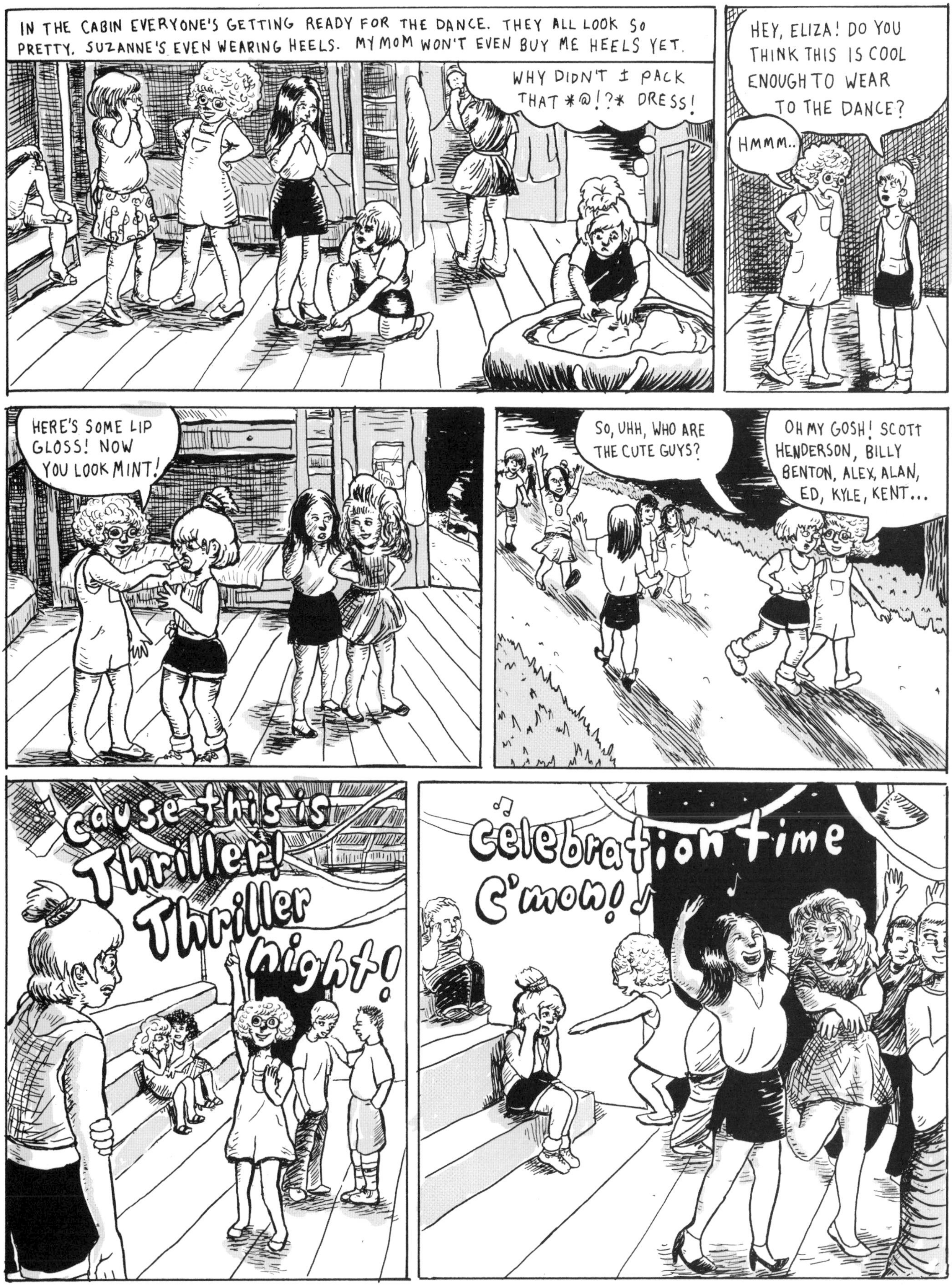
IN THE CABIN EVERYONE'S GETTING READY FOR THE DANCE. THEY ALL LOOK SO PRETTY. SUZANNE'S EVEN WEARING HEELS. MY MOM WON'T EVEN BUY ME HEELS YET.
WHY DIDN'T I PACK THAT *@!?* DRESS!
HEY, ELIZA! DO YOU THINK THIS IS COOL ENOUGH TO WEAR TO THE DANCE?
HMMM..
HERE'S SOME LIP GLOSS! NOW YOU LOOK MINT!
SO, UHH, WHO ARE THE CUTE GUYS?
OH MY GOSH! SCOTT HENDERSON, BILLY BENTON, ALEX, ALAN, ED, KYLE, KENT...
cause this is Thriller! Thriller night!
celebration time C'mon!

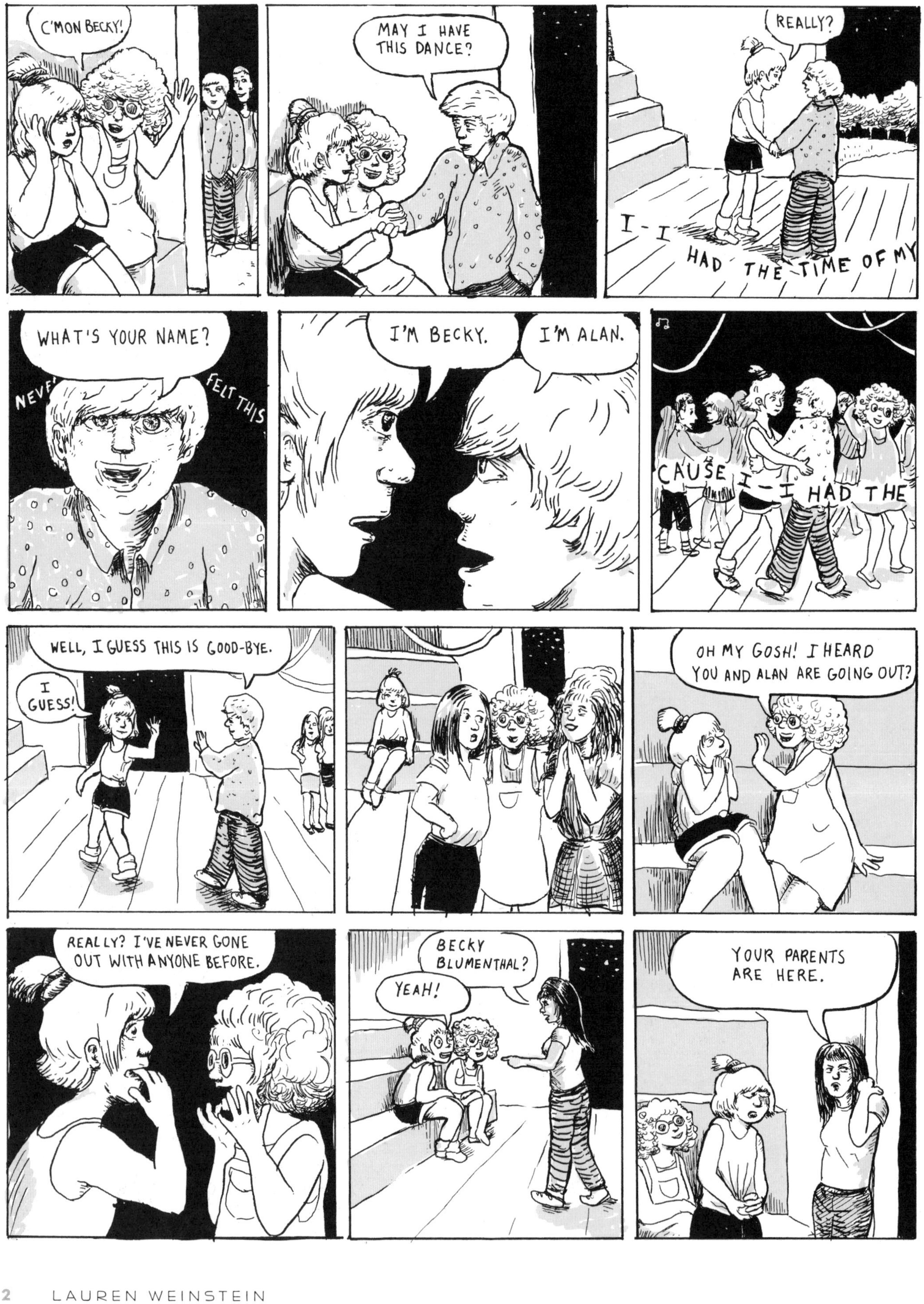
C'MON BECKY!
MAY I HAVE THIS DANCE?
REALLY?
I-I HAD THE TIME OF MY
WHAT'S YOUR NAME?
NEVE
FELT THIS
I'M BECKY.
I'M ALAN.
CAUSE I-I HAD THE
WELL, I GUESS THIS IS GOOD-BYE.
I GUESS!
OH MY GOSH! I HEARD YOU AND ALAN ARE GOING OUT?
REALLY? I'VE NEVER GONE OUT WITH ANYONE BEFORE.
BECKY BLUMENTHAL?
YEAH!
YOUR PARENTS ARE HERE.

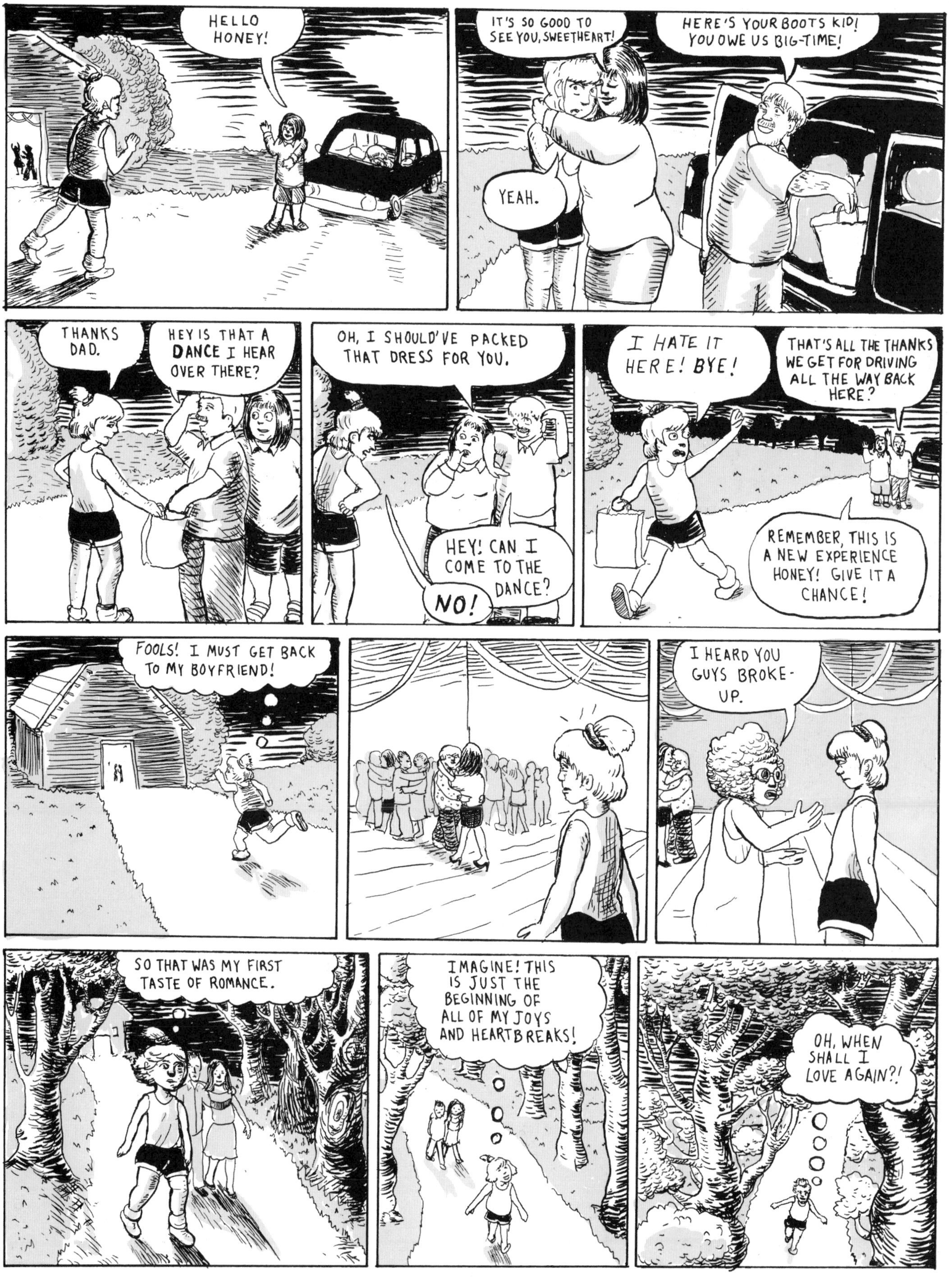
HELLO HONEY!
IT'S SO GOOD TO SEE YOU, SWEETHEART!
YEAH.
HERE'S YOUR BOOTS KID! YOU OWE US BIG-TIME!
THANKS DAD.
HEY IS THAT A DANCE I HEAR OVER THERE?
OH, I SHOULD'VE PACKED THAT DRESS FOR YOU.
HEY! CAN I COME TO THE DANCE?
NO!
I HATE IT HERE! BYE!
THAT'S ALL THE THANKS WE GET FOR DRIVING ALL THE WAY BACK HERE?
REMEMBER, THIS IS A NEW EXPERIENCE HONEY! GIVE IT A CHANCE!
FOOLS! I MUST GET BACK TO MY BOYFRIEND!
I HEARD YOU GUYS BROKE-UP.
SO THAT WAS MY FIRST TASTE OF ROMANCE.
IMAGINE! THIS IS JUST THE BEGINNING OF ALL OF MY JOYS AND HEARTBREAKS!
OH, WHEN SHALL I LOVE AGAIN?!

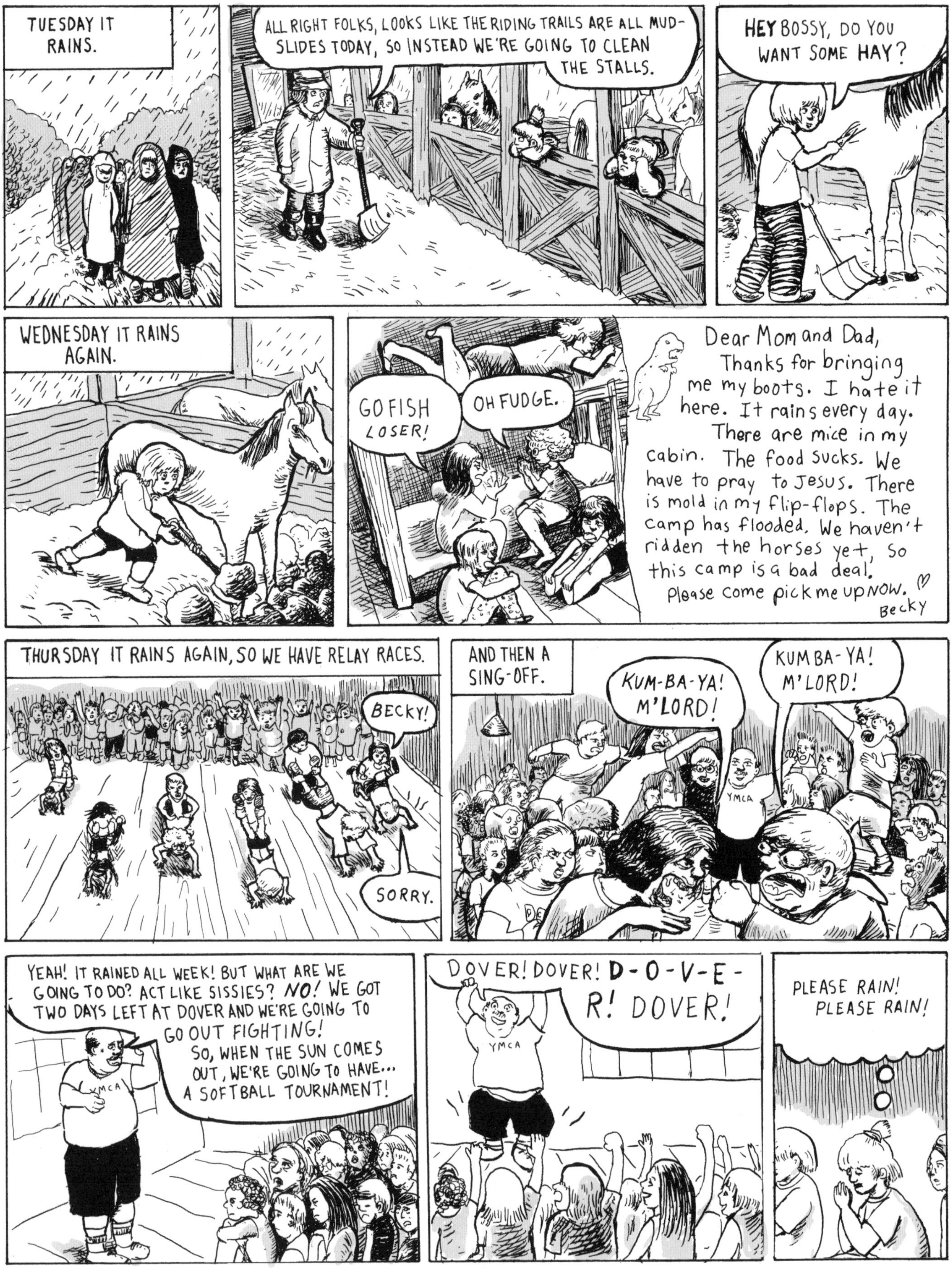
TUESDAY IT RAINS.
ALL RIGHT FOLKS, LOOKS LIKE THE RIDING TRAILS ARE ALL MUD-SLIDES TODAY, SO INSTEAD WE'RE GOING TO CLEAN THE STALLS.
HEY BOSSY, DO YOU WANT SOME HAY?
WEDNESDAY IT RAINS AGAIN.
GO FISH LOSER!
OH FUDGE.
Dear Mom and Dad,
Thanks for bringing me my boots. I hate it here. It rains every day. There are mice in my cabin. The food sucks. We have to pray to Jesus. There is mold in my flip-flops. The camp has flooded. We haven't ridden the horses yet, so this camp is a bad deal.
Please come pick me up NOW.
Becky
THURSDAY IT RAINS AGAIN, SO WE HAVE RELAY RACES.
BECKY!
SORRY.
AND THEN A SING-OFF.
KUM-BA-YA! M'LORD!
KUM BA-YA! M'LORD!
YMCA
YEAH! IT RAINED ALL WEEK! BUT WHAT ARE WE GOING TO DO? ACT LIKE SISSIES? NO! WE GOT TWO DAYS LEFT AT DOVER AND WE'RE GOING TO GO OUT FIGHTING!
SO, WHEN THE SUN COMES OUT, WE'RE GOING TO HAVE... A SOFTBALL TOURNAMENT!
YMCA
DOVER! DOVER! D-O-V-E-R! DOVER!
YMCA
PLEASE RAIN! PLEASE RAIN!

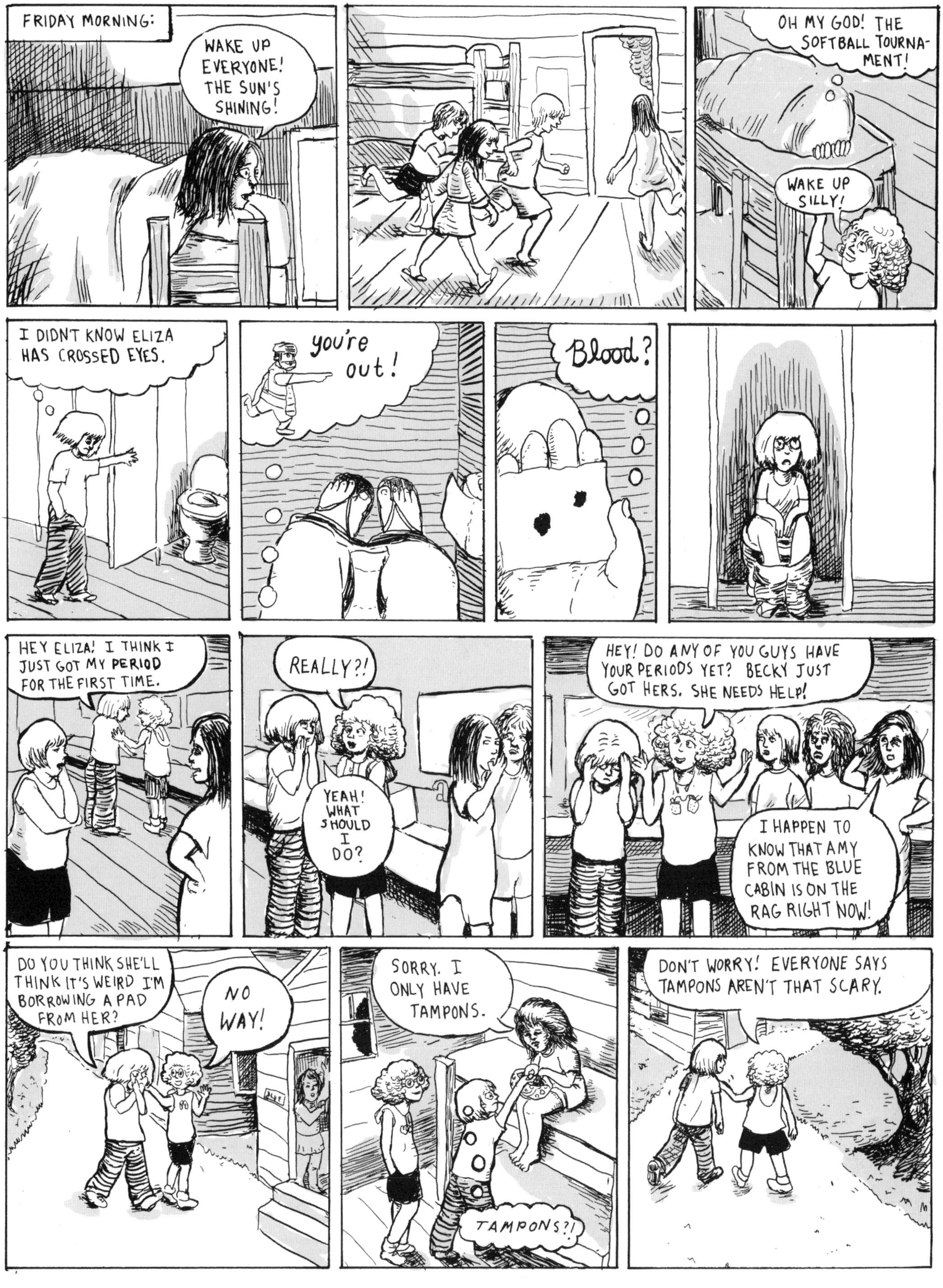
FRIDAY MORNING:
WAKE UP EVERYONE! THE SUN'S SHINING!
OH MY GOD! THE SOFTBALL TOURNAMENT!
WAKE UP SILLY!
I DIDN'T KNOW ELIZA HAS CROSSED EYES.
you're out!
Blood?
HEY ELIZA! I THINK I JUST GOT MY PERIOD FOR THE FIRST TIME.
REALLY?!
YEAH! WHAT SHOULD I DO?
HEY! DO ANY OF YOU GUYS HAVE YOUR PERIODS YET? BECKY JUST GOT HERS. SHE NEEDS HELP!
I HAPPEN TO KNOW THAT AMY FROM THE BLUE CABIN IS ON THE RAG RIGHT NOW!
DO YOU THINK SHE'LL THINK IT'S WEIRD I'M BORROWING A PAD FROM HER?
NO WAY!
SORRY. I ONLY HAVE TAMPONS.
TAMPONS?!
DON'T WORRY! EVERYONE SAYS TAMPONS AREN'T THAT SCARY.

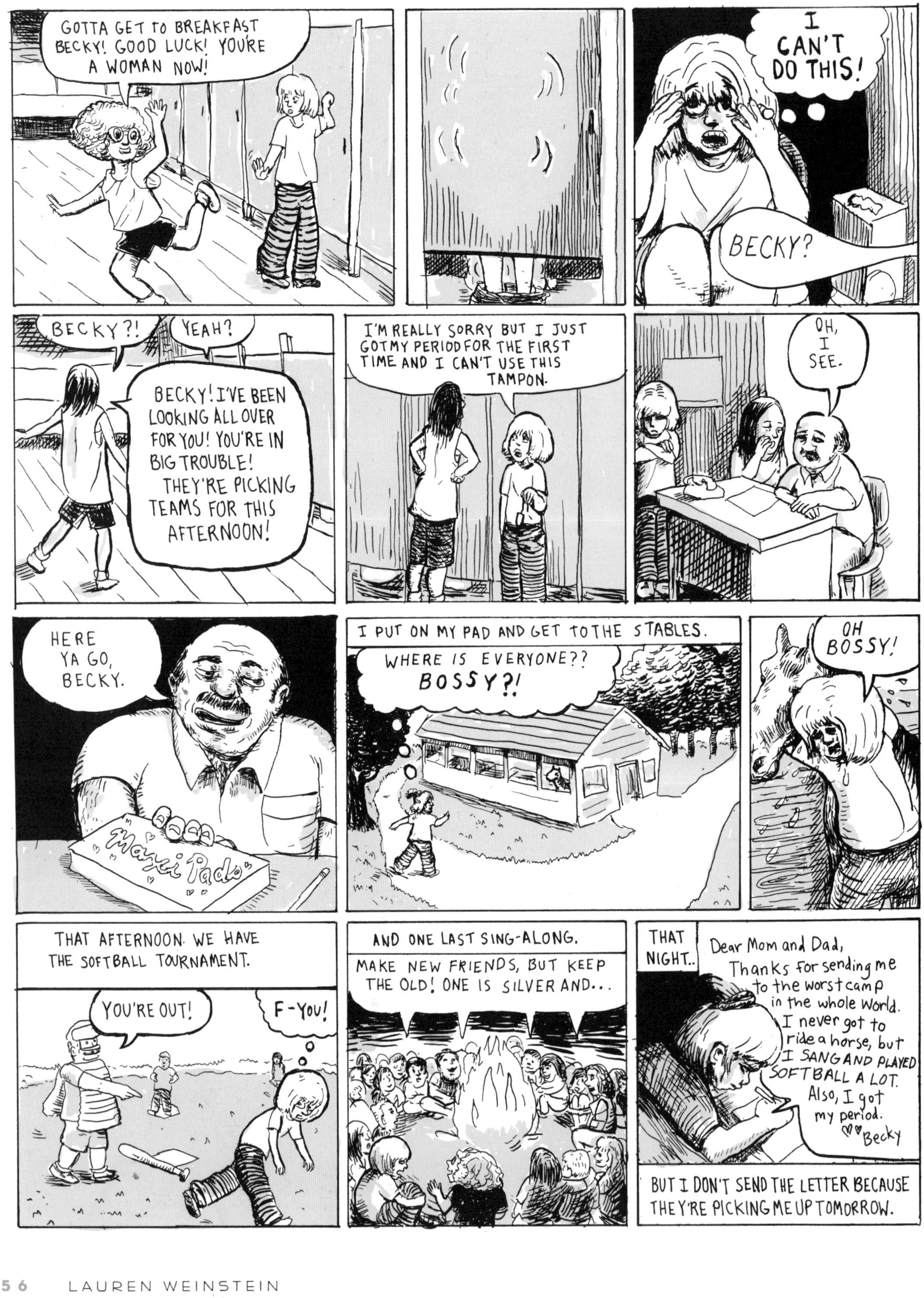
GOTTA GET TO BREAKFAST BECKY! GOOD LUCK! YOU'RE A WOMAN NOW!
I CAN'T DO THIS!
BECKY?
BECKY?!
YEAH?
BECKY! I'VE BEEN LOOKING ALL OVER FOR YOU! YOU'RE IN BIG TROUBLE! THEY'RE PICKING TEAMS FOR THIS AFTERNOON!
I'M REALLY SORRY BUT I JUST GOT MY PERIOD FOR THE FIRST TIME AND I CAN'T USE THIS TAMPON.
OH, I SEE.
HERE YA GO, BECKY.
Maxi Pads
I PUT ON MY PAD AND GET TO THE STABLES.
WHERE IS EVERYONE?? BOSSY?!
OH BOSSY!
THAT AFTERNOON WE HAVE THE SOFTBALL TOURNAMENT.
YOU'RE OUT!
F-YOU!
AND ONE LAST SING-ALONG.
MAKE NEW FRIENDS, BUT KEEP THE OLD! ONE IS SILVER AND...
THAT NIGHT..
Dear Mom and Dad, Thanks for sending me to the worst camp in the whole world. I never got to ride a horse, but I SANG AND PLAYED SOFTBALL A LOT. Also, I got my period. Becky
BUT I DON'T SEND THE LETTER BECAUSE THEY'RE PICKING ME UP TOMORROW.

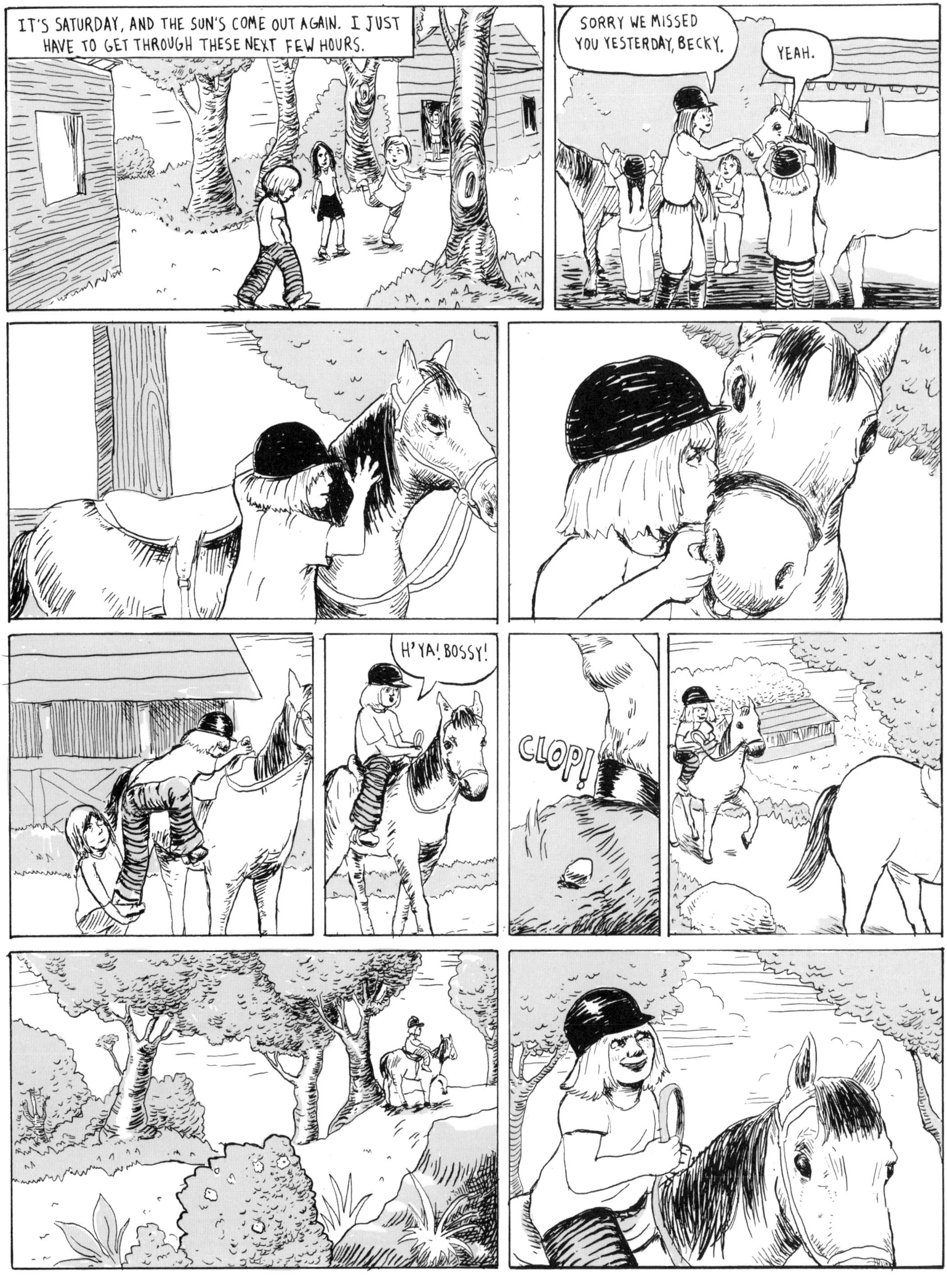
IT'S SATURDAY, AND THE SUN'S COME OUT AGAIN. I JUST HAVE TO GET THROUGH THESE NEXT FEW HOURS.
SORRY WE MISSED YOU YESTERDAY, BECKY.
YEAH.
H'YA! BOSSY!
CLOP!

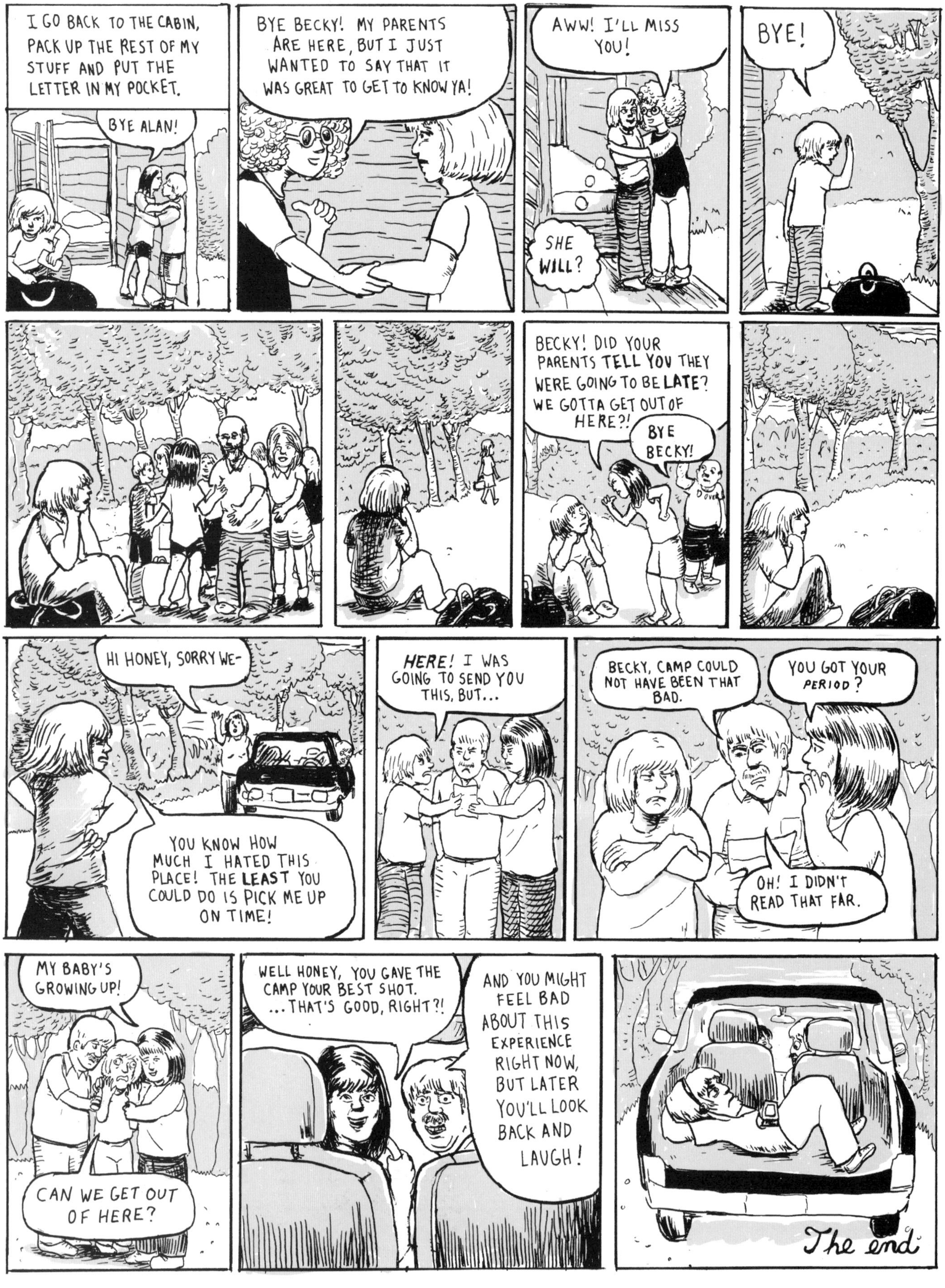
I GO BACK TO THE CABIN, PACK UP THE REST OF MY STUFF AND PUT THE LETTER IN MY POCKET.
BYE ALAN!
BYE BECKY! MY PARENTS ARE HERE, BUT I JUST WANTED TO SAY THAT IT WAS GREAT TO GET TO KNOW YA!
AWW! I'LL MISS YOU!
SHE WILL?
BYE!
BECKY! DID YOUR PARENTS TELL YOU THEY WERE GOING TO BE LATE? WE GOTTA GET OUT OF HERE?!
BYE BECKY!
DOVER
HI HONEY, SORRY WE-
YOU KNOW HOW MUCH I HATED THIS PLACE! THE LEAST YOU COULD DO IS PICK ME UP ON TIME!
HERE! I WAS GOING TO SEND YOU THIS, BUT...
BECKY, CAMP COULD NOT HAVE BEEN THAT BAD.
YOU GOT YOUR PERIOD?
OH! I DIDN'T READ THAT FAR.
MY BABY'S GROWING UP!
CAN WE GET OUT OF HERE?
WELL HONEY, YOU GAVE THE CAMP YOUR BEST SHOT. ...THAT'S GOOD, RIGHT?!
AND YOU MIGHT FEEL BAD ABOUT THIS EXPERIENCE RIGHT NOW, BUT LATER YOU'LL LOOK BACK AND LAUGH!
The end

JIM HOOVER

A Relationship in Eight Pages

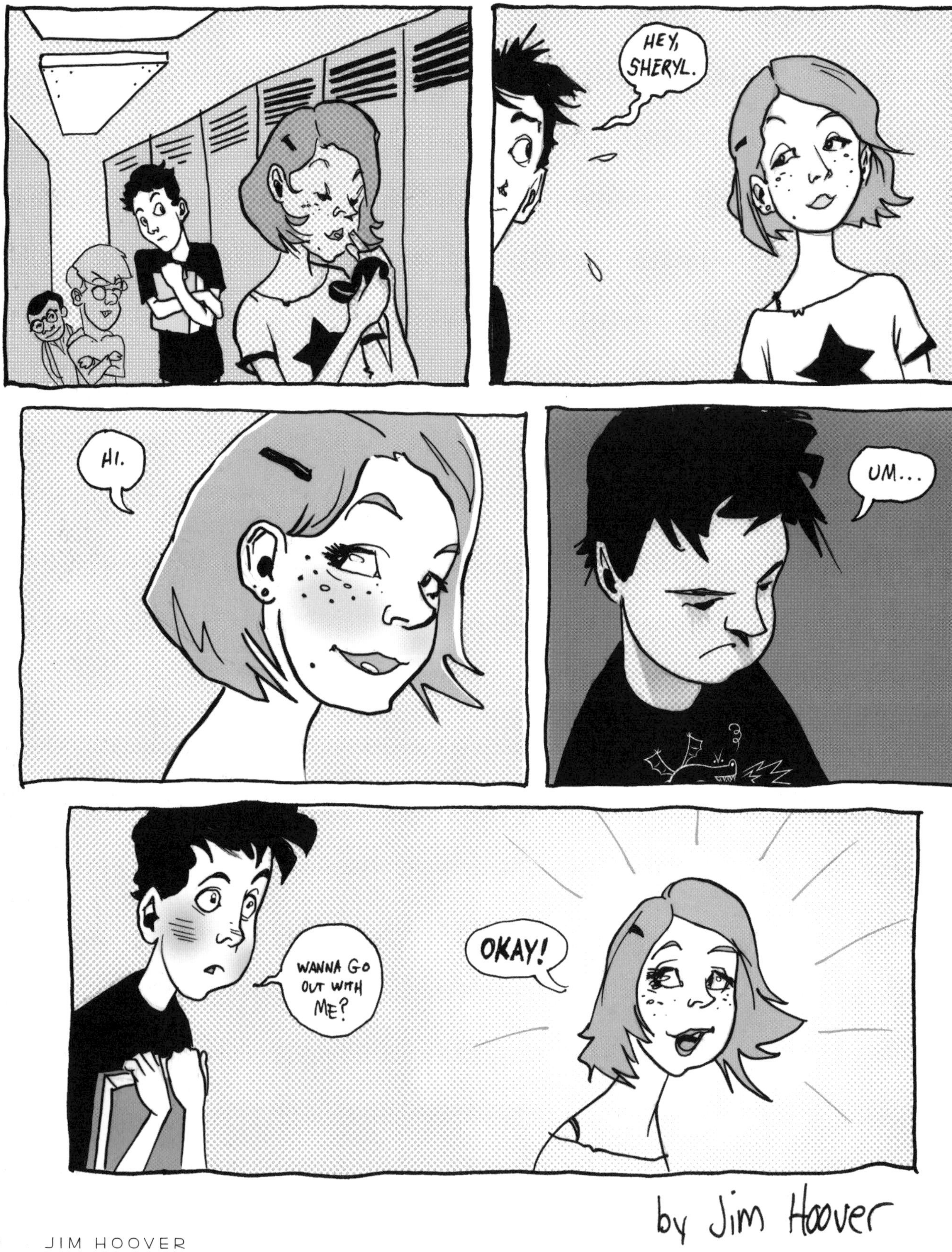

HEY, SHERYL.
HI.
UM...
WANNA GO OUT WITH ME?
OKAY!

by Jim Hoover

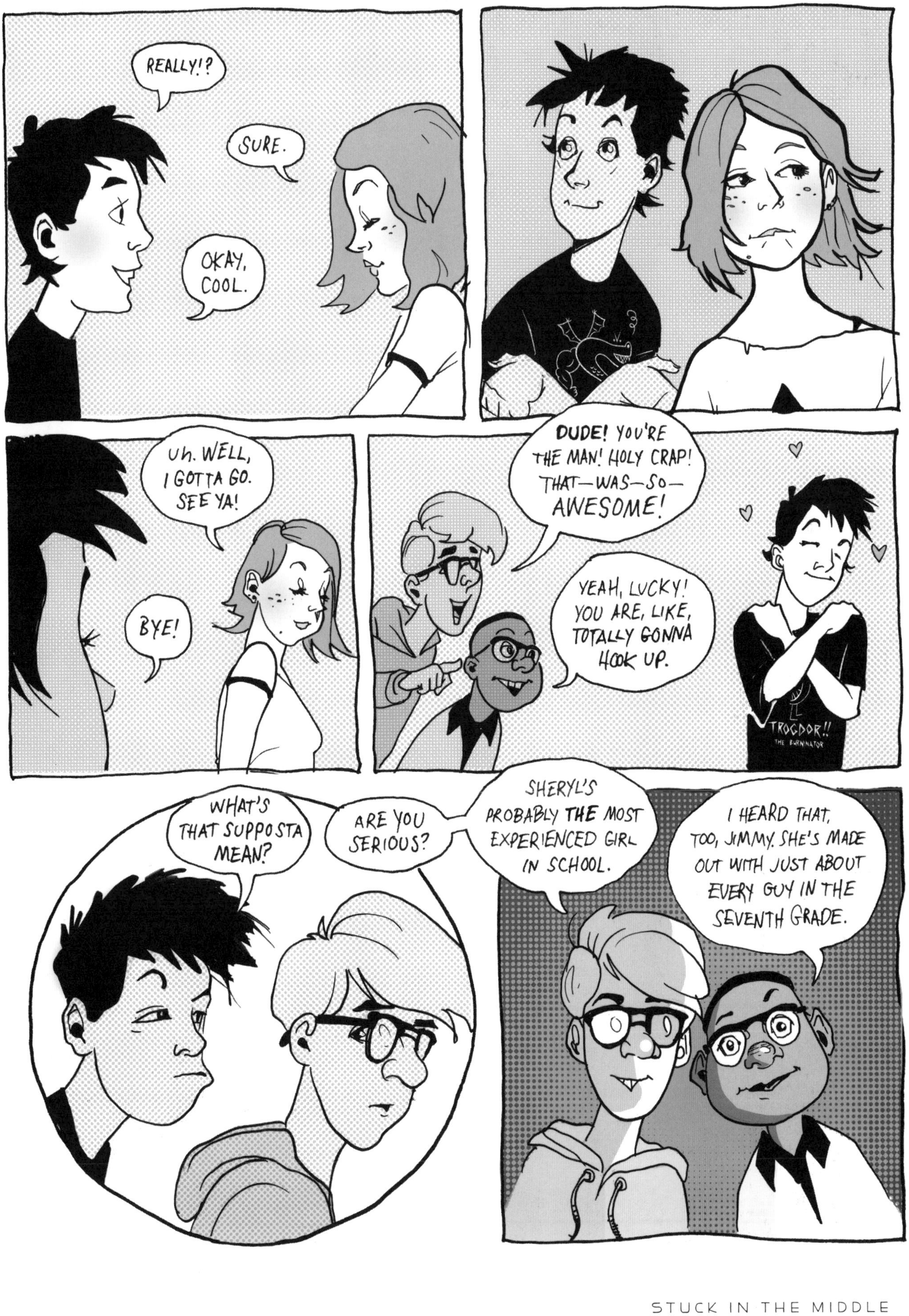
REALLY!?
SURE.
OKAY, COOL.
Uh. WELL, I GOTTA GO. SEE YA!
BYE!
DUDE! YOU'RE THE MAN! HOLY CRAP! THAT—WAS—SO—AWESOME!
YEAH, LUCKY! YOU ARE, LIKE, TOTALLY GONNA HOOK UP.
TROGDOR!! THE BURNINATOR
WHAT'S THAT SUPPOSTA MEAN?
ARE YOU SERIOUS?
SHERYL'S PROBABLY THE MOST EXPERIENCED GIRL IN SCHOOL.
I HEARD THAT, TOO, JIMMY. SHE'S MADE OUT WITH JUST ABOUT EVERY GUY IN THE SEVENTH GRADE.

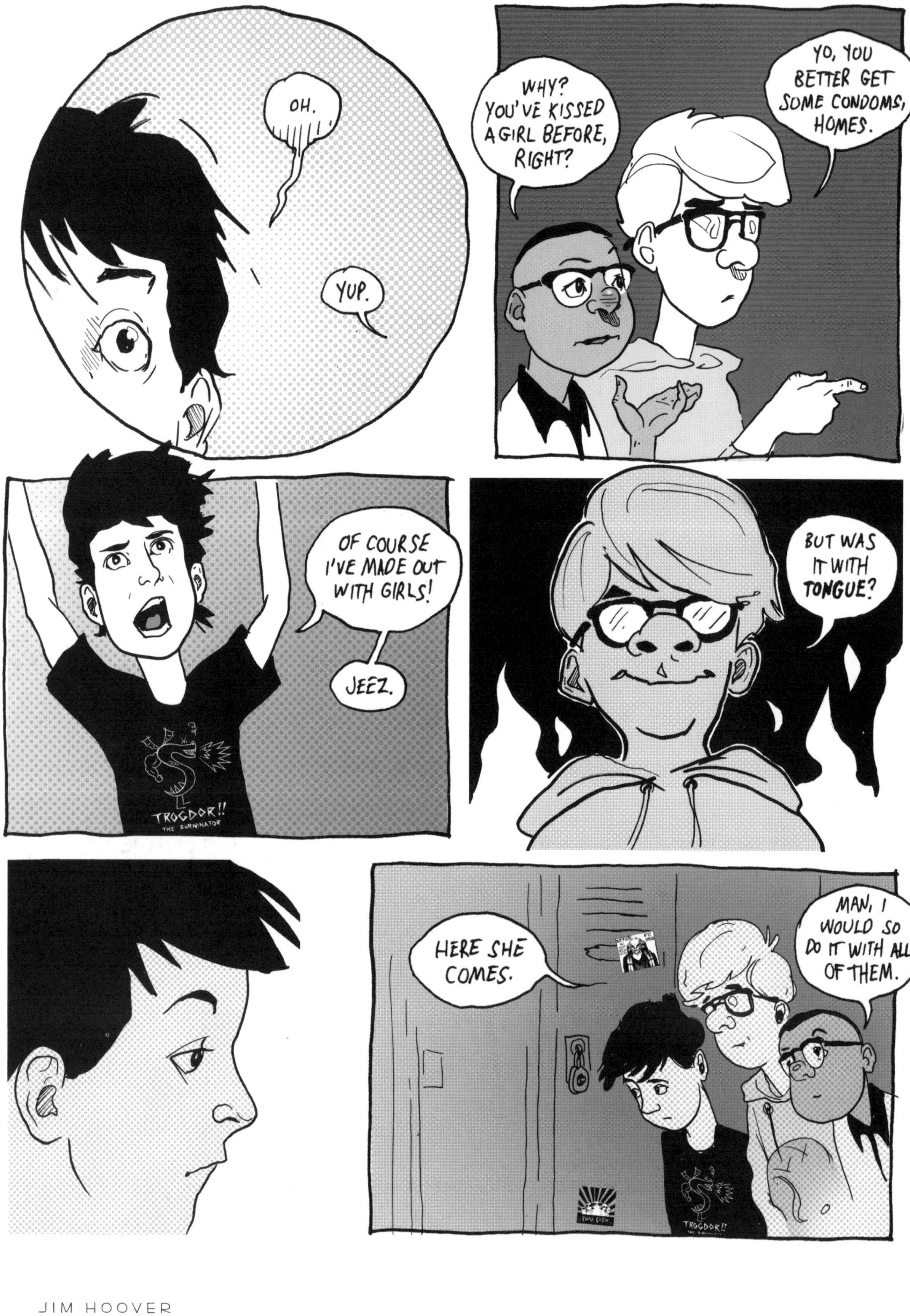
OH.
YUP.
WHY? YOU'VE KISSED A GIRL BEFORE, RIGHT?
YO, YOU BETTER GET SOME CONDOMS, HOMES.
OF COURSE I'VE MADE OUT WITH GIRLS!
JEEZ.
TROGDOR!! THE BURNINATOR
BUT WAS IT WITH **TONGUE?**
HERE SHE COMES.
MAN, I WOULD SO DO IT WITH ALL OF THEM.
TROGDOR!!

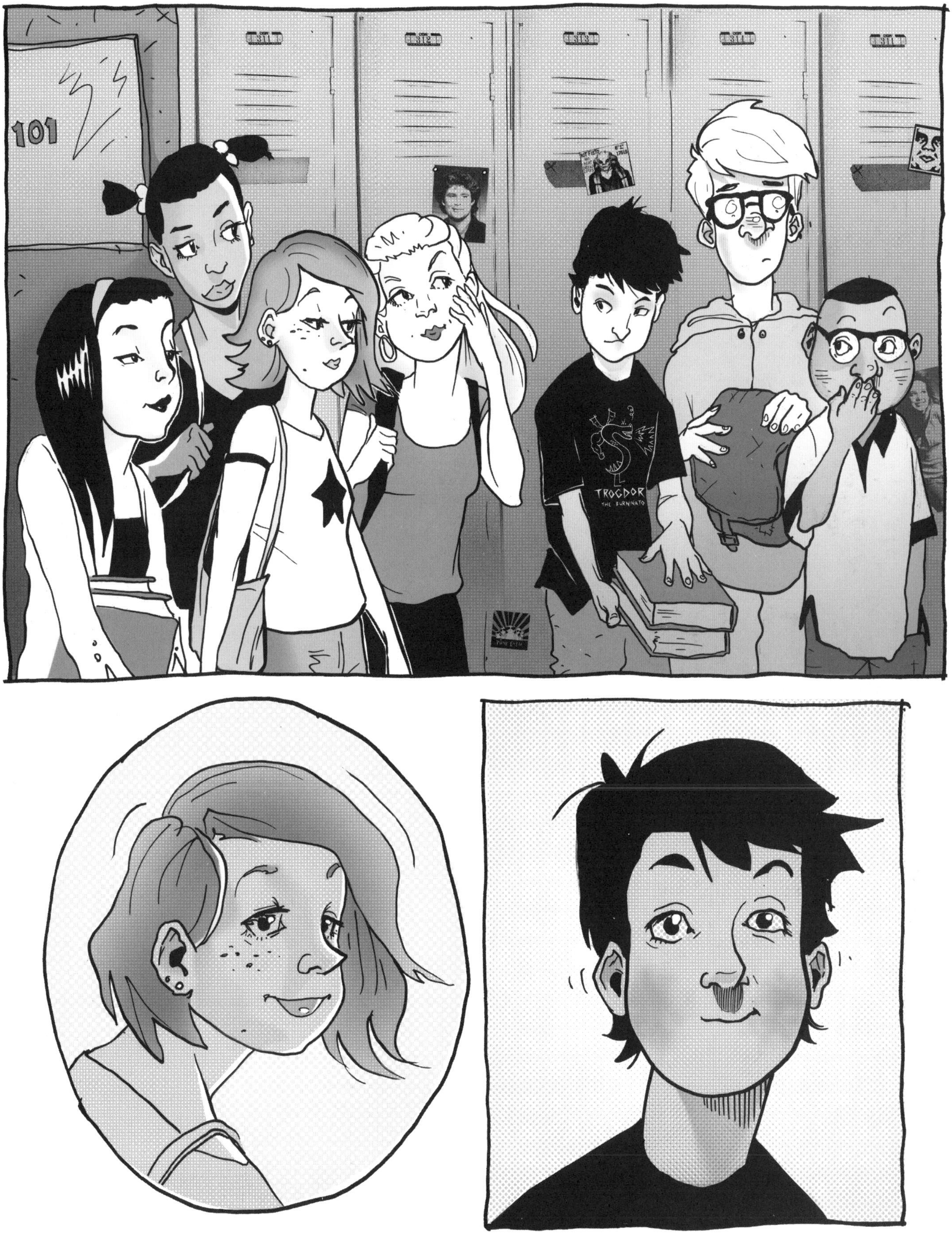
101
TROGDOR

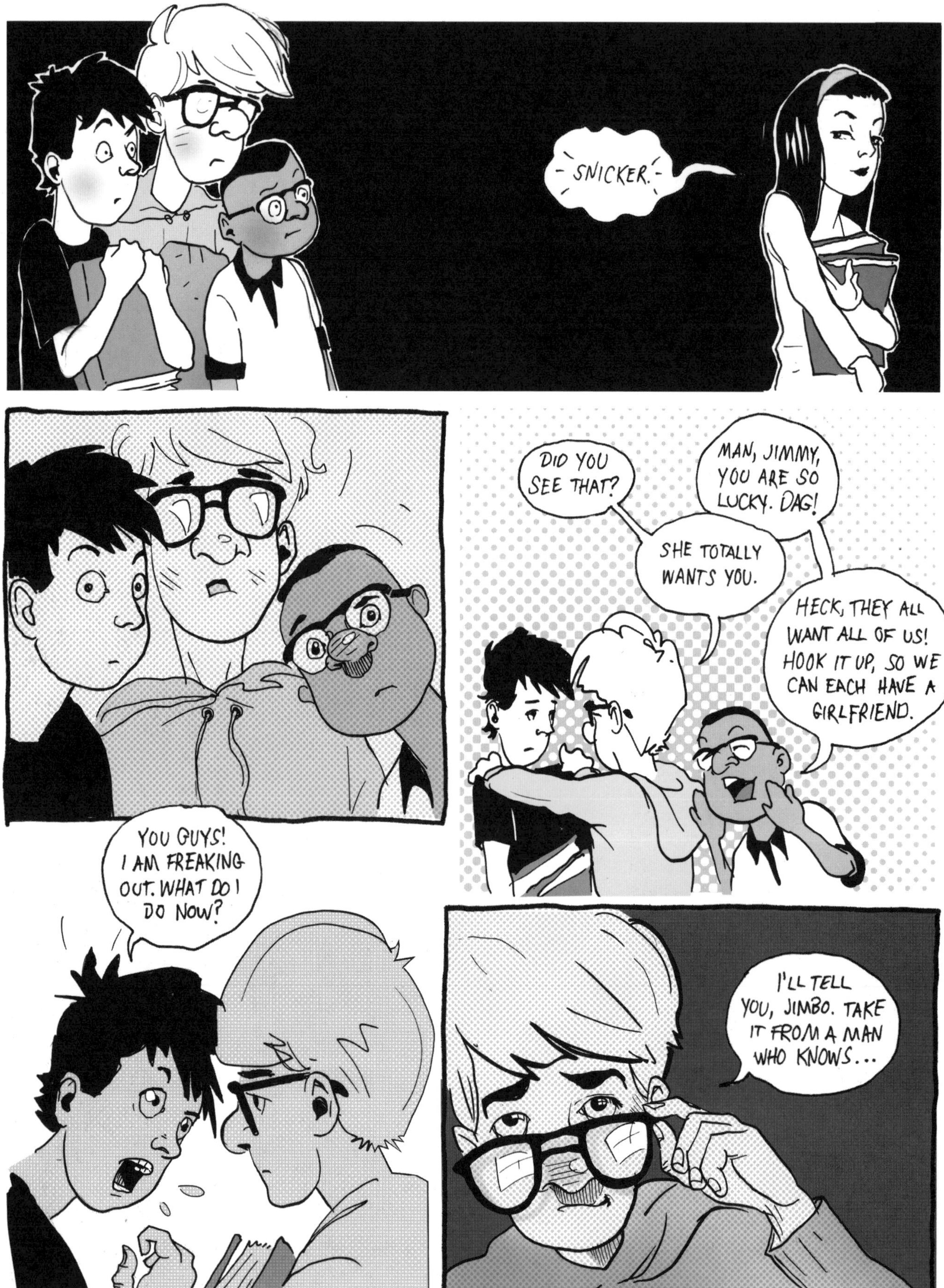
SNICKER.
DID YOU SEE THAT?
MAN, JIMMY, YOU ARE SO LUCKY. DAG!
SHE TOTALLY WANTS YOU.
HECK, THEY ALL WANT ALL OF US! HOOK IT UP, SO WE CAN EACH HAVE A GIRLFRIEND.
YOU GUYS! I AM FREAKING OUT. WHAT DO I DO NOW?
I'LL TELL YOU, JIMBO. TAKE IT FROM A MAN WHO KNOWS...

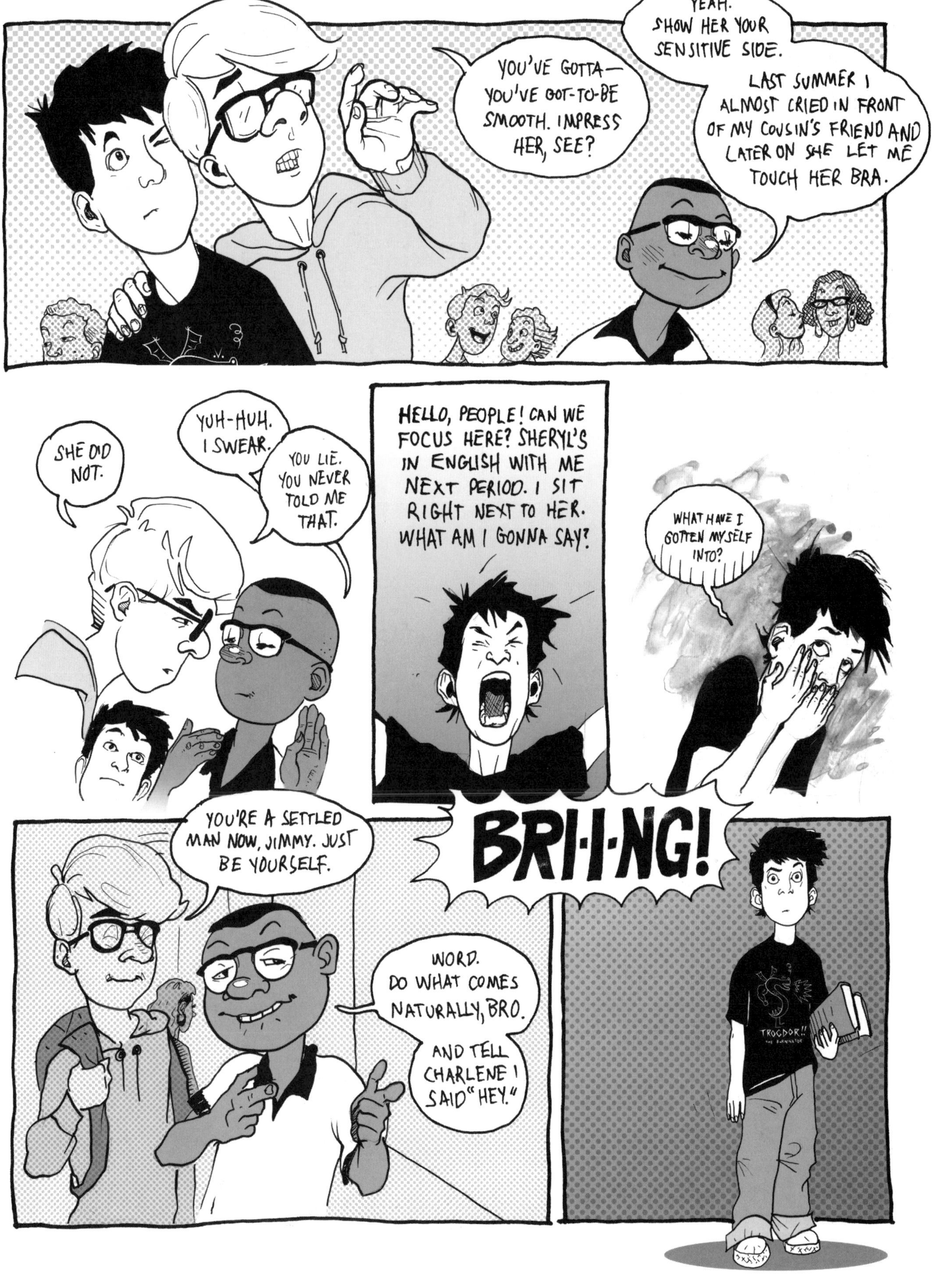
YOU'VE GOTTA— YOU'VE GOT-TO-BE SMOOTH. IMPRESS HER, SEE?
YEAH. SHOW HER YOUR SENSITIVE SIDE.
LAST SUMMER I ALMOST CRIED IN FRONT OF MY COUSIN'S FRIEND AND LATER ON SHE LET ME TOUCH HER BRA.
SHE DID NOT.
YUH-HUH. I SWEAR.
YOU LIE. YOU NEVER TOLD ME THAT.
HELLO, PEOPLE! CAN WE FOCUS HERE? SHERYL'S IN ENGLISH WITH ME NEXT PERIOD. I SIT RIGHT NEXT TO HER. WHAT AM I GONNA SAY?
WHAT HAVE I GOTTEN MYSELF INTO?
YOU'RE A SETTLED MAN NOW, JIMMY. JUST BE YOURSELF.
WORD. DO WHAT COMES NATURALLY, BRO.
AND TELL CHARLENE I SAID "HEY."
BRI-I-NG!
TROGDOR!!

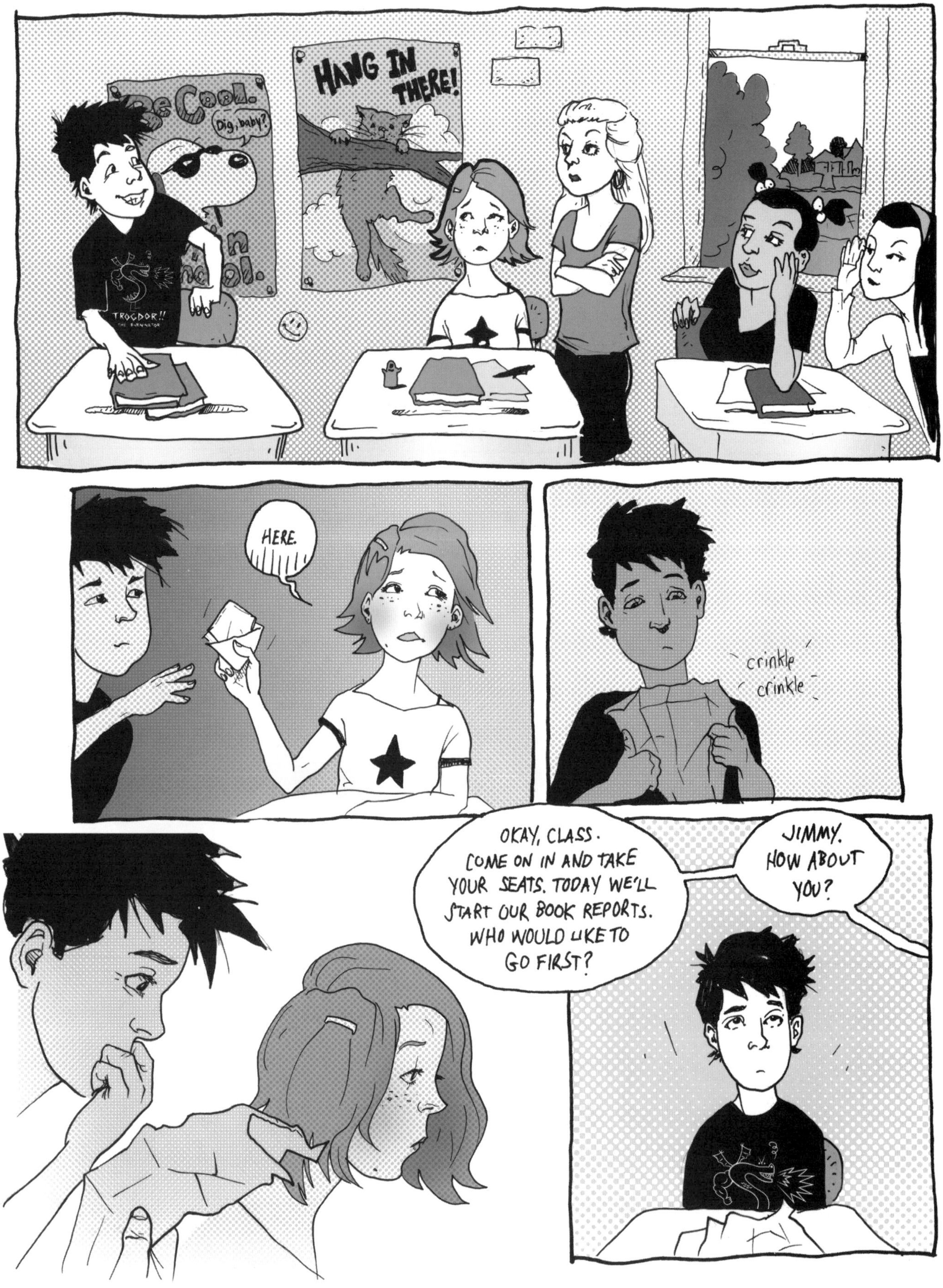
Be Cool.
Dig, baby?
HANG IN THERE!
TROGDOR!!
HERE.
crinkle
crinkle
OKAY, CLASS. COME ON IN AND TAKE YOUR SEATS. TODAY WE'LL START OUR BOOK REPORTS. WHO WOULD LIKE TO GO FIRST?
JIMMY. HOW ABOUT YOU?

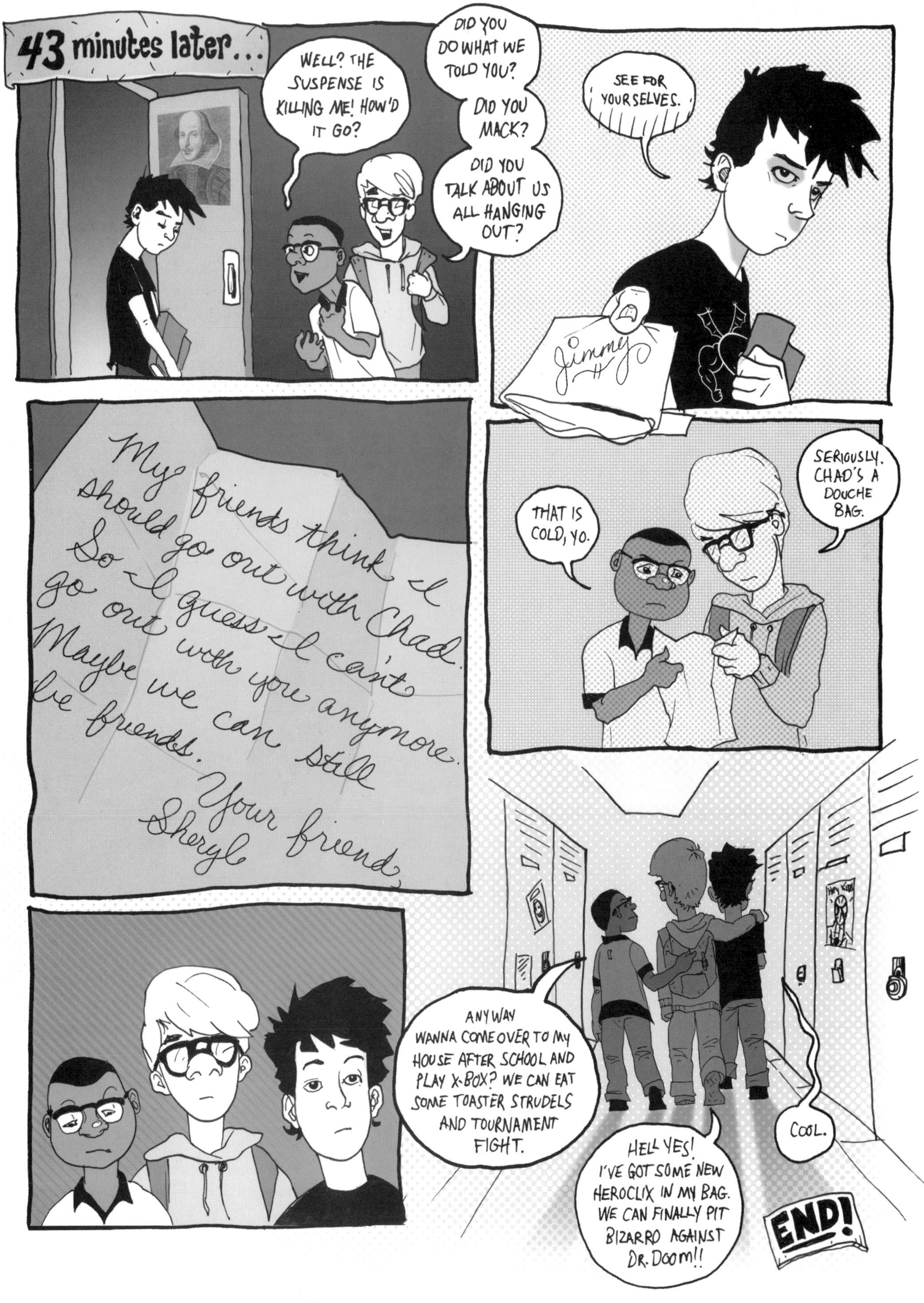
43 minutes later...
WELL? THE SUSPENSE IS KILLING ME! HOW'D IT GO?
DID YOU DO WHAT WE TOLD YOU?
DID YOU MACK?
DID YOU TALK ABOUT US ALL HANGING OUT?
SEE FOR YOURSELVES.
Jimmy
My friends think I should go out with Chad. So I guess I can't go out with you anymore. Maybe we can still be friends.
Your friend,
Sheryl
THAT IS COLD, YO.
SERIOUSLY. CHAD'S A DOUCHE BAG.
ANYWAY WANNA COME OVER TO MY HOUSE AFTER SCHOOL AND PLAY X-BOX? WE CAN EAT SOME TOASTER STRUDELS AND TOURNAMENT FIGHT.
HELL YES! I'VE GOT SOME NEW HEROCLIX IN MY BAG. WE CAN FINALLY PIT BIZARRO AGAINST DR. DOOM!!
COOL.
END!

ROBYN CHAPMAN

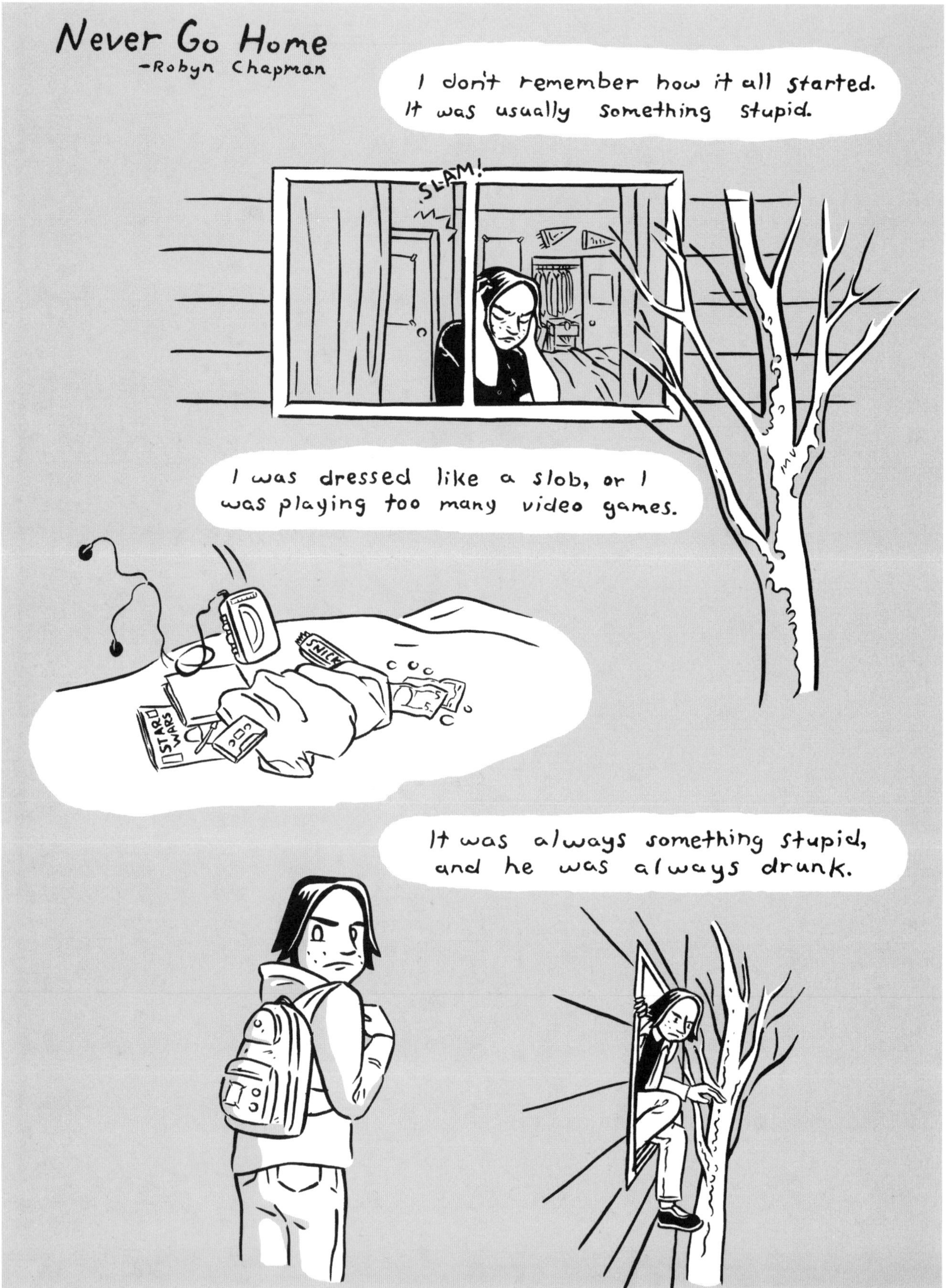

Never Go Home
-Robyn Chapman
I don't remember how it all started. It was usually something stupid.
SLAM!
I was dressed like a slob, or I was playing too many video games.
STAR WARS
It was always something stupid, and he was always drunk.

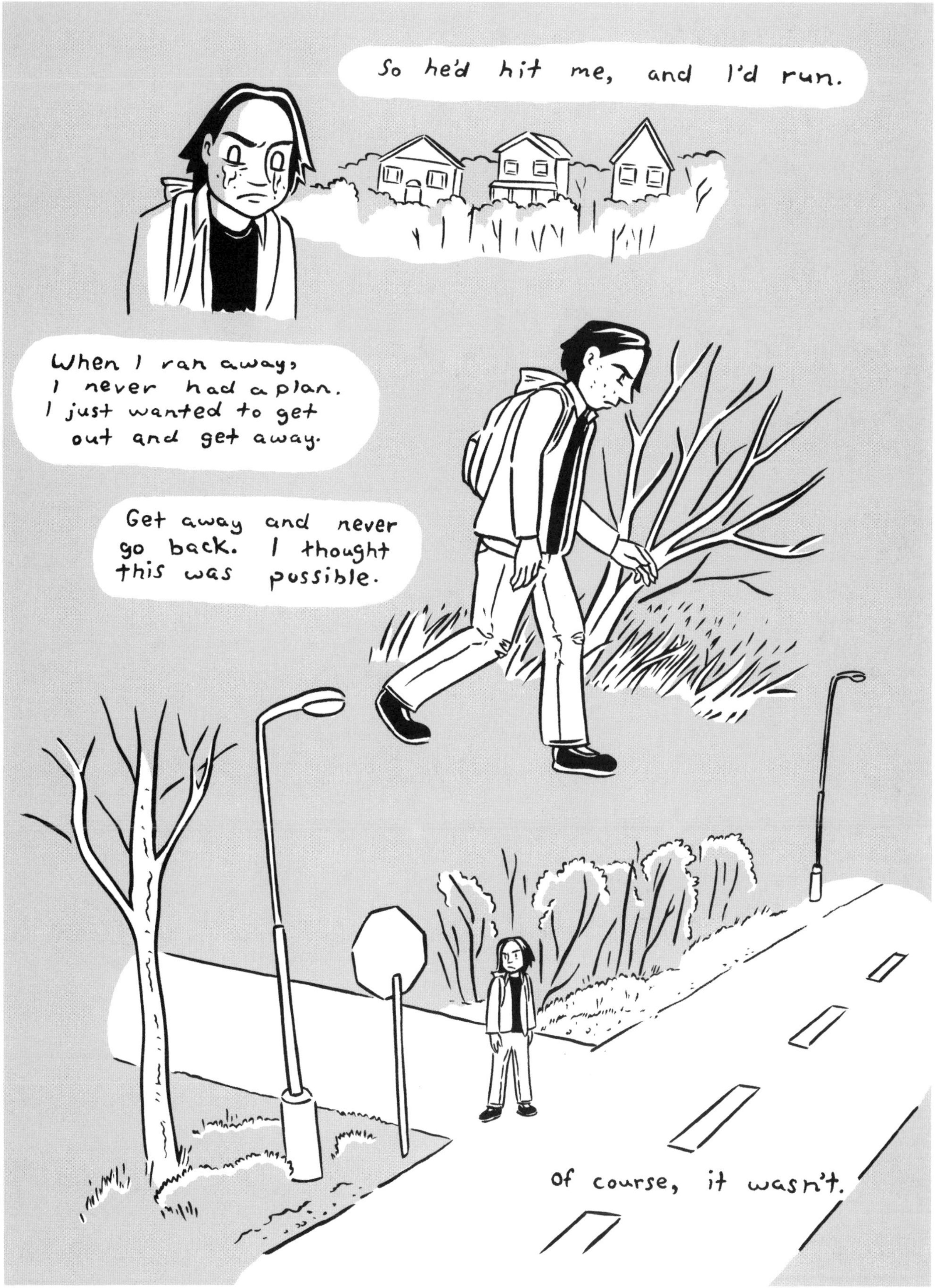
So he'd hit me, and I'd run.
When I ran away, I never had a plan. I just wanted to get out and get away.
Get away and never go back. I thought this was possible.
Of course, it wasn't.

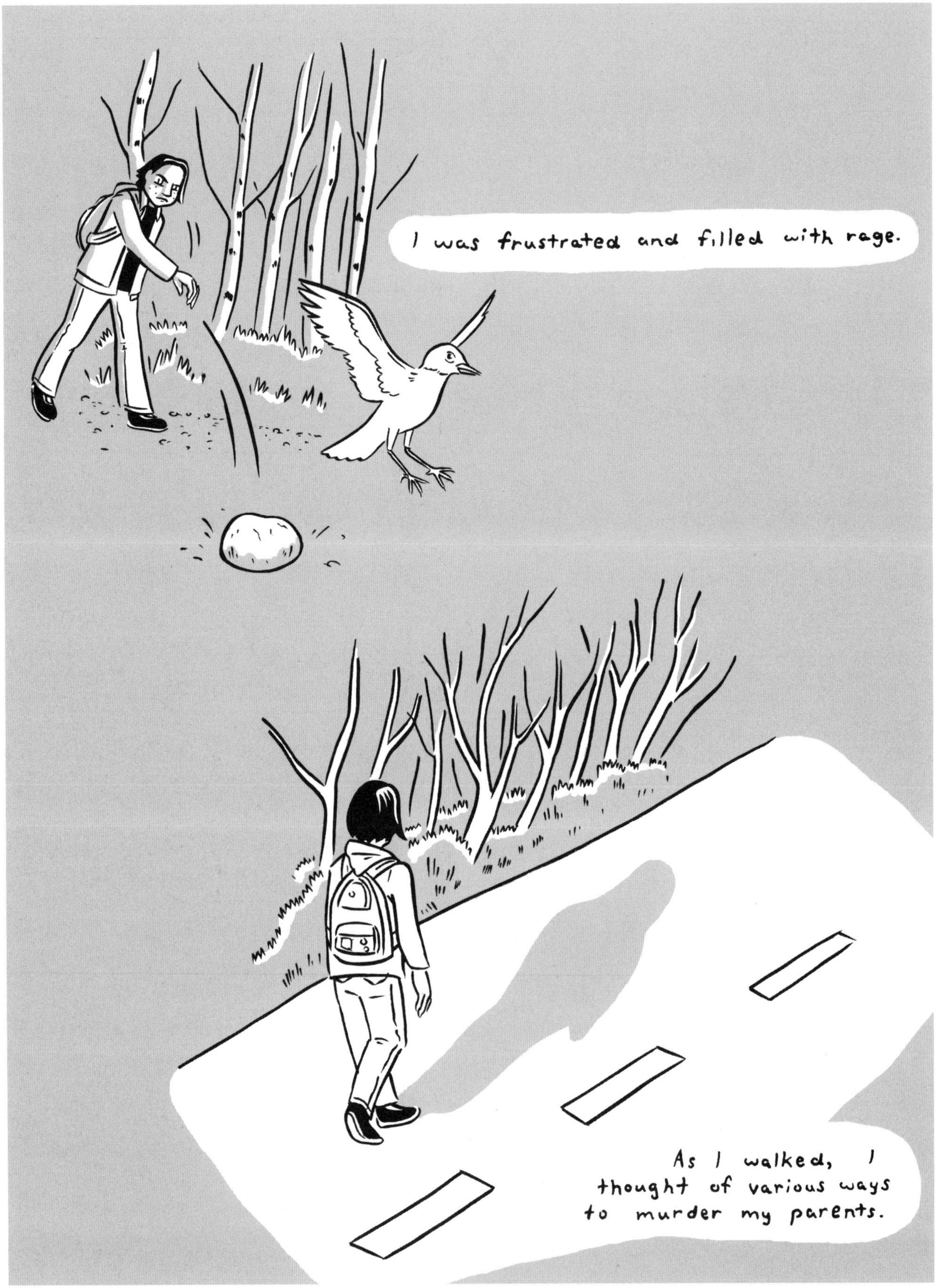
I was frustrated and filled with rage.
As I walked, I thought of various ways to murder my parents.

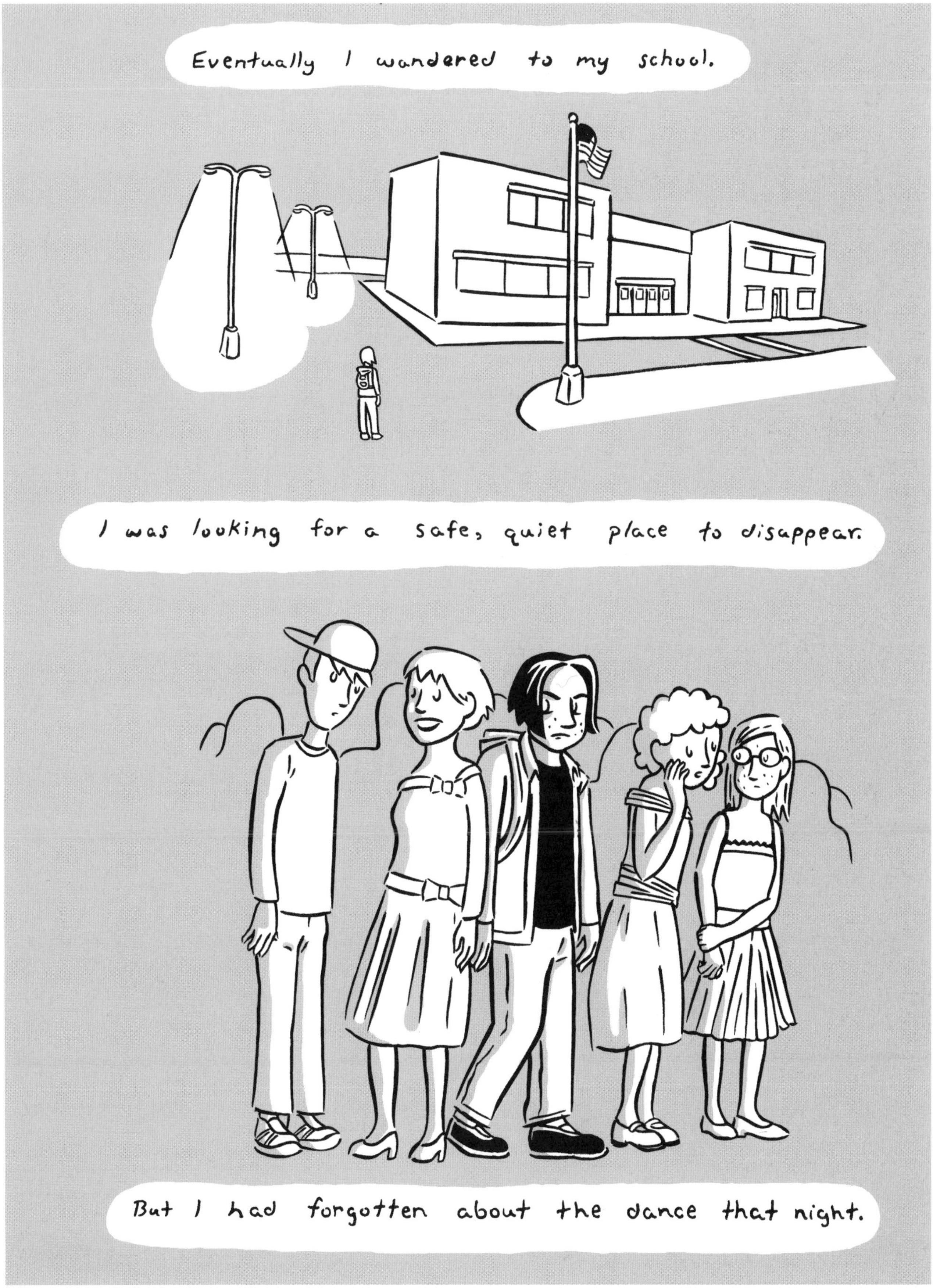
Eventually I wandered to my school.
I was looking for a safe, quiet place to disappear.
But I had forgotten about the dance that night.

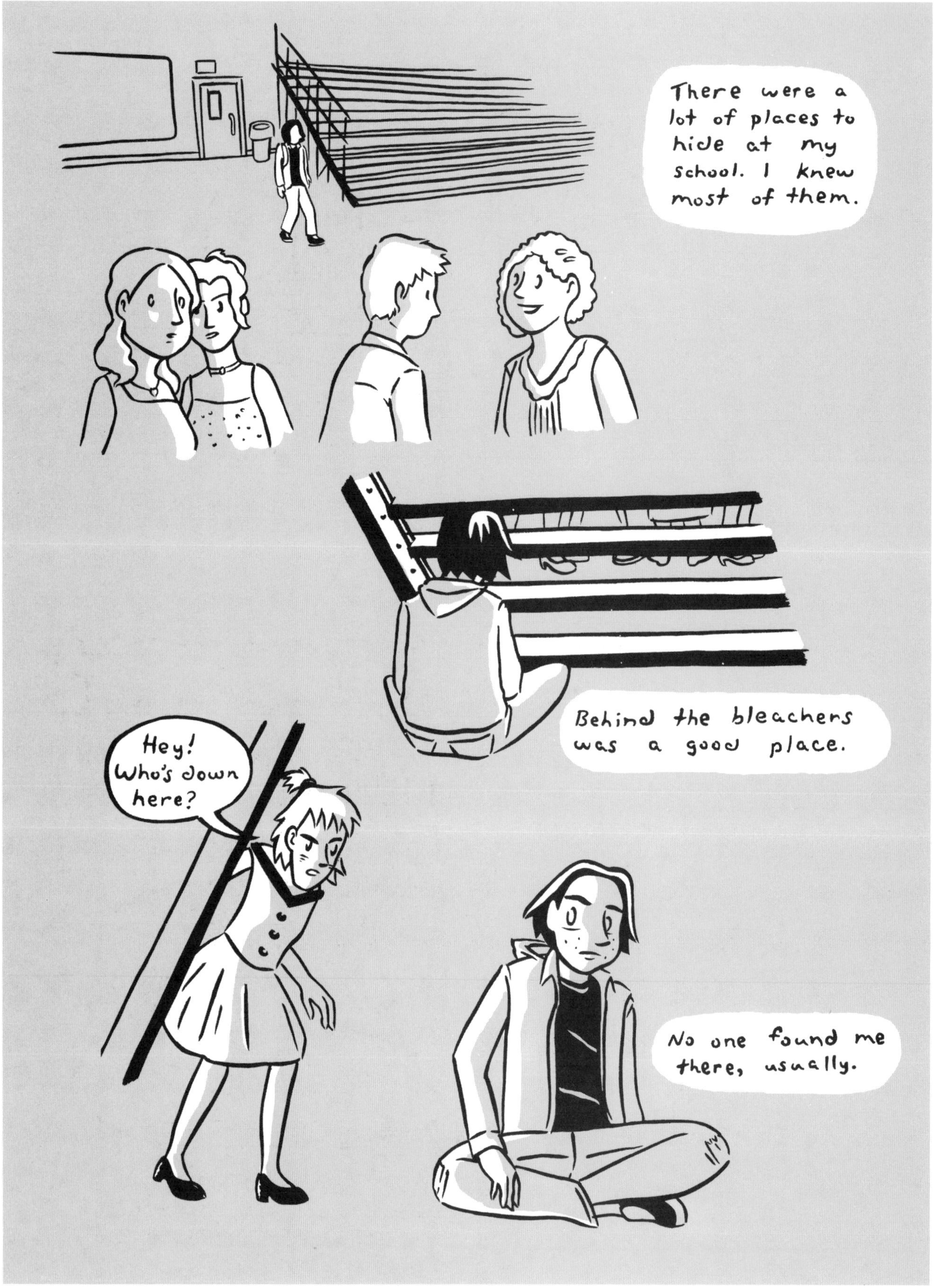
There were a lot of places to hide at my school. I knew most of them.
Behind the bleachers was a good place.
Hey! Who's down here?
No one found me there, usually.

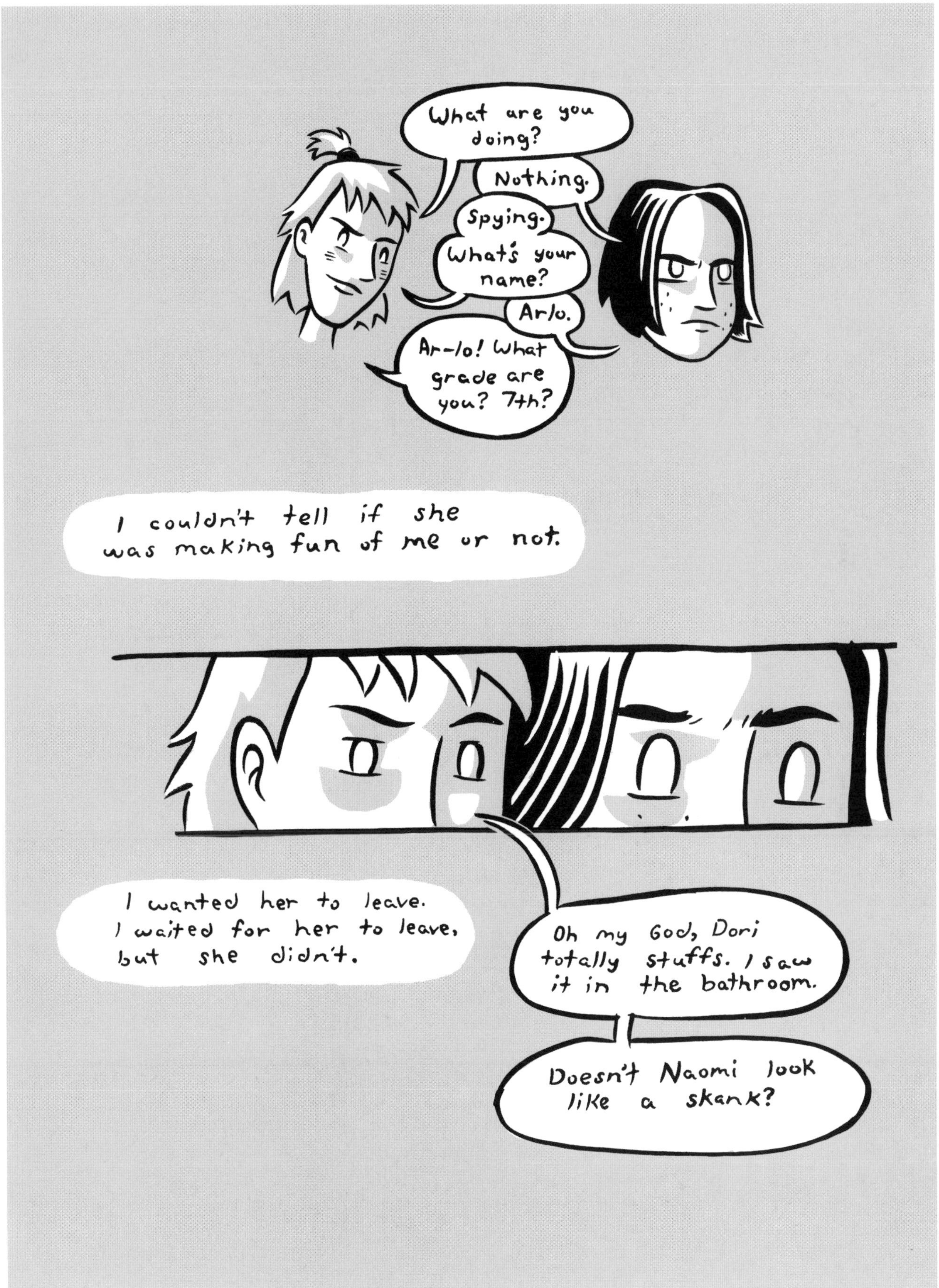
What are you doing?
Nothing.
Spying.
What's your name?
Arlo.
Ar-lo! What grade are you? 7th?
I couldn't tell if she was making fun of me or not.
I wanted her to leave. I waited for her to leave, but she didn't.
Oh my God, Dori totally stuffs. I saw it in the bathroom.
Doesn't Naomi look like a skank?

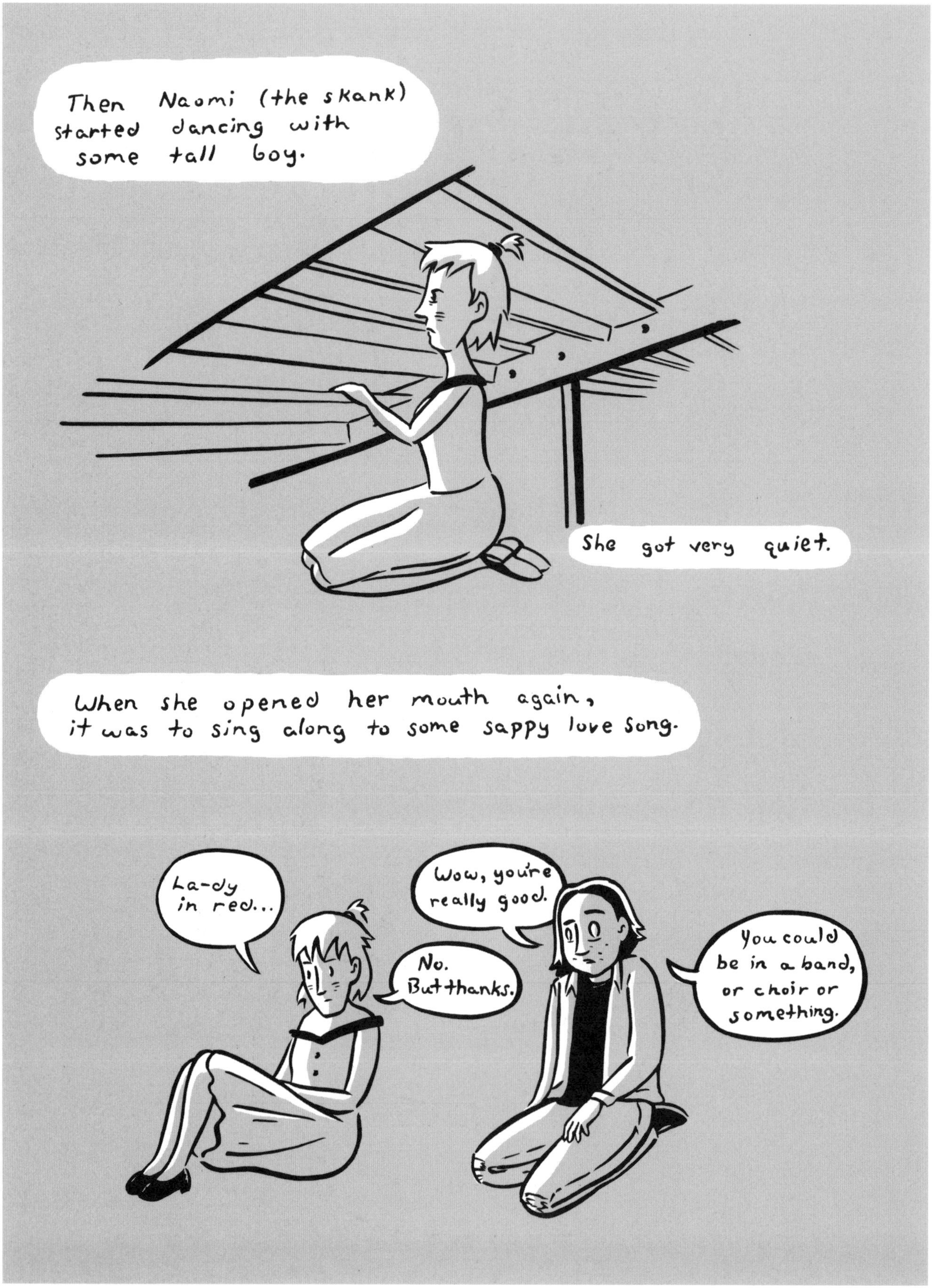
Then Naomi (the skank) started dancing with some tall boy.
She got very quiet.
When she opened her mouth again, it was to sing along to some sappy love song.
La-dy in red...
Wow, you're really good.
No. But thanks.
You could be in a band, or choir or something.

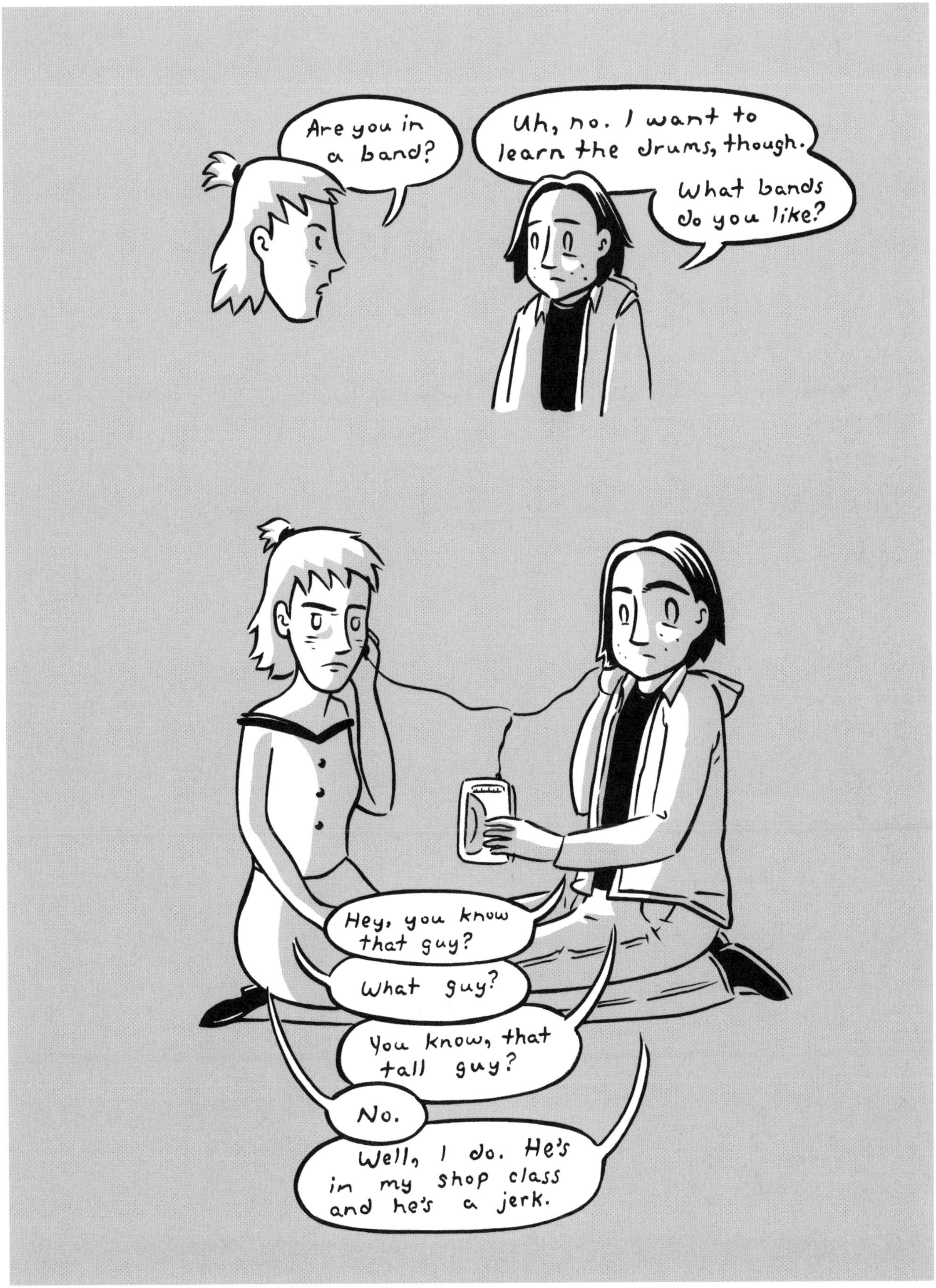
Are you in a band?
Uh, no. I want to learn the drums, though.
What bands do you like?
Hey, you know that guy?
What guy?
You know, that tall guy?
No.
Well, I do. He's in my shop class and he's a jerk.

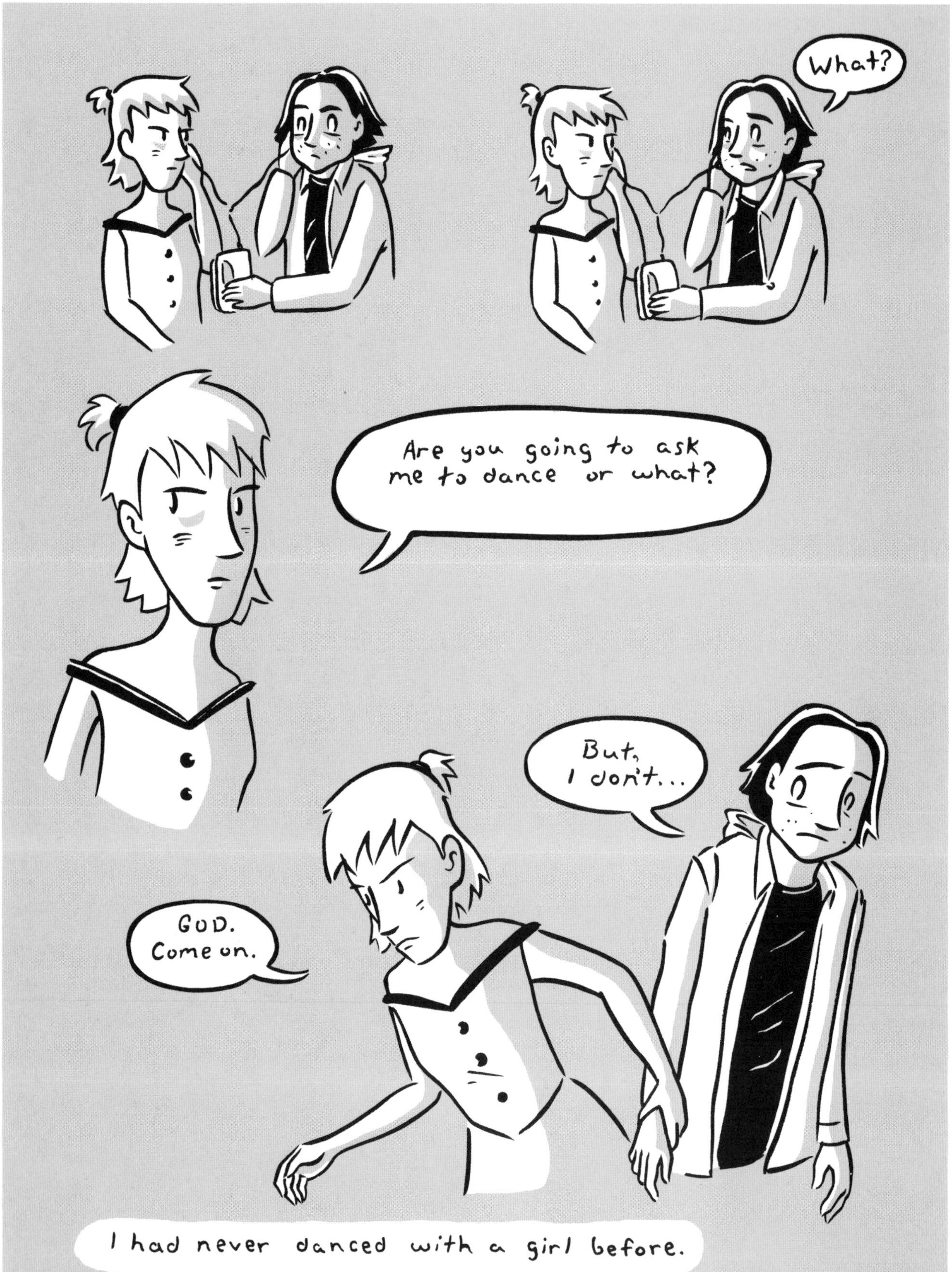
What?
Are you going to ask me to dance or what?
But, I don't...
GOD. Come on.
I had never danced with a girl before.

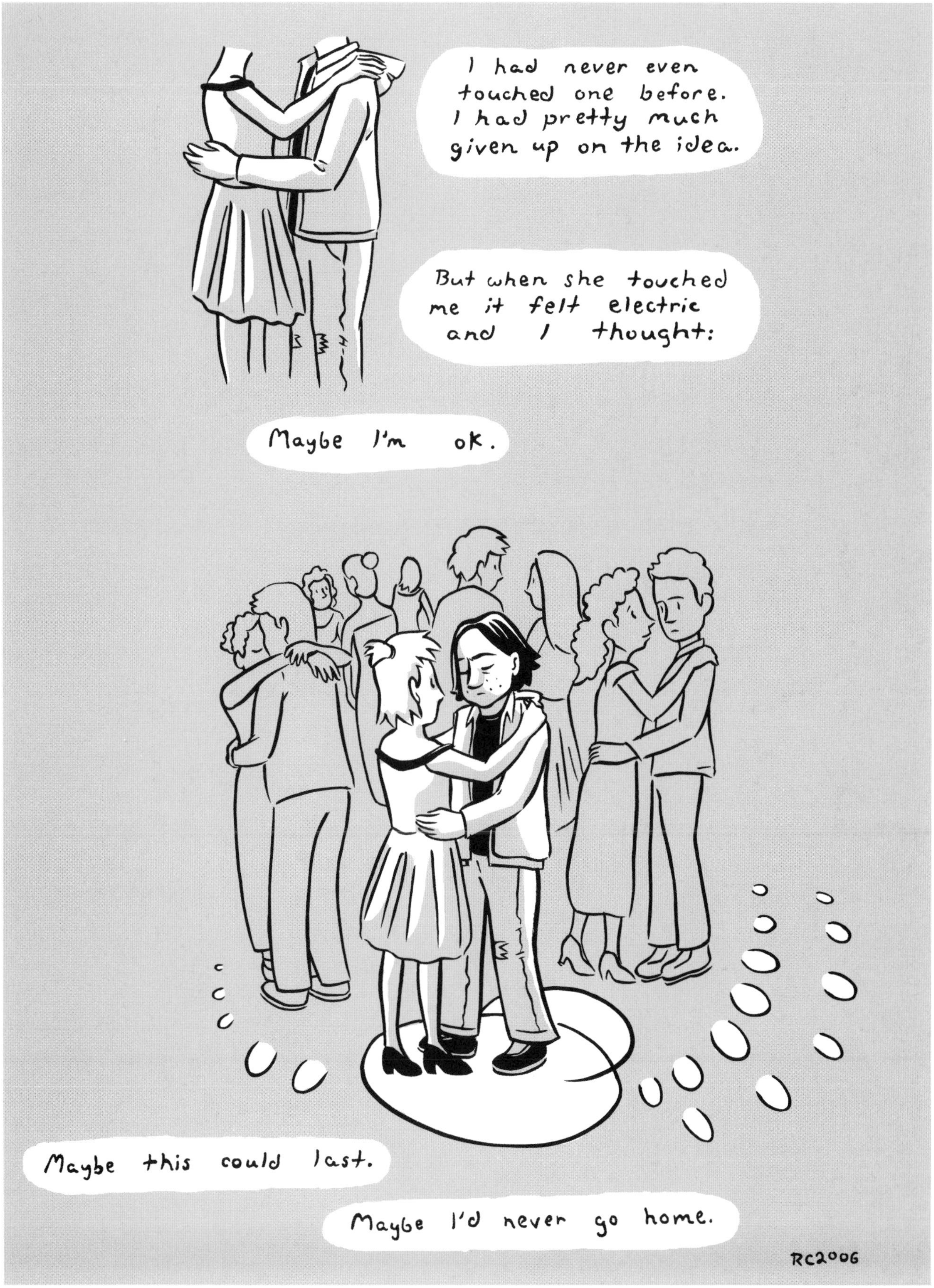
I had never even touched one before. I had pretty much given up on the idea.
But when she touched me it felt electric and I thought:
Maybe I'm ok.
Maybe this could last.
Maybe I'd never go home.
RC2006

ARIEL BORDEAUX

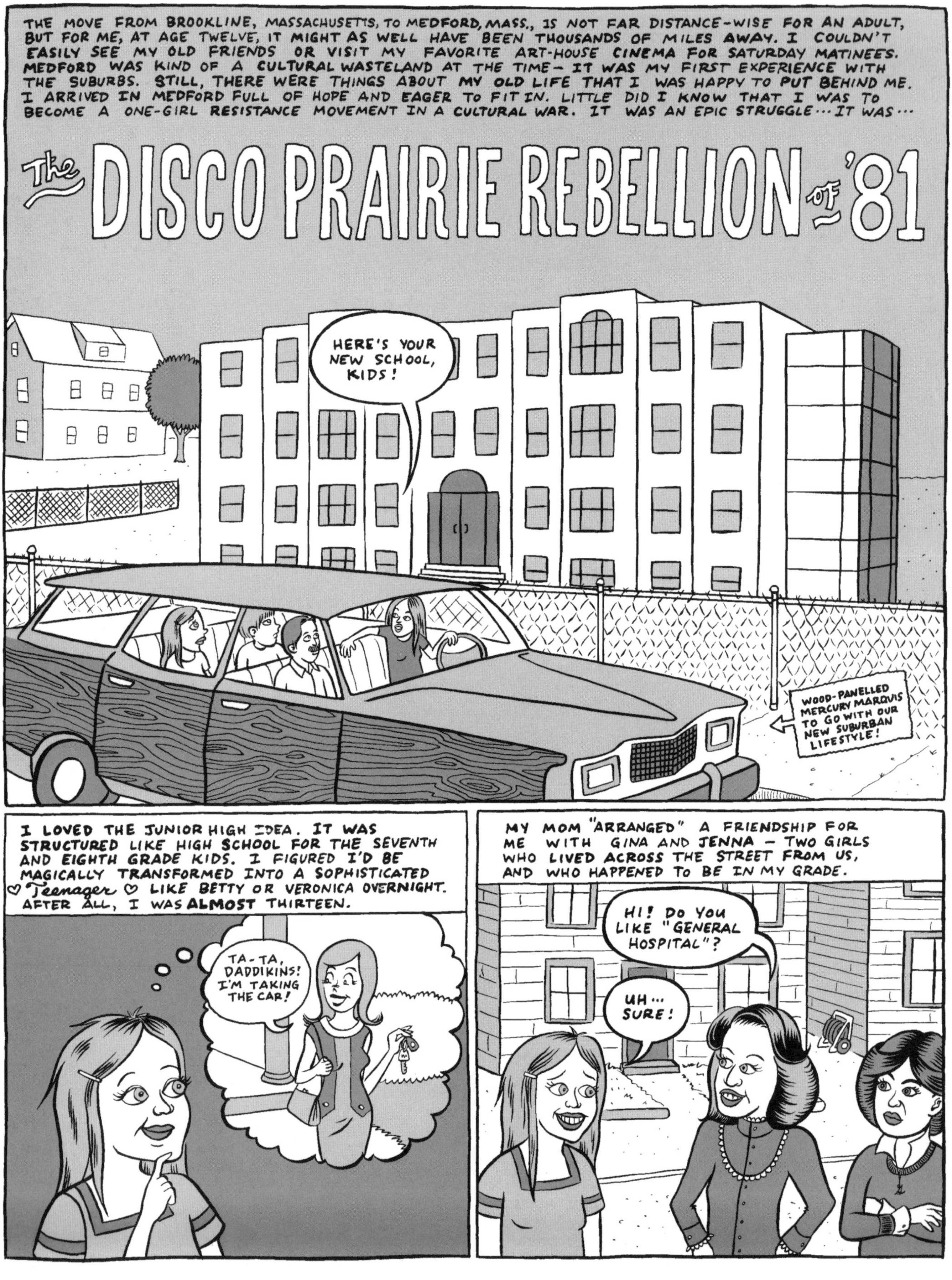

THE MOVE FROM BROOKLINE, MASSACHUSETTS, TO MEDFORD, MASS., IS NOT FAR DISTANCE-WISE FOR AN ADULT, BUT FOR ME, AT AGE TWELVE, IT MIGHT AS WELL HAVE BEEN THOUSANDS OF MILES AWAY. I COULDN'T EASILY SEE MY OLD FRIENDS OR VISIT MY FAVORITE ART-HOUSE CINEMA FOR SATURDAY MATINEES. MEDFORD WAS KIND OF A CULTURAL WASTELAND AT THE TIME- IT WAS MY FIRST EXPERIENCE WITH THE SUBURBS. STILL, THERE WERE THINGS ABOUT MY OLD LIFE THAT I WAS HAPPY TO PUT BEHIND ME. I ARRIVED IN MEDFORD FULL OF HOPE AND EAGER TO FIT IN. LITTLE DID I KNOW THAT I WAS TO BECOME A ONE-GIRL RESISTANCE MOVEMENT IN A CULTURAL WAR. IT WAS AN EPIC STRUGGLE... IT WAS...
The DISCO PRAIRIE REBELLION of '81
HERE'S YOUR NEW SCHOOL, KIDS!
WOOD-PANELLED MERCURY MARQUIS TO GO WITH OUR NEW SUBURBAN LIFESTYLE!
I LOVED THE JUNIOR HIGH IDEA. IT WAS STRUCTURED LIKE HIGH SCHOOL FOR THE SEVENTH AND EIGHTH GRADE KIDS. I FIGURED I'D BE MAGICALLY TRANSFORMED INTO A SOPHISTICATED ♡ Teenager ♡ LIKE BETTY OR VERONICA OVERNIGHT. AFTER ALL, I WAS ALMOST THIRTEEN.
TA-TA, DADDIKINS! I'M TAKING THE CAR!
MY MOM "ARRANGED" A FRIENDSHIP FOR ME WITH GINA AND JENNA - TWO GIRLS WHO LIVED ACROSS THE STREET FROM US, AND WHO HAPPENED TO BE IN MY GRADE.
HI! DO YOU LIKE "GENERAL HOSPITAL"?
UH... SURE!

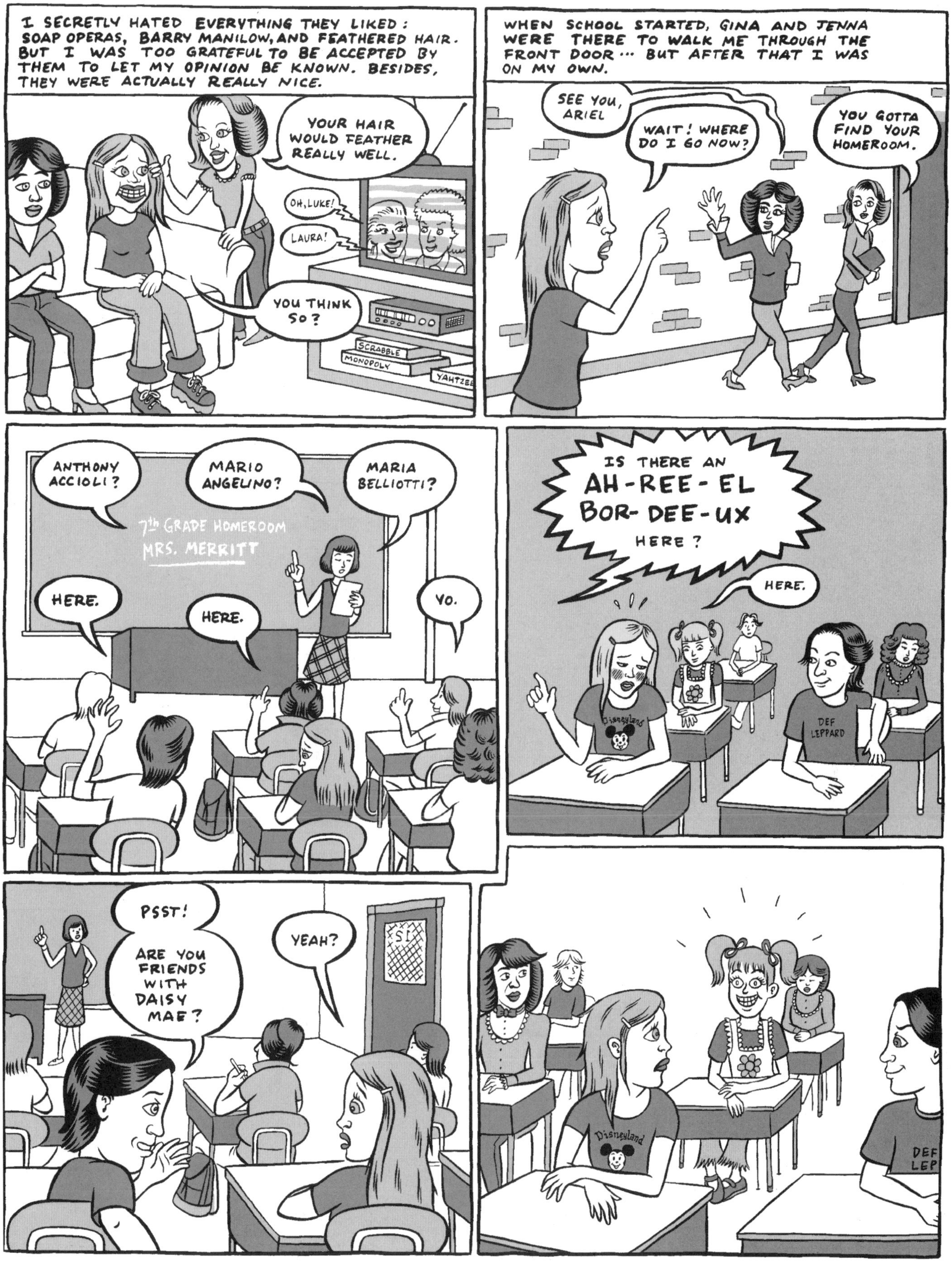
I SECRETLY HATED EVERYTHING THEY LIKED: SOAP OPERAS, BARRY MANILOW, AND FEATHERED HAIR. BUT I WAS TOO GRATEFUL TO BE ACCEPTED BY THEM TO LET MY OPINION BE KNOWN. BESIDES, THEY WERE ACTUALLY REALLY NICE.
YOUR HAIR WOULD FEATHER REALLY WELL.
OH, LUKE!
LAURA!
YOU THINK SO?
SCRABBLE
MONOPOLY
YAHTZEE
WHEN SCHOOL STARTED, GINA AND JENNA WERE THERE TO WALK ME THROUGH THE FRONT DOOR... BUT AFTER THAT I WAS ON MY OWN.
SEE YOU, ARIEL
WAIT! WHERE DO I GO NOW?
YOU GOTTA FIND YOUR HOMEROOM.
ANTHONY ACCIOLI?
MARIO ANGELINO?
MARIA BELLIOTTI?
7th GRADE HOMEROOM
MRS. MERRITT
HERE.
HERE.
YO.
IS THERE AN AH-REE-EL BOR-DEE-UX HERE?
HERE.
Disneyland
DEF LEPPARD
PSST!
ARE YOU FRIENDS WITH DAISY MAE?
YEAH?
Disneyland
DEF LEP

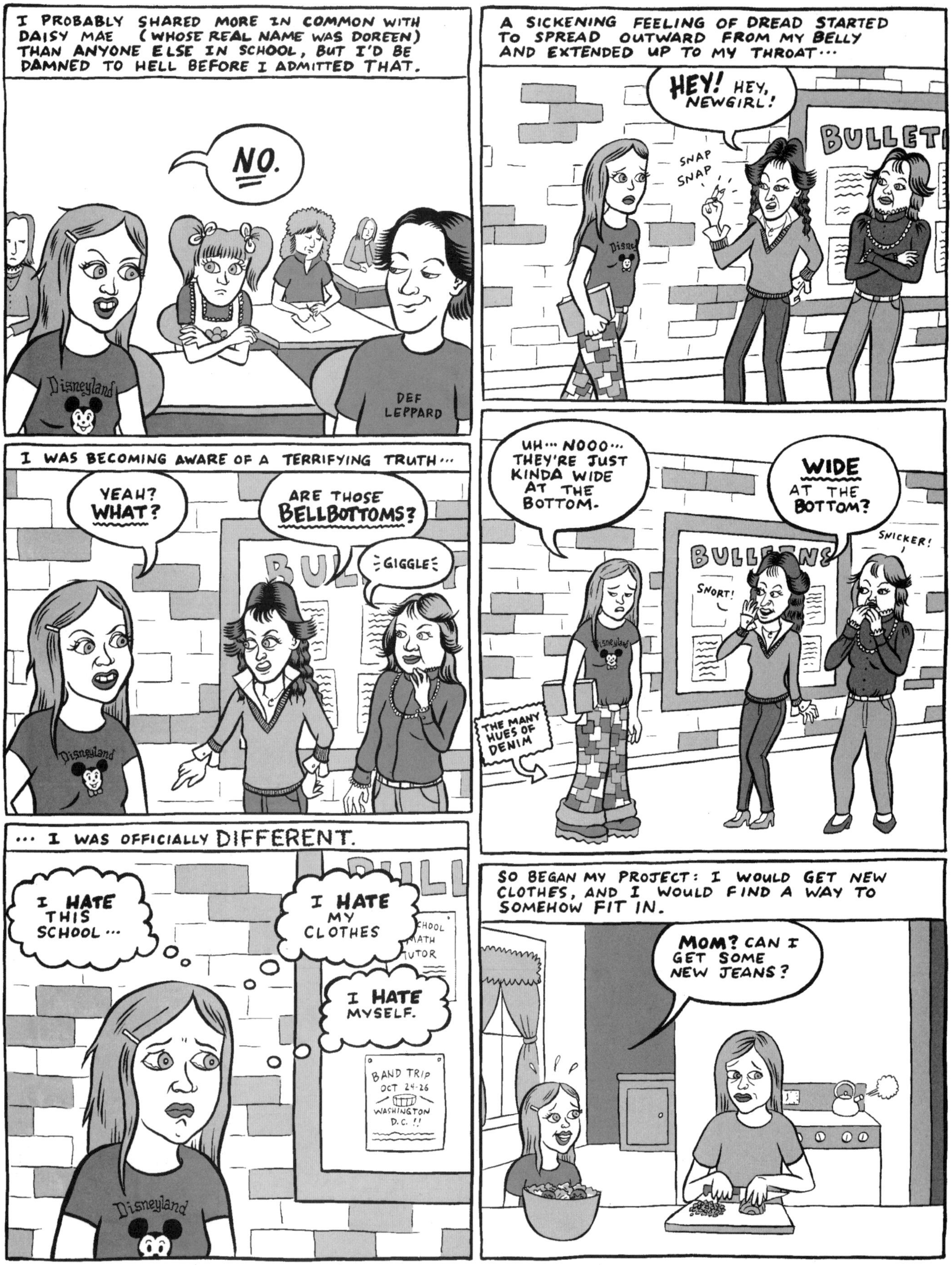
I PROBABLY SHARED MORE IN COMMON WITH DAISY MAE (WHOSE REAL NAME WAS DOREEN) THAN ANYONE ELSE IN SCHOOL, BUT I'D BE DAMNED TO HELL BEFORE I ADMITTED THAT.
NO.
Disneyland
DEF LEPPARD
A SICKENING FEELING OF DREAD STARTED TO SPREAD OUTWARD FROM MY BELLY AND EXTENDED UP TO MY THROAT...
HEY! HEY, NEWGIRL!
SNAP SNAP
BULLETI
I WAS BECOMING AWARE OF A TERRIFYING TRUTH...
YEAH? WHAT?
ARE THOSE BELLBOTTOMS?
GIGGLE
Disneyland
UH... NOOO... THEY'RE JUST KINDA WIDE AT THE BOTTOM.
WIDE AT THE BOTTOM?
SNICKER!
SNORT!
BULLETINS
THE MANY HUES OF DENIM
... I WAS OFFICIALLY DIFFERENT.
I HATE THIS SCHOOL...
I HATE MY CLOTHES
I HATE MYSELF.
BAND TRIP OCT 24-26 WASHINGTON D.C. !!
Disneyland
SO BEGAN MY PROJECT: I WOULD GET NEW CLOTHES, AND I WOULD FIND A WAY TO SOMEHOW FIT IN.
MOM? CAN I GET SOME NEW JEANS?

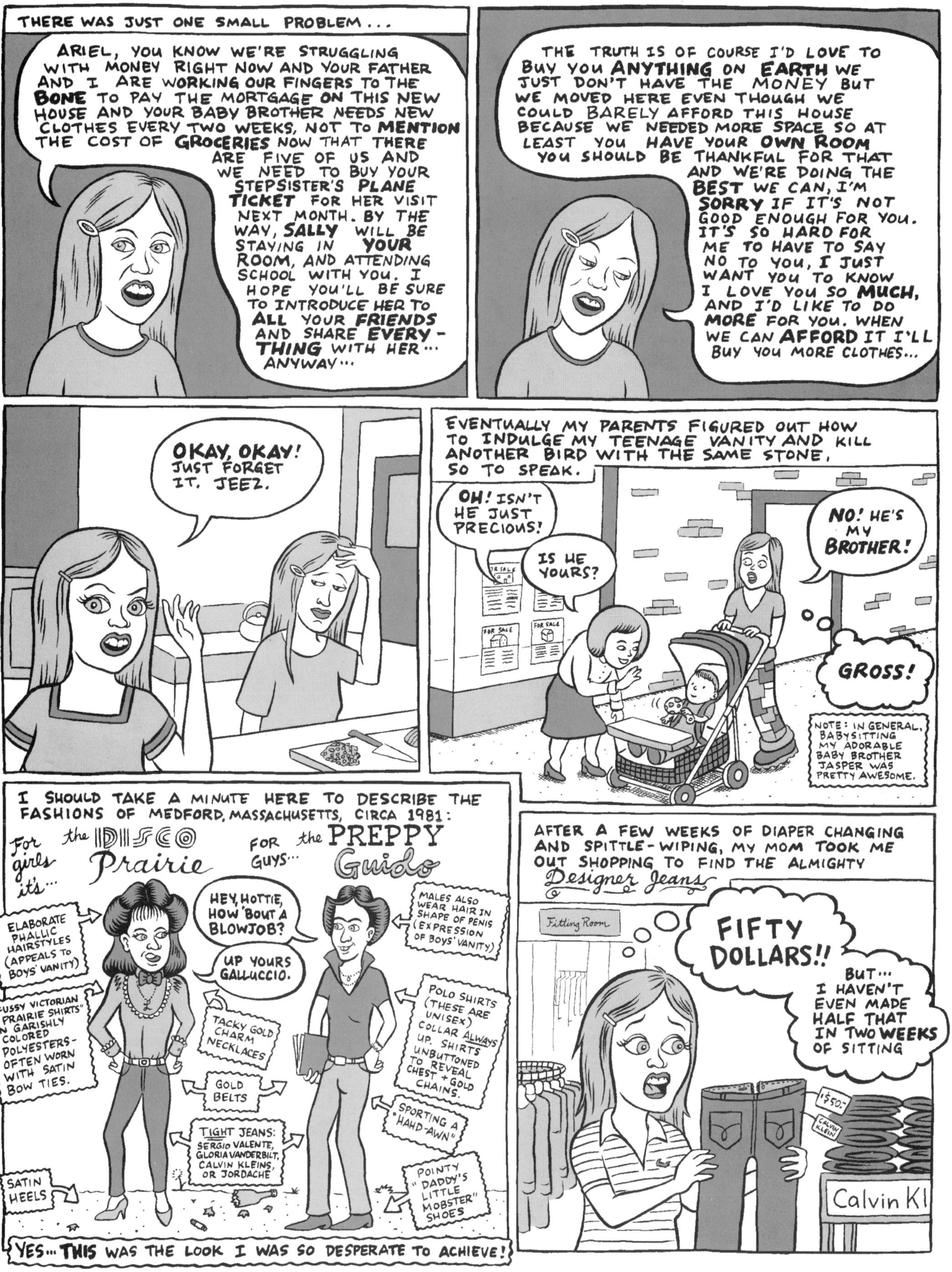

THERE WAS JUST ONE SMALL PROBLEM...
ARIEL, YOU KNOW WE'RE STRUGGLING WITH MONEY RIGHT NOW AND YOUR FATHER AND I ARE WORKING OUR FINGERS TO THE BONE TO PAY THE MORTGAGE ON THIS NEW HOUSE AND YOUR BABY BROTHER NEEDS NEW CLOTHES EVERY TWO WEEKS, NOT TO MENTION THE COST OF GROCERIES NOW THAT THERE ARE FIVE OF US AND WE NEED TO BUY YOUR STEPSISTER'S PLANE TICKET FOR HER VISIT NEXT MONTH. BY THE WAY, SALLY WILL BE STAYING IN YOUR ROOM, AND ATTENDING SCHOOL WITH YOU. I HOPE YOU'LL BE SURE TO INTRODUCE HER TO ALL YOUR FRIENDS AND SHARE EVERY-THING WITH HER... ANYWAY...
THE TRUTH IS OF COURSE I'D LOVE TO BUY YOU ANYTHING ON EARTH WE JUST DON'T HAVE THE MONEY BUT WE MOVED HERE EVEN THOUGH WE COULD BARELY AFFORD THIS HOUSE BECAUSE WE NEEDED MORE SPACE SO AT LEAST YOU HAVE YOUR OWN ROOM YOU SHOULD BE THANKFUL FOR THAT AND WE'RE DOING THE BEST WE CAN, I'M SORRY IF IT'S NOT GOOD ENOUGH FOR YOU. IT'S SO HARD FOR ME TO HAVE TO SAY NO TO YOU, I JUST WANT YOU TO KNOW I LOVE YOU SO MUCH, AND I'D LIKE TO DO MORE FOR YOU. WHEN WE CAN AFFORD IT I'LL BUY YOU MORE CLOTHES...
OKAY, OKAY! JUST FORGET IT. JEEZ.
EVENTUALLY MY PARENTS FIGURED OUT HOW TO INDULGE MY TEENAGE VANITY AND KILL ANOTHER BIRD WITH THE SAME STONE, SO TO SPEAK.
OH! ISN'T HE JUST PRECIOUS!
IS HE YOURS?
NO! HE'S MY BROTHER!
GROSS!
FOR SALE
FOR SALE
NOTE: IN GENERAL, BABYSITTING MY ADORABLE BABY BROTHER JASPER WAS PRETTY AWESOME.
I SHOULD TAKE A MINUTE HERE TO DESCRIBE THE FASHIONS OF MEDFORD, MASSACHUSETTS, CIRCA 1981:
For girls it's... the DISCO Prairie
FOR GUYS... the PREPPY Guido
HEY, HOTTIE, HOW 'BOUT A BLOWJOB?
UP YOURS GALLUCCIO.
ELABORATE PHALLIC HAIRSTYLES (APPEALS TO BOYS' VANITY)
MALES ALSO WEAR HAIR IN SHAPE OF PENIS (EXPRESSION OF BOYS' VANITY)
FUSSY VICTORIAN "PRAIRIE SHIRTS" IN GARISHLY COLORED POLYESTERS-OFTEN WORN WITH SATIN BOW TIES.
TACKY GOLD CHARM NECKLACES
POLO SHIRTS (THESE ARE UNISEX) COLLAR ALWAYS UP. SHIRTS UNBUTTONED TO REVEAL CHEST + GOLD CHAINS.
GOLD BELTS
SPORTING A "HARD-AWN"
TIGHT JEANS: SERGIO VALENTE, GLORIA VANDERBILT, CALVIN KLEINS, OR JORDACHE
SATIN HEELS
POINTY "DADDY'S LITTLE MOBSTER" SHOES
YES... THIS WAS THE LOOK I WAS SO DESPERATE TO ACHIEVE!
AFTER A FEW WEEKS OF DIAPER CHANGING AND SPITTLE-WIPING, MY MOM TOOK ME OUT SHOPPING TO FIND THE ALMIGHTY Designer Jeans
Fitting Room
FIFTY DOLLARS!!
BUT... I HAVEN'T EVEN MADE HALF THAT IN TWO WEEKS OF SITTING
$50.-
CALVIN KLEIN
Calvin Kl

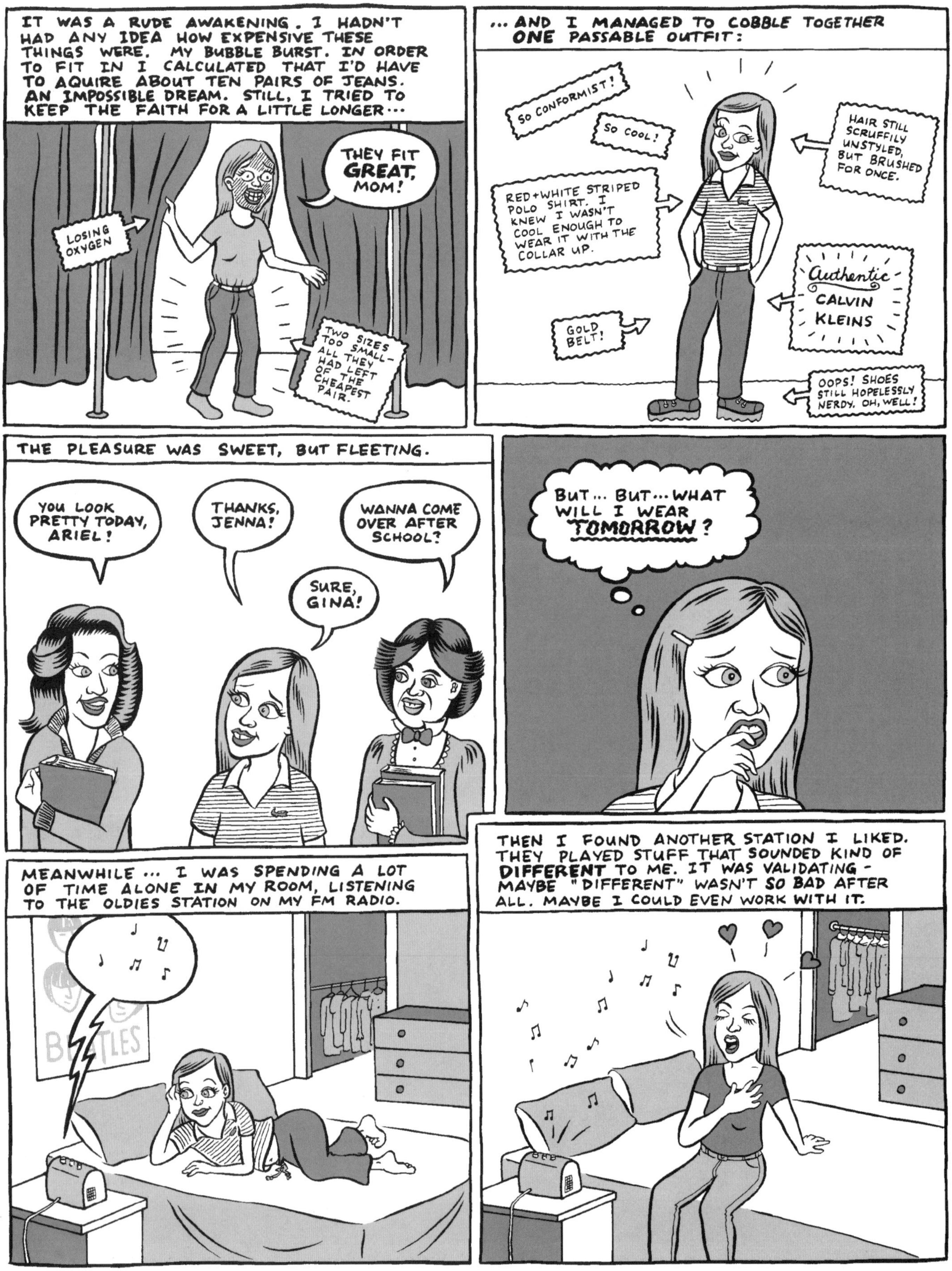
IT WAS A RUDE AWAKENING. I HADN'T HAD ANY IDEA HOW EXPENSIVE THESE THINGS WERE. MY BUBBLE BURST. IN ORDER TO FIT IN I CALCULATED THAT I'D HAVE TO AQUIRE ABOUT TEN PAIRS OF JEANS. AN IMPOSSIBLE DREAM. STILL, I TRIED TO KEEP THE FAITH FOR A LITTLE LONGER...
THEY FIT GREAT, MOM!
LOSING OXYGEN
TWO SIZES TOO SMALL—ALL THEY HAD LEFT OF THE CHEAPEST PAIR.
...AND I MANAGED TO COBBLE TOGETHER ONE PASSABLE OUTFIT:
SO CONFORMIST!
SO COOL!
HAIR STILL SCRUFFILY UNSTYLED, BUT BRUSHED FOR ONCE.
RED+WHITE STRIPED POLO SHIRT. I KNEW I WASN'T COOL ENOUGH TO WEAR IT WITH THE COLLAR UP.
Authentic CALVIN KLEINS
GOLD BELT!
OOPS! SHOES STILL HOPELESSLY NERDY. OH, WELL!
THE PLEASURE WAS SWEET, BUT FLEETING.
YOU LOOK PRETTY TODAY, ARIEL!
THANKS, JENNA!
WANNA COME OVER AFTER SCHOOL?
SURE, GINA!
BUT... BUT... WHAT WILL I WEAR TOMORROW?
MEANWHILE... I WAS SPENDING A LOT OF TIME ALONE IN MY ROOM, LISTENING TO THE OLDIES STATION ON MY FM RADIO.
BEATLES
THEN I FOUND ANOTHER STATION I LIKED. THEY PLAYED STUFF THAT SOUNDED KIND OF DIFFERENT TO ME. IT WAS VALIDATING - MAYBE "DIFFERENT" WASN'T SO BAD AFTER ALL. MAYBE I COULD EVEN WORK WITH IT.

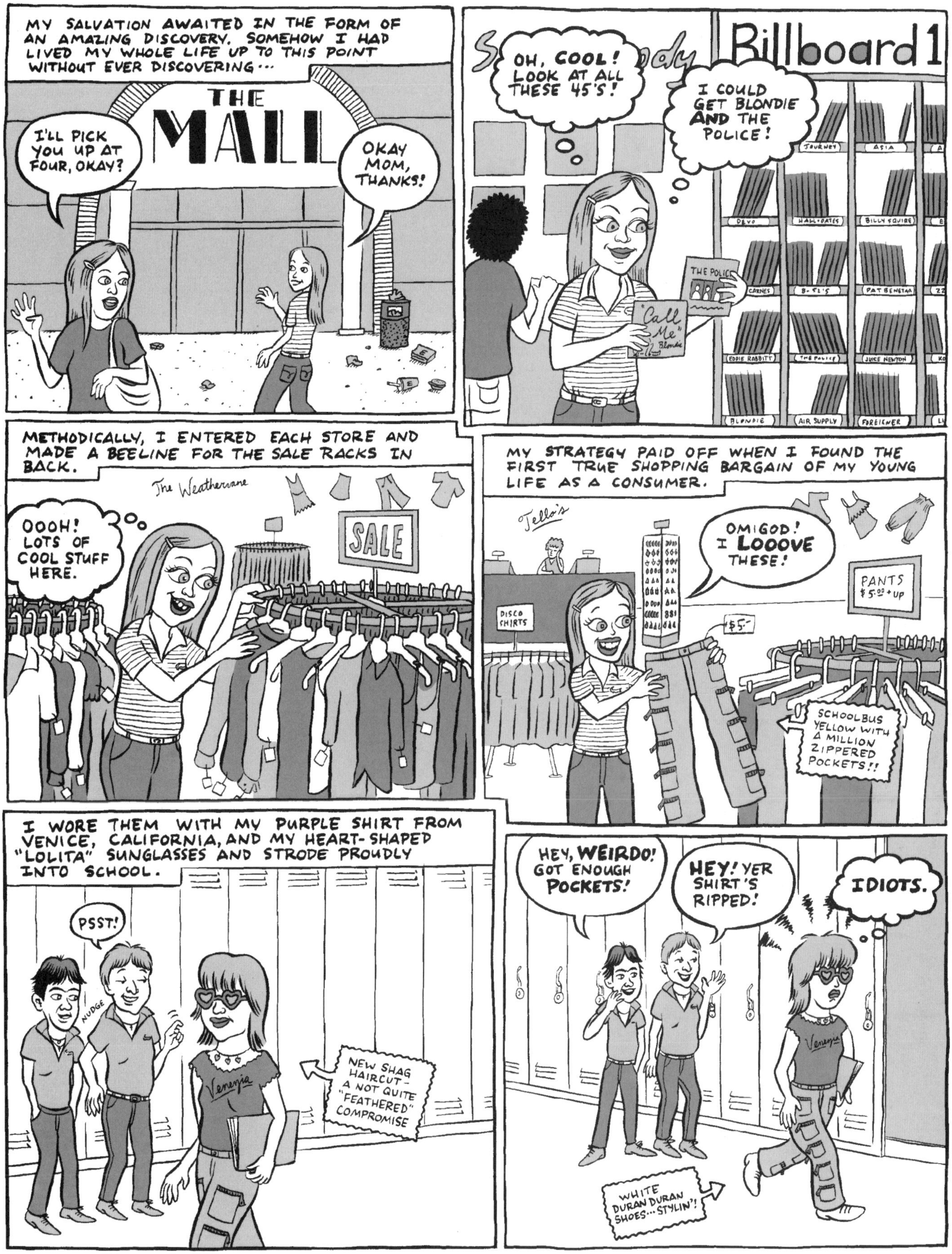
MY SALVATION AWAITED IN THE FORM OF AN AMAZING DISCOVERY. SOMEHOW I HAD LIVED MY WHOLE LIFE UP TO THIS POINT WITHOUT EVER DISCOVERING...
THE MALL
I'LL PICK YOU UP AT FOUR, OKAY?
OKAY MOM, THANKS!
Billboard 1
OH, COOL! LOOK AT ALL THESE 45'S!
I COULD GET BLONDIE AND THE POLICE!
THE POLICE
"Call Me" Blondie
JOURNEY
ASIA
DEVO
HALL+OATES
BILLY SQUIRE
CARNES
B-52'S
PAT BENETAR
EDDIE RABBITT
THE POLICE
JUICE NEWTON
BLONDIE
AIR SUPPLY
FOREIGNER
METHODICALLY, I ENTERED EACH STORE AND MADE A BEELINE FOR THE SALE RACKS IN BACK.
The Weathervane
OOOH! LOTS OF COOL STUFF HERE.
SALE
MY STRATEGY PAID OFF WHEN I FOUND THE FIRST TRUE SHOPPING BARGAIN OF MY YOUNG LIFE AS A CONSUMER.
Jello's
OMIGOD! I LOOOVE THESE!
DISCO SHIRTS
$5.-
PANTS $5.00 + UP
SCHOOLBUS YELLOW WITH A MILLION ZIPPERED POCKETS!!
I WORE THEM WITH MY PURPLE SHIRT FROM VENICE, CALIFORNIA, AND MY HEART-SHAPED "LOLITA" SUNGLASSES AND STRODE PROUDLY INTO SCHOOL.
PSST!
NUDGE
Venezia
NEW SHAG HAIRCUT - A NOT QUITE "FEATHERED" COMPROMISE
HEY, WEIRDO! GOT ENOUGH POCKETS!
HEY! YER SHIRT'S RIPPED!
IDIOTS.
Venezia
WHITE DURAN DURAN SHOES...STYLIN'!

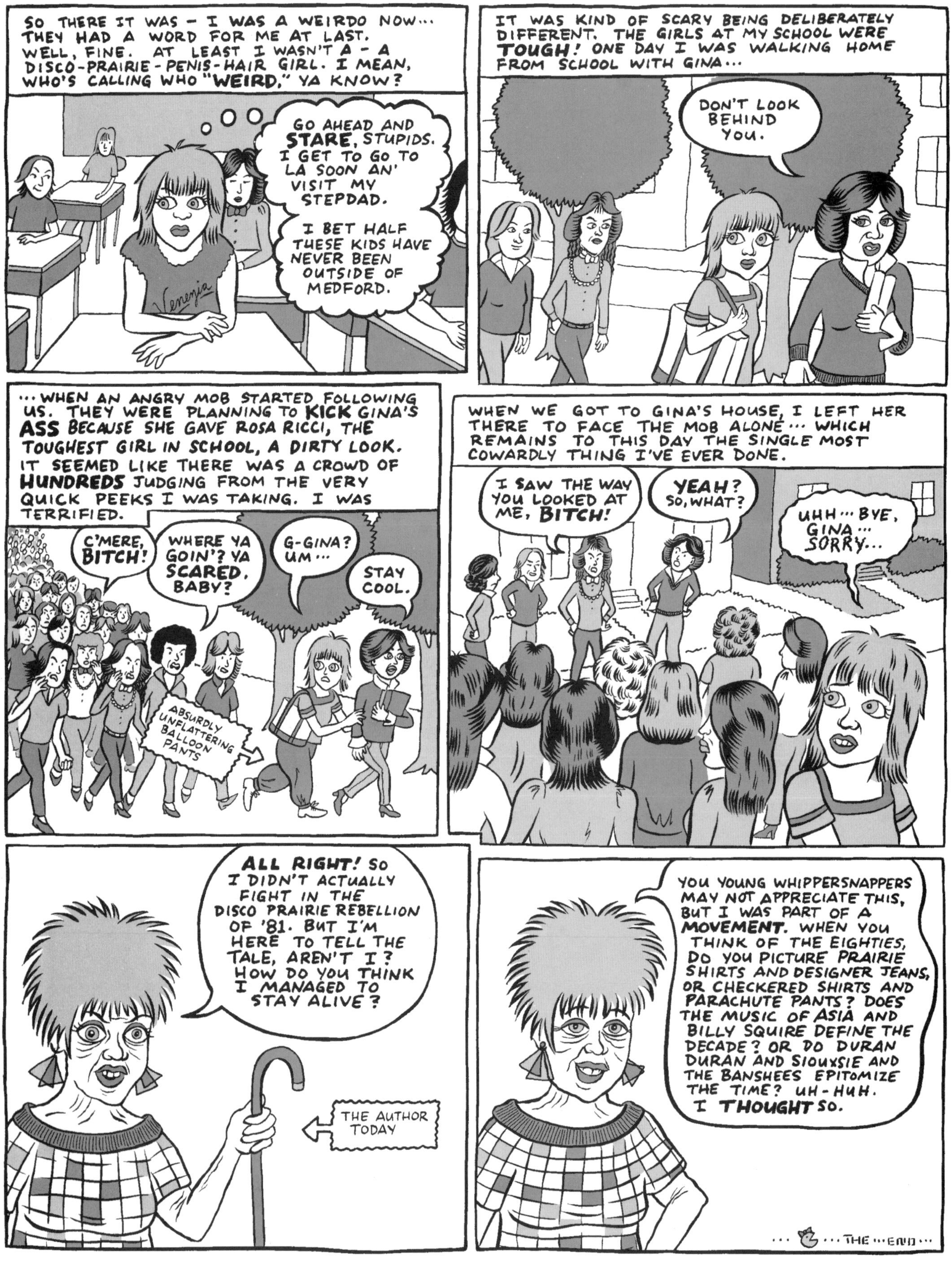
SO THERE IT WAS – I WAS A WEIRDO NOW… THEY HAD A WORD FOR ME AT LAST. WELL, FINE. AT LEAST I WASN'T A – A DISCO-PRAIRIE-PENIS-HAIR GIRL. I MEAN, WHO'S CALLING WHO "WEIRD," YA KNOW?
GO AHEAD AND STARE, STUPIDS. I GET TO GO TO LA SOON AN' VISIT MY STEPDAD.
I BET HALF THESE KIDS HAVE NEVER BEEN OUTSIDE OF MEDFORD.
Venezia
IT WAS KIND OF SCARY BEING DELIBERATELY DIFFERENT. THE GIRLS AT MY SCHOOL WERE TOUGH! ONE DAY I WAS WALKING HOME FROM SCHOOL WITH GINA…
DON'T LOOK BEHIND YOU.
…WHEN AN ANGRY MOB STARTED FOLLOWING US. THEY WERE PLANNING TO KICK GINA'S ASS BECAUSE SHE GAVE ROSA RICCI, THE TOUGHEST GIRL IN SCHOOL, A DIRTY LOOK. IT SEEMED LIKE THERE WAS A CROWD OF HUNDREDS JUDGING FROM THE VERY QUICK PEEKS I WAS TAKING. I WAS TERRIFIED.
C'MERE, BITCH!
WHERE YA GOIN'? YA SCARED, BABY?
G-GINA? UM…
STAY COOL.
ABSURDLY UNFLATTERING BALLOON PANTS
WHEN WE GOT TO GINA'S HOUSE, I LEFT HER THERE TO FACE THE MOB ALONE… WHICH REMAINS TO THIS DAY THE SINGLE MOST COWARDLY THING I'VE EVER DONE.
I SAW THE WAY YOU LOOKED AT ME, BITCH!
YEAH? SO, WHAT?
UHH… BYE, GINA… SORRY…
ALL RIGHT! SO I DIDN'T ACTUALLY FIGHT IN THE DISCO PRAIRIE REBELLION OF '81. BUT I'M HERE TO TELL THE TALE, AREN'T I? HOW DO YOU THINK I MANAGED TO STAY ALIVE?
THE AUTHOR TODAY
YOU YOUNG WHIPPERSNAPPERS MAY NOT APPRECIATE THIS, BUT I WAS PART OF A MOVEMENT. WHEN YOU THINK OF THE EIGHTIES, DO YOU PICTURE PRAIRIE SHIRTS AND DESIGNER JEANS, OR CHECKERED SHIRTS AND PARACHUTE PANTS? DOES THE MUSIC OF ASIA AND BILLY SQUIRE DEFINE THE DECADE? OR DO DURAN DURAN AND SIOUXSIE AND THE BANSHEES EPITOMIZE THE TIME? UH-HUH. I THOUGHT SO.
…THE…END…

AARON RENIER

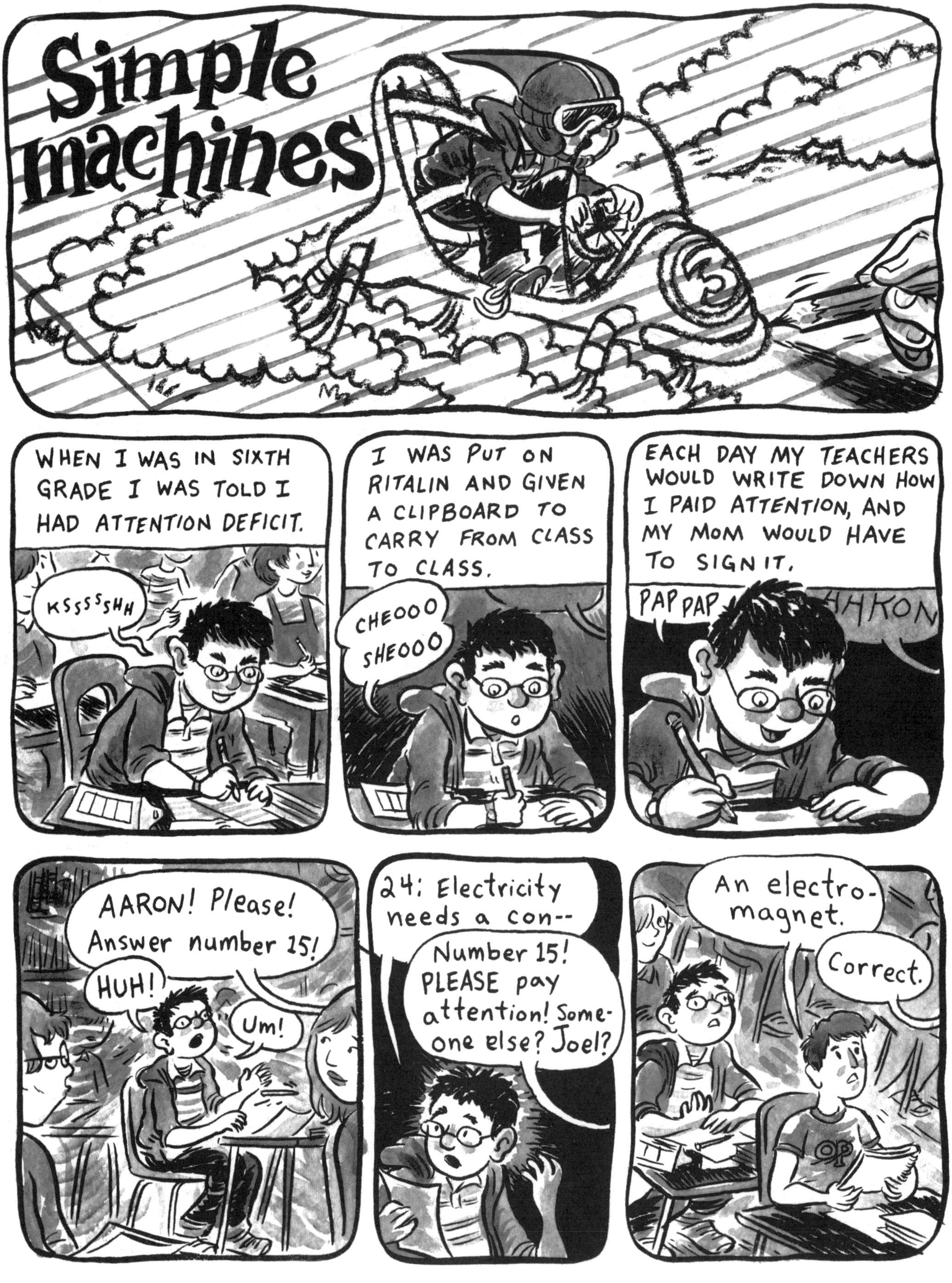
Simple machines
WHEN I WAS IN SIXTH GRADE I WAS TOLD I HAD ATTENTION DEFICIT.
KSSSSSHH
I WAS PUT ON RITALIN AND GIVEN A CLIPBOARD TO CARRY FROM CLASS TO CLASS.
CHEOOO SHEOOO
EACH DAY MY TEACHERS WOULD WRITE DOWN HOW I PAID ATTENTION, AND MY MOM WOULD HAVE TO SIGN IT.
PAP PAP
HHKON
AARON! Please! Answer number 15!
HUH!
Um!
24: Electricity needs a con--
Number 15! PLEASE pay attention! Someone else? Joel?
An electro-magnet.
Correct.

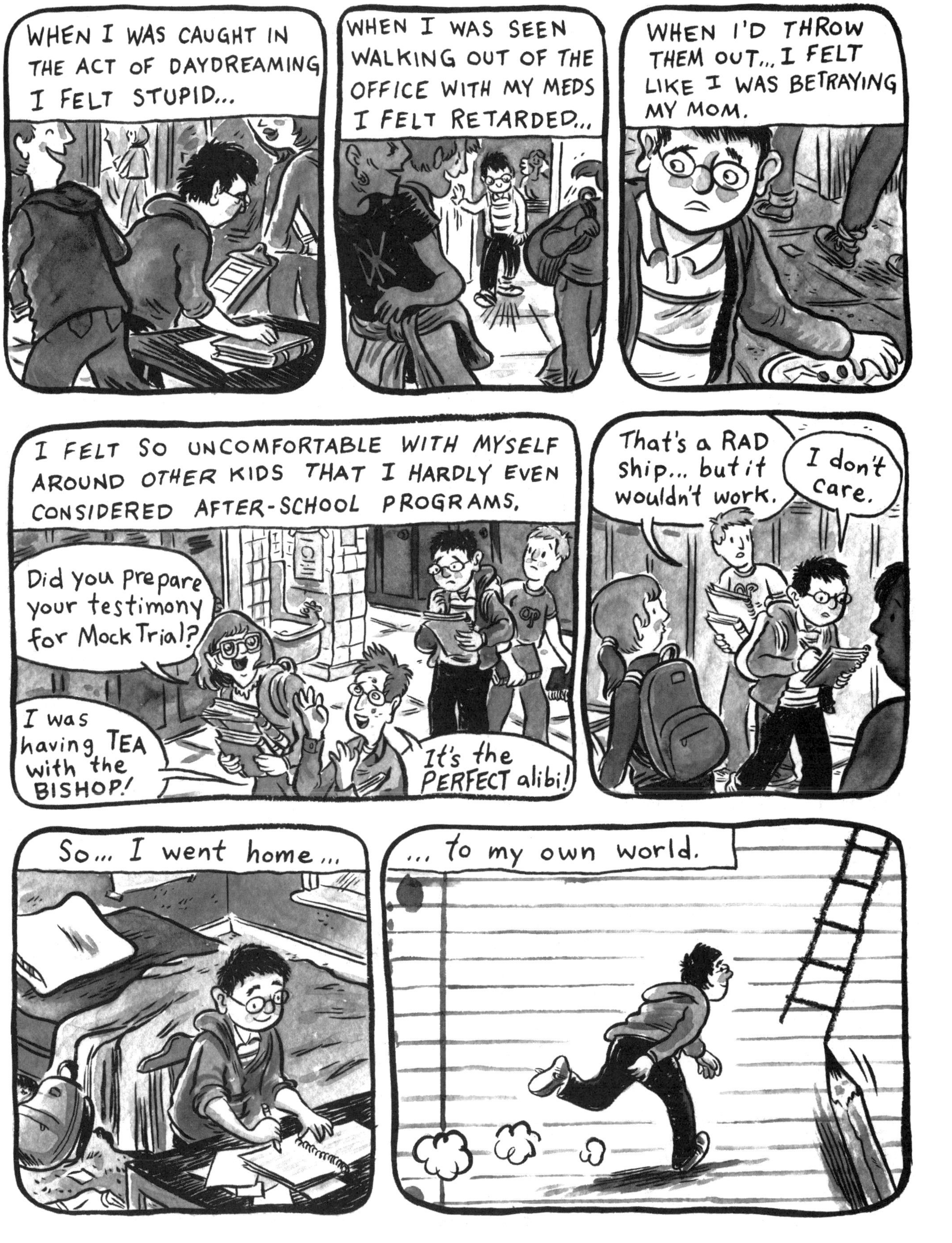
WHEN I WAS CAUGHT IN THE ACT OF DAYDREAMING I FELT STUPID...
WHEN I WAS SEEN WALKING OUT OF THE OFFICE WITH MY MEDS I FELT RETARDED...
WHEN I'D THROW THEM OUT... I FELT LIKE I WAS BETRAYING MY MOM.
I FELT SO UNCOMFORTABLE WITH MYSELF AROUND OTHER KIDS THAT I HARDLY EVEN CONSIDERED AFTER-SCHOOL PROGRAMS.
Did you prepare your testimony for Mock Trial?
I was having TEA with the BISHOP!
It's the PERFECT alibi!
That's a RAD ship... but it wouldn't work.
I don't care.
So... I went home...
... to my own world.

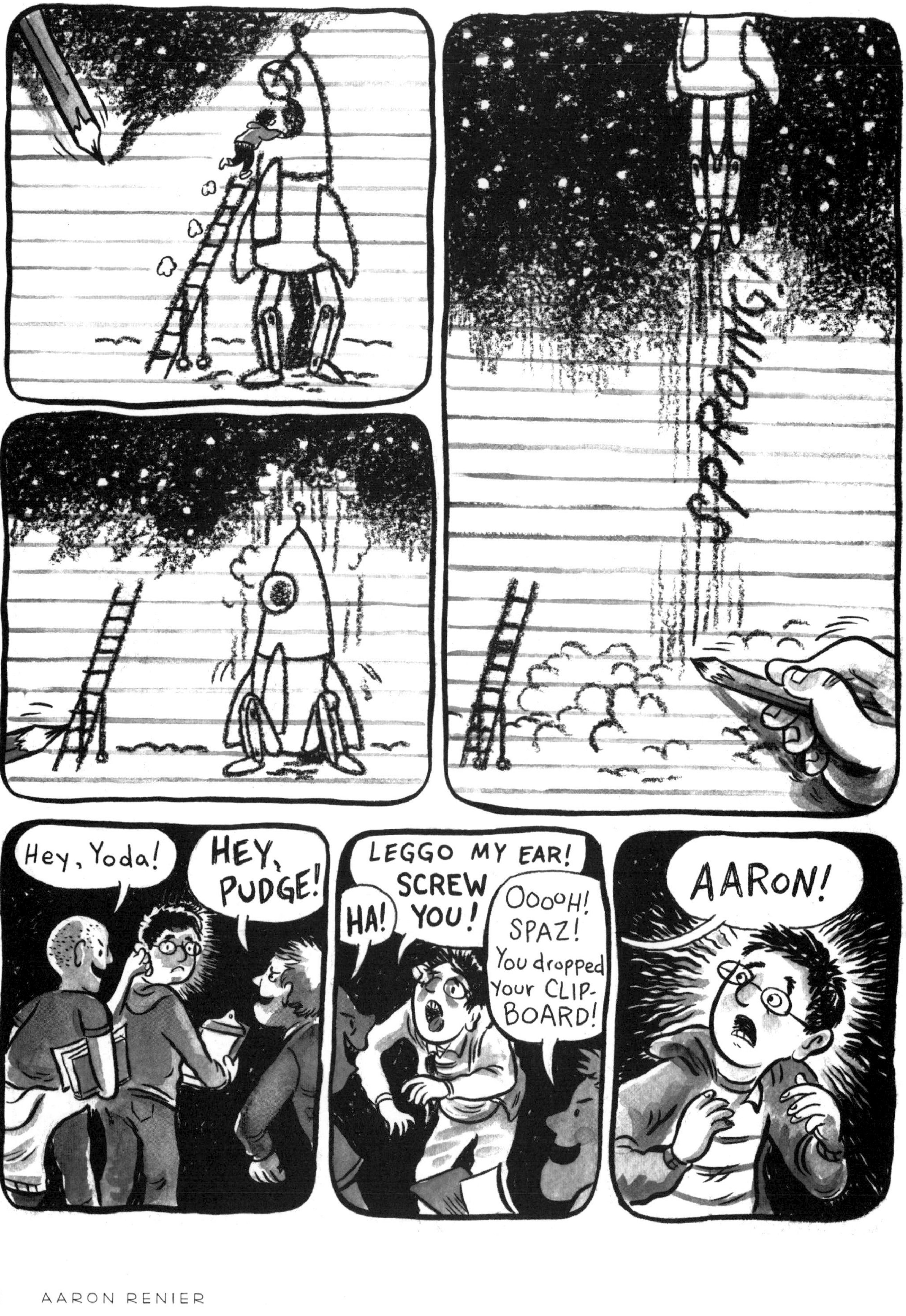
Hey, Yoda!
HEY, PUDGE!
LEGGO MY EAR!
HA!
SCREW YOU!
OooOH! SPAZ! You dropped your CLIP-BOARD!
AARON!

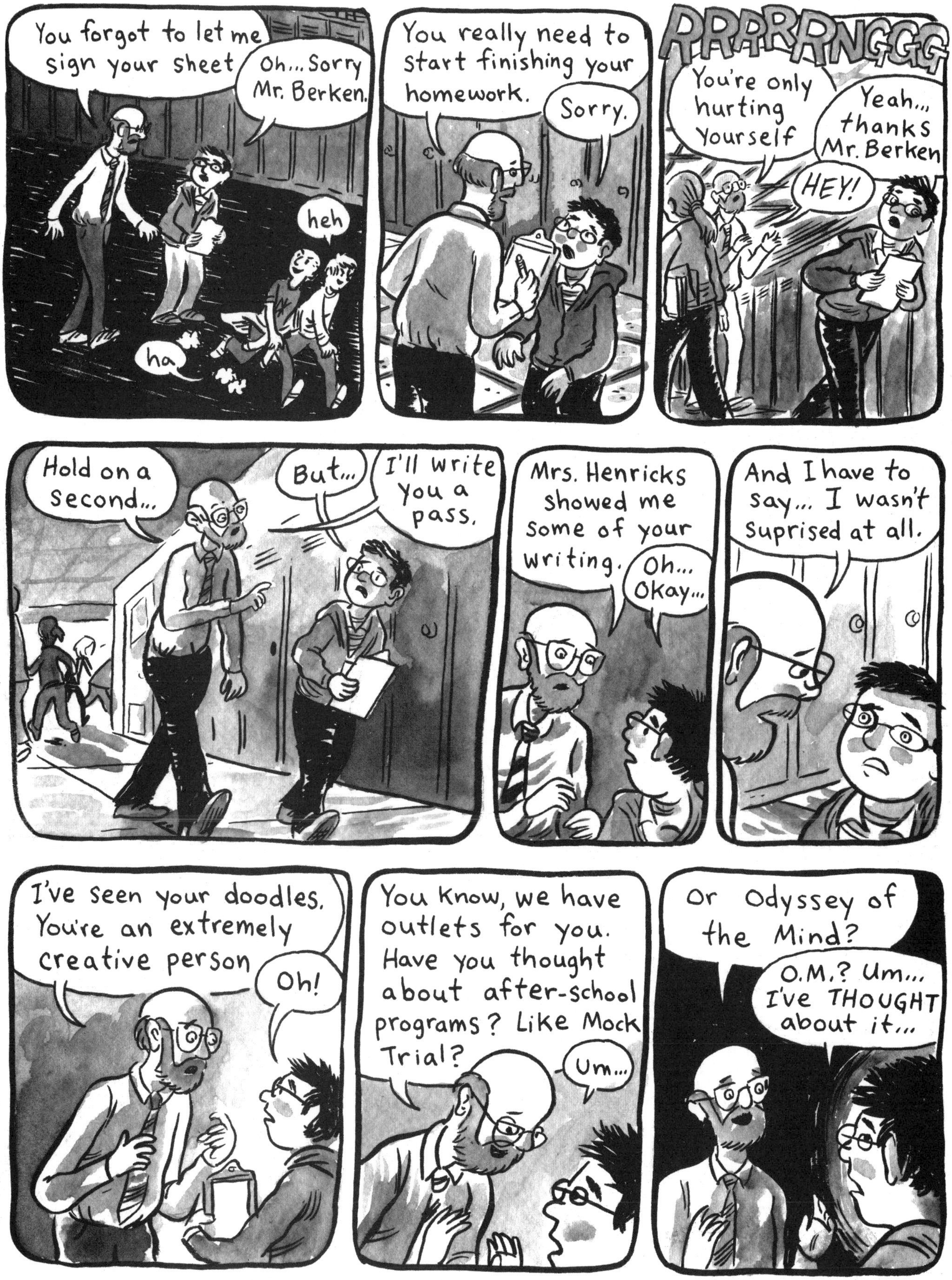
You forgot to let me sign your sheet
Oh... Sorry Mr. Berken.
heh
ha
You really need to start finishing your homework.
Sorry.
RRRRRNGGG
You're only hurting yourself
Yeah... thanks Mr. Berken
HEY!
Hold on a second...
But...
I'll write you a pass.
Mrs. Henricks showed me some of your writing.
Oh... Okay...
And I have to say... I wasn't suprised at all.
I've seen your doodles. You're an extremely creative person
Oh!
You know, we have outlets for you. Have you thought about after-school programs? Like Mock Trial?
Um...
Or Odyssey of the Mind?
O.M.? Um... I've THOUGHT about it...

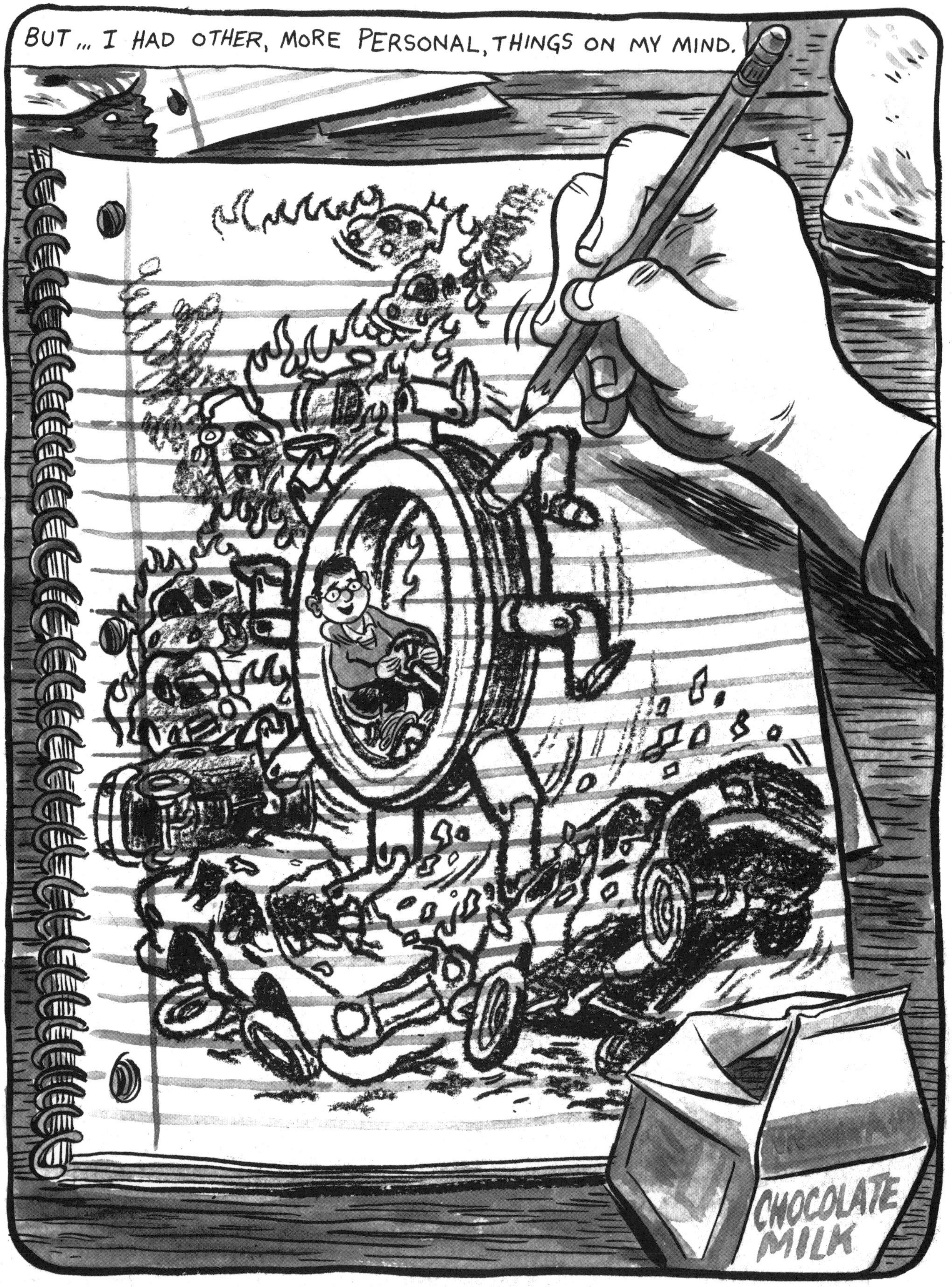
BUT... I HAD OTHER, MORE PERSONAL, THINGS ON MY MIND.
CHOCOLATE MILK

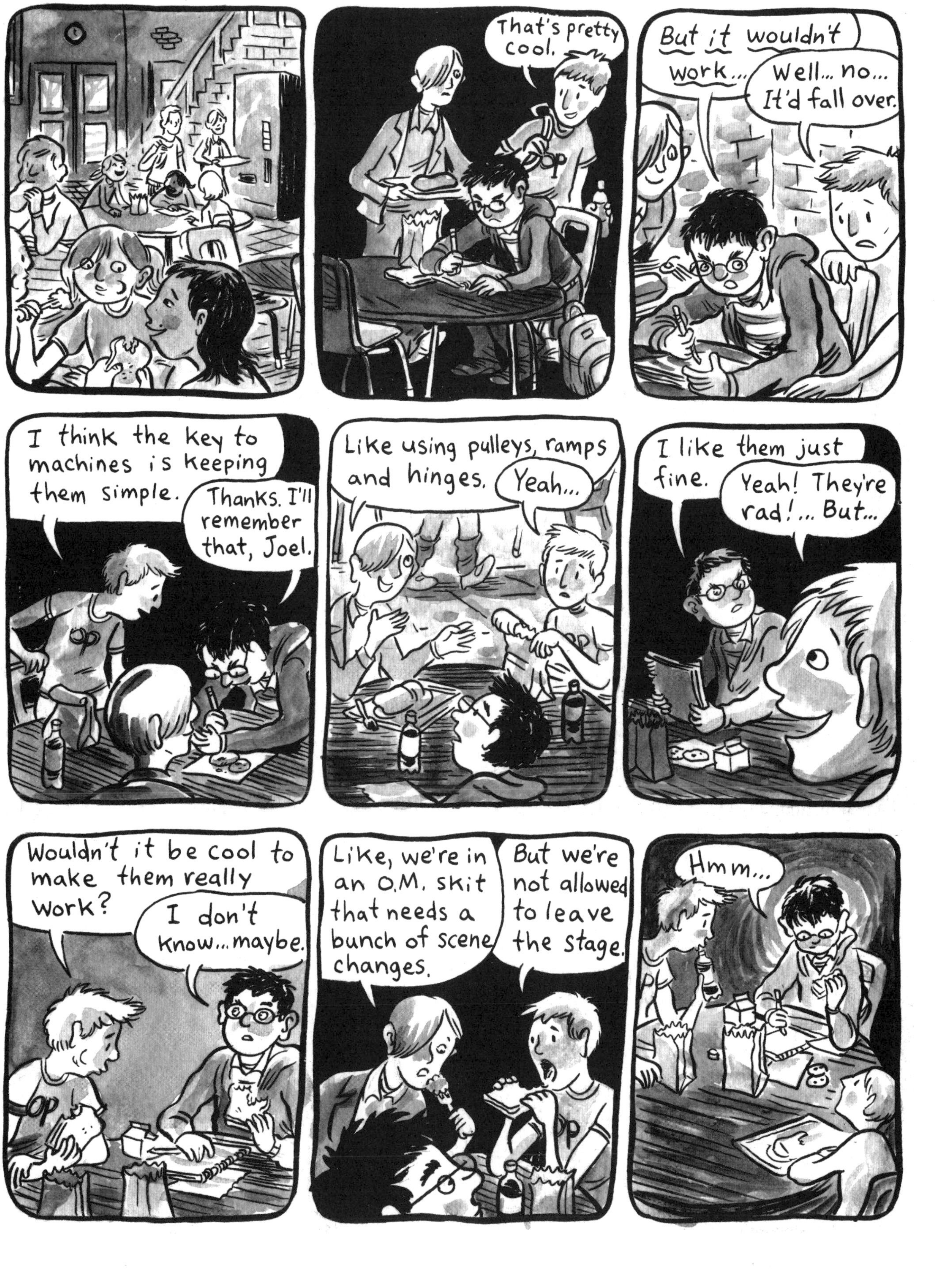

That's pretty cool.
But it wouldn't work...
Well... no... It'd fall over.
I think the key to machines is keeping them simple.
Thanks. I'll remember that, Joel.
Like using pulleys, ramps and hinges.
Yeah...
I like them just fine.
Yeah! They're rad!... But...
Wouldn't it be cool to make them really work?
I don't know... maybe.
Like, we're in an O.M. skit that needs a bunch of scene changes.
But we're not allowed to leave the stage.
Hmm...

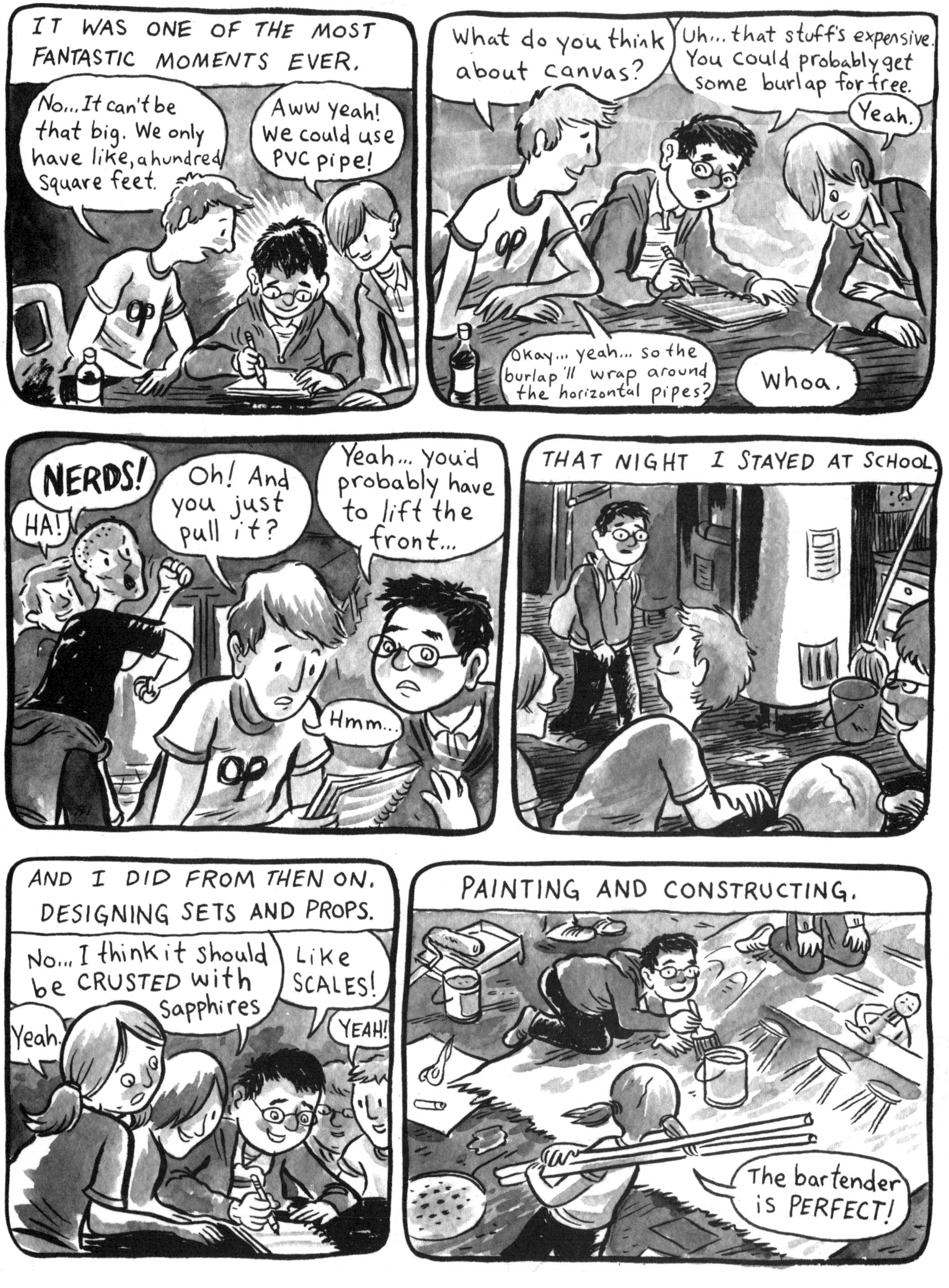
IT WAS ONE OF THE MOST FANTASTIC MOMENTS EVER.
No... It can't be that big. We only have like, a hundred square feet.
Aww yeah! We could use PVC pipe!
What do you think about canvas?
Uh... that stuff's expensive. You could probably get some burlap for free.
Yeah.
Okay... yeah... so the burlap'll wrap around the horizontal pipes?
Whoa.
NERDS!
HA!
Oh! And you just pull it?
Yeah... you'd probably have to lift the front...
Hmm...
THAT NIGHT I STAYED AT SCHOOL.
AND I DID FROM THEN ON. DESIGNING SETS AND PROPS.
No... I think it should be CRUSTED with sapphires
Like SCALES!
Yeah.
YEAH!
PAINTING AND CONSTRUCTING.
The bartender is PERFECT!

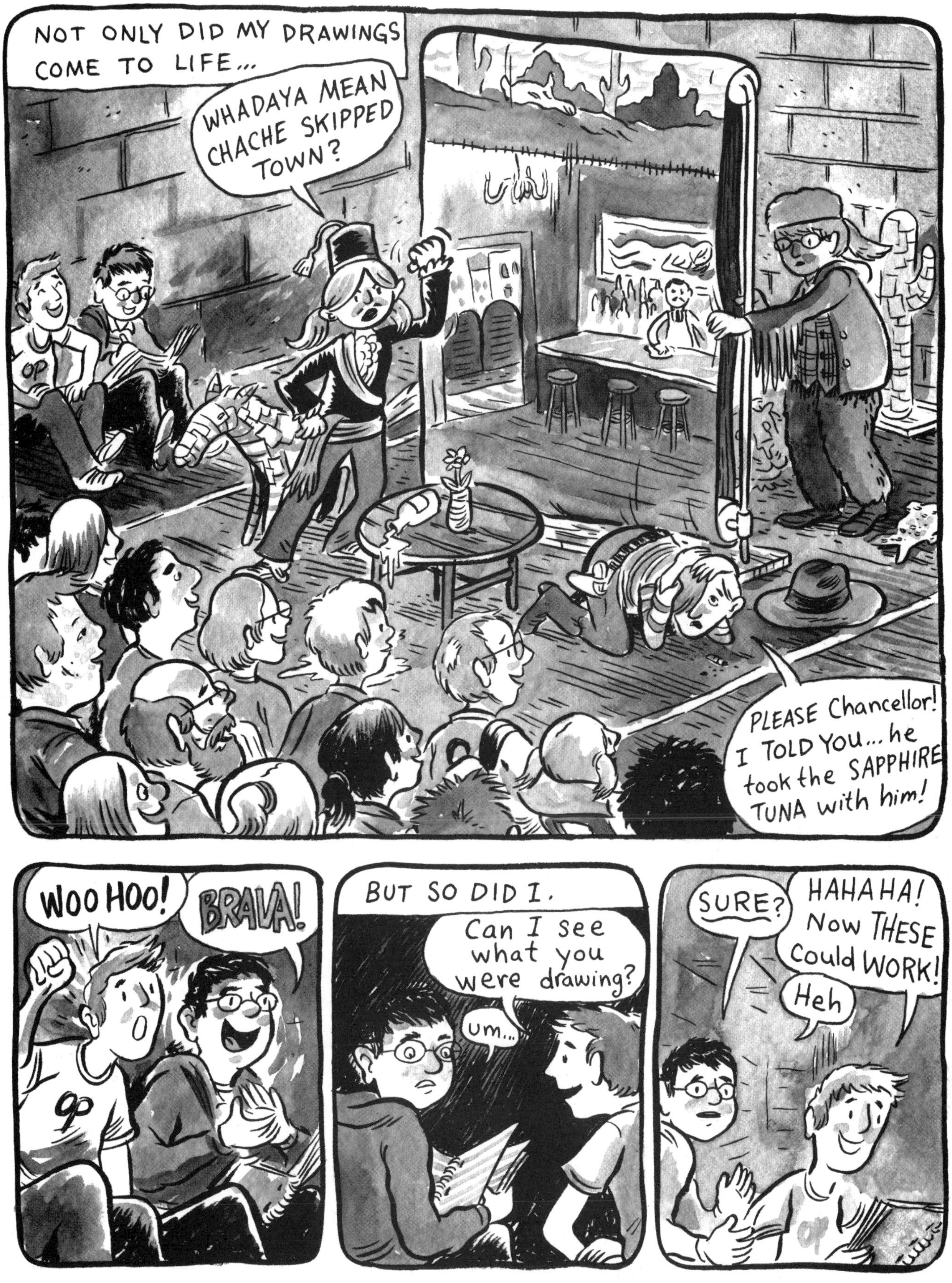
NOT ONLY DID MY DRAWINGS COME TO LIFE...
WHADAYA MEAN CHACHE SKIPPED TOWN?
PLEASE Chancellor! I TOLD YOU... he took the SAPPHIRE TUNA with him!
WOO HOO!
BRAVA!
BUT SO DID I.
Can I see what you were drawing?
um...
SURE?
HAHAHA! Now THESE Could WORK!
Heh

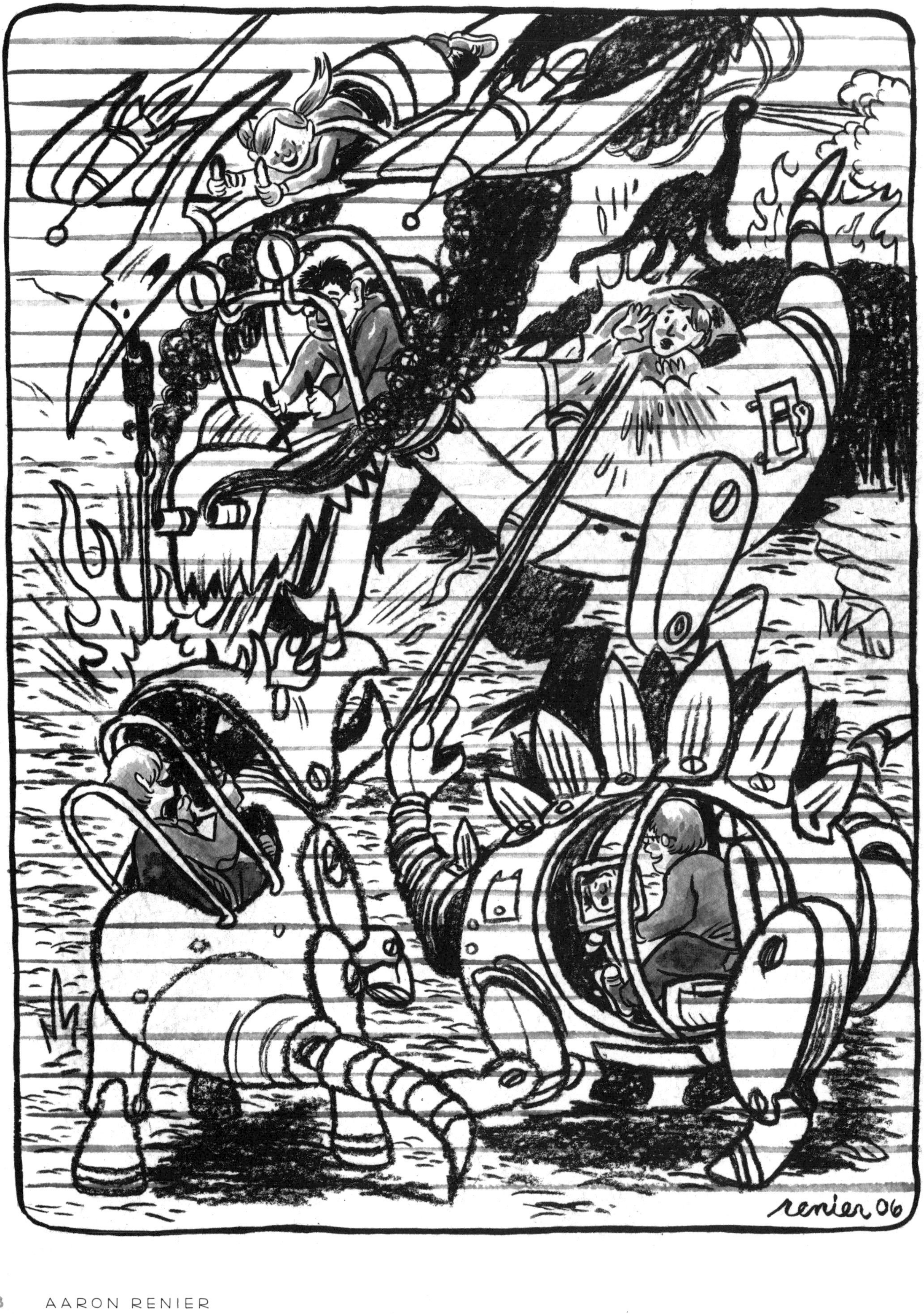
renier 06

ARIEL SCHRAG

Ariel schrag

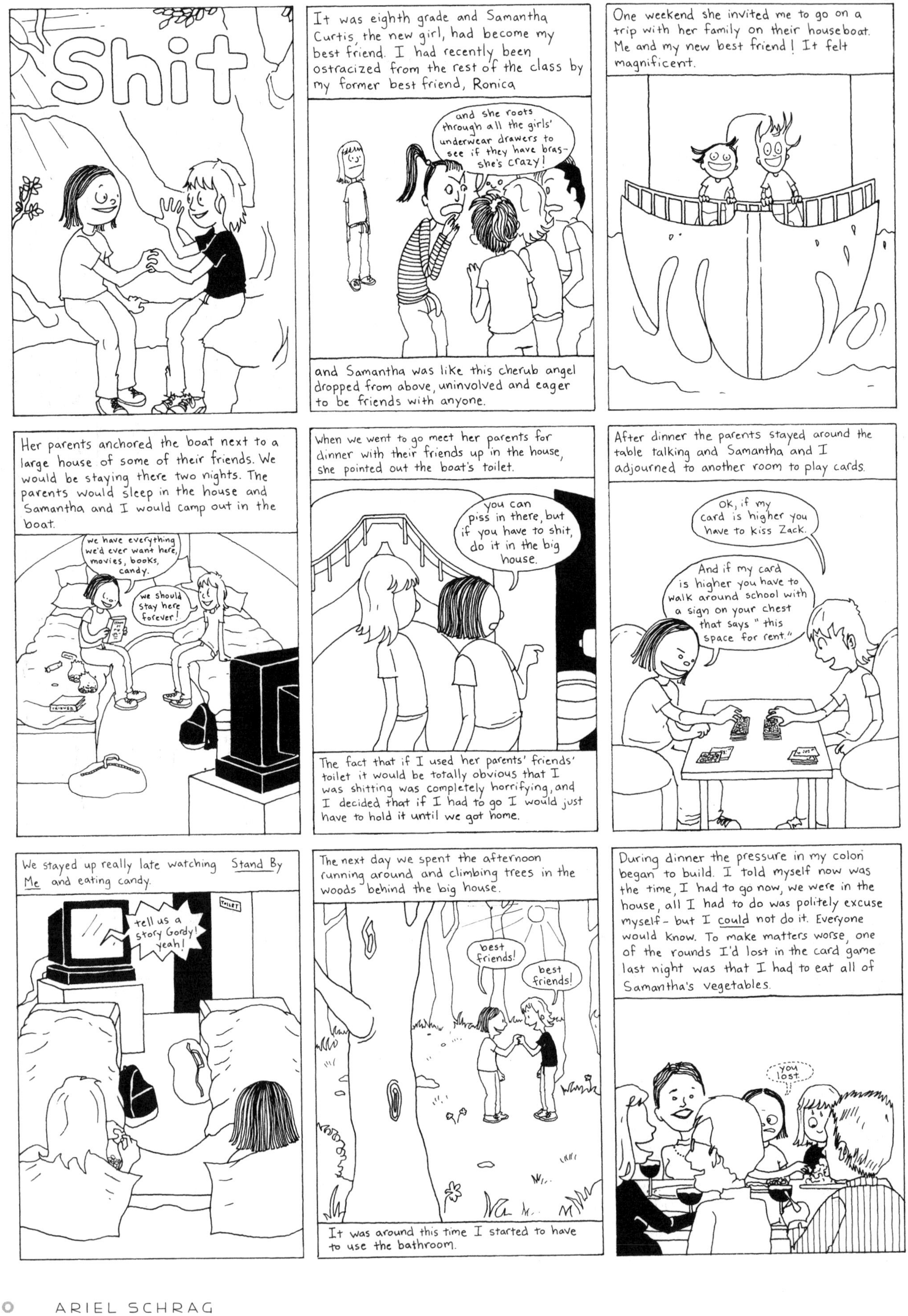
Shit
It was eighth grade and Samantha Curtis, the new girl, had become my best friend. I had recently been ostracized from the rest of the class by my former best friend, Ronica
and she roots through all the girls' underwear drawers to see if they have bras- she's crazy!
and Samantha was like this cherub angel dropped from above, uninvolved and eager to be friends with anyone.
One weekend she invited me to go on a trip with her family on their houseboat. Me and my new best friend! It felt magnificent.
Her parents anchored the boat next to a large house of some of their friends. We would be staying there two nights. The parents would sleep in the house and Samantha and I would camp out in the boat.
we have everything we'd ever want here, movies, books, candy.
we should stay here forever!
When we went to go meet her parents for dinner with their friends up in the house, she pointed out the boat's toilet.
you can piss in there, but if you have to shit, do it in the big house.
The fact that if I used her parents' friends' toilet it would be totally obvious that I was shitting was completely horrifying, and I decided that if I had to go I would just have to hold it until we got home.
After dinner the parents stayed around the table talking and Samantha and I adjourned to another room to play cards.
OK, if my card is higher you have to kiss Zack.
And if my card is higher you have to walk around school with a sign on your chest that says " this space for rent."
We stayed up really late watching Stand By Me and eating candy.
TOILET
tell us a story Gordy! yeah!
The next day we spent the afternoon running around and climbing trees in the woods behind the big house.
best friends!
best friends!
It was around this time I started to have to use the bathroom.
During dinner the pressure in my colon began to build. I told myself now was the time, I had to go now, we were in the house, all I had to do was politely excuse myself- but I could not do it. Everyone would know. To make matters worse, one of the rounds I'd lost in the card game last night was that I had to eat all of Samantha's vegetables.
you lost.

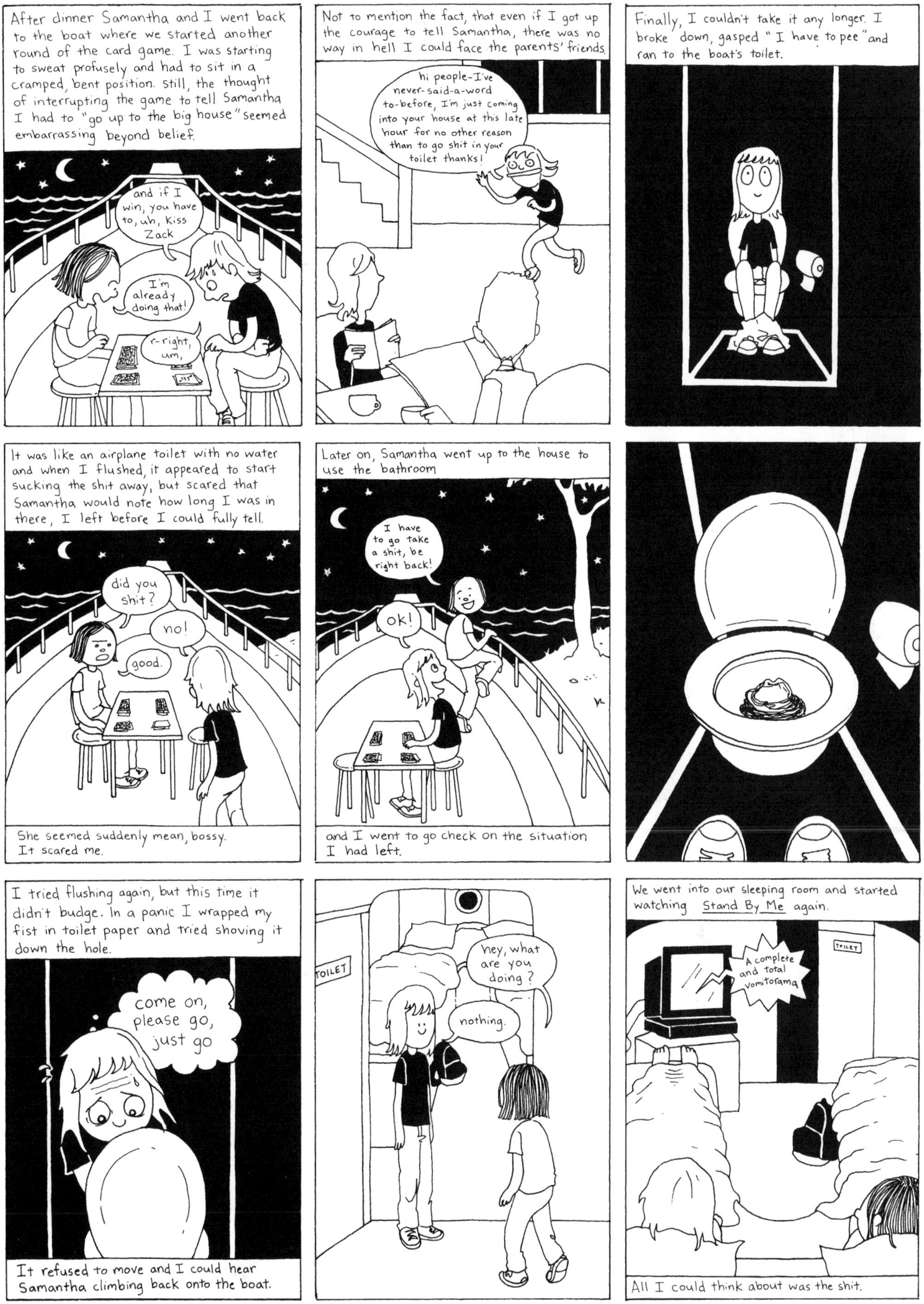

After dinner Samantha and I went back to the boat where we started another round of the card game. I was starting to sweat profusely and had to sit in a cramped, bent position. Still, the thought of interrupting the game to tell Samantha I had to "go up to the big house" seemed embarrassing beyond belief.
and if I win, you have to, uh, kiss Zack
I'm already doing that!
r-right, um,
Not to mention the fact, that even if I got up the courage to tell Samantha, there was no way in hell I could face the parents' friends.
hi people-I've never-said-a-word to-before, I'm just coming into your house at this late hour for no other reason than to go shit in your toilet thanks!
Finally, I couldn't take it any longer. I broke down, gasped "I have to pee" and ran to the boat's toilet.
It was like an airplane toilet with no water and when I flushed, it appeared to start sucking the shit away, but scared that Samantha would note how long I was in there, I left before I could fully tell.
did you shit?
no!
good.
She seemed suddenly mean, bossy. It scared me.
Later on, Samantha went up to the house to use the bathroom
I have to go take a shit, be right back!
ok!
and I went to go check on the situation I had left.
I tried flushing again, but this time it didn't budge. In a panic I wrapped my fist in toilet paper and tried shoving it down the hole.
come on, please go, just go
It refused to move and I could hear Samantha climbing back onto the boat.
TOILET
hey, what are you doing?
nothing.
We went into our sleeping room and started watching Stand By Me again.
TOILET
A complete and total vomitorama
All I could think about was the shit.

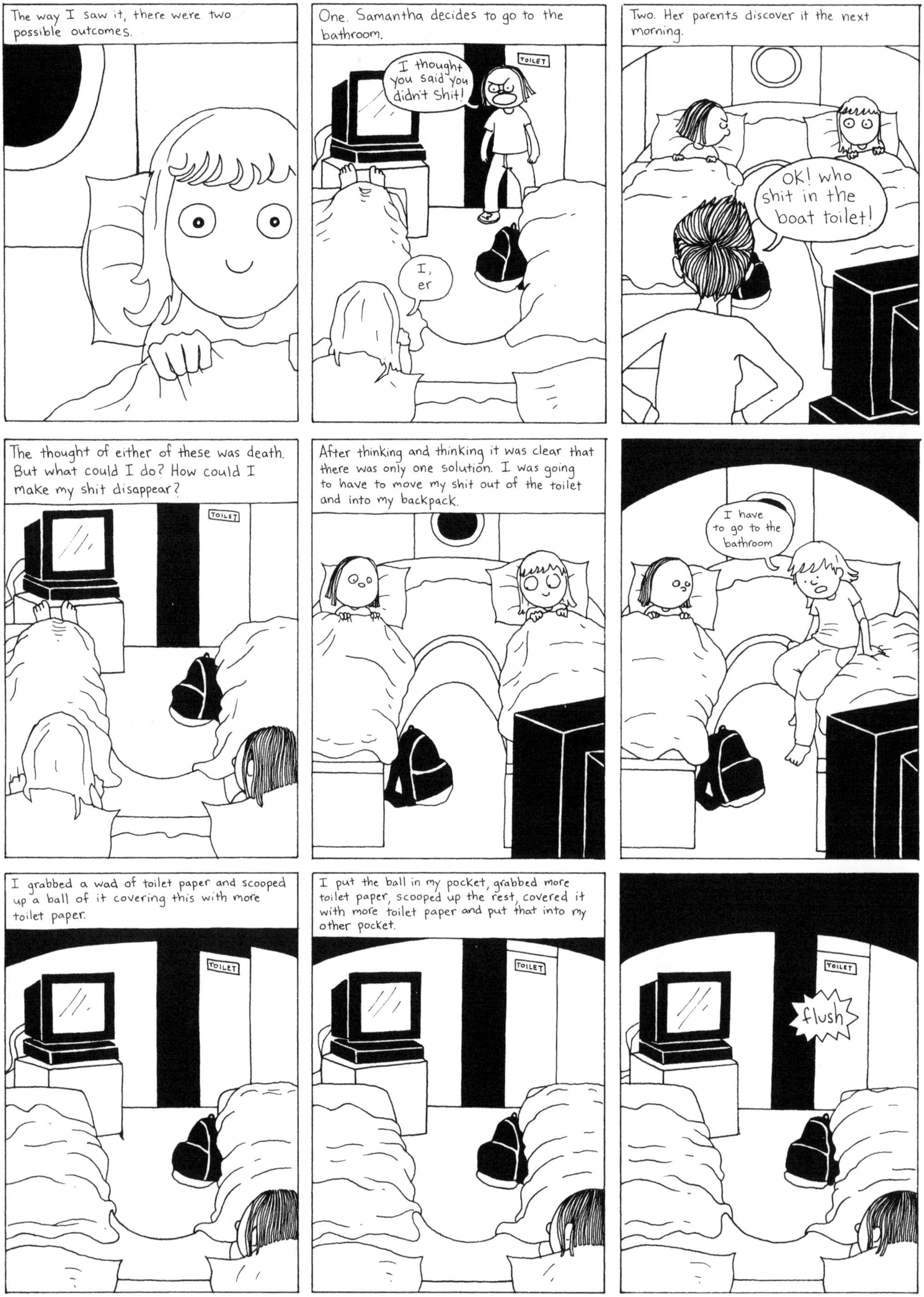

The way I saw it, there were two possible outcomes.
One. Samantha decides to go to the bathroom.
TOILET
I thought you said you didn't shit!
I, er
Two. Her parents discover it the next morning.
OK! who shit in the boat toilet!
The thought of either of these was death. But what could I do? How could I make my shit disappear?
TOILET
After thinking and thinking it was clear that there was only one solution. I was going to have to move my shit out of the toilet and into my backpack.
I have to go to the bathroom
I grabbed a wad of toilet paper and scooped up a ball of it covering this with more toilet paper.
TOILET
I put the ball in my pocket, grabbed more toilet paper, scooped up the rest, covered it with more toilet paper and put that into my other pocket.
TOILET
TOILET
flush

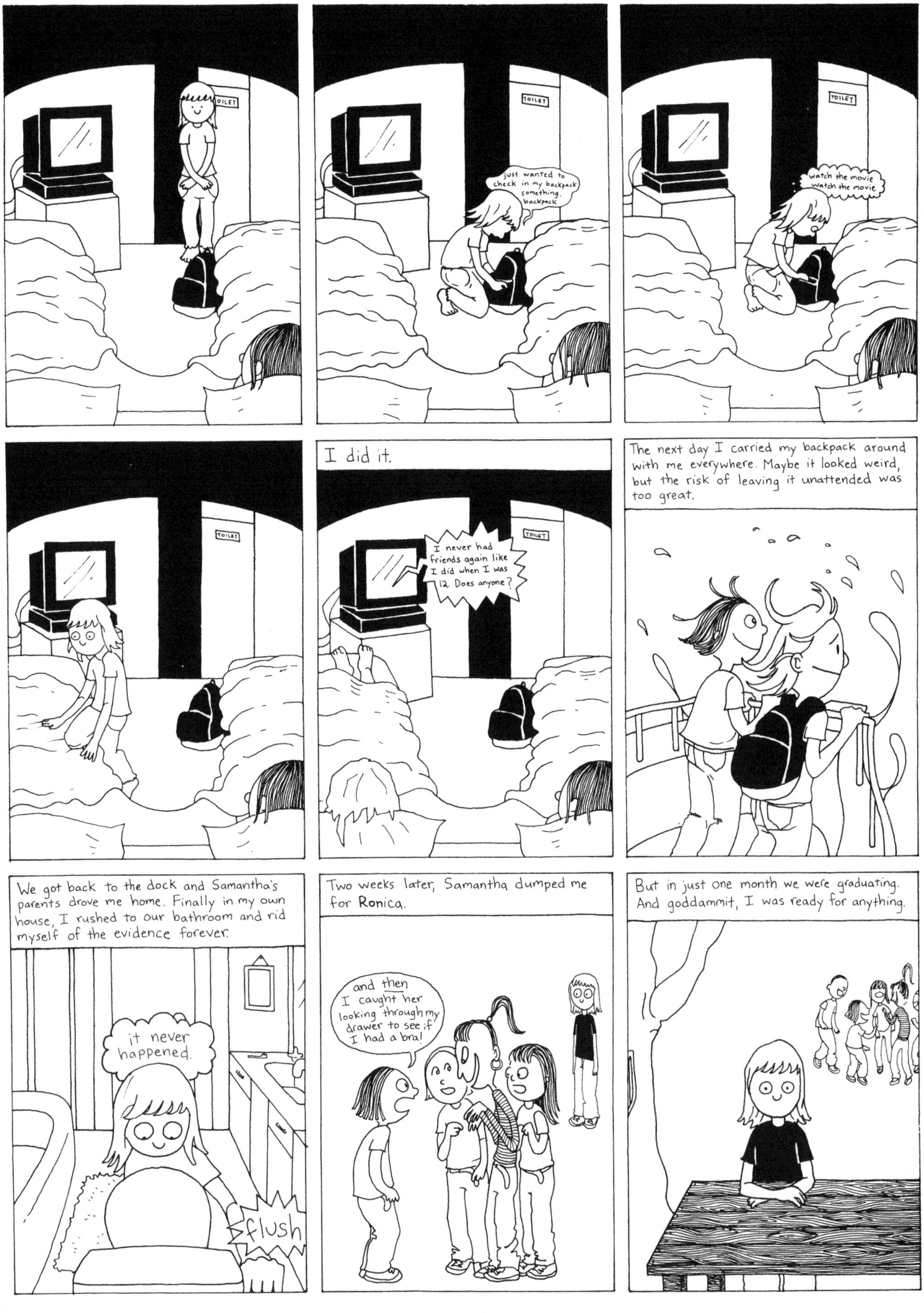
TOILET
TOILET
just wanted to check in my backpack something. backpack
TOILET
watch the movie watch the movie
TOILET
I did it.
TOILET
I never had friends again like I did when I was 12. Does anyone?
The next day I carried my backpack around with me everywhere. Maybe it looked weird, but the risk of leaving it unattended was too great.
We got back to the dock and Samantha's parents drove me home. Finally in my own house, I rushed to our bathroom and rid myself of the evidence forever.
it never happened.
flush
Two weeks later, Samantha dumped me for Ronica.
and then I caught her looking through my drawer to see if I had a bra!
But in just one month we were graduating. And goddammit, I was ready for anything.

CONTRIBUTORS

VANESSA DAVIS was born in 1978 and grew up in West Palm Beach, Florida. Until she went to middle school, she knew almost only Jewish people. She started drawing comics because she loves drawing and telling stories about herself and the people she knows. In 2005, *Spaniel Rage*, a collection of her diary comics, was published by Buenaventura Press.

JOE MATT, born in 1963, grew up in the suburbs of Philadelphia. His collecting habit manifested early at the age of six when he began trimming the comic strip "Li'l Abner" from the daily newspaper. A strict Catholic upbringing afforded him numerous opportunities for developing neurotic and compulsive behavioral habits.

A graduate of the Philadelphia College of Art, he went on to create the autobiographical comic book series Peepshow in 1991. Pages from his collection *Fair Weather*, which documents a weekend of his childhood, appear in the book you are currently holding. Joe Matt lives in Los Angeles without a car or a computer.

TANIA SCHRAG was born in Berkeley, California. She started drawing comics at age fourteen having been inspired by her older sister, Ariel Schrag, and a recent event in her life. She collected her work into a self-published volume, titled *Tales of a Teenage Nothing*, and began selling it at comic conventions nationwide. She is currently working on several stories, including a comic about Chicago, where she lived while attending the University of Chicago, and a comic titled, "The Autistic Lover" detailing the experience of her first year in New York, where she currently lives. After two years of being a high school Latin teacher, she now works for the Civilian Complaints Review Board investigating New York City police officers.

ERIC ENRIGHT was born and raised in New Jersey, where he attended the ironically named Our Lady Queen of Peace School through the eighth grade. It continues to be the most miserable experience of his life. Eric has worked in a variety of media, mass and otherwise. He is currently pursuing his M.A. in Media Studies at The New School in New York City, where he resides with his fish, Gil.

ARIEL SCHRAG

In seventh grade Ariel Schrag started a sketchbook/journal, which came to be known as "Black Book." Black Book started out wholesome, with Ariel and friends filling its pages with lyrics to oldies songs, inside jokes, and poems. The book took a quick turn to the dark side, however, when Ariel's best friend lied to her about going on a ski trip with another girl and Ariel drew a huge grotesque caricature of the best friend and showed it to anyone that came over to her house. Soon everyone wanted to draw a mean caricature of the person they hated, and Black Book became a hotbed of preteen revenge and spite. At one point a teacher at the school found out about Black Book and made an announcement in front of the entire class that she was going to burn it. Ariel shouted out, "You can't burn it! It's my diary!" Ariel likes to think of *Stuck in the Middle* as the "socially acceptable" version of Black Book.

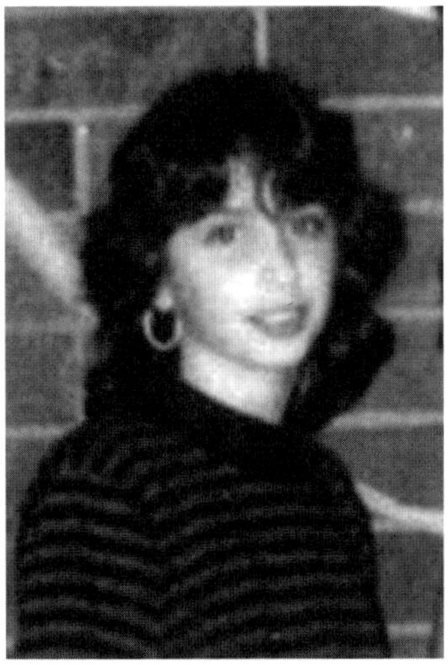

JACE SMITH (a.k.a. Rascal Smith) is a Boston born, Brooklyn, New York-based comic artist and illustrator who has been producing D.I.Y. 'zines and comics for about seven years. Jace is the creator of *The Pac-Man Fever Fanzine* and has had several solo shows in New York City, as well as the greater New England area. Jace's comics often deal with issues of gender, sexuality, and politics, as well as the depiction of adult-kid culture. Jace is currently pursuing a Bachelor of Fine Arts Degree in illustration at the School of Visual Arts in New York City.

DANIEL CLOWES

Ghost World and *David Boring* are just two of the books that emerged from Daniel Clowes's long-running comic series *Eightball*, which is published by Fantagraphics. His other books include *Pussey!*, *Ice Haven*, *The Manly World of Lloyd Llewellyn*, *Caricature*, and *Like a Velvet Glove Cast in Iron*. With Terry Zwigoff, he adapted *Ghost World* into an Oscar-nominated film; their latest film collaboration, *Art School Confidential*, also adapted from *Eightball*, was released in the spring of 2006. Clowes lives in Oakland, California, with his wife and son, where in addition to drawing comics, he is writing the screenplay for a film about a shot-by-shot remake of *Raiders of the Lost Ark*.

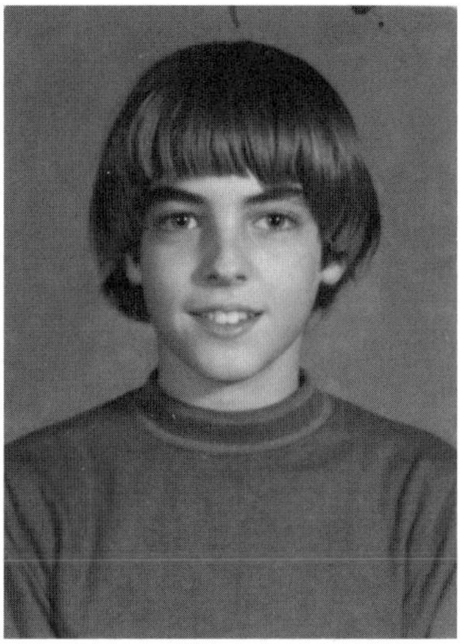

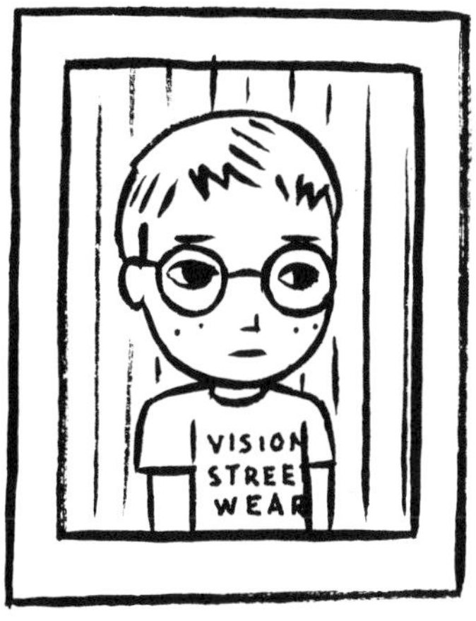
VISIO
STREE
WEAR

COLE JOHNSON was born in 1977. He attended middle school in San Antonio, Texas, where he had the misfortune of being the new boy at a number of schools. Cole now lives in Philadelphia, Pennsylvania, with his wife and daughter. You can see more of his work at www.sleepovercomics.com.

NICK ELIOPULOS began working as a batboy for a minor-league baseball team when he was in the eighth grade. His parents reasoned that the experience would build his character, but whether or not it worked is still up for debate. Today he lives in Manhattan, where he works in children's publishing and enjoys harassing his roommates' dog, a quarrelsome pug named Paisley. "The Adventures of Batboy and Starling" is his first published work. You can learn more about Nick at www.myspace.com/neliopulos.

GABRIELLE BELL was born in London, England, and raised in Northern California. She has contributed to several anthologies, including the acclaimed *Kramers Ergot*, *Mome*, and the *Drawn & Quarterly Showcase*. She is the author of the books *When I'm Old and Other Stories* and *Lucky*. She lives in Brooklyn, New York.

DASH SHAW

Dash Shaw spent the majority of his middle school career playing Dungeons and Dragons. Now he's a full-time illustrator and cartoonist. His comic books include *The Mother's Mouth*, *Goddess Head* (a collection of short stories), and *Love Eats Brains!* Please visit www.dashshaw.com for more information.

LAUREN WEINSTEIN is a cartoonist who lives in Brooklyn with her husband and dog, Dr. Buddy. Her newest jumbo comic book, titled *Girl Stories*, is about a teenager who goes from being a total nerd to being kind of cool. Her other book of comic strips, *Inside Vineyland*, won the Xeric Grant. She has also received the Ignatz Award for promising new talent. Lauren has done comics for *Glamour*, *McSweeney's*, *The Stranger*, and the *L.A. Weekly*. She is currently working on a sequel to *Girl Stories* titled *Calamity*. Check out www.girlstoriescomics.com for more information.

JIM HOOVER attended middle school in his hometown of Dover, Delaware. It was there, in eighth grade, that his career path was forged: he landed in detention for two days after his science teacher found a notebook Jim had filled with comics that made fun of most of the teachers in school. Having suffered for his art, he wasn't about to turn back. He went on to earn his college degree from the Rhode Island School of Design, then headed to New York City to join the fast-paced, glamorous world of children's publishing. Now he gets to work with other artists and pick out colors and fonts and be a designer (didn't he do a great job laying this book out?). He has worked with DreamWorks, Simon & Schuster, and Puffin Books, and is now Assistant Art Director for Viking Children's Books.

ROBYN CHAPMAN was born and raised in Alaska. She now lives in White River Junction, Vermont, where she works for the Center for Cartoon Studies. Robyn's work has been featured in several anthologies and magazines, including *Storylines*, *Scheherazade*, and *The Utne Reader*. She is the editor and publisher of a hand-crafted journal dedicated solely to eyeglasses titled *Hey, 4-Eyes!*.

ARIEL BORDEAUX used to do this mini-comic in the early nineties called "Deep Girl," plus she did a book called *No Love Lost*. Ariel's comics have been in a bunch of publications such as *Action Girl*, *Bizarro Comics*, *Bust* magazine, *Secrets & Confidences: The Complicated Truth about Women's Friendships*, *Scheherazade*, and *The Stranger*. She also does illustrations for magazines and bands, and participates in group gallery shows in the United States and Europe. Ariel had to be the new girl in school four different times, and had three different dads by the time she reached seventh grade. She got to go thrifting on Melrose in Los Angeles on visits to her ex-stepdad, and she discovered the comics that rocked her world in Seattle when visiting her real dad, so it wasn't always so bad. Now she lives in Rhode Island with her cartoonist husband Rick Altergott, two very overindulged cats, a clownfish, a kole tang, and a couple of really cool sea anemones.

AARON RENIER was born in Green Bay, Wisconsin, in 1977. He attended Vince Lombardi Middle School and first started drawing comics in his notebooks there. The program Odyssey of the Mind (O.M.) stuck with him through high school, as did comics. He became the art editor of the school's newspaper, went to state competition twice for O.M., and won the coveted Ranatra Fusca for creativity. He then went to the Milwaukee Institute of Art and Design to be an illustration major. There he continued his interest in comics by starting a school paper with his friend, and drawing a weekly comic strip for another local college. He left Milwaukee during the first half of his senior year to go to the School

of Visual Arts in New York to study comics specifically. He then moved to Portland, Oregon, where he did illustrations for the local newspaper *The Mercury* and created his first graphic novel, *Spiral-Bound*, for Top Shelf Productions. He recently moved back to New York and is working on his new graphic novel *Walker Bean*. He spends a lot of his time playing with his dog, Beluga, and riding his bike. He recently won an Eisner award for "Talent Deserving Wider Recognition."

Autographs

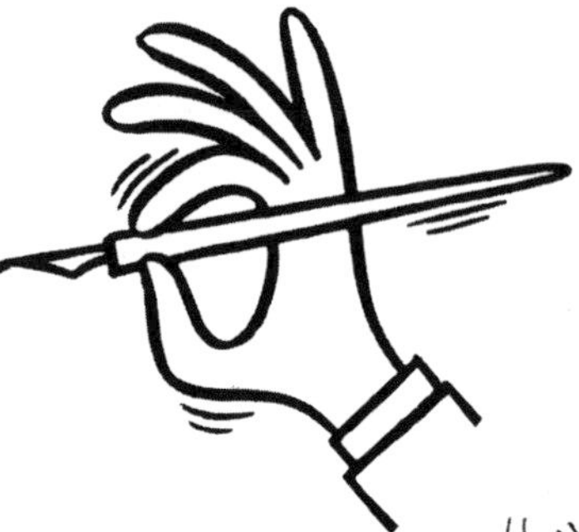

$WEE¢T!

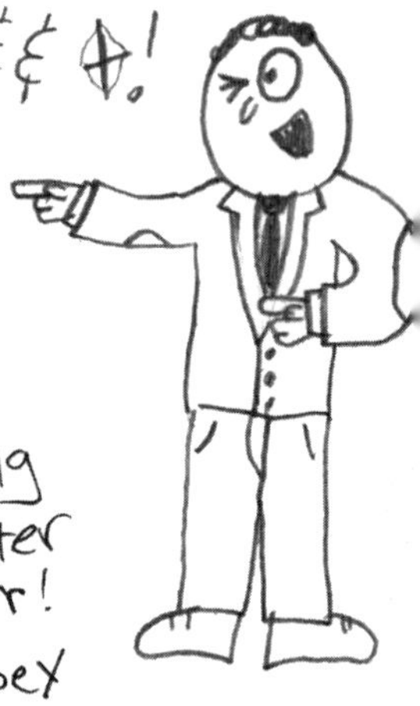

hmmph!

Have fun doing nothing with your sister [redacted] this summer! Hah! — Joey

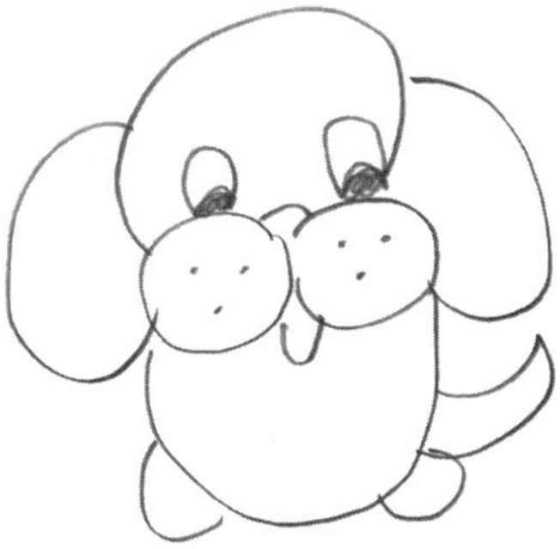

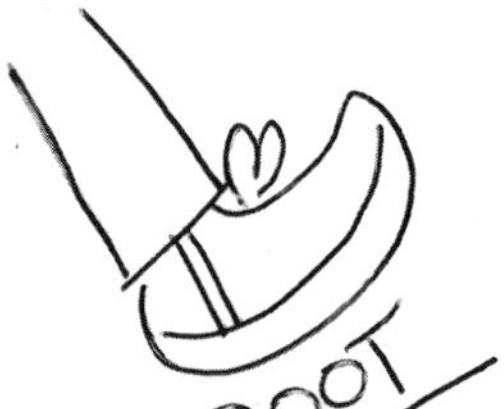

BOOT

BFF!

DEAREST SALLY-
IT'S SO HOT! THE SUMMER'S FINALLY HERE! I SWEAR TO GOD I'M GONNA GET LAID IN FRANCE (JOKE-KINDA!)
CALL ME!
-ALEX THE STUDLIEST DUDE OF THEM ALL

URAQTSS!!!

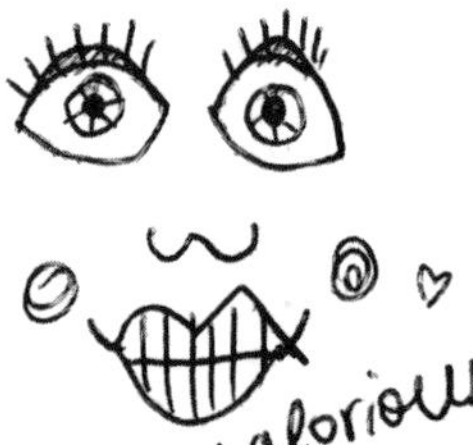

have a glorious, happy, sunfilled, funfilled, boyfilled, amefilled summer!

Dear Emily-
Even though we will most likely see eachother this summer I am sad. Goodbye.
It seems like the year has dragged on so horribly but now it is OVER
see ya.
bye.
—Kate

Dear Suellen,
It was a pleasure having you in my class.
Mr. Watson

Don't forget me from the activity bus! stay cool and K.I.T. this summer. — Nico

BOOTSOCK

BRAD WAS HERE

Hey chris, Is it true you got beat up by Brent + Drea? I bet that hurt. — [redacted]

— ALVIN

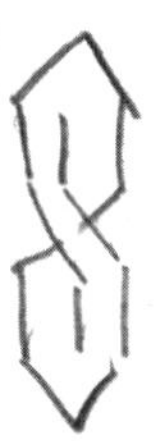

coldy moldy vs. Oatmeal honey heather feather

First to sign your crack!

Jim

I PEED

2 ugly
+ 2 B
4 gotten!

Thanks for not calling me names.
-Nick

yours till cream puffs,
Eric

Stay sweet!
♡ Vanessa

we survived carpool!
Chloe

I can't believe 7th grade is over! Remember Mrs. Allen's class? Cowpie lady! LOL! Call me this summer.
LYLAS!!!
KLL

dear Walrus,

As I said before shoe lives no more. It was stupid huh? I think so! Magic wand was ruled out and peace man and vibrations came into the picture. I hate the bricks and Corduroy and Mushroom and they can all die.

Only for us, OK?

Pelican

Have a great summer! You seem really nice and I wish I had gotten to know you better.
-Gabrielle

best friends 4-eva!

Sike!

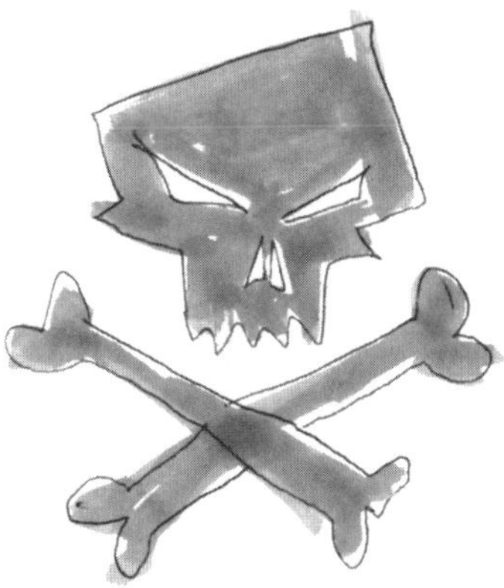

You're a wicked cool kid. Have a wicked awesome summer.

Luv ya,
Joy

Workbook Attack!

I pity the river,
I pity the brook,
I pity the fool,
that steals this book.

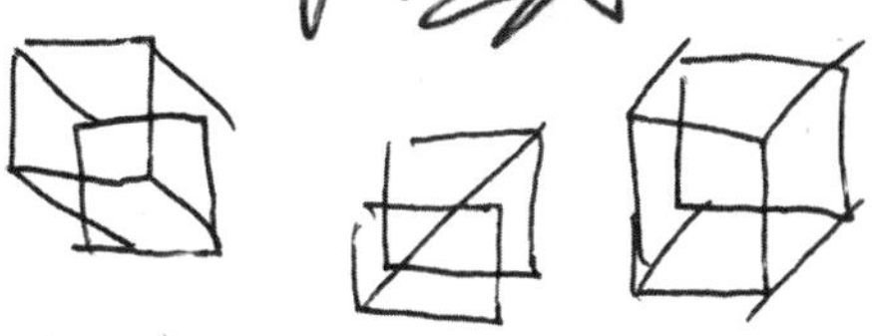

C U l8R

xo, Lucy

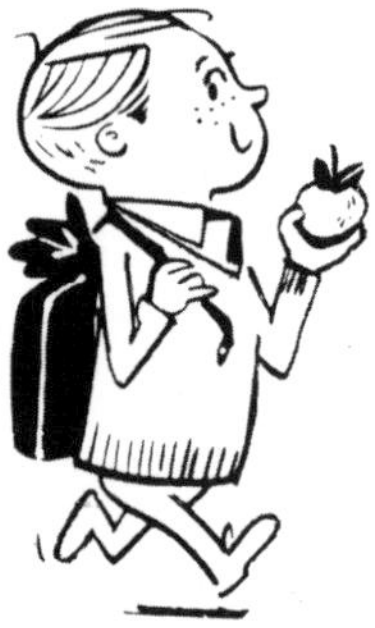

This book was printed on 100% paper. It is very nice.
Please avoid vigorously rubbing the edges with your fingers,
as paper cuts can really sting.